Deerfield Public Library
920 Waukegan Road
Deerfield, IL 60015

W9-AUI-934
DEERFIELD PUBLIC LIBRARY

3 9094 03158 8062

WITHDRAWN

SPRING FEVER

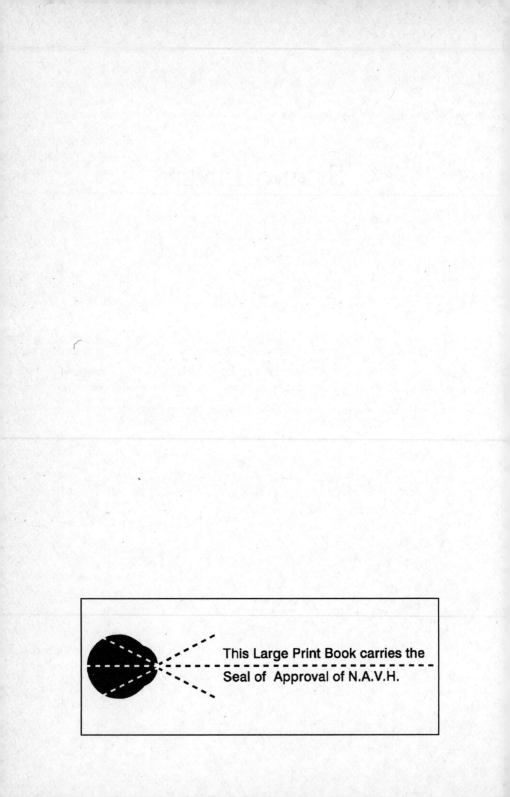

This Large Print Book carries the
Seal of Approval of N.A.V.H.

SPRING FEVER

MARY KAY ANDREWS

WHEELER PUBLISHING
A part of Gale, Cengage Learning

GALE
CENGAGE Learning·

Detroit • New York • San Francisco • New Haven, Conn • Waterville, Maine • London

GALE
CENGAGE Learning®

Copyright © 2012 by Whodunnit, Inc.
Excerpt from "The Runaway Bunny" copyright © 1942 by Harper & Row Publishers. Text copyright renewed 1970 by Roberta Brown Rauch.
Wheeler Publishing, a part of Gale, Cengage Learning.

ALL RIGHTS RESERVED
This is a work of fiction. All of the characters, organizations, and events portrayed in this novel are either products of the author's imagination or are used fictitiously.
Wheeler Publishing Large Print Hardcover.
The text of this Large Print edition is unabridged.
Other aspects of the book may vary from the original edition.
Set in 16 pt. Plantin.

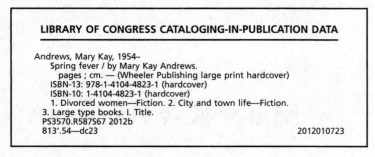

LIBRARY OF CONGRESS CATALOGING-IN-PUBLICATION DATA

Andrews, Mary Kay, 1954–
   Spring fever / by Mary Kay Andrews.
     pages ; cm. — (Wheeler Publishing large print hardcover)
   ISBN-13: 978-1-4104-4823-1 (hardcover)
   ISBN-10: 1-4104-4823-1 (hardcover)
    1. Divorced women—Fiction. 2. City and town life—Fiction.
3. Large type books. I. Title.
   PS3570.R587S67 2012b
   813'.54—dc23   2012010723

Published in 2012 by arrangement with St. Martin's Press, LLC

Printed in the United States of America
1 2 3 4 5 6 7 16 15 14 13 12

0 3158 8062

For Griffin, the new kid on the block,
with a heart full of love

ACKNOWLEDGMENTS

The author wishes to thank:

Thomas Norris for explaining tricky legal stuff. If I got it wrong, it's not his fault.

The Ritchie family of Salisbury, North Carolina, and the fine folks at Cheerwine for explaining how you make and market a delicious regional soft drink. If I got it wrong, it's not their fault.

Jack Reimer and Sharon Stokes and Beth Fleishman and Richard Boyette, who let me run away to their mountain cabins to work on the book, and who helped with some more stuff. I don't know what happened to all the good wine you guys thought you'd hidden, but it could be my fault.

Meg Walker, of Tandem Literary, who told me about marketing stuff, and who, in fact, is a genius at what she does.

The aptly named Grace Quinn, who keeps the wheels from falling off the bus on a weekly basis.

The Women of Weymouth: Alexandra

Sokoloff, Bren Witchger, Diane Chamberlain, Katy Munger, Margaret Maron, and Sarah Shaber — and honorary chair Nancy Olson — who are absolutely essential to the writing process, and who beat me at Scrabble every time.

The divine Jennifer Enderlin, who somehow managed to slap me and my manuscript into some kind of shape. Again. Huge thanks also to the whole team at St. Martin's Press. If the book works, it's definitely your fault.

Stuart Krichevsky, the best damn agent in the business. Here's to more ice cream and roses.

My family, listed last, but first in my heart. Tom, Katie, Mark, and Andy. Nothing works without you.

1

From her seat in the sanctuary of the Church of the Good Shepherd, Annajane Hudgens wondered if there had ever been a more flawless day for a wedding.

Spring had arrived spectacularly early in Passcoe, North Carolina. Only the first week in April, yet the dogwoods and azaleas were already burst into bloom, and the weeping cherry trees lining the walkway to the church trailed fingertips of pale pink onto a blue and white carpet of violets and alyssum.

It was as if the bride, the equally flawless Celia Wakefield, had somehow managed to *will* perfect weather. Or perhaps she'd specified blue skies and color-coordinated bursts of blooms in one of her famously precise memos. If anybody could do that, Annajane mused, it would be Celia.

Could there be a more beautiful setting? Baylesses had been getting married at the Church of the Good Shepherd for nearly two hundred years. Not in this grand sanctuary, of course. The original church was a quaint, stoop-shouldered gray granite affair, with uneven oak floors, a single Gothic-arched leaded-glass window above the altar, and two rows of ten primitively wrought pine pews built by black laborers from the casket factory in Moore County, twenty minutes down the road.

Annajane could remember sitting beside her best friend, Pokey, in the Bayless family pew after countless Saturday-night sleepovers, back when they were both still in pigtails. By then, Pokey's grandmother had already started her slow descent into senility, although Annajane had not known that. Miss Pauline, for whom Pokey had been named, seldom spoke, but she was content to sit in church on Sunday mornings and smile and nod to the hymns, dabbing at her cataract-clouded blue eyes with her ever-present handkerchief and patting Annajane's hand. "She thinks you're me," Pokey would whisper, giggling at her grandmother's confusion and grimacing and holding her nose when Miss Pauline passed gas, which she did frequently.

When the "new" Church of the Good Shepherd was built in the early '90s, with reproduction Tiffany stained-glass windows, solid cherry pews, and a custom-built German pipe organ, the old church was renamed the Woodrow Memorial Chapel in memory of Pauline Woodrow, who died in her sleep the year Pokey and Annajane turned fourteen.

Annajane's own wedding had been held in the chapel, the one concession her new in-laws made to what they considered Anna-jane's "quaint" ideas. Since she'd paid for the wedding herself, she'd insisted on having an intimate affair, just family and close friends, fewer than forty people, with Pokey as her only attendant. It had rained the November evening of her nuptials, and at the time she'd considered it wildly romantic that the loud thrum of the rain on the church's tin roof threatened to drown out the wedding march played on the chapel's original wheezy pump organ.

Had it been only seven years ago? Some-times she wasn't sure any of it had really hap-pened at all, that it wasn't something she'd just remembered from a long-ago dream.

Today's affair was nothing like Annajane's modest wedding. The sanctuary was at capac-ity — beyond capacity, if you went by the county fire code, which said the church could hold five hundred people. It seemed to Anna-jane that every living person who had ever known or done business with the Bayless family, or even just sipped a bottle of their Quixie cherry soft drink, had crammed themselves into one of the polished wooden pews beneath the soaring exposed rafters of the imposing Episcopal church.

Annajane felt her eyelids droop now. It was too warm in the church, and the scent of the lilies and roses banking everything that didn't move was overpowering. She'd had almost no sleep the night before, and not much more sleep the night before that. And, yes, she'd had herself a good stiff drink, Quixie and bourbon on the rocks, back at the house, after she'd finished dressing and before she'd left for the church. She closed her eyes, just for a moment, felt her chin droop to her chest, and the next moment, she felt a sharp elbow dig into her ribs.

Pokey had managed to wedge herself into the pew. "Wake up and slide over!" she ordered.

Annajane's eyes flew open, and she looked up, just in time to see Sallie Bayless, seated in the front row, two pews ahead of them, turn and shoot Pokey a stern look of warning. Sallie's gleaming auburn hair shone in the candlelit church. She was sixty-four, but still had the dewy complexion, sparkling brown eyes, and slender figure of a woman twenty years younger. Now, those eyes narrowed as they took in Pokey's tardy and disheveled appearance.

Pokey gave her mother a grin and a finger wave, and Sallie's head swiveled back around, eyes front, head held high, the Bayless pearls, a double strand, clasped firmly around her neck.

12

Annajane offered an apologetic smile to the elderly woman to her right. The woman frowned, but begrudgingly inched aside to allow the new arrival to be seated.

As usual, Pokey Bayless Riggs took no notice of the stir she'd caused. She'd been causing a stir nearly every day of her thirty-five years, and today, her brother's wedding day, was no different.

The boatneck collar of Pokey's expensive new red silk jacket had slipped off her right shoulder, exposing a leopard-print bra strap and an unseemly amount of cleavage. Little Clayton was two years old, but Pokey was still struggling to lose her baby weight. She'd managed to pop one of the jacket's rhinestone buttons, and the tight silk skirt had somehow twisted around so that the zipper was now in the front, rather than on the side. She was bare-legged, which was a scandal in and of itself, but now Annajane noticed that her best friend had ditched the Sallie-mandated sedate dyed-silk slingback pumps in favor of a pair of blinged-out silver flip flops.

Pokey's thin, poker-straight blond hair had already lost its beauty-salon bounce, and now hung limply on either side of her full pink cheeks. Her lipstick was smeared. But her eyes, her amazing cornflower-blue eyes, glinted with mischief.

"Busted!" Annajane whispered, not daring to look at her best friend.

"Christ!" Pokey muttered. "This is so not my fault. I couldn't find a parking spot! The church lot's full and the whole block is lined with cars on both sides of the street. I had to leave the Land Rover clear down the block in front of the gas station and run all the way here."

"Aren't you supposed to be up there with your mom and everybody else in the family?" Annajane asked. "I mean, you *are* the groom's only sister."

"Screw that," Pokey said swiftly. "I refuse to make nice with that woman. Mason knows I don't like her. Mama knows it too. I'm taking a moral stand here."

"Who the hell are all these people anyway?" she asked, glancing around at the packed church and zeroing in on the bride's side of the aisle. "Not family, right? Since poor lil' Celia is an orphan, and the only family she could produce is that elderly great aunt staying over at Mama's house. Did Celia charter a bus or something?"

Annajane shrugged. "You're apparently the only person in Passcoe who *doesn't* think that Celia Wakefield is the best thing since flush toilets and sliced store-bought bread."

"Don't give me that. You hate her as much as I do," Pokey said under her breath.

"Not at all," Annajane replied. "I'm happy for them."

"Yippy-fuckin'-skippy," Pokey drawled.

14

"Happy, happy, happy. It's fine for you. In less than a week, you'll pack up your U-Haul and head for Atlanta and your nice new life without even a glance in the rearview mirror. New man, new job, new address. But where does that leave me? Stuck here in stinkin' Passcoe, with my mama, my evil brother Davis, and good ole Mason and his new bride, Cruella de Vil."

"Poor, poor Pokey," Annajane mocked her right back. "Richest girl in town, married to the second richest man in town."

"Third richest," Pokey corrected. "Or maybe fourth. Davis and Mason have way more money than Pete, especially since people quit buying furniture made in America."

"Speaking of, where is Pete?" Annajane asked, craning her neck to look for him. Instead of spotting Pokey's tall redheaded husband, Pete, her eyes rested on another tardy couple, Bonnie and Matthew Kelsey, hurrying up the right-side aisle of the church.

Bonnie Kelsey's eyes met Annajane's. She blushed, and looked away quickly, clutching Matthew's arm and steering him into a pew as far away from Annajane's as she could manage in the overcrowded church.

Pokey saw the maneuver for what it was. "Bitch," she said.

"It's all right," Annajane said smoothly. "I mean, what do you expect? Matt and Mason

15

play golf every week. From what I hear, Bonnie and Celia get along like a house afire. Best friends forever! Anyway, Bonnie's not the only one to sign up for Team Celia. Every woman in this room has been staring daggers at me since I walked into this church. I knew when I agreed to come today that it would be awkward."

"Awkward?" Pokey laughed bitterly. "It's freakish, is what it is. Who else but you would agree to show up at her ex-husband's wedding?"

2

Out of the corner of her eye, Annajane saw more people eyeing her with undisguised curiosity. She gave a tight smile and looked away.

"I had to come today," Annajane reminded Pokey. "For Sophie. She made me promise. In fact, it's the only way she'd agree to be in the wedding. It's also my last official company function."

"I still can't believe you're leaving Quixie," Pokey said. "After how many years?"

"Too many," Annajane murmured. "I never should have stayed after the divorce. I just didn't have the gumption to get out and start a new life for myself. And then there was Sophie, of course."

"You spoil that child rotten," Pokey said, tsk-tsking. "And Mason is even worse."

But before she could launch into her lecture about the kind of strict parenting her niece really needed, the soft strains of organ music that had been playing as guests drifted into the church segued into harp music.

"A harp?" Pokey turned and craned her neck to look in the direction of the choir loft. "Where the hell did she find a harp in Passcoe?"

Annajane gave a little shrug. "The harp made its first appearance at the rehearsal dinner last night. Which you somehow managed to miss?"

"I had one of my migraines," Pokey said quickly. "I was all dressed and everything when it hit me. Pete gave me one of my pills and put me to bed at eight o'clock."

"Migraine or not, you are officially on your mother's list today, as if you didn't already know that," Annajane told her.

"I do not understand why Mama and my brothers have suddenly allowed Celia free reign with the company bank accounts," Pokey said. "If Daddy were alive, he would be shittin' kittens at the way they're throwing money around. Pete doesn't like it either. He says . . ."

Suddenly, the harpist was joined by a violin and a flute, the tempo of the music quickening.

"Shh," Annajane said. "It's starting."

A door beside the altar opened, and three men in dark tuxes emerged following the pastor, a personable young priest from Boston, Father Jolly, who'd only been at the church for a few months. He even looked the part, Annajane reflected bitterly, short and stout, with a fringe of dark bangs and a beaming choir-boy countenance. Perfect, perfect, perfect.

But it wasn't the priest Annajane was staring at. She involuntarily held her breath at the sight of Mason Bayless, in his flawlessly cut charcoal-gray Armani tuxedo. At thirty-nine, he still had the build of an athlete, broad shoulders, narrow hips, long, muscled neck. He looked like the baseball player he'd been in his college years. His dark blond hair had been carefully combed back from his high forehead, slicked into place with some kind of hair goo, a style he'd adopted only recently, since Celia came into his life. He was paler than usual, and those cornflower-blue eyes and ridiculously long curly lashes seemed focused on the floor, and not on the congregation eagerly awaiting the upcoming ceremony.

As Mason took his place to the right of Father Jolly, his younger brother, Davis, slid easily to his side. Pokey might have been the youngest of the three Bayless progeny, but Davis was now, and always, the baby of the family.

Twenty months younger than Mason, Davis was half a head shorter and easily weighed forty pounds more than his older brother. While Mason and Pokey had the Bayless blue eyes and dark blond hair coloring, Davis,

19

alone among the children, took after his mother Sallie's people. He had the Woodrow snapping dark eyes; thick, wavy dark hair; and the high cheekbones Miss Pauline always claimed came from their long-ago Cherokee ancestors. Davis looked eagerly around the room, tugging at the collar of his starched white tux shirt, nodding at friends and acquaintances, exchanging a sly wink with somebody, a woman, no doubt, seated on the far left side of the church.

Pokey caught the wink, too, and clucked her tongue in disapproval. "I did not think she would have the nerve to show up here today. Obviously, I have once again underestimated the low moral fiber of another of Davis's women."

"Who is she?" Annajane asked eagerly, studying the left side of the church.

"Name is Dreama, if you can believe it. Works at the bottling plant in Fayetteville. Not but twenty-two. Married, of course."

"Of course," Annajane agreed. "Does your mama know?"

"Does Sallie ever miss anything? She knows, but she's choosing to act like it's not happening. Denial is mama's religion. She made Davis ask Linda Balez as his 'official date' for the weekend. You remember Linda, right? She was in my deb group, went to Sweetbriar? She's living over in Pinehurst, does some kind of tax planning or something."

"Tall brunette? Little bit of an overbite? I think I met her last night."

"That's the one," Pokey said, nodding. "Sweet girl, really. Mama insisted that she stay in the guest room at Cherry Hill, but of course Davis has got little old Dreama stashed in the Davis Bayless Honeymoon Suite over at the Pinecone Motor Lodge."

"So that's why he left the party so early last night," Annajane said. "I was walking out to my car at nine thirty, when he went whizzing past me in the Boxster. I did see a woman in the front seat, but it was dark, and I just assumed it was his date."

"Doubtful," Pokey said. "I saw Linda at the brunch up at the house this morning, and Davis was nowhere to be found, the little shit. I don't know why any of us put up with his crap, do you?"

"We just do," Annajane said quietly.

Annajane returned her attention to the groomsmen. Pokey's husband, Pete, had taken his place to the left of Father Jolly. His bright red hair had just started showing gray at the temples, and his beard was neatly clipped. His tux fit him like it had been custom tailored, and his broad, toothy smile seemed to take in everybody in the packed sanctuary.

"Gawwd," Pokey moaned, gesturing at her husband. "Would you look at that man? Could you not eat him up with a spoon? It's just not fair. After all these years, even after everything he's put me through, I swear to goodness, if he asked me to, I would take his hand, leave this church right this minute, follow him out to the car, and drop my panties in a New York minute."

The blue-haired matron sitting beside Annajane gasped, clutched her yellowing pearls, and scooted over another six inches to the right.

"Nice visual," Annajane whispered, putting her lips to Pokey's ears. "But could you keep it down? I think you just gave one of your mother's bridge partners heart palpitations."

"Serves her right for eavesdropping," Pokey said. She leaned back and studied Annajane for the first time since she'd arrived at the church.

"You look amazing," Pokey said. She touched the cap sleeve of Annajane's dress. "Is this new?"

Annajane looked down at her cocktail dress. The fabric was a thick satin, the color of new ferns, cut close to the body, with a deep squared-off scoop neck and dressmaker details like tiny covered buttons, an inset waist, and a wide, shell-pink satin belt with a large rhinestone and pearl-encrusted buckle.

"This old thing?" she laughed. "It's vintage. Although I don't think it had ever been worn. I found it last year at the Junior League Thriftique. It still has the original satin Bonwit

Teller label sewn in."

"Love that bracelet, too," Pokey commented. "Don't tell me you found that around Passcoe."

Annajane flexed her hands for her friend's inspection. She wore a wide antique cuff bracelet of rhinestones and pearls. "Sallie actually gave me this bracelet for Christmas the first year Mason and I were married. I think it was your grandmother's."

"I don't remember ever seeing it before," Pokey said.

Annajane's brow furrowed. "Oh. Damn." She fumbled with the bracelet clasp. "Bad form, wearing the Bayless family jewels to his wedding, right? I swear, it didn't dawn on me until just now. Just give it back to Sallie later, after I'm gone."

"Stop," Pokey said, closing her hand around Annajane's. "If Mama gave you this bracelet, I'm sure she wants you to keep it. Besides, she probably only gave it to you because it's costume jewelry."

"In the back of her mind, Sallie was probably saving back the good stuff for her *next* daughter-in-law," Annajane said. "Oh. Sorry. Didn't mean to sound bitter."

Pokey tapped the thick twist of silver on Annajane's left ring finger and then twisted her own two-carat diamond engagement band. "I still can't believe you gave back Grandmama Bayless's ring."

23

"I love *this* ring," Annajane said, lifting her chin. "Shane designed it himself."

"Sweet," Pokey said, with a dismissive sniff. "Although I never heard of an engagement ring without some kind of precious stone. And I still think you should have kept Mason's ring. You could just wear it on your right hand."

"It was a family heirloom," Annajane said quietly. "I'm not a Bayless anymore. I'm not sure I ever was one. It should go to you, or one of your boys. Or Sophie."

"Daddy would have wanted you to keep it," Pokey said. "He's the one who insisted Mason give you that instead of a new ring. He said you'd earned it. And you have. No matter what Mama or anybody else thinks."

Pokey held up her hand, left pinky extended. Annajane sighed, and linked her own pinky through her best friend's, just as they always had, since they were six years old.

"I notice Celia didn't get Grandma Bayless's ring," Pokey said.

"No, but she got one with a waaay bigger diamond, which I understand she picked out herself," Annajane said. "I don't imagine somebody like Celia Wakefield would want anything as old-fashioned as your grandmother's engagement ring."

"Hope she chokes on it," Pokey said pleasantly.

Without warning, Annajane suddenly began

tearing up.

"Are you okay?" Pokey asked, digging in her evening bag for a tissue. "Honey, I really, really think it is not a good thing for you to watch this whole charade."

"I'm fine," Annajane insisted, refusing the tissue. "Really. Pinky swear. This is a good thing. For Mason, for Sophie, for the family. This is closure for me. Honestly. Step one, Mason marries Celia. Step two, Annajane marries Shane. End of story. Everybody lives happily ever after."

"You're nuts," Pokey said. She jerked her head in the direction of the altar, where her big brother Mason stood, hands clasped behind his back, legs slightly apart, rocking back and forth slightly on his heels.

"He's nuts, too," Pokey continued. "And he is *so* not over you."

"Wrong," Annajane snapped. "He's been over me for years. And I am over him. Finally. Totally. Completely. Over. Him."

3

Getting over Mason Bayless was easier said than done. How do you stop caring for somebody you've loved your whole life? Five years ago, right after their breakup, when she'd cried herself to sleep every night for months and months, Annajane decided loving Mason might be like having some insidious virus. She could go for days, not allowing herself to think of him, ignoring his phone calls and e-mails, or speaking to him coolly, with complete detachment, her emotional firewall firmly intact. And then, one day, for no reason at all, she would have what she came to think of as a flare-up.

He'd swing through the office, with his rolling, loping gait, maybe flash that grin of his to one of the other girls in the office. Oh, that grin. When he gave the slow "hey-howyadoin" smile that exposed the chipped left incisor he'd broken during a teenage wrestling match with Davis, Annajane would come completely unglued. She'd have to get up from her desk, run to the lady's room, lock herself in, and bawl like a baby.

Sometimes the flare-ups happened in the car. She'd be driving along, and she'd hear their song. "Don't Stop Believin' " . . . Journey. Once she nearly ran a motorcyclist off the road, when she was driving home from the plant late at night when the song came on the radio. She'd had to pull off the highway, roll down the windows, and force herself to let the cold damp February air roll over her flaming cheeks and snap her back to reality before she could drive on.

She'd even tried her own version of an exorcism to get over Mason. Three years ago, on the two-year anniversary of their divorce, she'd snuck back to the lake cottage that held so much of their history.

A light winter rain was falling as she navigated the rutted gravel road that led through thick woods back to the lake. Officially the lake's name was Lake Wesley Forlines Jr., after a local decorated World War I hero. But everybody around Passcoe always just called it Hideaway Lake, because county budget cuts had long ago closed the only public beach and boat ramp. Now the only access to the lake was through the Bayless's property. Private property.

Weeds and sapling trees had sprung up in the narrow lane, and it struck Annajane that since she and Mason had moved out, the rest of the family had very likely forgotten the place even existed. Maybe, she thought, in one panicky moment, the house had finally succumbed to the inevitable, and simply tumbled all the way to the ground.

But the little stone cottage was still there, nestled beneath the leafless limbs of a huge old water oak. Acorns crunched under her tires as she rolled to a stop a few yards away from the house, and, as she stepped out of the car, she glimpsed the gray-green glimmer of the lake through a raggedy hedge of privet that had replaced the lawn Mason had so carefully cultivated.

Briars caught at the legs of her jeans as she pushed open the rickety cedar gate. Annajane plucked a dried bud from the canes of the New Dawn roses that twined through the pickets of the fence. The rosebushes, two of them, had been a wedding gift from her stepfather, who'd planted them himself, promising that the fast-growing climbers would blanket the fence with carefree pink blossoms within a year. And they had. The rosebushes had survived, even if the marriage had withered.

Annajane frowned when she got to the front door of the cottage. The periwinkle-blue paint she'd coated the old door with only three years earlier was already cracked and peeling. Worse, a rusting iron hasp and shiny new padlock had been fastened to the door. They'd never even had a key to the house when they'd lived there. But now that it was abandoned, somebody had seen fit to lock the house up tight. She tried to peer in through the front windows, but the inexpensive bamboo blinds were drawn, and anyway the windows were caked with dirt.

She walked around to the rear of the house and tried the back door, which led onto a small utility room. The wooden door was spongy with rot, but it had apparently been latched from the inside, and she was afraid if she tugged too hard the whole door would collapse on top of her. Which wouldn't do. Annajane didn't want to advertise her visit to the cottage.

So she moved over to the left, to the wide set of triple windows that looked out over the lake. Or at least, they'd looked out on the lake when it was their master bedroom. Now those windows mostly looked out on the tops of dead weeds. A lanky camellia bush partially blocked the center window, but she managed to slither behind it, praying as she did so that no snakes were hidden in the thick carpet of dead leaves underfoot. She grasped the window sill with both hands, grunted and shoved the window upward. She climbed inside.

Instantly she wished she hadn't. Her muddy shoes left footprints in the thick carpet of dust on the worn wooden floor, and cobwebs festooned the ceiling fan overhead. The furniture in the room, an old wooden dresser, matching mahogany four-poster bed, and chest of drawers of no particular vintage or value, had come from Cherry Hill's attic. But Mason hadn't bothered to remove any of it when he moved out. Now a pale green mist of mold dotted the dark varnished wood surfaces. Some kind of animal had been chewing at the bare mattress.

Annajane walked around the room, her shoulders sagging, fingers trailing across the walls she'd repainted three times in one crazy, Quixie-fueled weekend, before arriving at the exact right shade, Benjamin Moore Morning Sky Blue, cut to half-strength.

She shouldn't have come. She opened the closet, so small they'd once joked that it wouldn't hold even one of the Bayless family secrets. Not much left there. Some rusty wire coat hangers, a folded green wool blanket on the one shelf. On a hook on the back of the door she found a faded plaid flannel shirt of Mason's, which he'd worn for yard work. On the floor she spied his mud-spattered laceless work boots lined up companionably next to a pair of her own grungy tennis shoes. Without thinking, Annajane pulled the flannel shirt on over her own denim shirt. She burrowed her nose into the collar, seeking some sense memory of her former husband, of those happy times they'd spent making this cottage their own. Instead, she sneezed violently, expelling a tiny dried-up spider into the mildew-scented air.

Her footsteps echoed in the closed-up house as she walked from room to room. To be precise, the house only had three rooms, the bedroom, an L-shaped living-dining room, the kitchen, and of course a bathroom, which was not much bigger than their bedroom closet.

One by one, she opened and closed the kitchen cupboards. The cabinet beside the stove held a yellowing box of pancake mix and an opened carton of baking soda. Kernels of rice trailed from a sack of Mahatma, where a mouse had nibbled a hole in the plastic bag. The cupboard by the refrigerator held two mismatched coffee mugs and a stack of green-tinted Quixie promotional glasses. Rust spots freckled the fridge.

Annajane stood in front of the window over the sink and looked out at the lake. From here, she could see the weather-beaten dock that stretched out into the water. They'd sunned themselves on that dock, dove naked into the surprisingly cool water on moonlit summer nights, paddled out into the middle of the lake on another night to make a drunken attempt at lovemaking in the bottom of the old wooden rowboat, an attempt that had ended up dunking them both into the lake.

They'd had big plans once: to build a double-decker boathouse at the end of the dock, one with a deck and a screened porch and a stone fireplace up top, for cookouts and parties, with davits below to hold the *Sallieforth,* a derelict 1967 seventeen-foot Chris-Craft ski boat that Mason hoped to eventually restore to working condition.

So many plans. Once that lake had been a clear blue-green, lapping wavelets against a shore lined with the blue hydrangeas, red geraniums, and drifts of Shasta daisies planted by the original caretaker's wife. Now weeds and water lilies choked the shoreline and obstructed the water views. She felt a melancholy, as cold and gray as the winter lake, seep into her soul.

Turning away from the window, she wandered into the living room, where the only furniture that remained was a lumpy brown sofabed, handed down from one of Mason's college roommates. The sofa faced the fireplace, where a stack of half-burned logs perched atop a small mound of coals. The old copper tub on the hearth had once held pieces of kindling, matches, and twists of newspaper. She reached in, found a couple sizable twigs, a long wooden kitchen match, and some yellowing newspaper.

Annajane placed the newspaper and the kindling on top of one of the half-burned logs, lit the match, and held it to the paper until it caught fire. In a moment, the dry sticks were burning merrily. She sat on the edge of the sofa, watching, waiting for the fire to build. When it threatened to die down, she searched around the house until she found an old phone book. She ripped out the pages, wadded them up, and tossed them onto the fire, crouching in front of the fireplace, ready to feed the fire more paper, lest the blaze die down again.

Finally, the logs caught, too. She could feel fingers of warmth creeping into the chill, stale air. She sat back on the sofa, watched and waited. Waited for what, she asked herself? Some catharsis? A cleansing? A healing? Coming here had been a mistake. She stood, stripped off the flannel shirt, and tossed it onto the flames, which claimed it with a whoosh of orange and red flames.

She let herself out the window, closed it, and drove off without a backward glance.

Three years later, Annajane forced herself to study her ex-husband, standing there on the altar, waiting for his new bride. Marrying Mason off to Celia was the final step in her self-prescribed cure. It was the only solution. And once it was done, once she heard Father Jolly pronounce the happy couple Mr. and Mrs. Mason Sheppard Bayless, Annajane could move on with her own life. Away from

Passcoe, the Bayless family, and, yes, even dear old Quixie, the Quicker Quencher.

Everybody in town said that if you were born in Passcoe, North Carolina, the home of Quixie and the Quixie Beverage Company since 1922, you were born with the cherry-flavored cola running through your blood. It wasn't quite true of Annajane Hudgens.

Ruth, her mother, always claimed she couldn't stand the taste of the stuff, but Annajane knew the truth of the matter was that it was the Bayless family who left a bad taste in Ruth Hudgens's mouth.

Annajane always secretly wondered if Ruth hated the Baylesses because her daddy, Ruth's first husband, Bobby Mayes, had been killed by a drunk driver while driving a Quixie truck, when Annajane was barely two years old. Ruth had married Leonard Hudgens a year later, and Leonard quietly adopted the little girl when she was four. Even though Leonard worked at the plant, Ruth wouldn't allow Quixie in her house, and she certainly wouldn't allow her only child to drink the stuff. No, it was milk or apple juice or lemonade for Annajane, never Quixie.

Annajane could still remember the first time she tasted Quixie. It was in kindergarten, when she was invited to Pokey Bayless's fifth birthday party.

Her mama had thrown the pink engraved

invitation right into the trash. "Think they're better than us and everybody else in town," she'd overheard Ruth tell Leonard. "Probably only asked Annajane because they want to lord it over us."

"Ruth, for Pete's sake, the girls go to kindergarten together. They're friends," Leonard had protested. "Just 'cuz you can't stand the parents, that don't mean those little girls can't play together." In the end, Annajane cried and begged, until, finally, Leonard had persuaded Mama to let her go to Pokey's party.

It was a tea party, and for the event a caterer set up a big round table draped in pink tulle on the front porch at Cherry Hill, the Baylesses' rambling old Greek Revival estate.

The table was set with a child-sized bone china tea set that had been one of Pokey's birthday presents, and there were real sterling silver forks and spoons and cloth napkins. Each of the six guests — all girls — was presented with her own silver sequined tiara and a pink feather boa. And at every place setting on the table stood a perfectly chilled chubby little bottle of Quixie soda with a pink and white striped straw sticking out of the neck.

Annajane could still remember that first icy sip. She'd never tasted a carbonated beverage before, and the bubbles tickled her nose and gave her the hiccups.

To her, Quixie didn't taste like cherry Kool-Aid or cherry Life Savers, or even cherry Popsicles. The fruit flavoring was bold and spicy and tart and sweet all at the same time, like a sour cherry exploding on her tongue with sparkly after-notes, and Annajane had never tasted anything as delicious in her entire life.

Besides the bottles of Quixie, the party refreshments included trays of tiny little crustless tea sandwiches and cookies and petit fours and a three-tiered Care Bears birthday cake that Mrs. Bayless had ordered from a bakery in Pinehurst, but for Annajane, nothing could match that first taste of Quixie.

Pokey's daddy, who'd played butler and head waiter at the party, had been delighted at Annajane's enthusiasm for the family product, and he had gladly replaced that first empty soda bottle with two more bottles in quick succession.

When the party was over, each girl in attendance was given a huge goodie bag containing a full-sized Cabbage Patch doll, a monogrammed grosgrain ribbon hair bow, and yet another bottle of Quixie cola, this one with a special commemorative label that said: IN CELEBRATION OF POKEY BAYLESS'S FIFTH BIRTHDAY. A VERY SPECIAL DAY.

Even at five, Annajane knew better than to

36

share all the details of the party menu with her mama. She hid the commemorative bottle of Quixie at the bottom of her toy box, and two hours after she got home from the party, still wearing her treasured silver tiara and feather boa, she found herself crouched over the commode, silently retching up the contraband soft drink.

But the upset stomach did nothing to dim Annajane's enthusiasm for Quixie, or for her new best friend, Pokey, who'd earned the nickname because she'd been born nearly two weeks after Sallie's due date.

Pokey was as blond and fair-skinned and round as Annajane was dark and skinny. To Ruth Hudgens's consternation, the girls became inseparable, alternating sleepovers at each other's house nearly every weekend. Ruth never said a word to Annajane against Pokey — how could she? Silly, sunny-natured, fair-haired Pokey was the golden child everybody — even Ruth, against her will, loved.

As for Sallie Bayless, she was always cordial to Pokey's best friend, but as Annajane grew older, she came to realize that she would never measure up to Sallie's standards. Not as a friend, and certainly never as a daughter-in-law.

At the Bayless house, Pokey's brother Davis was an annoying constant in the girl's lives, bossing, teasing, and tormenting the girls until they would retreat, in tears, to

Annajane's house, out of his reach. Annajane heard a lot about Mason, the adored oldest brother, who was four years older than Pokey, but she saw him rarely. Mason went to boarding school in Virginia and spent summer vacations sailing and water-skiing at Camp Seagull on the coast. According to Pokey, Mason was very near to a saint. He was the hero who stood up for her against Davis, whipped everybody at every sport, and, during summer vacations, when the family spent a month at their house at Wrightsville Beach, took her fishing and taught her to play spades.

On the handful of occasions when she'd been around Mason as a kid, Annajane had been so tongue-tied in his presence that she was sure they'd never even exchanged more than a "hey-howyadoin?"

Every summer, the Baylesses would invite Annajane to join them for their August trip to the beach, and every summer, Ruth would refuse to let her go. Sallie Bayless would write Ruth Hudgens a polite note on her pale blue engraved stationery, and when that didn't work, Pokey's father, Mr. Glenn Bayless, would seek out Annajane's stepfather, Leonard, at the plant, clap him on the back, and declare loudly, "Now, Leonard, my daughter Pokey is fussin' and fumin' at me because y'all won't let your little Annajane come to the beach with us. It'd sure give me some rest if you could do without her for a week or so."

But Leonard had his orders. "I'm sorry, Mr. Bayless," he'd say firmly. "But August is when we get together up in the mountains with Annajane's grandma and aunts and uncles. I'd have the whole family down on my neck if I messed with the family reunion."

So every summer, Annajane obediently joined her mother's relatives in a crowded, damp mountain cabin on a dirt road, where the relatives played cards and listened to gospel music and the cousins slept on pallets on the porch, played endless games of Clue, and griped about the lack of television.

Finally, miraculously, the summer when Annajane was fifteen, Ruth announced that they would not be going to the mountains. Her sister and brother-in-law had sold the cabin and were moving to Florida and taking Annajane's grandma with them.

Annajane was on the phone with Pokey moments later. "Guess what?" she said breathlessly. "No more stinkin' mountains for me! I've got the whole summer to do whatever I want!"

"Guess what else?" Pokey countered. "Daddy says he'll give us jobs at the plant this summer, if we want. Real jobs! With name badges and paychecks and everything."

"No way!" Annajane squealed with delight.

"Our own money. No more babysitting for me."

The Monday after school was out found Annajane reporting to the Quixie front office, where Voncile, Glenn Bayless's assistant, seemed surprised to see her.

"Mr. Bayless has a job for me," Annajane said quietly. "Pokey said so."

"Of course," Voncile had said, smiling and leafing through some papers on her desktop. Growing up, Annajane and Pokey had always had the run of the Quixie plant. Voncile looked up at Annajane, standing there in the neatly pressed plaid dress Ruth had sewn just for this occasion. "Where is Miss Pokey this morning?"

"Oh. I thought she'd be here already," Annajane said, her spirits sinking. Pokey had promised to meet her at the plant at nine sharp.

"Well. Do you know how to type?"

"Yes ma'am," Annajane said proudly. "Forty-five words a minute."

"Wonderful," Voncile said. She ushered Annajane into a tiny windowless office not far from the reception room. A long table and two folding metal chairs were in the center of the room, and an enormous canvas mail bin sat beside the table, where a computer had been set up. A large plastic tub held boxes of business-sized white envelopes, and a smaller one held glossy Quixie coupons.

"Here we go," Voncile said. She gestured at the mail bin. "Are you familiar with our Quixie Quickie summer promotion?"

"I don't think so," Annajane replied, trying not to giggle.

Voncile picked up a bulky padded envelope and ripped it open. Five distinctive red and green Quixie screwtop bottle caps tumbled out. Voncile swept them into the trash with one hand, and extracted a piece of paper from the envelope.

"This," she said, waving the slip of paper, "is what we're after. We've asked Quixie lovers to mail in five bottle caps, along with their name and mailing address, for a chance to win one of those." She gestured to a row of gleaming red Coleman coolers against the far wall. Each of the coolers was printed with the oval Quixie logo, the one with the Quixie Pixie, leaning against a Quixie bottle, smiling and winking impishly.

Annajane counted two dozen coolers.

"So," Voncile said briskly, handing the slip to Annajane. "You'll type the name and address into our database. Right?" She leaned over the computer, tapped a few keys, and brought up a blank spreadsheet. "Just type on each line, and hit tab when you come to the end of the address. You can do that, can't you?"

"Yes ma'am," Annajane said.

"Then," Voncile said, "Come to my office

and let me know when you've typed in all these addresses. I'll print them out onto labels, and then you'll put the labels on those envelopes." She plucked an envelope from a box and showed it to Annajane. The Quixie logo was printed in the upper-left-hand corner of each one. "You'll put one coupon for a free twelve-ounce bottle of Quixie in each envelope, seal up the envelope, and put it in that other bin. How does that sound?"

"Fine," was all Annajane could think of to say.

"Good," Voncile said, glancing at her watch. "I've got a meeting right now, but you just sit right down here and get started, and I'll come back afterwards to see how you're doing. All right?"

"Yes ma'am," Annajane said. She sat down at the computer, flexed her fingertips, and got started. It was slow going at first, ripping open the envelopes, sorting out the addresses, and then counting out the bottle caps. She was shocked to discover some envelopes didn't actually contain five bottle caps. Others might contain three or four Quixie caps, but with a non-Quixie cap thrown in to fill out the mix. Annajane counted Coke caps, Pepsi caps, Dr Pepper caps, even a few Hires and Barq root beer bottle caps. These she indignantly threw in the trash, along with the sender's entry blank. Who did these people think they were fooling?

42

After an hour or so, she got a system going, opening twenty-five envelopes at a time, scanning the caps, and then typing the names into the computer. Every once in a while, she'd get up, walk around the room, and peek out the door, wondering what was taking Pokey so long. Hadn't they agreed they would start their careers today?

At noon, her stomach started to growl. Her shoulders ached, and she was getting a headache from staring at the flickering computer screen. She wished she'd thought to bring along a lunch. At one, she walked over to Voncile's office, to inquire about taking a break. But the office was empty, and Mr. Bayless's office door was closed, too.

Finally, she remembered the break room, where she and Pokey had played restaurant as little girls, serving paper cups of Quixie from the fountain machine to the plant workers and being treated to packages of Tom's salted peanuts or Cheetos from the vending machines.

She was back at her computer, sipping from a cup of Quixie and nibbling a Mr. Goodbar when the door flew open.

"Come on, you little brat," a man's deep voice called. "Mama sent me to take you to lunch." He stepped into the room, and Annajane was so flustered by an in-the-flesh glimpse of Mason Bayless that she knocked over her drink.

Speechless, she watched a bright red river of soda splashing onto the stack of contest entry blanks she'd just stacked beside the computer.

"Oh no," she cried, jumping up. She reached into the trash bin and grabbed a discarded envelope and started madly dabbing at the mess. But it was too late. She'd greedily poured herself a huge cup of Quixie, and now everything on the tabletop was soaked.

"Damn," she wailed, mopping and breathing hard, and trying not to look up at her best friend's big brother. When she realized that she'd cursed out loud, she blushed harder and mopped faster.

Mason Bayless was sunburned, which made his blue eyes look bluer, and his dark blond hair needed cutting because it brushed down his high forehead and across his thick dark eyebrows. His prominent nose had a bump across the bridge, but he had perfect white teeth, except for one chipped incisor. He was dressed in faded blue jeans and well-worn high-top leather work boots and a green Quixie Beverage Company uniform shirt with red pinstripes and an embroidered patch over his breast that said MASON.

Not that he needed a name patch. Not much. Every one of the three hundred employees at Quixie Beverage Company knew Mr. Glenn Bayless's oldest boy, as did just about everybody in the community. Passcoe was a company town, and Quixie and Passcoe had been inextricably linked for more than seventy years.

Mason's uniform shirt was untucked and the top three buttons unfastened. After a moment, he grabbed another envelope and began sweeping the ruined papers into the trash.

"Sorry," he drawled. "Didn't mean to scare you like that. I was looking for my sister."

"Oh, wait," Annajane said, grabbing for the trash can. "I can't, I mean, those are contest entries. And I've got to type them into the computer. Maybe I can get them dried out . . ."

"Forget it," Mason said. "Those are toast."

"But I'm supposed to type them all in. It's a contest, and the winner gets a cooler, and it's not fair . . ." she sighed. "I'll have to tell Voncile, I guess. I don't know what she'll say."

"Voncile won't give a rat's ass," Mason said. He smiled. "I'll just tell her I did it. Which is kinda true. It was my fault."

He cocked his head and considered her. "Hey. You've got stuff on your dress." He reached out and his fingertip brushed the sleeve.

She jumped several inches.

He laughed. "Sorry. You're kinda jumpy, aren't you?" He held out her hand. "I'm Mason Bayless. I don't think I've seen you around the plant before. Are you new?"

"I know," Annajane said, "I mean, I know you're Mason." Idiot! He'd think she was stalking him. She blushed and tried to start over. "Well, I mean, we've met, but it's been a long time. I'm Pokey's friend, Annajane Hudgens." She smiled nervously, glancing down at the large red stain blossoming across the front of her new dress.

"Pokey's friend," he said. "The one who disappears every August. Hell yeah. So you're working here?"

"Just for the summer," Annajane said. "Your dad gave us jobs. It's my first day."

"And where's my bratty sister?" Mason asked. "Did she bail on you already?"

"Um," Annajane stalled, not wanting to rat out her best friend.

Mason rolled his eyes. "That's what I thought. She never even showed today, did she?"

"She might have had summer school this morning," Annajane lied. "She's trying to get her Spanish grade up to a B."

"Riiight," Mason said. "What do you wanna bet her lazy behind is lying right beside the pool at the club, while you're stuck here at the plant, counting bottle caps?"

"Summer school could have run late," Annajane said, loyal to the end.

"If you do see Pokey, tell her I came by," Mason said. "I'll stop by Voncile's desk and

46

let her know I kinda messed things up in here."

"Thanks," Annajane breathed.

"And don't worry," he added. "I won't blow Pokey's cover story. Not this time, anyway."

4

Annajane never told Mason she'd fallen in love with him that first day at the plant. She'd never told anybody. Not even Pokey. After all, she'd been fifteen, he was nineteen, working in the warehouse for the first time that summer after his freshman year of college, at his father's insistence. As far as Mason Bayless was concerned, Annajane was just some goofy girl who hung out with his baby sister.

He hadn't given her a second thought, or a second glance. It would be another four years before they exchanged their first kiss.

Her cheeks burned now at the thought of that first time. She shook her head violently, trying to dislodge the memory.

"You okay?" Pokey whispered. "It's not too late to make your escape."

But it *was* too late. The music swelled again, and the violins and flutes and organ began the fluttering notes of the Pachelbel's Canon in D. Every head turned toward the back of the church.

"Ahh." Annajane heard the chorus of approving sighs, and in a moment she spotted Sophie.

The five-year-old tiptoed slowly up the aisle. Somebody had attempted to tame the wild mane of blond curls, but the circlet of baby's breath and pink rosebuds rested at a crooked tilt, listing slightly over her right ear. She was angelic in the ankle-length pink organza dress with its delicate pin-tucked bodice and bell-shaped sleeves. Annajane held her breath as Sophie made her way up the aisle, flinging fists full of rosebuds from the satin basket dangling from her skinny wrist. Her sparkly pink cat-eye glasses slid down her nose, and she paused once, to push them back into place.

The sight of Mason's daughter caused Annajane unexpected tears. Sophie was not her child, although she should have been. Mason had fathered her during a brief one-night stand not long after their separation and had legally adopted her after the mother couldn't care for the baby.

People in Passcoe expected that Annajane would be outraged by the child's birth, so soon after her split from Mason, but Sophie had stolen her heart the first time she held her in her arms. How could anybody resent bossy, enchanting, Disney-princess-loving Sophie? Her Aunt Pokey's house was Sophie's second home, and since Pokey's best friend, Annajane, was there nearly as often as the child, Sophie considered her family. Which she was. Sort of. Leaving Sophie, losing her to Celia — the prospect of it felt like the unkindest cut of all to Annajane.

As always, Sophie seemed to move to her own inner soundtrack, which was unfortunately nowhere in sync to Canon in D. The little girl was anxiously scanning the aisles as she walked, looking, Annajane knew, for familiar faces. Finally, she spotted Annajane and her aunt Pokey and nodded solemnly. But behind the thick lenses of her glasses, her usually impish gray eyes were dark-rimmed and heavy-lidded. Her cheeks were hot pink in contrast to her alabaster skin.

Pokey leaned into the aisle. "You're doin' great, baby," she whispered encouragingly, and Annajane nodded silent agreement and blew her a kiss. Finally, the child gave a tremulous smile and pressed a wad of rosebuds into Pokey's outstretched hand. As she moved past, Annajane noticed that the streamers of the long satin sash were lopsided, and wet, which surely meant that the sash had somehow gotten dunked during a prewedding potty stop.

Why, Annajane wondered, hadn't somebody spotted the wet sash? Perhaps, somebody like Sophie's about-to-be stepmother? The dress was Celia's own design, and no matter what

50

Pokey or Annajane thought of her as a person, it was no secret that Celia's successful children's clothing business, Gingerpeachy, had recently sold to a national chain, netting Celia and her backers a rumored ten million dollars.

A few steps past their pew, two-thirds of the way to the altar, Sophie came to a dead stop. She was looking uncertainly, right to left. The music kept playing, but Sophie was not moving. Annajane held her breath.

She looked up at the altar. Father Jolly seemed oblivious, but Davis and Pete were frowning, exchanging worried asides. Mason had taken a couple steps forward. He was half-kneeling, smiling, his arms extended to his little girl, encouraging her to finish her triumphant voyage up the aisle.

Annajane could read his lips, even from this far way. "Come on, sweetheart," he was telling her. "You can do it."

She could not see the child's face, only the slightest nod of her head, and then Sophie began to tiptoe forward again.

Only a few steps behind Sophie came a willowy redhead in an ankle-length cerise organza gown, cut so tightly through the skirt, she was forced to take tiny, mincing geisha-girl steps. The woman was in her late twenties and looked as though she'd just stepped off a Paris runway.

"Who's that?" Annajane asked.

51

Pokey shrugged. "Never laid eyes on her before. Just another of Celia's legions of best girlfriends, probably."

Six more women in silk gowns of the same hue followed the maid of honor. Annajane knew most of the women, some of them only slightly. But when she saw a familiar brunette with long, wavy, blond highlighted hair, Annajane felt a stab of jealousy. McKenna Murphey Kelleher was *her* friend. They'd known each other since junior high, and Annajane had introduced McKenna to Jimmy Kelleher, the man she'd ended up marrying. When had McKenna defected to Team Celia?

There was no time for further discussion. The processional music faded, and the heavy wooden doors at the rear of the church opened with a theatrical boom. The congregation stirred and stood, and in the brief silence the rustle of satin, silk, and good wool filled the church.

Annajane's eyes were riveted on the bride, the future Mrs. Mason Bayless.

Celia Wakefield was teacup-sized, with short, silvery hair and huge doelike liquid-dark eyes that were today emphasized with the most extravagant false eyelashes Annajane had ever seen. She seemed even smaller than usual, standing back there, poised and alone, framed by the twelve-foot oak door.

Mason, on the other hand, was at least eighteen inches taller than his new bride. He was solidly built, not heavy, but she estimated he weighed close to a hundred pounds more than Celia.

What, Annjane wondered idly, was sex like between the two of them? She squeezed her eyes shut, trying to dislodge the image of Mason and Celia, naked. After all, she was in church, not exactly the same church where she and Mason had been married, but it was still church, and the eyes of God and all of Passcoe were watching. *Must stop thinking about sex in church,* Annajane vowed.

Strings and woodwinds warbled, a lovely classical piece that seemed hauntingly familiar. "What's that song?" Annajane asked, craning her neck to get a better look at the bride.

Must not think of sex in church. Must not think of sex in church. Must not think of Mason naked.

Instead, she tried to think of Shane, naked. Her fiancé had a perfectly nice body, tall and rangy, and he had long, artistic fingers, but he was just the slightest bit self-conscious, even in bed, which she thought must be unusual. Weren't musicians supposed to be wildly uninhibited? Oh, but Mason, naked! Annajane felt herself shiver at the memory.

Fortunately, her best friend didn't notice. She was humming the processional under her breath. Pokey had taken piano for years at Sallie's insistence, and was actually a credible musician, when she cared to be. She gave a sniff of disapproval. "Handel. *Arrival of the Queen of Sheba.* As if."

The bride took her first step down the aisle.

Celia was tiny, dainty, exquisite, a queen of Sheba in miniature, Annajane thought. Her gown, another of her own designs, was a severe architectural strapless column of lustrous ivory satin, its only ornament a series of stiff fabric folds forming an accordion-pleat fan at the alarmingly low-cut bodice.

Seeing the regal bride, Annajane felt instantly five sizes larger, dowdy in her fussy vintage dress with its prissy row of buttons and old-fashioned buckle. She'd dressed with such care only a few hours earlier, and dulled her inhibitions with bourbon, but now, she decided, she'd seriously overdressed and undermedicated herself. What the hell had she been thinking?

"Geezus H!" Pokey chortled, elbowing Annajane in the ribs again. "That's some dress. I think I can actually see her nipples."

"Hush," Annajane said halfheartedly, looking around in panic for an escape route. But her pew was packed butt to butt. It was standing room only in the church, with latecomers lolling against the walls on the side aisles, and the bride about to process down the center aisle. No, not even Houdini could have extricated himself from such a tight prison. She would have to stay and see the cure all the way through to the bitter end.

The bride paused for a moment, basking in this, her moment of glory. She adjusted her train, raised her chin, and began to glide down the white-carpeted aisle. Celia's ensemble was simplicity itself. She wore no jewelry other than her engagement ring, except a pair of shoulder-brushing diamond drop earrings, and in the now-darkened church, the diamonds spun kaleidoscopic reflections on the ceiling. She clutched a single immense calla lily — the size of a majorette's baton — in her elbow-length gloved hands.

Halfway up the aisle, Celia's cloak of poise slipped, just a bit. She frowned and slowed her gait.

The music was still playing. Annajane turned toward the altar, to see what was holding things up. Father Jolly, Pete, and Davis stood expectantly, watching the proceedings with detached solemnity.

Mason's back was ramrod straight. His lips were curved in a slight, frozen smile, but the rest of his face seemed a mask, his eyes flickering rapidly, side to side.

Sophie had stopped again, this time only a few yards from the altar. She was looking around, studying the flowers, her grandmother and cousins in the front pew, waving shyly at her adored nanny, Letha, in the row directly behind Sallie Bayless and family.

Letha leaned out into the aisle. "Go on,

baby," she whispered. "You're doing great."

So what if the groom was nervous? Annajane thought. This meant nothing. It was perfectly natural. Mason had been single for five years. Since their divorce, he'd certainly played the field, dated his share of women, most of them wildly inappropriate, and one of those flings had resulted in Sophie, whose appearance, literally on the Bayless family doorstep, had at first been a shock and then what they'd all come to unanimously regard as a blessing.

She had to give Mason credit. Faced with a six-month-old baby and apparently irrefutable proof of the child's paternity, he had done the right thing. The Baylesses did not shirk responsibility. He had been forced to, as Davis so cynically put it, "man up." Letha had been hired as a nanny, and a nursery was established in Mason's house, just down the street from the Bayless compound.

Sophie, who'd been a spindly, colicky infant when she came to them, had slowly begun to blossom. Mason's responsibilities for Quixie had formerly kept him on the road four days out of every week, but after Sophie arrived, he'd reshuffled his responsibilities to allow him to spend most evenings with her. And he had fallen head over heels in love with his little girl.

Mason had a lot on his plate, Annajane thought. He had a first wife who still worked for the company, right under his nose, at least for the time being; a faltering business to run; and a crazy family to try to ride herd over. And any moment now, she thought, he would be adding a second wife and stepmother to that mix.

He seemed to be holding up reasonably well under the pressure, Annajane decided, studying him again. He rocked back slightly on his heels, and his lips tried, but failed, to form a smile as Celia began moving closer.

Annajane stared, her face growing hot again. A muscle twitched in Mason's jaw. He worked to erase it with his right index finger, but it twitched again. For a second, only a second, she felt Mason's eyes meet her own. And then his jaw muscle twitched six times in rapid succession, and he looked away.

Not soon enough. Annajane's pulse quickened and her throat caught. She felt dizzy and grabbed Pokey's arm for support.

It was a tell! How many times had she seen that involuntary signal? Across the room at a boring dinner party, in the middle of a contentious meeting with his mother or his brother? And yes, during the worst moments of their doomed marriage. When Mason was feeling trapped, desperate to flee, he would rock back on his heels, and his jaw muscle would twitch like a frightened rabbit's ears.

He wants out, Annajane thought. He does not want to marry this woman.

As she watched, she felt the past come rushing back with a ferocity that nearly knocked her down. And it struck her, this was not just a flare-up she was experiencing, not just a bout of spring fever. This was full-blown passion.

This can't happen. She can't have him. I want him back.

Her fingers gripped Pokey's arm in a death lock.

"Heey," Pokey whispered, giving her a worried look. "What's up? Are you okay?"

Annajane couldn't speak.

The music kept playing. Celia floated past them in a cloud of perfume. Annajane took a half step to the left, sending Pokey half-sprawling into the aisle, but Celia never noticed.

Stop that woman! Annajane wanted to scream. But the words wouldn't come out. And Celia was nearly at the altar. Father Jolly was beaming. Mason's jaw was twitching so violently now, even Davis was looking at him oddly.

No, no, no! Annajane cleared her throat. She was going to do it. She had to do it.

But suddenly, a forlorn, high-pitched wail rose above the violins and the piccolos.

It was Sophie. Just a few feet from the altar, she crumpled to the carpet in a pink tulle heap. She was writhing and clutching her tummy. She howled. "It hurts! Daddy, it hurts!"

5

For a moment, nobody moved. An instant later, Mason was kneeling at Sophie's side. He gently scooped her into his arms, and she twisted like a caged animal. Worse than screaming, she was only whimpering now, words Annajane couldn't quite make out.

The music kept playing. Father Jolly held a whispered conference with Pete and Davis, who were helplessly shaking their heads, looking around for some kind of direction. Celia reached the altar, but there was nobody there to meet her, because her groom was rushing toward the side exit. She stood, momentarily stunned, tightly gripping her oversized calla lily.

"Oh my God," Pokey whispered. "What on earth?" People were murmuring, heads turning, but mostly they were frozen in place.

Annajane didn't wait to hear any more. She managed to slide past Pokey, and now she was sprinting for the front of the church. She had to get to Sophie.

As she reached the door to the robing room, she heard Father Jolly's voice from the lectern. "Uh, folks," he said tentatively. "We've got a sick little girl on our hands here. If you would, I'd like to ask you all to bow your heads and pray for God's blessing."

She found Mason seated on a brocade loveseat in the robing room, cradling Sophie across his lap. She was moaning, and her face was gray and beaded with perspiration. Mason was smoothing her hair with one hand, and fumbling with a phone on a table with the other.

"Here," Annajane said, sliding onto the sofa beside him and extending her arms to the child. "Let me take her. Have you called for an ambulance?"

Sophie whimpered a little, but settled quickly into Annajane's arms. The child's body was hot to the touch, and as Annajane stroked her face, Sophie's face contorted. She shuddered, coughed, and vomited. And vomited again.

"Oh my God," Mason said, dropping the phone. "What . . . what should I do?"

Annajane grabbed for a box of tissue beside the phone and began mopping Sophie's face. "I'm sorry," the little girl sobbed. "I'm sorry." She vomited again.

"It's okay, baby," Annajane said. "It's okay." She wiped Sophie's face clean again, and poised her hand over the little girl's abdomen. "Can I touch your tummy? Just for a minute?"

The child nodded. Annajane placed the palm of her hand flat against Sophie's stomach, but even the lightest touch resulted in a yowl of pain.

"Jesus," Mason said, shakily. "What do you think's wrong?"

The robing-room door opened, and Celia rushed in. "Is she all right?" Celia started to ask. When she saw the vomit spattered across Sophie and Annajane, she took a step backward. Then she swallowed hard, bent down, and took Sophie's hand.

"Where does it hurt, honey?" she asked softly. "Tell Celia."

Sophie moaned and pressed her feverish face against Annajane's chest.

Celia patted Sophie's damp curls. "Poor baby."

She gave Mason an exasperated shake of the head. "She ate a lot of junk at lunch today. I personally saw your brother sneaking her at least two bowls of that damned Quixie ice cream. It's probably just a combination of an upset tummy and all the excitement."

"You think?" Mason asked hopefully, his hand hovering over the phone.

Celia looked over at Annajane, treating her to a conspiratorial smile. "Maybe you could be an angel and go get Letha and ask her to take Sophie home and put her to bed?"

"I don't think so," Annajane said. "This isn't just a bellyache. I'm sorry, Celia, but we need to get her to the hospital. Right now. She's burning up with fever."

"Excuse me?" Celia tilted her head, as though she hadn't heard correctly. "We've got five hundred people sitting in that church out there. We've got a soloist from the North Carolina Symphony, and over at the country club, we've got lobster thermidor and a steamship of roast beef. My great-aunt Eleanor flew in this morning from Kansas City. With an *oxygen* tank."

There was a quick knock at the door, and Father Jolly poked his head inside. "How's the patient?" he inquired. "I hate to intrude, but people are concerned." He shrugged apologetically. "Mason, your mother and sister wanted me to see how the little girl is doing. Mrs. Bayless doesn't want anybody to panic."

Celia stood and hiked up the sagging bodice of her dress. "Tell Sallie everything is fine." She gave Annajane a pointed look. "There is no need to overreact. We just need *somebody* to fetch Letha, and then, I think, we can go ahead with the ceremony. Right, darling?" She rested her hand lightly on Mason's broad tuxedo-clad shoulder, letting her fingertips drift down the lapel of his jacket. It was a clear signal of ownership, to

63

Father Jolly, Mason, and most important, Annajane.

He is mine. I am in charge. The show must go on.

Mason glanced from his ex-wife to his next. He cleared his throat. "Well . . . uh . . ."

As if to settle the matter, Sophie moaned, coughed, and barfed again.

Annajane struggled unsteadily to her feet, clutching Sophie to her. She had had enough.

"Fine. You two do what you need to do. But in the meantime, Mason, I think you'd better call 911." She was making a deliberate effort to keep her voice calm. "Tell them we've got a five-year-old with abdominal pain and a high fever. Her belly seems rigid and tender to the touch. And tell them to please hurry."

"Excuse me?" Celia said. "What medical school did you say you attended?"

"My mother was a nurse for thirty years, and I was a candy striper all through high school," Annajane said calmly. "Anyway, it's just a matter of common sense. Feel her tummy, if you don't believe me."

Mason was dialing and reaching for Celia's hand. "I'm sorry," he said pleadingly. "But you understand. Right?"

Celia took only a moment to reevaluate the situation, shift tactics, and choose the proper response. "Of course," she cried. "Absolutely. Do you think it would be better to load her

64

into my car and take her over to the hospital ourselves?"

"Just a minute," Mason said, turning his attention back to the phone. "Right. This is Mason Bayless. I'm at the Church of the Good Shepherd in Passcoe. There's something wrong with my little girl. What? No, I don't know the address. It's on Fairhaven, about a block from downtown. It's the only Episcopal church in town, for God's sake. Don't you people have a computer or something?"

He listened impatiently. "Yes, that's it. Okay. She's five years old, and she just . . . suddenly collapsed. She's in a lot of pain. It's her stomach. She's got a high fever, and she's throwing up . . . No, she doesn't have any allergies that I know of. No! She hasn't gotten into poison. Who the hell do you think you're dealing with here?"

Annajane took the phone from him. "Listen, you need to send an ambulance. Now. I'm no nurse, but I think maybe it's her appendix. Fine. We'll meet you out front of the church."

The robing-room door opened and Pokey stepped in. "What's the news?" she started, and then wrinkled her nose. "Oh no. Stomach bug?"

"Annajane thinks it might be her appendix," Mason said gloomily. "They're sending an ambulance."

65

"What do you need me to do?" She was addressing her brother, ignoring his fiancée not something Celia was used to.

"Pokey, could you please ask Father Jolly to announce that the ceremony has been postponed?" Celia said, reasserting her authority. "Ask everybody to go ahead on over to the country club for the reception. Just say we're doing things backward. Reception, then ceremony. We've got all that food and champagne chilled down, and it'd be a shame to waste it. We'll try to get over there after we get Sophie taken care of at the hospital. But she's the first priority."

"We'll have to get all those cars cleared out of the driveway and the street outside, before an ambulance can get here," Pokey said. "And Mama's going to want to go to the hospital, too, I can tell you right now."

"Fine," Celia said impatiently. "You and Pete can take her, or Davis or somebody, but in the meantime, could you please get those cars moved?"

"Sure," Pokey said, bristling at being ordered around. She looked over at Annajane, who was pacing around the small room, softly humming to the whimpering Sophie. "I'll be right back after the announcement, and we'll get you some kind of clean clothes. You can't leave looking like that."

"I don't mind," Annajane protested. "Just do whatever you need to do, Pokey. I'm go-

ing to ride in the ambulance with Sophie." She glanced at Mason. "If that's okay with you?"

"Now, wait a minute," Celia snapped, not about to let Annajane usurp her authority. "Her father and I will ride in the ambulance. He's going to have to sign authorization for her to be treated. And I'm her, uh, I'm his wife."

Pokey turned to go. "Not yet, you're not." She said it under her breath, just loud enough for Celia to hear.

"Daddy," Sophie whimpered, reaching out an arm for her father.

"Right here, sugar," Mason said, stepping to Annajane's side and squeezing the little girl's hand. "We're going to get you to see a doctor right this minute. And guess what? You're gonna get to ride in an ambulance. What do you think about that?"

"Will it hurt?" Sophie asked, huge tears rolling down her pale cheeks.

"Not at all," Celia said brightly. "It'll be fun! I'll get them to blast the siren so everybody knows you're coming."

"It might hurt a little bit," Annajane said, shooting Celia a look. "But we'll be right there with you, the whole time. We need to get the doctors at the hospital to see what's wrong with your tummy. I think they'll give you something to make you sleep, and then they'll take a look and figure things out."

"Okay," Sophie said wearily. "Only, don't let me go, Annajane. Okay?" Her eyelids fluttered, and she dozed off, her forehead nestled against Annajane's ruined dress.

"I won't, baby," Annajane whispered. "I promise."

Mason reached over and gently removed the little girl's glasses, which had slid off the end of her nose, tucking them into the pocket of his tux jacket.

The door flew open again, and Sallie Bayless bustled in with Davis in her wake. "Pokey says there's some talk that it might be her appendix? And an ambulance is on the way? I just called Max Kaufman. He was on the third tee at the golf club when I reached him," she told her son. "He's going to meet you at the emergency room."

"Max Kaufman?" Celia asked.

"Chief of surgery at the hospital," Sallie said. "A very old family friend. He should have been sitting right out front in one of those pews, but Max is a hopeless philistine. Says he never goes to weddings or funerals. But he's a wonderful doctor, isn't he, Mason? He'll take very good care of the child."

"Mason and Annajane are going to the hospital, and I'll follow in my car. Maybe you could ride with me," Celia said.

Sallie shook her head. "Celia, dear, I think it would be better if you and I went on over to the club to greet our guests. Mason has his cell, and I have mine, and he can keep us posted."

"I don't know," Celia said, her brow furrowed prettily. "I think I need to be with Sophie . . ."

"Look, y'all, we don't all need to go to the hospital," Davis spoke up. "Mama, I'll take you and Celia over to the club for the reception. If there's nothin' seriously wrong with Sophie, Pokey can bring Mason back over there once Doc Kaufman gets it figured out. Hell, maybe it's nothing. It'd be a shame to cancel the party if it's only a bellyache."

He glanced toward the doorway, where Celia's sultry maid of honor leaned against the doorjamb, looking bored.

"Good idea," Mason nodded in agreement. He grasped Celia's arm and gently steered her toward the door.

"Well," Celia said hesitantly, "If you really think you can do without me . . ."

Mason walked her to the door. His hand rested lightly on the small of her back, and he brushed a kiss on Celia's forehead. "I knew you'd understand. Look, I'll call you the minute we know something. Maybe it's not really anything serious. In which case, I'll be at the club in an hour or so. Okay?"

Celia responded by wrapping her arms tightly around Mason's neck, molding herself to him, and kissing him deeply and passionately.

Sallie Bayless looked away politely. Finally, she cleared her throat. "Celia, dear, I think we'd better go. Your great-aunt is out there, and she's beside herself with worry . . ."

In the distance, they heard the approaching keen of a siren.

Mason peeled himself off the front of his bride's low-cut gown. "Better go," he said.

"Call me," Celia repeated, reluctantly allowing herself to be towed away.

When they were alone again, Mason went back to the settee, where Annajane was still holding Sophie in her arms.

"Let me take her," he whispered, holding out his arms.

"You'll ruin your tux," Annajane protested, but Mason was already sliding his arms under the child's limp torso. He straightened up and cradled Sophie against his chest.

"You really think it's her appendix?" he asked.

Annajane shrugged. "My cousin Nadine had appendicitis one summer when we were up at the cabin. Thank God Mama was there, because my aunt really thought Nadine was just constipated. Mama insisted they go to the emergency room, and, sure enough, that's what it was."

Mason blanched. "Maybe we should take her to Raleigh. Max Kaufman is a good enough country doc, from what I know, but

Passcoe Memorial is just a little old podunk hospital with, what, fifty beds? Maybe she should see a pediatric specialist . . ."

The siren was getting closer now.

"Mason, Passcoe Memorial is a fine facility," Annajane said. "It's small, but they have a state-of-the-art surgical wing, thanks to your father's Rotary Club, and Mama always said Dr. Kaufman was the best surgeon, the best diagnostician, she'd ever seen. If it really is her appendix, there's probably no time to take Sophie to Raleigh. If it's something else, something more serious, Dr. Kaufman can refer us to a specialist, but in the meantime, let's just take one thing at a time, please?"

Pokey rushed into the room, pink-faced and breathless.

"Okay, the cars are moved, and the ambulance is pulling around front," she said. She put one hand to Sophie's cheek. "Oh wow, she really does have a fever," she said. "How long has she been asleep?"

"Just a few minutes," Mason said.

"Where's the bride?" Pokey asked, looking around the room. "Checking her makeup?"

"Not funny," Mason snapped. "Mama persuaded her to go on over to the country club. Maybe you should join them."

"Not a chance," Pokey said. "Pete's taking the boys over there, but I'm going to the hospital."

6

Geographically, the distance from the church to the hospital, which was located on the bypass just outside the Passcoe city limits, was only seventeen miles.

To Annajane and Mason, the ride seemed to take a lifetime. Jammed into the back of the ambulance, perched on either side, with Sophie's tiny form on a gurney between them, they could only watch helplessly as she writhed in pain.

"She's hurting! Can't you give her something?" Mason growled at the emergency medical technician riding in the passenger seat.

"Sorry, Mr. Bayless, but with kids this young, we just make sure their pulse and breathing are stable," the EMT said. "We'll be at the hospital in fifteen minutes, and they'll probably give her something then."

"Daddy," Sophie whimpered. "Annajane. It hurts."

She was awake again, and she looked terrified. Annajane squeezed the child's hot, clammy hand and brushed back a strand of hair from her forehead.

"We're taking a ride to the hospital, sweetpea," Annajane said. "Can you tell how fast we're going? This old ambulance goes even faster than your daddy's fun car."

Mason laughed despite himself. The "fun car" was what Sophie called his restored candy-apple red 1972 Chevelle convertible. It had been Glenn Bayless's favorite big boy toy, handed down to Mason as a twenty-first-birthday gift.

The convertible was currently garaged in a truck bay at the bottling plant, brought out only occasionally, for Sunday drives to the coast, or as a special treat for Sophie, because there wasn't room for it in the two-car garage at the house, what with his own Yukon and Celia's Saab. And also because Celia had taken an instant disliking to — and distrust of — what she called his "middle-aged crazy car," or, worse, "your pimp-mobile."

"Why can't you buy a nice Porsche, like your brother's?" Celia had asked. "Or something with say, air-conditioning? Or satellite radio?"

The Chevelle's air probably hadn't worked all that well when it was new, and as for a radio, Mason preferred its tape deck, on which he listened to his stash of '80s hair bands.

He'd had some times in that Chevelle, for sure. In his youth, he'd ripped up and down the East Coast in it, ridden the length of the Outer Banks, the one summer of his youth when he hadn't worked at Quixie, his summer of rebellion, when he'd gotten a job working at a convenience store at Nags Head. He'd even driven to California and back, following the old Route 66, the summer he'd graduated from Penn.

Sophie's tear-swollen eyes widened. "Can you make the top of the amb'lance go down so I can see out?"

"I can't do that, sugar," Mason said soothingly, "but just as soon as we get your tummy better, I'm gonna take you all the way to the beach in the fun car. Just you and me."

"And Annajane," Sophie added. "Annajane loves the fun car, too."

Mason exchanged a look with his ex. Her cheeks colored and she looked away. He wondered if she remembered.

He'd been driving the Chevelle the second time he remembered an important encounter with Annajane Hudgens. She was what? Maybe nineteen? Which would have made him twenty-three.

It was summertime, and he'd somehow allowed himself to be roped into driving the convertible in the Passcoe Fourth of July parade, chauffeuring a local beauty queen,

74

Tamelah Dorman, who'd actually been crowned Miss Passcoe, although it should have been Miss Spray-Tan, because she was surely the most artificially overbronzed girl he'd ever encountered.

Anyway, he and Tamelah were having a pretty good time that day. She, perched on the back of the Chevelle, decked out in a short, low-cut spangly firecracker-red dress that definitely showed off her best assets, and he in shorts and a white Quixie Soda polo shirt. He'd filled a flask full of crushed ice, Captain Morgan rum, and Quixie, and he and good old Tamelah had emptied and refilled it before they got a quarter of the way down the Main Street parade route that morning.

The Fourth of July parade was always a major deal in Passcoe, and that year, the hundredth anniversary of the town's incorporation, made it an even bigger deal than usual. Thousands of people lined Main Street, seated on lawn chairs, standing in the shade of storefronts, or crouched on the curbs.

He'd hoped for a spot either at the very beginning or the very end of the parade lineup, but no such luck. They'd slotted him slap in the middle, between Patti-Jean's Twirling Tykes — three dozen tap-dancing, baton-twirling preschoolers, and the El-Shazaam Masonic Lodge's Shriner Klown Korps,

75

which consisted of ten middle-aged men in white face, baggy pants, and red fright wigs, perched atop souped-up lawn-mower chassis.

Their progress was agonizingly slow. The Tykes' twirling routines were limited to two songs — playing over and over again — which blared out from a huge boom box mounted on a wagon pulled by Patti-Jean herself, a Sousa march and *I'm a Yankee Doodle Dandy.* Behind him, the Klown Korps guys zigzagged crazily across the pavement, popping wheelies and running a dizzying series of figure eights that left an acrid cloud of gasoline fumes hanging overhead.

The sun was blazing down, and Mason worried that their snail's pace would cause the Chevelle's supercharged engine to overheat.

What with the heat and all, he and Tamelah had slain one whole bottle of the Captain and were shaking hands with another, and they still had half a mile to go before they would reach Memorial Park, where the parade ended and a huge citywide picnic and carnival was set up. If his memory served, Tamelah was so trashed that she'd given up her regal, queenly wave, and begun flipping off the good citizens of Passcoe seated on folding chairs along Main Street. Twice, when male admirers ran up alongside the car to snap photos of her, Tamelah had obliged by flashing them her boobs. She and Mason had already discussed a postparade meet-up back at his apartment later that evening.

At some point along the route, he'd glanced to the right and noticed that his wasn't the only Quixie soft drink unit participating in the parade.

There, pushing a hand cart and handing out complimentary cans of Quixie and fifty-cent coupons, was the company mascot, Dixie, the Quixie Pixie herself.

Somehow, somebody in the company had conned some poor sap into climbing into the pixie costume. Whoever it was, he thought, was probably ready to spontaneously combust in the outfit, which consisted of a long-sleeved green felt tunic, bright red tights, oversized green booties with curled-up toes, and a huge foam-rubber Pixie head, topped off with a pointy green and red elf cap.

Hell, he was roasting in the ninety-five-degree heat, and he was just dressed in shorts, flip flops, and a polo.

He slowed the Chevelle to a roll, waiting until the company mascot was right beside it. "Hey Dixie," he called over. "How's it goin'?"

The mascot head turned, and then the pixie made an exaggerated shrug and marched away at an accelerated pace. He studied the pixie's shape, trying to figure out who might be wearing the costume. The tunic was loose-fitting, but it was short, ending midthigh, and from the looks of the tights, he was pretty sure there was a girl under there. A girl with awesome legs.

"Whoossh that?" Tamelah demanded, whipping her head around to see what Mason was staring at.

"Why darlin', that's just our company mascot," Mason said, grinning.

"Zat a damned leprechaun?" Tamelah asked bleerily.

"Close. It's a pixie."

"What z'actly is a damned pixie?"

Mason gave it some thought. "A mischevious elf. Plus, it was the only word my grandmother could think of that rhymed with Quixie."

"Hmmpph," Tamelah hmmpphed. "Pass me that flask, will ya?"

Mason handed the flask back to Tamelah and rolled up alongside the pixie again.

"Hey Dixie," he called. "Wanna ride?"

This time the pixie did not bother to turn around. She tossed three cans of sodas to a trio of cat-calling teenage boys in rapid succession, and then took off again, the brass bells stitched to her curly toes jingling merrily with every step.

Mason chuckled under his breath, and accelerated the Chevelle.

"C'mon," he called, sliding easily alongside Dixie again. "Who is that under there? We're almost at the park. You can tell me."

But now the pixie was very nearly trotting,

the cart bumping along on the street's uneven asphalt pavement, spewing chunks of ice in its wake. She managed to sidestep the baton twirlers, and then, suddenly, she disappeared into the crowd.

"That damned pixie just shut you down, Mason baby," Tamelah giggled. Mason turned his head, to tell her to pipe down, but he needn't have bothered, because right about then, Tamelah's eyelids fluttered, her head slumped to one side, and she rather inelegantly slid down onto the backseat of the Chevelle. Passed out cold. Or hot, in Tamelah's case, with her spangly dress hiked up nearly to her waist.

Shit. He hoped none of the Twirling Tykes had seen that little performance. Mason turned and yanked the hem of the dress down.

Thank God, he was within half a block of the park. He would have left the parade right then, but he was hemmed in tight.

Fifteen minutes later, he finally pulled the Chevelle into the shade of a towering oak in the parking lot at Memorial Park. He got out of the car and walked around to check on Tamelah. She'd slumped into a prone position on the convertible's white leatherette bench seat, her rhinestone tiara had fallen to the floor, and she was now snoring in a very unqueenly manner. Mason shrugged, again readjusted the hem of her dress for modesty's sake, and looked around.

It was nearly one o'clock, he was hungry, and the irresistible aroma of kettle corn and charcoal-grilled hotdogs was wafting through the treetops from the area of the food concession tents. He pocketed his car keys and set out to find himself some lunch.

The park was already mobbed with people. He had to bob and weave his way through the chest-high banks of shrubbery and flowers, and he was finally making a beeline for the Kiwanis Club's barbecue stand when he happened to see a flash of red out of the corner of his eye. He stopped short and grinned.

The slight figure of a girl in a green tunic and red tights was seated on a park bench a hundred yards away. The foam-rubber pixie head sat beside her on the bench.

Mason ducked behind an overgrown azalea bush, circled around, and came up to the bench from behind. He still couldn't guess the girl's identity. Without a word, he picked up the pixie head and sat himself down on the bench in its place.

"Well, hey there, Dixie," he drawled.

The girl turned and looked at him. It was her, his little sister Pokey's best friend, Annajane. She'd been a cute little kid when he'd seen her last, and he'd glimpsed her around the plant over the past two summers but had somehow never really run into her again.

He'd been right about the heat inside that pixie suit. Her hair was wet and plastered to her head, and her face was beet-red and slicked with perspiration. She'd taken off the oversized green booties, and was so busy rubbing her stocking feet that she hadn't seen his approach. Also, she appeared to be crying.

"Oh no," she said quietly, covering her face with her hands.

"No good," Mason told her. "I can still see you, even if you can't see me. It's Annajane, right?"

"No," she said, sniffing, and still not moving her hands. "I don't know any Annajanes. Go away, please."

He looked around. "Where's your cart?"

"G-g-gone," she wailed. "I was almost at the park, and this bunch of little thugs snuck up behind me. I could only see straight in front of me with that darned pixie head on. Two of the boys grabbed me by the arms and held me, and the others took off with the cart. I tried to chase after 'em, but I couldn't run in these stinkin' shoes. I tried, but I tripped and fell. I tripped and fell, and I've ripped these doggoned tights." She stuck her right leg out, and Mason could indeed see the stocking was torn and stained with blood.

"You're hurt," he exclaimed, bending over to get a closer look. He could see now that the sleeve of her tunic was also ripped and spotted with more blood.

"Just scrapes," Annajane cried. "But I've ruined the costume! And that cart — it was probably really expensive."

"Well, hey," Mason said. "It's not like it's your fault. Nobody's going to blame you. You were mugged!"

Annajane drew her knees up to her chest and clutched them tightly. "God! I just want to go home and take a cold shower and forget about today."

"Do you need a ride?" Mason asked. "How were you supposed to get the cart back to the plant today?"

She sobbed again. "I was supposed to call Voncile, and she'd have one of the route drivers pick me up once I got here to the park! I had my billfold and my car keys in the cart. And now it's gone! And I'd just cashed my paycheck yesterday, and I had a hundred and fifty dollars in it, and now it's all gone!" She buried her head and wept more bitter tears.

Mason looked around uneasily. He wasn't really good with girls who cried, but Annajane was about to break his heart.

He patted her back gingerly. "Hey, it's not the end of the world, you know."

She raised her head and looked at him, rivers of tears and rivulets of snot dripping down her crimson cheeks. "It is to me. I can't afford to lose a hundred and fifty dollars."

Mason felt like a heel. "I know. I'm sorry. I

shouldn't have said that. Look, sitting here crying isn't doing you any good. We should find a cop, and fill out a report. Did you see what the kids looked like?"

"Not really. Just teenaged boys. Maybe thirteen or fourteen. I didn't recognize any of them from around here."

"Okay," Mason said with a sigh. "I'll go see if I can find a cop. Listen, are you hungry? Have you eaten today?"

"No," she said, her voice wobbly. "I mean, no, I haven't eaten, and yeah, I'm starved. But I don't have any money."

He stood up quickly. "All right. I'll be right back. Hotdog or barbecue?"

"Hotdog."

"Ketchup or mustard?"

"Both."

"French fries or potato chips?"

"Chips," she said, and then, managing a wan smile, "please."

He found a cop lounging against the cotton candy stand and told him how the gang of adolescent boys had made off with the Quixie cart with Annajane's billfold and car keys.

"I'll put out a watch for the cart," the cop promised. "They probably just wanted the drinks, and with any luck, they'll dump it somewhere. Have your girlfriend come by the station later and fill out a report."

Mason was about to tell him Annajane wasn't his girlfriend, but something made him hesitate.

Fifteen minutes later, he was back at the bench with a grease-spattered paper sack containing three mustard-and-ketchup-soaked dogs, a bag of potato chips and a package of french fries, not to mention two huge Styrofoam cups of sweet iced tea.

He handed her one of the cups. "I figured you'd probably already had your fill of Quixie today."

She nodded gratefully and gulped a mouthful of icy tea. "Oh God, this tastes good," she said.

He sat down beside her again and parceled out their food. She gobbled down the hotdog and potato chips as though she hadn't eaten in a week.

Finally, she sat back and sighed.

"Feel any better?" Mason asked.

"Fuller, maybe," Annajane said. "Thank you for lunch." She craned her neck and looked past him.

"What happened to Miss Passcoe?"

"She, uh, was a little tired out after the parade," Mason said. "She was catching a catnap in the car."

"Stone-cold drunk, right?" Annajane guessed. "Tamelah was a year behind Pokey and me in high school. She could drink the whole football team under the table, no problem."

"It was pretty hot out there today," Mason

84

said, always the gentleman. "And we mighta had a little Captain Morgan's with our Quixie."

"A little?" Annajane raised one eyebrow. She'd somehow managed to clean herself up while he was on his food run. Her face had returned to its normal color, she'd fluffed her dark hair, and for the first time, he noticed her remarkable eyes, which were a light sea green in contrast to her thick, sooty eyelashes. She wasn't somebody you'd call beautiful. Her nose was kind of stubby, and her mouth was probably too wide for her face. But her eyes made you forget those inconsequential details.

"I should probably go check on Tamelah," Mason said reluctantly, balling up the paper sack. "What about you? Can I give you a lift back to your car?"

"You could," Annajane agreed, "but since I don't have my car keys, it won't do me much good."

"Riiight," Mason said thoughtfully. "Look. Come with me. We'll get Tamelah sorted out, and then I'll take you home. All right?"

She hesitated. "Actually, I was supposed to go over to your house this afternoon. My folks are gone for the weekend, and I'm spending the night with Pokey."

"Even better," Mason said, feeling his spirits unaccountably lifted. He stood and picked up the foam-rubber pixie head. "After you," he told her.

When they arrived back at the Chevelle, Tamelah was gone, tiara and all.

"Guess she had a better offer," Mason said, secretly relieved. He tossed the pixie head in the backseat and opened the passenger door for Annajane.

"Shouldn't we wait around, to see if she comes back? Maybe she just went to find the bathroom or get something to eat," Annajane suggested.

Mason checked his watch. "I'll give her ten minutes, and if she's not back by then, she's on her own."

Fifteen minutes later, he and Annajane were riding down the highway, listening to the radio and singing along at the top of their lungs. An hour later, they were headed for the lake house, which was nothing more than a run-down caretaker's cottage perched at the edge of the spring-fed lake they called Hideaway, on the Bayless estate. Pokey was nowhere to be found. But Annajane showered and changed into a bathing suit, and pretty soon they were cooling off in the lake, floating in a couple of old inner tubes Mason retrieved from the boathouse. Mason had been right about Annajane's legs. They were spectacular. And the rest of her wasn't bad either.

But the thing that did him in were her eyes. Those solemn, amazing green eyes. When she looked up at him through those lowered dark lashes, when she laughed, when she was surprised, or, later, as she dozed on a lounge chair, he couldn't quit thinking about those eyes.

He was stretched out on the chaise next to hers, on the dock, his head propped up on one elbow, staring at her when she woke up.

Her sunburned cheeks flushed a deeper pink. "What are you looking at?"

"You," Mason said. He leaned across and kissed her lightly on the lips. "Where have you been all my life, Annajane Hudgens?"

She blushed even deeper. "I've been right here. Pokey and I have been best friends since we were five. And I bet I've spent more nights at Cherry Hill these past five years than you have. You're the one who's never been around."

"That's about to change," Mason vowed. "Starting today." And for the next six weeks, they'd been inseparable. Knowing her mother's low opinon of the Baylesses, they deliberately kept their families in the dark about their relationship. Mason could never understand why Annajane wanted to keep him a secret. "Your mom doesn't even know me," he'd protested. "How do you know she wouldn't like me?"

"If your last name wasn't Bayless, she'd probably love you," Annajane finally admitted. "But Mama's funny. She's got some kind of bug up her rear about your family. She never has admitted she likes Pokey, even though we've been best friends our whole lives. Mama thinks your mother's stuck-up, that she looks down on anybody who doesn't belong to the country club."

"Well hell, she's right about that," Mason said with a laugh. "Mama is a big snob. But that doesn't make me one."

In the end, though, they both came to enjoy the illicit nature of the romance. Only Pokey was in on the secret. She'd meet Mason at the lake, or stay late after work, and they'd head over to Southern Pines for dinner and a movie. And on the last summer weekend before she had to go back to school at State, she fabricated a story about an all-day shopping trip to Charlotte with Pokey.

Instead, she and Mason snuck out to the lake house, where she gladly gave up her virginity on a creaky army-surplus cot.

The following Monday, Annajane went off to Raleigh for her sophomore year at NC State and Mason went off to grad school. It would be two years before she would see Mason Bayless again.

Her first few weeks back at school, Annajane told herself Mason hadn't called or e-mailed because he was busy with classes. Getting a master's in finance was no joke, she knew. The weeks stretched out, and he still didn't call or e-mail, and she was too proud to call him. She went home at Thanksgiving, but Mason didn't. When Christmas rolled around, she was sure she'd see him. The Baylesses made a big deal of Christmas, with a huge open house on Christmas Eve and an elaborate family dinner. But Mason, Pokey told her, had been invited to spend the holiday with a classmate, at his family's vacation home in Cuernavaca.

When Christmas morning came and went without so much as an e-mail from him, Annajane tore the card off the antique sterling silver cufflinks she'd bought for Mason and instead gave them to her stepfather, Leonard, who only wore short-sleeved dress shirts.

Stung by being so unceremoniously dumped, Annajane returned to school and threw herself into classwork and a rigorous social life. She dated with a vengeance, told herself she was in love with a cute but slightly dim-witted guy in her marketing class, slept with him once, and then swore off men who used more hair products than she did.

She found herself deliberately staying away from Passcoe, instead spending holidays with classmates, even taking a part-time job as nanny for one of her professor's bratty nine-year-old twins, so that she'd have an excuse to stay in Raleigh year-round instead of going home — and facing the possibility of seeing Mason riding around town in that shiny red car with a new girlfriend.

The summer before her senior year, she got an internship with a New York advertising agency and shared a roach-infested six-hundred-square-foot apartment in Brooklyn with two other girls from NC State. Annajane had herself a very large summer; got invited to house parties at the shore, and dated another intern, Nouri, who introduced her to Pakistani food and who promptly fell in love with her and begged her to transfer to Columbia and move in with him.

Instead, Annajane returned to Raleigh in late September, with highlighted blond hair, a discreet butterfly tattoo on her right hip, and a tiny silver nose ring, which she quickly discarded after the shock value wore off.

Somehow, she managed to avoid seeing Mason Bayless for nearly two years. Right up until the day Pokey got married. But that was another story.

7

True to his word, Max Kaufman was standing at the emergency room entryway when the ambulance pulled up the ramp at Passcoe Memorial Hospital. In his late fifties, with a close-shaven shock of graying hair and large, soulful brown eyes, Dr. Kaufman was already dressed in rumpled green surgical scrubs.

After Sophie had been moved to a gurney and brought inside, Dr. Kaufman nodded a brisk greeting to Mason and Annajane, and then was all business, feeling the listless child's forehead and gently probing her abdomen.

Sophie cried feebly at his touch. "It's okay, sugar," Mason said, clutching her hand. "Dr. Max is going to make you feel better." He leaned down, smoothed her hair from her face, and kissed both cheeks.

"We're going to take this little lady back and get her blood drawn right away, do a CT scan, and make her comfortable, but from what you've told me, I suspect it is her appendix, in which case, we'll just get that bugger out of there," Dr. Kaufman said. He nodded at the nurse hovering at his elbow, and she began to wheel Sophie away.

"Well, Miss Sophie," they heard the nurse say. "My name is Molly. And I've got a little girl just your age at home, and her name is Sophie, too. What do you think about that? I sure do love that pretty pink dress you're wearing. Did you have a birthday party today?"

"No," Sophie said. "We were getting my daddy married, but then I throwed up."

Dr. Kaufman chuckled, looking from Mason to Annajane, raising one bushy eyebrow at the groom's vomit-spattered tuxedo and his ex-wife's ruined dress. "Everybody good now? Fine. Fill out the paperwork, get yourself some of our world-famous crappy coffee, and I should be able to let you know something about the surgery in a few minutes."

"Is this really necessary?" Mason asked anxiously.

"What, an appendix?" Dr. Kaufman said, irritably. "Mason, nobody really needs an appendix, as far as we know. It's not terribly common for a five-year-old to have appendicitis, but it's not a rarity either. That said, if she does have a hot appendix, we need to remove it, or things will get really ugly really fast. So you need to let me go find out, all right?" Without waiting for an answer, he turned and disappeared behind the swinging door to the examining rooms.

"Thank you," Annajane called after him.

"Prick," Mason muttered. He turned without a word and went to the intake desk to start filling out the paperwork.

Annajane found herself alone in the emergency room waiting area, a cheerless room with beige linoleum floors, beige painted walls, and a row of army-green straight-backed leatherette chairs that faced a wall-mounted television showing a video of proper hand-washing techniques. The only other entertainment option in the room was a beige metal magazine rack holding a handful of well-thumbed copies of *Highlights for Children* and *Modern Maturity.*

Choosing *Modern Maturity* only because all the brain-teaser puzzles in *Highlights* had already been worked, she was idly scanning an article about prostate health when Mason returned, slumping into a chair once removed from her own. He sighed loudly and buried his head in his hands.

Annajane looked at the clock. "It's barely been fifteen minutes," she pointed out.

He didn't respond.

"She's a perfectly healthy little girl," Annajane added. "And Dr. Kaufman really does know what he's doing."

"I know that," Mason said, his voice muffled. "It's just . . . this place." He raised his head. His voice was strained and full of despair. "This place. You know?"

"I do know," Annajane said softly. She hesitated, but after a moment, she reached over and squeezed his upper arm. His hand found hers, and he patted it briefly before letting go. They both knew this room all too well.

A little over five years ago, she'd rushed into this same emergency room and found Mason sitting in almost the same place, slumped over, despondent, waiting for news from this same doctor, Max Kaufman. Only that time, the patient had been Mason's father, Glenn, and the news, when it did come, had been devastating.

Funny. That day was the beginning of the end of their marriage.

There had been other fights. Annajane wouldn't have called them fights, really. Quarrels, or tiffs, if anybody ever really used that word.

They'd been married less than two years, when the little fissures in their happiness began to appear.

Mason and Annajane were living in the caretaker's cottage at the lake. It was only a temporary address, Mason assured her, a rent-free solution until they saved enough money for a down payment on a house of their own.

The cottage had been abandoned for years. As children, she and Pokey had appropriated it for a playhouse, furnishing it with cast-off furniture from the big house, a wobbly kitchen table, a pair of rickety wooden chairs, and an army cot for campouts. They played at cooking with a battered saucepan, once nearly burning the place down after attempting to heat up a can of SpaghettiOs on Davis's Boy Scout camp stove.

And yes, she and Mason had snuck away to the caretaker's house for stolen hours in the first few months after they'd started dating.

At first, Annajane had been enchanted with the quaint honeymoon cottage, with its deeply pitched slate roof, leaded-glass windows looking out onto the lake, and stacked stone fireplace.

But living there was a different matter. The kitchen's warped wooden cabinets didn't close, the refrigerator barely cooled, and that adorable roof had a spot that leaked — directly over their bed. It was drafty in the winter and hot in the summertime, and damp and mildew from the lake seemed to creep in year-round. Also, there were mice. There was no washer or dryer, which meant they had to either troop into town to the coin Laundromat or drag their basket of dirty clothes up to the big house, like a couple of college students.

All that Annajane might have cheerfully accepted. She hadn't grown up in a mansion, as Mason had. Her family's two-bedroom brick ranch had one window air-conditioning unit — in Ruth and Leonard's bedroom — and just one bathroom. The real problem with the cottage was its location — directly in the looming shadow of Sallie Bayless, a constant presence in their lives, who was prone to dropping over uninvited to offer Annajane unsolicited advice on everything from housekeeping: "Annajane dear, you really must use lemon oil every week on Mason's grandmother's walnut dresser, to keep the wood from drying out"; to cooking, "Annajane dear, we never, ever use dark meat in chicken salad"; to marriage itself, "Annajane dear, no man wants to see his wife in the morning before she's fixed her hair and her makeup — and his breakfast."

Her mother-in-law never came right out and criticized the new bride in front of Mason. That wasn't Sallie's style, but the slow drip-drip-drip of her constant nitpicking had the effect of sand in Annajane's newlywed sheets.

Annajane knew it was no good trying to extricate their life from Mason's family, or his family's business. They were too tightly woven together now.

And it was all Pokey's fault.

She'd shown up, unannounced, at Annajane's studio apartment in Raleigh, on a freezing weeknight in February.

"Guess what?" she'd demanded, as soon as she'd stepped into the room. "I'm pregnant!" And next came, "You're gonna be my maid of honor. And I won't take no for an answer."

Pokey had been in no hurry to finish college. She'd declared herself on the six-year plan, until she met Pete Riggs at a fraternity party in Chapel Hill. He was from a wealthy Charleston family who owned a chain of fine furniture stores. He was tall and redheaded and had earned a full four-year golf scholarship to Wake Forest. Fun-loving Pokey called Annajane that night, dead serious, to announce that she'd met her future husband. And as always, what Pokey wanted, Pokey got.

Before Annajane knew it, she was being dragged to bridal boutiques for fittings and, yes, back to Passcoe, for a seemingly endless round of brunches, teas, dinners, and showers.

Mason was a no-show for all of the prenuptial hoopla. He was working as a regional manager for Dr Pepper, in Memphis, with his father's blessing, to gain experience outside his own family's business. He was, Pokey confided, being a major pill about the whole thing. "Mason doesn't approve of Pete, and he doesn't approve of me getting married and dropping out just a semester short of graduation, and he most definitely doesn't approve of me having a baby. He threatened to put a beat-down on Pete for knocking me up, until I admitted I actually got myself knocked up on purpose. But if you ever tell that to Sallie, I'll never speak to you again," Pokey said.

"Too bad," Annajane had murmured, trying to sound unconcerned about Mason's opinions. She was desperate to see him again, and desperate to pretend he'd never entered her life. It wasn't until she had to walk up the aisle on his arm, the day of Pokey's wedding, that Annajane allowed herself to remember how she felt when Mason Bayless touched her. It wasn't Mason, she told herself, it was just spring fever.

Still, she tried to avoid him at the reception, dancing with every man in the room who was under the age of seventy and hiding out on the veranda of the country club, behind a huge potted palm, between dances.

That's where he found her, leaning against the veranda railing, sipping a glass of lukewarm champagne toward the end of the evening.

"Shoes hurt that bad?" he'd asked, gesturing toward the high-heeled silver slingback sandals she'd slipped out of.

"They're killing me," Annajane said, taking a large sip of champagne, hoping he wouldn't notice her suddenly flushed face in the darkness.

He picked up the sandals and flung them high into the air and out over the women's practice green.

"Great," she said glumly. "Two hundred dollar shoes. Gone."

"I'll buy you another pair," Mason offered. "Maybe a pair you can actually walk in?"

She didn't smile. "What do you want, Mason?"

He sighed. "I really screwed up, didn't I?"

"Did you?"

"I was a shit heel," he said, resting his back against the railing.

"A deflowerer of virgins," she said, nodding her head in agreement.

He winced. "If I told you I never stopped thinking about you, all this time, would you believe me?"

"No," Annajane said, unsmiling. "Because if you'd thought about me, even once, I'm pretty sure you could have figured out how to get in touch with me over the past two years."

"You're not easy, are you?" Mason said, with an exaggerated sigh.

"Not anymore, no."

"Listen." He touched her elbow lightly, and she jerked it away, but he took it again. "Will you please listen?"

"No," Annajane said. But she didn't move.

"I fell hard for you that summer," Mason said.

She gave a snort of disbelief.

"I did. Honestly. But it wouldn't have worked out. Your mother made me realize that."

She whirled to face him. "My *mother?* What are you talking about?"

He raised one eyebrow. "She never told you she called me, did she?"

"No," Annajane said. "Why would Mama have called you? She didn't even know we were seeing each other."

"Your mother is not a stupid person, Annajane. She figured it out."

Annajane's jaw dropped, and she felt a shiver go down her spine. "All of it?"

"Yep," Mason drawled.

"Oh, God. And she never said a word to me. Never let on she knew." She grabbed Mason's arm. "What did she say?"

"Enough. She called me on my cell phone. From yours. I guess you'd left it lying around the house, and she took a look at the call history. Listened to some of the voicemails I'd left you . . . about meeting me out at the lake house."

Annajane remembered those voice mails. Her face burned with the memory of those sexy messages Mason loved to leave.

"Long story short, she told me to stay away from you. I tried to point out that you were nineteen, and legally of the age of consent, but that didn't cut much ice with your

100

mother. She was very clear that I should get the hell out of your life and stay out. And she made some threats that weren't very nice."

"My mother? Threatened you? And you believed her? My mother wouldn't hurt a fly."

"Your mother said she would call the sheriff and have me arrested for statutory rape. And even if the charges didn't stick, it would ruin my life and ruin my family's reputation. And she meant every word of it."

"But it's not true," Annajane said. "You didn't rape me. Nobody would have believed a story like that."

Mason shrugged. "Doesn't matter. She was so intent on getting you away from me, she would have eventually cooked up something that would work. Anyway, you had to go back to State, and I was headed off to Penn. I decided maybe we should just cool it."

"Nice of you to let me know," Annajane said. "Coward."

"You're right," Mason agreed. "I suck. And the longer I went without talking to you, to try to explain things, the easier it got to just avoid Passcoe, and you. Pokey gave me reports of what you were up to, though."

"She did?"

"I heard about the guy in your marketing class. An SAE, right?"

"He was an ATO actually," Annajane said. "And dumber than a box of rocks."

"And wasn't there some mysterious Asian

guy you went with in New York? Pokey said you got his name tattooed on your ass."

"His name was Nouri," Annajane said. "And he was Pakistani. And no, I did not get his name tattooed on my ass. It's a very small butterfly and it's on my hip."

"I'd like to see that," Mason said. "I'm very interested in entomology, you know."

"Fat chance."

"Pokey says you're currently unattached," Mason said.

"Pokey has a big mouth," Annajane said.

"You haven't asked me if I'm seeing anybody," he said.

She turned toward him and raised one eyebrow, almost afraid to ask. "Are you?"

"No," he said, drawing the tip of his finger up her forearm. "I've been saving myself for you."

Annajane gave him her sweetest smile. She plucked his hand from her arm and dropped it. "What a waste. Nice try, Mason."

She hopped off the flagstone veranda and set out onto the golf course in her bare feet.

"Hey! Where you going?" Mason called after her.

"To get my damned shoes," she muttered.

With a newly minted marketing degree in hand, Annajane took a job in Raleigh, working for a start-up fast food chain called PoBoyz. She set up PoBoyz promotions at high school football games, stock car race-tracks, and minor league baseball games. She worked eleven-hour days and got promoted twice within eighteen months. And then her supervisor called her in for a face-to-face on a Friday at four o'clock.

Phoebe, the department's administrative assistant, gave Annajane a dark look.

"What?" Annajane asked. "It might be good news. I totally killed with that football game promotion. The franchisees said they'd never had so many buy-one get-one coupons fulfilled."

"It won't be good," Phoebe warned. "She never hands out attaboys on Fridays. Mondays are for attaboys. Fridays are for . . . well, I hope I'm wrong."

Eileen, her supervisor, got up and closed the door as soon as Annajane walked into her office. One look at her boss's face and she knew Phoebe had been right.

"I'm sorry," Eileen said, without preamble. "This is awful. I hate this. But I have to let you go."

"Why?" Annajane knew it was bad form to ask, but she'd never been fired before.

Eileen stared down at her desktop. "Howard Dewberry's nephew just graduated from college."

"So?" But Annajane knew what was coming next. Howard Dewberry was one of the company founders.

"The kid needs a job, and he thinks market-ing would be 'fun,' " Eileen said. "And you know the kind of budget we're working with. I can't afford two marketing assistants. Anyway, Annajane, the truth is, you're too good for this job. You're smart and hardwork-ing, and you've outgrown PoBoyz. I'm doing you a favor, really."

Annajane got up with a sigh. "Funny, it doesn't feel like a favor."

She kicked around Raleigh for another six months, sending out résumés and doing temp work, but when her savings ran out, she faced the inevitable and moved back to Passcoe.

But not to her mother's house. Not after the blowout they'd had after Annajane con-fronted her about making threats to Mason.

Instead, she got a crappy job selling ads for the town's only radio station, and she rented a crappy half of a duplex on a crappy street on the outskirts of town.

It didn't take long for Pokey to start match-making once Annajane moved home.

"What did you say to Mason at my wed-ding?" she demanded one day while they were sitting at her kitchen table. Pokey was spooning cereal into Denning's mouth, and he was spitting it out just as fast as she shov-eled it in.

"Nothing," Annajane said. "I just let him know I wasn't interested in getting together."

"That's a big fat lie," Pokey said. "I saw

you watching him at the wedding. And he was watching you. For God's sake, why don't you just sleep with him and be done with all the cat-and-mouse games?"

"I did sleep with him, and then he dropped me like a bad habit," Annajane said. "Remember?"

"You were just kids," Pokey said. "Anyway, you can't keep avoiding him forever. He's moving back to town, you know."

Annajane's pulse gave a blip. "When? Why?"

"Daddy finally talked him into giving up the job at Dr Pepper," Pokey said. "He's coming to work at Quixie." She looked over at the kitchen clock. "And I'd say he should be getting into town right about now."

She gave Annajane an innocent look. "He hasn't seen the baby in months. I made him promise to stop by as soon as he gets in."

Annajane stood up abruptly. "Pokey! This isn't funny. You should have told me you were expecting Mason. I don't appreciate . . ."

The kitchen door swung open, and Mason stepped inside. He stopped in his tracks when he saw that his sister had company.

He looked from Pokey to Annajane and sighed. "She tricked you into coming here, didn't she?"

Annajane nodded. "She tricked you, too, didn't she?"

"Yup." They both turned to confront Pokey, who'd scooped the baby out of his highchair and was beating a fast retreat out of the kitchen.

"Traitor!" Annajane yelled.

Mason sighed. "Did she tell you I'm moving back?"

Annajane nodded.

Mason stared at her intently. "It's a small town, Annajane. You can't hide from me for the rest of your life."

"I haven't been hiding from you," she lied.

"Sure looks like it from where I stand," Mason said. "Maybe let the past be past? At least agree to be friends again?"

She bit her lip and looked out the window. Because she knew if she looked at him, she would cave. Wasn't there some cure for the way she felt every time she was with him? Wasn't it about time she outgrew this adolescent obsession with Mason Bayless?

He reached out and tucked a lock of her hair behind her ear. "Please? Gimme another chance?"

She did. Two months later, she signed on as assistant VP of marketing at Quixie, working for Davis Bayless. Six months later she and Mason were engaged.

While Annajane figured out how to work for her charming, hyper, demanding future brother-in-law, Mason was busy climbing the corporate ladder.

Within six months, he'd been named divisional sales manager. For the first time, he was working for, and with, Glenn.

Father and son were on the road constantly, meeting with supermarket chains and convenience stores, trying to gain a foothold for Quixie in new markets.

Which meant that Annajane was back at home in Passcoe, working long hours, and trying hard to prove her own worth as a professional to Davis, who still tended to treat her like an annoying little sister. Which might not have been so bad, except for the fact that she could hardly complain about her job to her husband or her best friend — since Davis was their brother.

Two short weeks before the wedding, Ruth abruptly announced that she and Leonard were selling their house to move to Holden Beach.

"Now?" a bewildered Annajane had said, looking around at the boxes her mother had seemingly packed overnight. Leonard smiled wanly from his reclining chair, then looked away.

"It's his heart," Ruth had said. "The doctor says he's got congestive heart failure. From working at that damned plant . . ."

"He said no such thing," Leonard objected. "My heart trouble ain't got a damned thing to do with Quixie or the Baylesses. Thirty years of smoking and that chronic obstructive whatever you call it, that's what's done a number on my heart."

"But why the coast?" Annajane had asked. "You don't know anybody there. Why not stay here, where your family and friends are?"

"Because it's high time we got out of Passcoe," Ruth declared. "We've always wanted to live at the beach. Watch the sunsets, play golf, eat seafood whenever we want. Enjoy our lives while we've still got time."

"Your mother's allergic to shrimp," Leonard put in. "And I don't know a putter from a driver. We'll be bored to death. But I can't do nothin' to change her mind."

A month later, Leonard suffered the first of two heart attacks, and the emotional tug-of-war began in earnest.

Annajane made the long drive to Holden whenever she could, but when she couldn't, Ruth's sniping was relentless.

"I guess you got better things to do with your fancy new family than come all the way down here," her mother would say, with a martyred sigh. "Probably there's something going on at the country club."

Whenever she did spend the weekend with her parents, she felt guilty for not spending the time with Mason. Although Mason, she noticed, seemed to have no problems keeping busy when she was away, and even some weekends when she was home. He'd always been a huge fan of college football and basketball, but after their marriage, it seemed to her, he spent an inordinate amount of time either watching UNC games on television or in person.

"You didn't even go to Chapel Hill," she fumed the Saturday after Thanksgiving as he waited for his father and Davis and some other buddies to pick him up for the big UNC-Duke game, only a few hours after he'd gotten home from a weeklong business trip. "I don't see why this is such a big deal for you."

The words sounded bitchy and whiny, even to her, but she couldn't help it. She hadn't seen Mason alone in nearly two weeks. As it stood now, he would get back from Chapel Hill around noon Sunday, then turn right back around and hit the road with his father again on Monday.

He'd looked incredulous, and then annoyed. "Are you serious? This is just the biggest game of the year in this state. I've been going to this game since I was five years old. My grandfather took me to my first Carolina-Duke game. And his grandfather took him. If you really wanted to go, I could get you a ticket."

"And spoil all your fun by making you be the only guy who has to drag his wife along? No thanks," she'd said quickly.

Home alone most weeknights, Annajane, in turn, felt resentment seeping into her usually cheerful demeanor. Pokey was busy chasing her toddler son, so they didn't see each other that much. Her other friends, young and living the single life, occasionally invited her to join them for drinks or dinner, but she no longer enjoyed staying out til two in the morning, only to stumble to work half-awake and half-sober. She made up excuses not to go. She stayed home and dined alone on canned soup and a vague, simmering sense of dissolution.

And when Mason made his nightly long distance phone call, reporting on the dinners he'd just shared with important accounts at four-star restaurants in Atlanta, Charlotte, Nashville, or Charleston, Annajane would silently contemplate the shabby little cottage and her lonely bed. This was not what she'd thought marriage would be.

If Mason noticed her misery, he never mentioned it. He and Glenn were engaged in a high-stakes battle, trying to place Quixie in Maxi-Mart, a huge regional discount supermarket chain with nearly three hundred outlets around the South, many of them in new markets for Quixie. The deal was potentially worth millions for the company.

Among the Maxi-Mart executives father and son were wooing was a woman named Eva. Mason referred to her frequently in those late-night phone calls. "Eva wants us to meet with the guys down in Orlando," he'd say. Or, "Sorry, babe, we won't be home tomorrow after all. Maxi-Mart is the sponsor of a charity golf tournament in Richmond, and Dad and I are gonna play in a foursome Eva put together. You understand, right?"

She wasn't the jealous type. She and Mason were still practically newlyweds. And after all, this was company business. He was doing this for the company, and for them. Just six more months, Mason promised, "Maxi-Mart will be signed and sealed and we'll start house hunting. Hell, you can start looking now. All I ask is that you find something with a den for my big-screen, and a master bedroom big enough for a king-size bed. And no leaks overhead!"

"And a nursery?" Annajane asked.

"And a nursery," Mason assured her.

Still, she heard whispers around the office about this Eva woman. Whispers she chose to ignore. She'd asked Mason about Eva once, on one of their rare weekends together. "Yeah," he said, "I guess she's all-right looking, if you like that type."

"What type is that?" Annajane wanted to know. "Sexy? Flirty?"

Mason shrugged. "I guess some guys might find her sexy. You know, high heels, expensive business suits. She's pretty buttoned-up."

"Not your type?"

Mason laughed and reached around and began to tug at the zipper on Annajane's

111

dress. "Nah, I'm more a zipper man my own-self."

And then Christmas rolled around.

Annjane had volunteered to plan the company Christmas party. She'd wangled a sizable budget out of Davis and spent weeks planning every detail, from hiring the perfect Santa Claus for the visit with the employees' children in the afternoon, down to the oyster appetizers and prime rib at the seated dinner at the country club. For the after-dinner, she'd rented a full-scale disc-jockey setup, with Mason spinning records for the first hour of dancing.

Mason and Glenn were scheduled to drive back from a four-day business trip to Atlanta that Friday, the day of the party.

With Mason out of town so much lately, their love life had definitely taken a backseat to business. But not that night, Annajane decided. She had a postparty seduction carefully planned out for her husband. She'd splurged on a new dress, a short, tight-fitting emerald green velvet sheath with a plunging neckline — cut as low as she dared to go in conservative Passcoe — to be worn with a pair of wickedly sexy five-inch-high stiletto heels. And underneath? She had a black-lace push-up bra and the merest suggestion of filmy black-lace panties. It was going to be, she vowed, an evening Mason would not soon forget.

At six o'clock that night, when she'd run home to change after the children's party, Annajane was chagrined by the fact that Mason's car was missing from the driveway. He'd promised to be back from Atlanta by 5:00 P.M., in time to shower and dress for the party. As she zipped herself into the green dress, she tried to ignore the fact that Mason's tux was still laid out on the bed, where she'd placed it earlier that morning.

She'd called his cell phone twice as she drove back to the country club, but both times her message went directly to voice mail.

By seven, when she stood at the door to the ballroom welcoming their guests, cell phone clutched in one hand in case he called, she was doing a slow burn.

Sallie, of course, noticed everything.

"What a lovely dress," she'd said, her eyes flickering on Annajane's daring décolletage. "But won't you be cold without a jacket or something?" Later, during dinner, Sallie walked past and noticed her constantly checking the phone and texting Mason. "Annajane, dear," she whispered, gently closing her hand over the phone. "This is business. Glenn and Mason are closing a deal. Sometimes things get complicated."

"But he promised to get here for the party!" Annajane whispered back. "And he hasn't called. Maybe something has happened."

Sallie had given her a tight, knowing smile.

"It's just business, Annajane. Get used to it. I have."

All that night, she'd endured the embarrassment of having her husband a no-show. She sweet-talked Pokey's husband, Pete, into stepping in as deejay; table-hopped and chatted with every employee in the room; and, in between, picked at her dinner and glowered at the empty chair beside hers. All that night, her phone did not ring. Finally, at nine o'clock, she tucked her phone into her evening bag, resigned to the fact that it probably wasn't going to ring.

At eleven, she said her good-byes and drove home alone. The temperature had begun to drop at sundown, and now snowflakes were softly falling. White Christmases were a rarity in North Carolina. Any other night, she might have stood at the bay window, watching with wide-eyed glee at the snow sifting onto the lake and accumulating on the shaggy green evergreens ringing the little cottage. But on that night, she shut off the twinkling white lights on the Christmas tree she'd decorated by herself. In the bedroom, she hung up the party dress and changed out of the black lingerie and into a frowsy flannel nightie.

Their room was freezing, and the window panes rattled as the wind howled outside. Part of her worried about Mason driving home on treacherously icy roads; another part of her burned with anger and disappointment.

Finally, she drifted off to sleep, only to awaken at the sound of a car driving up to the house. She checked the clock on the nightstand. It was nearly two. She heard the front door open, heard heavy footsteps on the floors, heard their bedroom door open.

In the half-light from the hallway, she saw Mason drop his suitcase. He walked over to their bed, leaned down, and kissed her cheek.

Annajane pretended to be asleep. She made a show of yawning and half-opening her eyes.

"Sorry to miss the party, babe," Mason whispered.

She wanted to sit up in bed and throw something at him. She wanted to scream her rage about broken promises and ruined evenings. Instead, she rolled over and faced the wall closest to her side of the bed, her body rigid with suppressed fury.

Mason sat on the edge of the bed and took off his shoes. She heard water running in the bathroom, and a moment later he slid into bed beside her. Surely, she thought, now he will apologize. Now he will explain why he didn't call, why he came home so late. Surely, now, he will make it all right.

Her husband curled up beside her in the bed. He yawned and coughed.

Despite herself, Annajane whispered. "Everything all right?"

"Great," Mason said wearily. "We closed

the deal! Three hundred new stores. But I'm beat."

Instead of an apology, he draped a proprietary arm over her shoulder, cupping one hand under her flannel-clad breast. A moment later, she heard his slow, deep, even breathing. And then, soft snoring.

8

Mason was still asleep. Annajane stared down at him, sprawled facedown across their bed. The covers had slipped, exposing his bare back and the waist of his pajama bottoms. It was nearly nine, and she had to go back to the country club to supervise cleanup after the party and to pack up the disc-jockey equipment for return to the rental company.

She'd halfway expected Mason to awaken early, maybe fix their coffee and bring it back to bed for her, the way he'd done the first few months of their marriage. Saturday mornings then were their sacred time. Mason liked — no, loved — sex in the morning. Later, he'd fix her cinnamon toast, and they'd lounge around the house for hours, laughing and talking and making plans for the weekend, eventually tumbling back into bed for another round of lovemaking.

Two years later, she couldn't remember the last time they'd had Saturday morning sex.

Her face hardened as she remembered the

previous evening. If Mason didn't wake up soon and start apologizing, she told herself, they might never have sex again! Not that she meant it. She loved her husband, and loved their lovemaking. But, really, something had to change. They could not go on this way.

With a sigh, she headed for the front door, vowing to have this conversation when she got back home from the country club.

She sighed again, noticing, with annoyance, that Mason's company car, a big white Yukon with the Quixie logo on the door, had her own Acura blocked into the driveway. For a second, she entertained malicious thoughts of waking him up and making him move the car. But she could just as easily take the SUV. It was a bitterly cold morning, with at least an inch of snow on the ground. Mason wouldn't be going anywhere this morning, and if he did have plans, he could just take the Acura.

Annajane eased herself into the Yukon. She fumbled with the control buttons and adjusted the seat for her own frame, which was four inches shorter than Mason's. She backed the big car carefully down the driveway and was soon driving past the ornate wrought-iron Cherry Hill gates.

As she went through her mental checklist of everything she needed to accomplish at the club, Annajane absentmindedly punched the radio button on the Yukon's console. She wanted to hear the day's weather report, and then maybe some Christmas music might put her back into the holiday spirit.

Instead of the weather, though, she heard a sultry woman's voice singing "At Last." Etta James? Since when did Mason listen to the likes of Etta James? She'd have bet money Mason had never heard of the woman. With one gloved finger, she tapped the tracking button. The next song was even odder: "Let's Get It On," by Marvin Gaye. She punched the eject button and grabbed the CD as it slid out of the player.

It was a homemade mix, and written on the silvery disc in purple Sharpie, in a woman's handwriting, was, "Merry Christmas, baby. Think of me, cuz I'm thinking of you."

Annajane felt the blood drain from her face. Her hands were shaking so hard she had to pull the SUV onto the shoulder of the road. She sat there for five minutes, staring at the CD, considering the implications.

Think of me? Who was the me? The owner of the purple Sharpie? Eva? The Maxi-Mart exec? Was it Eva who'd made the mix of love songs? She bit her lip so hard it drew blood. Was this inevitable? After all, Mason was a competitor. He had to win, at any cost. And if it took sleeping with a sexy woman like Eva in order to close the deal, would he say no?

Would he?

Somehow, she pulled herself together and

drove on to the country club. She managed to direct the workers who were loading up the sound equipment onto a truck for return to the rental company. She stayed until she was satisfied that the club's ballroom had been restored to its formerly pristine condition. Annajane was walking out the front door of the club when her mother-in-law arrived with her two best friends, Martha and Corinne.

"Oh good, Annajane dear," Sallie exclaimed, clutching her arm. "You're just the girl we need. We can have a nice lunch, and then, since Gaynelle has a cold, you can make up our fourth for bridge."

Annajane couldn't remember Sallie ever inviting her to join her foursome before, and she could not think of anything she'd rather do less. "I can't," she blurted. "I'm awful at bridge. And . . . Mason is expecting me back at the house."

But Sallie had insisted she stay for lunch with her friends, refusing to take no for an answer. Annajane managed to choke down just enough of the green salad and crab bisque to persuade her mother-in-law that she was all right. Finally, after an agonizing hour, she'd begged to be excused.

When she got back to the cottage, her Acura was parked in the same spot it had been that morning. Mason was sitting in the living room, dressed in faded jeans and his favorite raggedy Penn sweatshirt, watching a football game.

Without a word, she tossed the CD at him, bouncing it off his chest.

"Ow," he'd said, more surprised than angry. "What the hell is this?"

"You tell me," Annajane said, planting herself directly in front of the television. "It was in your car this morning. Interesting song selection."

Mason turned the CD from one side to the other. "It's not mine," he said. He tossed it aside. "Do you mind? Carolina is driving the ball."

Annajane picked the CD up and held it up. "Oh really? Not yours? But it looks like it's got a message for you. 'Merry Christmas, Baby. Think of me, cuz I'm thinking of you?' In a woman's handwriting? Purple Sharpie? Sound familiar?"

Mason shook his head. "Still not mine. Have we got anything to eat?"

"So you're telling me an alien broke into your car and planted a CD of love songs there?" Annajane repeated.

Finally, she had his attention. He looked up at her, his blue eyes narrowed. "What I am telling you is I'm hungry. Also, that is not my CD."

She thrust the CD into his hands. "Whose handwriting is this? Are you telling me it's not that Eva woman's?"

121

He took the CD and examined it. "I suppose it could be hers. I don't really know. Or care. And I don't get why you're getting so worked up about this."

"I'm worked up because you came home nine hours late last night," Annajane said. "And when I got in your car this morning, I found this CD. Are you trying to tell me you weren't with that woman?"

"Hell, yeah, I was with her," Mason said, standing now. "I told you, we finalized the Maxi-Mart deal last night. Dad and I took Eva and the others to dinner at the Ritz-Carlton around eight to celebrate. It was business, Annajane. That's what I do. I sell cherry soda. We ran into some people she knew at the restaurant, and we had to invite them to join us at the table, and by the time we got the check and got out of there, it was after ten, and there was a truck overturned on I-85. You know what the weather was like last night. We're lucky we got home when we did."

"It was two in the morning! Are you sure you and Eva didn't slip upstairs to her room while you were at the Ritz?" She hurled the words at him, blind with anger.

He stared. "Did you really just say that? Did you accuse me of having an affair?"

"Aren't you?"

"Have I ever lied to you, Annajane?" Mason's voice was level, which was infuriating.

122

"Have I ever given you a reason to doubt me?"

"What about last night?" she ignored his first question. "It was the company Christmas party. You were supposed to be there! Everybody was expecting you. I was expecting you. Do you know how humiliated I was? I worked my ass off putting that party together. For you. And your family and the company. But you didn't even call. If you went to dinner at eight, you knew there was no way you'd be back in Passcoe. But you didn't even call to let me know?"

He shrugged. "Okay, my bad. I should have called. But Dad was with me. And we had Eva and the Maxi-Mart folks with us, and everybody wanted to head out and celebrate. I would have looked like a wuss if I'd begged off. What was I gonna say? 'Hey y'all, I can't go to dinner. I gotta call my wife.' "

"And that's worse?" Annajane asked. "Than letting me down? Breaking a promise to your wife?"

Mason was still holding the remote control. He tossed it onto the chair where he'd been sitting. "Okay. This is ridiculous. I was late last night. I missed the Christmas party. I should have called. For that, I am guilty, and I apologize." He turned and stomped toward the front door.

"Wait a minute," Annajane cried. "We're not through here." She shook the CD. "Just tell me how this got in your car."

Mason had his hand on the doorknob. "I'm through. I am not talking about this anymore. Either you believe me or you don't."

"Where are you going?"

The door was open and he didn't look back. "I'm going over to Mama's. She's always got something to eat. Unlike here." He didn't slam the door. In fact, he didn't even bother to close it all the way.

Half an hour later, Annajane did slam the door. And she didn't bother to lock it as she left. Nobody locked doors in Passcoe, especially at Cherry Hill. She tossed a hastily packed overnight bag in the backseat of her Acura, backed out of the driveway, and headed for the main gate. The snow had already begun to melt, and the ancient oak trees lining both sides of the drive looked menacing, with their twisted gray limbs blocking out the weak winter sunlight. A carpet of acorns crunched beneath her tires. A rusted-out pickup truck with an enormous Fraser fir poking out of the bed rolled past her, headed toward the big house. She gave a dispirited wave to Nate, the Bayless's yard man. At the end of the drive, she picked up the remote from the passenger seat, mashed the button, and waited impatiently while the wrought-iron gates slowly creaked open.

Ten minutes later, she was on the bypass. At some point, she realized she didn't really

124

have a destination in mind. All she knew was that she had to get out of Passcoe and away from the Bayless compound.

An hour later, her cell phone rang. She picked it up, and, seeing the screen, tossed it back onto the passenger seat without answering. Mason. She blinked back tears, and a moment later heard the phone buzz, letting her know he'd left a voice mail.

Five minutes later, it rang again. Annajane's hand hovered over the phone. She even picked it up, but then changed her mind. Let him call.

Two hours later, when she pulled into the driveway of the modest little frame house at Holden Beach, she paused before turning off the ignition. Had she really just done this? Picked a fight with Mason? Accused him of cheating, and then run home to Mama? This was crazy. She should turn around, go home, and talk things out calmly with Mason. Make him understand how badly he'd hurt her.

It was full dark. Multicolored lights were strung all across the eaves of her parents' house. A silly plastic light-up snowman was posed on the front steps. Annajane and her mother hated that snowman and tried to persuade Leonard how tacky it was, but her stepfather delighted in hauling it out of storage every Christmas. She could see the glow of the artificial tree through the drapes. Somehow, she felt reassured. Maybe things

125

weren't as bad as they seemed.

Before she could change her mind and turn around to head home, Ruth was opening the aluminum storm door, but instead of surprise or pleasure at seeing her only daughter, Annajane recognized something else in her mother's face.

She jumped out of the car and ran to the door. "Mom? What is it? Is it Leonard? Is he okay?"

Ruth's face was pale. "Leonard's fine. Have you talked to Mason?"

"No," Annajane said bitterly. "Don't tell me he called you."

Ruth held out her own phone. "Here. You need to call him."

Annajane shook her head stubbornly. "Let him stew. Did he tell you what he did to me? He missed the Christmas party? Stood me up? Mama, I think maybe . . ."

Ruth shook the phone in her daughter's face. "You are not listening. Honey, you need to call Mason right this minute. It's Glenn. He's . . . Just call Mason. All right?"

Her mind was a blank. Her hands were trembling. Ruth dialed and handed her the phone.

"Mason? I just got to Mama's. She said . . ."

"It's Dad," Mason said. He sounded calm, detached even. "It's bad. They think he's had a heart attack. We're at Passcoe Memorial."

"Oh my God," Annajane breathed. "When?

How long ago?"

"We're not sure. Mom found him on the floor of the bedroom when she got home this afternoon. They're working on him, but . . . we just don't know anything. Dr. Kaufman is in with him."

"I'm so sorry," Annajane said. "Mason, I am so, so sorry. I'm coming back. Right now."

"All right," he said. "I've gotta go. The nurse is coming out to talk to us."

"Call me," Annajane said. "Let me know what they say. I'm on the way."

She found Mason alone in the waiting room at the hospital, slumped forward in one of those hard-backed green chairs. Even with the harsh fluorescent overhead lights the beige room was wreathed in shadows. He didn't look up when she sat down and called his name.

"Where's Sallie?" she asked, looking around the room. "And Pokey?"

"Pokey had to go home," Mason said, his voice a monotone. "To nurse the baby. Mama's in the room with Dad. They tried to make her leave, but she raised holy hell and threatened to sue everybody, so they finally let her stay."

"What about Davis?"

Mason shrugged. "He went up to Boone early this morning, to go skiing. Phone reception is lousy up there."

"Is there . . . any change?"

"No," Mason said. He sat up and stared at the television. "It's not good," he said bleakly. "Dr. Kaufman says his brain had likely been without oxygen for at least an hour or more by the time Mama found him. The EMTs managed to get his heart started in the ambulance, but Dr. Kaufman told us, even if he does make it, he won't be the same. You know."

Annajane nodded mutely. "I prayed the whole way back," she said finally. "For your daddy. I don't think I've ever prayed so hard in my life."

"Okay," Mason said. "That's nice. Mama will appreciate it."

They sat like that, not talking for another hour. Finally, she could stand the silence no more. "I'm gonna get some coffee," she said, standing and stretching. "I'll get some for you, too."

"No thanks," Mason said.

She got up and walked over to the coffee station in the corner, taking her time with sugar packets and instant creamer. She was about to sit down again when Sallie Bayless appeared in the doorway.

She was still dressed in the elegant black cashmere sweater and slacks she'd been wearing hours and hours ago, when Annajane had sat through that awful luncheon. But Sallie's usually perfectly arranged hair was a tangled mess. Her face was pale, her lipstick chewed off, her eyes red-rimmed.

"Mama?" Mason stood.

She nodded. "He's gone. They did everything they could, but your daddy is gone, son." She burst into tears, and threw herself into her oldest child's arms, while Annajane stood by, mute and heartbroken.

The next few days and weeks after the funeral were a blur.

Glenn Bayless's sudden death shook his family, and the company, to its core. Sallie, his widow, wept constantly and seemed unable to cope with even the simplest detail of day-to-day life. The first few nights after Glenn's death, she declared herself afraid to stay alone in the rambling old house. It fell to Mason, the oldest son, to move into his old bedroom down the hall to keep her company.

After two weeks, Sallie's doctor prescribed sleeping pills, and Mason came home. To the lumpy pullout sofa.

He plunged into the work of settling his father's estate and came home exhausted and ashen-faced from endless meetings with the lawyers. If Annajane inquired, he brusquely replied that everything was "fine."

But things were not fine. Without confiding in his son, Glenn had quietly begun acquiring expensive parcels of land for a new bottling plant in the southern part of the state, anticipating increased demand for Quixie. But the owner of the key parcel, the only acreage with the direct rail access a plant would require, had suddenly backed out of the sale. The company was stuck with the land, bought at a top-of-the-market price, with a correspondingly high interest rate.

At the same time, Quixie's sales had taken a worrisome dip. Vitamin waters, energy drinks, and flavored bottled iced teas were eroding their share of the soft drink market.

And Annajane and Mason hadn't had sex since before the ill-fated Quixie Christmas party. They lived in the same house and worked for the same company, their offices only feet apart, but the chasm between them seemed to widen every day. When Leonard Hudgens fell and broke his hip and died of pneumonia a month after the death of Glenn Bayless, Annajane spent two weeks in Holden Beach with her mother. By the time she got back to Passcoe, Mason had moved out of the caretaker's cottage. And the marriage was over.

9

The nurse who'd wheeled Sophie back to the exam room beckoned. "Dr. Kaufman wanted me to tell you that he's gonna go ahead and take out her appendix," she said hurriedly. "They're prepping her now. You can go back, but only for a minute."

They found Sophie clutching a teddy bear, with an IV-drip tube connected to her arm. Nurse Molly patted the child's hand. "She's been such a good girl," she told Mason. "Didn't even cry when we stuck her for blood or put in the IV needle."

Mason laid his cheek against Sophie's. "Hey kiddo," he said softly. "Dr. Max is gonna fix up your tummy now."

Her eyelashes fluttered. "Daddy?" she said woozily. "I got a new bear."

"I see that," Mason said.

Annajane took Sophie's hand. "What have you got there?"

Clenched in the palm of her hand was an empty glass vial, probably from some drug that had been injected into her IV tube. Sophie was a magpie. From the moment she'd first started to crawl, she had a habit of picking up random small items. A misplaced earring, paper clip, discarded gum wrapper, all of these were treasures to Sophie, who would carefully tuck them in a pocket or hide them under her pillow. Or more often than not lately, in her treasured pink plastic pocketbook.

"It's a baby bottle. For my new bear," Sophie said.

"I'll keep it for you," Annajane promised, carefully placing the vial on the table out of Sophie's reach. "Does the bear have a name?"

"Mittens," Sophie said. "I'm sooo sleepy."

"You rest," Mason told her. "And when you wake up, I'll be right here."

"Annajane, too?"

"Me, too," Annajane said. "I'm not going anywhere."

And then they were wheeling her into surgery.

When they got back to the waiting area, Pokey was there. She'd changed out of her wedding attire and was wearing jeans, tennis shoes, and a T-shirt. "The nurse told me they're gonna operate?"

Mason nodded tersely. "Did you go by the club? How's Celia?"

"Fine, I guess," Pokey reported. "Pete took Letha to help out with the boys. She made

132

me promise to call her as soon as we know something. I talked to him a little while ago. He said people were a little shocked at first, just kinda standing around, staring at each other, but then Mama took charge, got the waiters passing appetizers and the bar up and running, and the band warmed up. Everybody's dancing and having a high old time."

She pulled her cell phone from her back pocket. "Mama has ordered me to make sure you call her with an update on Sophie."

He exhaled loudly. "I can't deal with her right now." He looked at Annajane. "Could you?"

Annajane was in no mood for a long conversation with Sallie Bayless either, but she took the phone, made the call, and reassured her former mother-in-law that Dr. Kaufman had things firmly in hand. She heard the sound of music in the background, the clink of glasses and ice, and voices.

"Thank you for calling, Annajane dear," Sallie said finally. "I know this can't be easy for you."

"Sophie is a little trouper," Annajane said. "But yes, I'll feel better once she's out of surgery."

"I meant the wedding," Sallie said.

Annajane allowed herself a wry smile. "I'm happy for Mason. And Celia," she added.

"Of course," Sallie said. Her tone said otherwise.

When she rejoined the others, Mason was thumbing through e-mails on his BlackBerry, and his sister was staring at the television with a blank expression on her face.

"Hey," Pokey said, standing up quickly. "C'mon, let's go raid the vending machines. I'm starved. Mase? Can we bring you anything?"

"Nothing," he said without looking up.

Annajane trailed along after Pokey. They found a bank of vending machines outside the hospital's cafeteria, which was closed.

Pokey dug in the pocket of her jeans and came up with a handful of coins. She studied the candy machine. "Hmm. Almond Joy or Butterfinger?"

"Nothing for me," Annajane said. "Maybe a bottle of water or something." She looked at the other machines. "Although I could use some aspirin or ibuprofen or something for this headache."

"Hangover?" Pokey gave her a surprised look. Annajane was almost never sick, and almost never drank to excess.

Her friend sighed. "I dosed myself with bourbon before leaving for the church this afternoon. Should have known it would come back later and bite me in the butt."

Pokey fed coins into the soda machine and bought bottled water for both of them, then, moving over to the next machine, bought a packet of Aleve for Annajane.

"Let's sit in here," she said, gesturing to the half-darkened cafeteria.

They found a table near the door, and Annajane gratefully swallowed the pain medicine with a swig of water.

"Something I need to ask you," Pokey said, leaning across the table. "And don't bullshit me, okay? We've known each other too long for that."

"Oh God," Annajane said warily. "What is it now?"

"I saw the look on your face in church today, when Celia came down the aisle. I saw the look on Mason's face, too. And I know him just as well as I know you."

"And?" Annajane wished she had not followed her friend out of the waiting room. She'd walked right into Pokey's trap.

"And I got the distinct feeling, right before Sophie got sick, that you were about to make a big move."

"That's crazy," Annajane said, laughing uneasily. "I don't know what you're talking about."

"Sure you do," Pokey said. "You shoved me into the aisle. I don't care what you say. I know you, Annajane Hudgens. And I know you are not over him. You are still in love with my brother."

"Absolutely not," Annajane said automatically. "I'm in love with Shane. I've moved on."

"You are *so* not over Mason. And I've got a news flash for you. He's not over you, either."

"You're delusional," Annajane said, taking another swig of water. "Either that, or smoking crack. Hey. What were *you* drinking before the wedding?"

"Skim milk. Straight up. Iron supplement chaser." Pokey said. "I'm pregnant."

Annajane nearly spit out her water. "Again! Oh my God, Pokey, are you sure?"

Pokey took a big bite of her Butterfinger and chewed for a moment. "The fourth time around, you tend to know these things. And the EPT test I took Monday confirmed it. Yup. Just call me Fertile Myrtle. Knocked up again."

Annajane grasped both her friend's hands in hers. "Oh honey, that's great. I mean, I know Clayton isn't even two, but you really were born for motherhood. Are you okay with it? What does Pete say?"

Pokey laughed. "I'm fine with popping 'em out one, two, three. And four. As for Pete, he did allow that he wouldn't *mind* having a girl this time around. I pointed out to him that he's the one shooting all the blue bullets so far. Anyway, don't try to change the subject. We were talking about how you and my brother are still stupid in love with each other."

Annajane sighed. "I'll admit it was hard today, being in church, facing the reality of, well, everything. Mason truly was my first love. Yeah, I dated around in college, but nobody else ever came close. I guess I just had the world's biggest, longest crush on him. But marriage is different. It's real life, not a fairy tale. You can't sustain a crush when bad things happen, when people hurt each other. When they *cheat* on each other and won't even be honest enough to admit what they've done. If Mason had just apologized, if he'd just acknowledged what had happened, maybe things would have been different. But I'm not going to dwell on that anymore. I've found a man I can love as well as trust. Shane would never cheat on me. He just wouldn't."

"Stop!" Pokey exclaimed. "I will *never* believe Mason ever loved anybody but you. So maybe he screwed up, maybe he slipped up. He's a man, and gawd knows none of 'em are perfect. Especially the *Bayless* men."

"What's that supposed to mean?" Annajane asked.

Pokey shrugged. "What it sounds like. Look at Davis. What a man whore! He sleeps with any and every girl that comes along, single or married, and he gets away with it because he's Davis. He behaves like a goat in rut and we all just roll our eyes and laugh. And my daddy? Annajane, you know there was never a bigger daddy's girl than me. I loved my daddy and I miss him every day, but I'm not dumb, and I'm not blind. I know he . . .

fooled around on Mama."

Annajane had heard rumors about her former father-in-law's conquests over the years. After all, even in his sixties, Glenn Bayless was a startlingly handsome man, with a full head of hair that had turned silver in his early forties, piercing blue eyes, and a lean athlete's build honed from hours in the gym he'd set up in the basement of Cherry Hill, not to mention twice-weekly games of cut-throat tennis with partners half his age.

Still, this was not a topic she had ever discussed with anybody in the family. "You really believe all those old stories?"

"I just know, okay?" Pokey said. "The crazy thing is, I don't think it affected their marriage. Daddy worshipped the ground Mama walked on. I think he just, you know, liked the ladies. And they liked him back. But I am here to tell you that Mason isn't like that."

"And what makes Mason so different?" Annajane said flippantly.

"Because he knew Daddy screwed around on Mama," Pokey said flatly. "And it wasn't just a rumor. If you must know, Mason and I caught him at it. Red-handed. And Mason never forgave him for it."

Caught off guard, Annajane sat back in her chair and regarded Pokey, who was calmly finishing off the last bite of her candy bar.

"Mason never said a word," Annajane said.

"We swore to keep it a secret," Pokey said.

"We didn't even tell Davis. It was awful. For both of us. You remember that summer Mason moved away? Right after graduation? The only summer he didn't work at the plant?"

Annajane nodded. What she remembered most was the way her heart beat faster the first time she saw Mason Bayless roaring through town in the red convertible, headed for a summer job at the Outer Banks, and how her sixteen-year-old self pined for a man who barely knew she existed.

"Daddy said he was giving Mason the Chevelle as a birthday present. But really? It was a bribe. Or maybe a peace offering. Mason wasn't even speaking to Daddy at that point. I don't think he spoke to him that whole summer."

"But Mason came back home in the fall. And he went back to work for Quixie," Annajane pointed out. "And I never heard him say a single bad thing about your dad. I always thought it was so sweet, the way they worked together."

"They patched things up," Pokey agreed. "But they were never as close again as they were before that summer. Mason loved Daddy, but he didn't respect him."

Annajane shook her head. "I don't even know why we are having this conversation. The past is past." She held up her left hand, and wiggled her ring finger pointedly. "I've

139

got a new life; Mason has a new life. It's time, all right?"

Pokey rolled her eyes.

"I know you don't like Celia," Annajane went on. "And no, she's not who I would have picked for Mason, but the important thing is, he picked her, and he apparently loves her, and I honestly think she'll be good for him and for the company."

"The company!" Pokey exclaimed. "Who gives a rat's ass about Quixie? We are talking about my brother's happiness. And yours. Celia is totally wrong for him. Did you notice he only asked the bitch to marry him *after* you announced your engagement? And don't get me started on the topic of Celia as mommy material."

"Sophie seems okay with Celia," Annajane broke in.

"Sophie doesn't know her like we do. But I don't care what kind of show she puts on; Celia just barely tolerates Sophie. I mean, Sophie is another woman's baby, not hers. Celia doesn't have a maternal bone in her body. The woman is an ice queen. And as for her company — so what if she made money selling kids' clothes? That doesn't mean she can keep Quixie from going down the tubes. Soft drinks are an entirely different ball game. I don't care if she is Miss Congeniality. I don't like her and I don't trust her. What do we really know about this woman, aside from what she's told us?"

"We know Mason wants to marry her," Annajane said softly. "Anyway, much as I love you and the rest of your crazy clan, Pokey, the company is no longer my problem. In case you forgot, I'm moving to Atlanta in five days. I have a new job, and I'm starting a new life. Going to the wedding was about closure. I'm engaged to Shane, remember?"

"Closure?" Pokey scoffed. "And you really intend to marry a guy named Shane? Really? Shane? What kind of name is that for a grown man? Is he a cowboy or something?"

It was Annajane's turn for an eyeroll. "Hello, Pokey? May I remind you that you named your own sons Glenndenning, Peterson, and Clayton? And that you have brothers named Mason and Davis?"

"Those are family names, and you know it," Pokey said.

"Fine. I think Shane is a perfectly nice name. And he's a nice guy, and he loves me and I love him."

A wicked, familiar glint shone in Pokey's eyes. "How's the sex?"

"None of your business."

"I knew it," Pokey crowed. "You've been dating, what, six months, and you haven't fucked him?"

"I hate that word," Annajane said irritably. "And our sex life is perfectly normal. Divine, if you must know. Although, remember, we

141

do live four hours apart. And up until this week, I still had my job here."

"If you were really attracted to him, you'd be screwing like a pair of jackrabbits," Pokey said, "instead of hanging around here in Passcoe. You think I don't know how you and Mason used to be when you were engaged? Jesus! We never once had Sunday dinner on time in the old days, because you two were always off over at the lake, getting it on."

Despite herself, Annajane blushed. "You knew?"

"*Everybody* knew. Mama, Daddy, hell, I think even Nate the yard man knew what you two were up to, and he's nearly senile. Those windows didn't get steamed up by themselves. My point is, if you are really this hot for this Shane guy, nothing could keep you apart. Hey!" she said, brightening, "maybe he's gay."

Annajane stood up abruptly. "I think we're done here. Nice talking to you."

"You still can't admit it, can you?" Pokey taunted.

"Admit what?"

"You can't admit that you were wrong to end your marriage to Mason. That the divorce was a huge mistake. That you loved him then and you love him now, and you would take him back in a minute if you could."

"But I can't," Annajane pointed out, gripping her water bottle so tightly she heard the plastic crumple. "I'm engaged to another man. To Shane. And Mason's wedding was postponed, not called off. And as soon as Sophie is well again, this wedding is going to happen."

"*Fuck* the wedding," Pokey said fiercely. "You're still not being honest with me. You're still bullshitting me. Come off it, Annajane. We have been best friends since we were five years old. Just be straight with me. Will you?"

Annajane walked over to a trash bin and tossed in the water bottle.

"All right," she said finally. "Okay, maybe there is still something there. It's probably just jealousy, wanting what I can't have. But yes, I had a twinge when I saw Mason standing there at the altar."

She allowed herself a sad, lopsided smile. "Happy now?"

"Yesss!" Pokey said, fist-pumping.

"I don't know what to do," Annajane heard herself admitting. "I can't believe I am saying this out loud."

"Tell him," Pokey advised. "It's not too late. Just be straight with him. If not for yourself, then at least for Sophie's sake."

"I can't," Annajane said. "I am engaged to another man. He is engaged to Celia. This is hopeless. And pointless."

"Then I will," Pokey vowed.

"No!" Annajane clutched Pokey's arm. "Don't you dare. If you say a word about this

143

to Mason, I swear, Pokey, I will never speak to you again. I mean it. Just stay out of it, please?"

"This is so stupid," Pokey said stubbornly. "He will ruin his life, and Sophie's if he goes through with this charade and marries Celia."

"But it's his life," Annajane said. "Not yours."

They heard the voice as they were rounding the corridor back to the waiting room.

"Now, darlin', you've got to eat something," Celia cooed. "I fixed up this basket just for you. Maybe just a ham biscuit, or some of the tenderloin. I had the waiter slice it from the rare end, just like you like it."

Annajane felt her spine stiffen. Beside her, Pokey made a soft gagging noise.

She wanted to turn around and run out the door. Instead, she forced herself to keep walking back to the waiting room.

Celia had changed out of her wedding gown and was wearing an aqua velour tracksuit, with the jacket unzipped far enough to reveal a tantalizing amount of cleavage. A huge picnic basket sat by her feet, and she'd dragged a table over to the seating area, where she was unwrapping foil packages and plastic cartons.

"Hey there!" she said, as she saw the two women approaching. "I hope you're still hungry, because Sallie had the catering

144

people pack enough food for the Russian army."

"I've eaten," Pokey said bluntly.

"Annajane?" Celia held out a petite yeast roll stuffed with blood-red prime beef and a leaf of arugula.

"Oh, nothing for me," Annajane said, as her stomach grumbled the message that she hadn't eaten since breakfast. She looked at Mason, who'd removed his tux jacket and rolled up the sleeves of his dress shirt. "Any news about the patient?" she asked.

"The nurse just came out and said Sophie's doing fine," Celia volunteered. "So I was hoping maybe I could lure this crazy man of mine into finally relaxing and eating something." She reached over and gave Mason's knee an affectionate squeeze.

"And I was just trying to tell her that this hospital gives me the creeps, and I really don't want to eat anything here," Mason said, looking up at Annajane with an expression she couldn't quite fathom.

"Well," Annajane said brightly, looking from Mason to Celia to Pokey. "It's been a long day. And if the nurse says Sophie's all right, that's a huge relief. Maybe I'll go on home and check back here in the morning. I'll get here early, hopefully before she wakes up."

"I think that's a very sensible idea," Celia agreed, nodding her head vigorously. "There's really nothing you can do here tonight, Anna-jane. The nurse said they'll only let *family* back, once she's in the recovery room. Mason and I will keep a vigil, won't we, darlin'?"

Mason frowned slightly. "Annajane is family."

Celia laughed a silvery, hollow little laugh. "Of course. But she probably wants to go home and shower and get out of that stinky dress, don't you think?" She studied Anna-jane's face dispassionately. "Don't take this the wrong way, but you do look pretty beat."

Annajane looked down at herself. Her shoes were spattered with something unspeakable, her stockings had runs in both legs, and the dress was history. She felt her shoulders slump. She was no match for Celia's effortless perfection. She should go.

"I'll call you if there's any change," Mason said as he stood.

Clearly, Annajane thought, he wants to be alone with his bride.

"I'd better get home to make sure Pete puts the little heathens to bed," Pokey announced.

"I'll walk you both to your cars," Mason offered.

10

"I'm right there," Pokey said, pointing to the Range Rover she'd parked in the ambulance loading zone.

Mason and Annajane watched Pokey scramble into the driver's seat and zoom off into the darkness.

It wasn't until she saw her friend's taillights disappear that Annajane remembered that she'd arrived at the hospital in the ambulance — and that her own car was parked back at the church.

"Oh hell," she told Mason. "I don't have a car here, and neither do you."

"That's right." Mason scratched his neck absentmindedly.

"I'll call her and get her to come back for me," Annajane said, reaching in her purse for her cell phone. A moment later she disconnected. "She must still have her phone turned off," she said.

Mason reached in his pocket and brought out a set of keys. "I'll give you a ride," he

147

said. "We can take Celia's Saab." He pointed in the direction of the parking lot and started walking. "It's right over there."

"Shouldn't you check with her?" Annajane said uneasily.

"I don't have to ask Celia's permission to give you a ride, Annajane," Mason snapped. "She's my fiancée, not my supervisor. And she trusts me."

That last sentence hung in the air. Trust. Celia trusted him. Annajane hadn't. And here they were, many years later. Some things hadn't changed.

"Suit yourself," Annajane said finally. "I just meant maybe you should let her know you'll be gone for thirty minutes. So she won't think you've disappeared."

He scowled. "Be right back."

Fifteen minutes passed. It was getting dark, and the temperature had started to dip as the sun dropped. Annajane hugged herself and rubbed her arms, shifting from one foot to the other in an attempt to keep warm. But she would not go back inside the waiting room. Obviously Mason had underestimated his need for Celia's approval for this little outing.

She grinned and wished Pokey were around to enjoy the drama.

Finally, Mason strode through the emergency room doors. "Let's go," he said brusquely.

An uneasy silence fell between them as Mason expertly shifted the Saab into gear.

"Everything okay?" Annajane asked.

"It's all good," he said, keeping his eyes on the road. "Thank you for insisting we get Sophie to the hospital. I guess . . . I guess I was kidding myself thinking the wedding could go on."

"I'm sorry about your wedding. Celia was a beautiful bride. But I'm glad things turned out all right with Sophie," Annajane murmured.

"Celia really adores Sophie," he blurted out a moment later.

"I'm sure she does," Annajane said, although she was certain of no such thing.

"It's a lot for anybody to deal with," Mason went on. "Not just being a stepmother, but, you know, taking on my, uh, daughter by a woman she's never met."

As far as Annajane knew, nobody in the family had ever met Sophie's mother.

One day, while they were still legally separated, but before the divorce was final, Mason knocked on her office door and stepped in and closed it carefully.

The visit took Annajane by surprise. Since their split, Mason had gone out of his way never to be alone with her.

He sat stiffly on the edge of the chair facing hers and cleared his throat.

"Look," he said finally. "I've got something I need to tell you. I was seeing this woman . . ."

Annajane held up her hand. "Stop right there, Mason. You're single now, and who you see, or what you do, no longer affects me on a personal level."

He scowled. "Will you just listen? This is important. The thing is, we're not really together now, this woman and I. We were only together for a short time, actually, and then she got pregnant. But I only recently found out about the baby."

Annajane heard herself gasp out loud.

Mason cleared his throat and plunged ahead. "Sophie is three months old now. Her mother, Kristy, is single, divorced, actually. And she and the baby had been living with Kristy's mom, down in Jacksonville. But Kristy's mom just died of breast cancer. And Kristy — she's not a bad person, but she's probably not mother material. She could handle the baby, while her mom was living there and helping out. Now, though . . . she's pretty overwhelmed. She wants to go back to her job, and Sophie is kind of cranky, I guess you'd say, right now. So, uh, here's the deal. Sophie's coming to live with me."

Annajane laughed despite herself. "Right. You're gonna be raising a baby. Three men and a baby. Only not."

"Yes," he said, glaring at her. "I am. Is this

somehow funny to you?"

At that moment, it dawned on her that Mason was perfectly serious.

"Are you telling me that you're an unwed father?" she said finally.

He shook his head in disgust. "If that's what you want to call it." He stood. "Okay, I can see this was a mistake. I just thought I owed you an explanation, because I realize, as soon as it gets out that I've adopted Sophie, some people are going to just assume I was having an affair with Kristy while I was married to you."

Annajane swallowed. "Were you?"

"No," Mason said quietly, getting up from his chair. "I never met Kristy until after we were separated. You can take my word for it or not, but as God is my witness, that's the truth, Annajane."

Sophie's arrival had, as Mason predicted, stirred up a lot of gossip in Passcoe. And although the knowledge that Mason fathered a child with another woman had come as yet another searing blow to Annajane's already-battered ego, she found herself curiously drawn to the motherless infant.

"Is she not the yummiest little thing you've ever seen?" Pokey crooned, the first time she held the sleeping child in her arms. "No denying she's a Bayless, either. Look at those eyebrows! And that high forehead. She is Mason made over."

"Actually, she looks enough like you that she could be yours," Annajane pointed out.

"She is just perfect," Annajane said, gazing down into Sophie's familiar blue eyes. She touched a fingertip to the baby's hand, and Sophie's fingers instinctively curled around her own. Annajane was enchanted.

She found herself dropping by Pokey's whenever she knew Sophie was in residence. Annajane had always adored Pete and Pokey's three boisterous sons, but her attachment to Mason's daughter was somehow deeper, and mutual.

As soon as Sophie was walking, she would run immediately to Annajane. When she could speak, Annajane's was one of the first names she said, right after Daddy and Pokey. If she was fussy, as she often was until she was almost two, Annajane was often the only one who could soothe her or rock her to sleep.

And if Mason was uncomfortable with his daughter's obvious preference for his ex-wife, he never showed it. He might be stiff or distant with Annajane when they were alone together, but he seemed genuinely grateful for her relationship with Sophie, and he made it a point to include Annajane in any family function centered on the child, to his mother's obvious annoyance.

When Annajane mentioned Sallie's pointed coolness toward her after Sophie's third birthday party, Pokey laughed it off. "Mama's just jealous," she said. "Sophie won't even look at her if you're in the room."

As she sat beside Mason now, on his ruined wedding day, Annajane wondered, once again, if Celia would attempt to discourage Sophie's relationship with her. And she had no intention of sharing her reservations about Celia's parenting skills or maternal temperament.

"Celia is an extremely competent person," Annajane said guardedly. "I'll bet she's never failed at anything. She'll handle this, too."

"What do you mean, handle?" Mason asked, frowning.

"Nothing," Annajane said.

"Pokey hates Celia," Mason said. "I wish she'd lighten up a little. I think she'd like Celia, if she gave her half a chance."

"Maybe," Annajane said, wishing he would change the subject. "You know Pokey. Nothing if not opinionated."

Mason tapped his fingertips on the steering wheel. "So," he said, after a long silence. "How's it feel to be moving away after all these years in Passcoe?"

Annajane exhaled slowly. "Good." She hesitated, looking out the window. Wildflowers bloomed in roadside ditches, and she caught a glimpse of a bluebird, perched on a power line. "Scary."

"Change is good," Mason said, nodding for

emphasis. "I mean, don't get me wrong, you'll be missed. You've done a damned good job for us. I don't think Davis is gonna know what to do without you."

She wished, fleetingly, that Mason had said *he* didn't know what he'd do without her. "Davis will figure it out. And Tracey, the new girl, she's a fast learner."

"Farnham-Capheart is lucky to be getting you," Mason said. "I told Joe Farnham that when he called to make sure I didn't have any problem with his hiring you."

"He checked with you? Before offering me the job?" Annajane couldn't believe it. Farnham-Capheart had been Quixie's advertising agency for years, and Annajane had worked closely with Lacey Parini, the account exec assigned to Quixie. When Lacey decided to become a stay-at-home mom after the birth of her second child, she'd encouraged Annajane to apply for her old job.

Annajane had had lots of job offers over the years, but it wasn't until Celia Wakefield joined Quixie that she'd ever considered a career change.

"He called me as a professional courtesy," Mason assured her. "You know how Joe is. I guess we're probably his biggest account, and he didn't want to rock the boat."

She didn't know what to say, didn't know why she hated the idea that Joe Farnham thought he had to get Mason's approval before offering her a job. Suddenly, a thought occurred to her. Maybe Mason had actually asked Farnham to find a job for her. Maybe he thought it would be just too awkward to have his ex-wife working with his new wife.

Or maybe it had all been Celia's idea. Annajane clenched her teeth, thinking of the indignity of it. Never mind. It didn't matter how her new job came about. She'd wanted a change; she'd gotten a change.

Mason obviously knew he'd somehow strayed into dangerous territory. He cleared his throat.

"So," he said, casually. "Have you, and uh, your fiancé set a date?"

"Shane," Annajane said. "His name is Shane. We're thinking fall, probably."

"Not til then, huh?" Mason sounded surprised. "Any reason for waiting?"

"Shane's a musician, you know," Annajane said. "He plays Dobro in a bluegrass band, and spring and summer is their busiest time, with all the outdoor music festivals. I want to get settled into my new job before I have to worry about planning a wedding. Not that we're planning anything elaborate."

"Gotcha," Mason said, nodding his head. "Bluegrass? What's the name of his band, if you don't mind my asking?"

"I don't mind at all," Annajane said proudly. "It's called Dandelion Wine. They have a CD coming out in September. Shane

155

wrote most of the songs himself."

"Have to look into that," Mason said.

Annajane laughed. "Oh please. You always hated bluegrass. And country."

"No!" Mason exclaimed. "You've got me all wrong. I love Alison Krauss."

"Okay, whatever," Annajane said, unconvinced. "I'll send you one when it comes out."

"Sweet."

He made the turn onto Main Street, where Annajane rented a loft above the old K&J Drygoods Store. "What's Ruth think about all this?"

"She's happy for me," Annajane said briefly. "Although I'll be a lot farther away in Atlanta. With Leonard gone, I hate to think about her living alone down there on the coast. I'm trying to talk her into moving. My aunt Nancy's a widow now, too, and she'd like Mama to come live with her down in Florida. But you know Mama. She's pretty set in her ways."

"What's she think about you getting remarried?"

"She *loves* Shane," Annajane said. "They've gotten really close. His own mother died when he was twenty, and I think Mama always wanted a son."

"Good for him," Mason said. "I'm glad she approves of the new guy, since she never cared for me."

Annajane sighed. They both knew that was putting it mildly. Ruth Hudgens didn't like

Mason any better than she liked his parents. The night Annajane came home with Mason's engagement ring on her finger, mother and daughter had the biggest fight of their lives. Annajane had fled the house and moved in briefly with Pokey and Pete. Leonard, always the peace maker, had brokered an uneasy truce between mother and daughter, but the damage had been done.

Ruth adamantly refused to take any part in the planning of Annajane's wedding, and Annajane had just as adamantly refused to let Leonard pay for any of it.

Mason pulled the car to the curb in front of her second-floor loft. "Okay," he said, obviously still uneasy at being alone with her. "Here you go."

"Thanks for the ride," she said. It was so weird, so awkward, having him drop her off like this. She flashed back to all those nights years ago, when he would park his car down the block from her parents' house, so they could exchange their urgent, passionate good nights without Ruth's knowing who she'd been out with. There would be no kisses, no desperate groping, no disheveled clothes to rearrange tonight.

"G'night," she said, jumping from the car.

11

Mason woke with a start. He sat up in bed and listened intently. For a moment, he thought maybe he'd heard Sophie, oak floorboards creaking gently underfoot as she crept down the hallway to his bedroom, as she used to do before Celia moved in and put a firm but loving stop to that.

And then he remembered, Sophie was in the hospital. It was his wedding night, and he was alone.

He swung his legs over the side of the bed and rubbed his eyes. He needed sleep, and yet he couldn't sleep. It was 3:00 A.M. Too early to call the hospital to check on Sophie. He'd wanted to stay in the waiting room last night, in case she awakened and asked for him, but the nurses chased him off, telling him that Sophie would be just fine without him and promising to call if she did awaken.

Celia had decided to stay with her great-aunt in one of the guest rooms at Cherry Hill. The old lady was overwrought from all the excitement of the day, and Sallie had hinted broadly that she herself was in no condition to play nursemaid.

Just as well, Mason thought. He was in the damnedest mood. Jumpy and irritable. Well, the day had been a disaster, hadn't it?

He'd left Celia in tears, back at Cherry Hill.

"Our beautiful day," she'd said, peeling off the false eyelashes and depositing them in the ashtray of the Saab. "All our plans, everything. Ruined."

"I know," he'd said, kissing her, trying to soothe her. "And I'm so sorry. But it wasn't really ruined, was it? I mean, you looked amazing, and everything was just the way you planned it."

She pulled away and stared at him. "Are you out of your mind? Your daughter collapsed at the altar and had to be rushed to the hospital. All of our guests were just sitting there . . . stunned. And don't forget, we never did actually get married. There's a $3,500 wedding cake at the country club, getting stale even as we speak."

"The cake? Can't we just, freeze it or . . ."

"No," she cut him off. "We can't."

"Oh-kaaay," Mason said, trying to tread lightly. "But we will get married. I promise. We'll do it all over again. We'll get another cake. Just as soon as we get Sophie home and recovered from surgery."

"It won't be the same," Celia said sorrowfully. "You're a man, and you've already had one wedding. I guess I can't really expect you to understand. A girl dreams of her wedding day her whole life. She has just one shot at one perfect moment. No matter how hard you try, you don't get that moment back again."

"I'm sorry." It was all he could say. As she'd pointed out, he couldn't fix it, no matter how hard he tried.

He got up to go to the bathroom and stubbed his toe hard on the foot of a damned chair. Christ! Since Celia had redecorated the house, or decorated it, since, as she aptly pointed out, it had never been decorated at all before she moved in, he was always bumping into things, knocking things over, breaking things.

Mason limped downstairs and into the kitchen. He stood in front of the open refrigerator door, not really hungry, but wanting . . . what?

Celia's nonfat yogurt containers were lined up in neat rows, as were the bottles of mineral water. Half a roast chicken nested on a plate under a tinfoil wrapping. There were containers of strawberries and blueberries and raspberries, packages of cheeses he'd never heard of, a crisper drawer full of things like scallions and leeks and arugula, carrots and baby spinach and celery sticks. Everything looked healthy and wholesome and totally uninteresting. At the very back of the top shelf, he spied the comforting sight of a tall-necked brown bottle.

He took the beer and a chunk of the least stinky cheese he could find and went into the room Celia called his study.

It was a handsome room, he had to admit. Celia had taste to spare, even Pokey grudgingly gave her that. She'd had the builder-beige Sheetrock walls covered with weather-beaten boards taken out of an old barn out at the farm, had bookshelves built to line two walls, and had conjured up rows and rows of old leather and vellum-bound books to line the shelves. He'd opened one once, just to see what she thought he should be reading. But it was in German. He didn't know German. The rug underfoot was some kind of rope-textured thing, sisal maybe — and it felt sandpaper-rough under his bare feet. He'd asked about keeping the old red and blue oriental rug he'd originally brought over from the attic at Cherry Hill when he'd bought the house, but Celia had just laughed and promised she'd find a better place for it when she finished redecorating.

He sat down at his desk and thrummed his fingers on the leather top. The desk was one of the very few things he'd insisted on keeping from his short-lived bachelor years. It had come out of his grandfather's old office at the bottling plant. It was beat-up mahogany, with two banks of drawers that stuck and a deep knee-hole recess, where he could remember playing with his army action figures as a little kid, pretending that he was in a bunker. The chair had been his grandfather's, too; it was high-backed, with cracked and peeling green leather upholstery that creaked loudly when he reclined in it.

Mason switched on his computer and idly glanced at his e-mails. Nothing that wouldn't keep. He'd inherited Voncile as his assistant after his father's death, and she was ruthless about weeding out e-mails he didn't need to deal with — especially since he was supposed to be on his honeymoon right this minute.

His honeymoon! A week in Aruba, their own villa overlooking the ocean. He shrugged. Knowing Voncile, he was sure she'd gone straight to the office from the church, and begun canceling flights and arranging for refunds.

Thinking of the office reminded him of Annajane, and he frowned. Stuffed in the back of that ambulance, and then later, in the waiting room at the hospital, he'd seen glimpses of the old Annajane. She was as terrified as he, but they were together again, if only briefly, as a team. And then, in the car, she'd been so prickly, hostile almost.

She really thought she was something, getting remarried, telling him all about this Shane guy.

As though he hadn't already thoroughly checked him out.

Mason clicked a few keys and opened up the file he'd started on this Shane Drummond clown the day Annajane returned from a trip to Atlanta — and announced her engagement.

From what Pokey told him, Annajane had only been seeing the guy since early fall. And three months later they were engaged? Fast work.

Voncile had been only too happy to conspire on this little research project. She'd nosed around the Internet for a few days, made some discreet calls to a security firm recommended by a business associate in Atlanta, and put together a fascinating dossier.

He was looking at that dossier now. Voncile had even managed to scrounge up photographs. Mason studied the largest of these, a color publicity still she'd found on Drummond's agent's Web site. So *this* was the kind of guy Annajane was attracted to?

In the photo, Drummond was dressed in a plaid lumberjack-type jacket and scruffy jeans. His curly hair looked unkempt, and he had those dark, brooding, soulful-looking eyes women like Annajane probably found irresistible. And was that a tiny gold hoop earring in his left ear? What the hell was it with women and musicians? Why did chicks always fall for the bad boys?

He shook his head and returned to the document Voncile had assembled.

Hmm. Matthew Shane Drummond, thirty-two. Hah! A younger man. Annajane had resorted to robbing the cradle. Born in Gastonia, he'd received a bachelor's degree in English at Middle Tennessee State University. He'd knocked around the country for the past few years, working as a bartender and a short-haul truck driver, but mostly earning a living playing in country music dives.

From what Mason could tell, Annajane's fiancé had formed his current group, Dandelion Wine, in 2008. He found a brief mention of the group in an obscure music magazine, about a recording contract with a Nashville label he'd actually heard of. So what? Did that mean this guy was the next Rascal Flatts? Mason highly doubted it.

Drummond owned a car, a 1999 Dodge Aerostar van, and a house, located in what looked like a rural area outside Atlanta, and valued, for tax purposes, at $82,700.

End of report. Mason scratched his chin and thought. Nothing sinister here. The guy was no tycoon, but he apparently also wasn't a destitute bum. He owned an old vehicle — a van he probably used for gigs for his band. He owned his own house. It wasn't a mansion, but it probably wasn't a chicken shed either.

He scowled and closed the file. Nothing of

interest here. Annajane was her own woman. If she wanted to marry an itinerant musician and spend the rest of her life living in a log cabin on a dirt road, driving around in a beat-up Aerostar van with him, that was her right.

The question that had been nagging at him ever since he'd left her earlier that evening was, Why? Why Shane Drummond? Why Atlanta? Why now?

And more important, why did he care so much?

12

Annajane sighed as she opened the door to the loft. She hated living in chaos. Half-packed boxes littered the floor and covered every surface in the living room. She knew without looking that her sink was piled with unwashed dishes and her bedroom floor covered with clothing. This was not like her. Not at all. She had let things get away from her. She picked her way through the boxes and went into the bathroom, where she stripped and tossed everything, except her bracelet, into the trash.

When she emerged from the shower wrapped only in an oversized towel, she pushed aside a stack of unfolded laundry and collapsed onto the bed. Her head still hurt. She was tired, and worried about Sophie. But mostly, she was worried about her own screwed-up emotions.

How could this happen? How could she possibly be falling for Mason Bayless again? And what could she do about it?

Forget it. Forget him, she vowed. Think of Shane. Of her new life. And get the hell out of Passcoe.

She could still make a clean break. By the end of the week, she would, by God, finish packing and get everything loaded in the rental van. By next Saturday, she'd be moving into her own studio apartment in a close-in Atlanta neighborhood. She would be with Shane, who was good and true and loved her without reservation.

And I love Shane, too, she thought fiercely. *I do. I really do. Shane is my future.*

And the Monday after the move, she would start her first day of work at the ad agency. She'd be so busy, there'd be no time to think about everything she'd left behind in Passcoe.

She found a clean T-shirt and pair of jeans among the jumble of clothes on her bed, got dressed, and got busy.

For three hours, she worked feverishly, packing up a lifetime's worth of belongings. The quicker she got it done, the sooner she could see Passcoe — and the Bayless family — in her rearview mirror.

Annajane abandoned any semblance of order or organization in her packing. Emptying kitchen cupboards, she dumped spice containers in with dishes, cookware in with cookbooks.

She took grim satisfaction in assembling

167

the flattened cardboard boxes, filling them, and then snapping a length of shipping tape across the intersecting flaps to seal them shut.

From the kitchen she moved into the living/dining room. She positioned a box in front of the bookcases and began unloading the shelves with a long sweep of her arm. A slip of paper escaped from one of the books and fluttered to the floor.

Stooping to pick it up, Annajane froze. It was a picture, an old snapshot of her and Mason, arms wrapped around each other, sitting on the front steps of the lake cottage.

She sank to the floor and studied the photo. They looked so young! Her hair was in a ponytail, and she wore a pink polka-dot halter top and white shorts and was sunburned, with a bad case of raccoon eyes from her sunglasses, and her mouth was wide open, in midlaugh. Mason was tanned and shirtless, his sunglasses obscuring his eyes, but his smile was wide and matched her own. The picture was undated, but she knew it had to be from their first summer together, when she was only nineteen. Funny, she remembered that top, bought on sale at the Gap for six bucks, but she couldn't remember the circumstances surrounding that picture. Most likely it had been taken by Pokey.

There were no other photos of them together. Annajane had burned them all, the day her divorce was final. They'd made a nice blaze in a rusty old grill in her mother's backyard at Holden Beach. How, she wondered idly, had this picture survived the fire?

Not that it mattered. She stood up and tucked the photo back into the book, but instead of dumping the book back in the box with the others, she walked into her bedroom and placed it on her nightstand. Thinking better of it, she put it under her pillow.

Then she picked up the phone and called Shane. His voice, when he answered, was husky.

"Oh no," Annajane said softly. "You were asleep. I thought you'd just be getting in from your gig. I'm sorry. Go back to bed. I'll call you in the morning."

"No, no," Shane said. "Don't hang up, baby. It's fine. I wasn't even in bed. Must've just dozed off in front of the television. What time is it?"

"Past three," Annajane said.

"What are you doing up so late?" Shane asked. "Something wrong?"

"Nothing's wrong," she said quickly.

Liar. Liar. Liar. Her subconscious taunted her even as she spoke the words.

"I just needed to hear your voice," she said, and that part was true.

It was his voice, deep, honeyed, and southern as sorghum syrup that had melted her heart the first time they met.

She'd gone down to visit her mother at

Holden Beach back in September. After two lo-o-o-n-g evenings of watching *Wheel of Fortune* and *Golden Girls* reruns, in desperation one night, after Ruth went to bed at nine, she went out for a drive. She'd seen the Holiday Inn sign and noticed they had a lounge, and since her mother was a teetotaler and didn't keep any liquor in the house, she decided to go in and get a drink on the spur of the moment.

The Sandpiper Lounge, as it turned out, was the happening nightspot for locals. A band called Dandelion Wine was playing to a packed house that night. Annajane sat at a table near the bar, slowly sipping a glass of wine. The band played mostly bluegrass, with a little country and rockabilly, which she was surprised to discover she enjoyed. There were two long tables close to the stage, both of them packed with women, maybe two dozen, who all seemed to know each other and the band. The women seemed to range in age from early twenties to early sixties, but they were drinking and having a great time, singing along to every song, whooping and clapping at their favorites. The lead singer and Dobro player seemed to be their favorite.

And why not? He was tall and lanky, with a mop of satiny deep brown curls and the dark, gorgeous eyes of a poet. He had dimples, and just a hint of five-o'clock shadow, and he wore a faded plaid flannel shirt and jeans

170

with worn-out knees.

When he'd start in on a song, the women whooped and called his name, "Shane! Shane!" He'd look up, smile shyly, and maybe treat them to a playful wink, but mostly he sat on a battered wooden barstool and played and sang.

Annajane had never believed any of that stuff she'd always heard about women falling for musicians. Until she met Shane Drummond.

She supposed she must have heard the song before, probably at those long-ago family reunions at her aunt's cabin. "On the Other Hand" was an old country standard, he told her much later, and it had been covered by greats like George Jones, Keith Whitley, and Randy Travis. But she'd never heard the song about a married man tempted to cheat like she heard Shane sing it that night.

His voice was deep and true and fine, and he managed to wring emotion from every word, and as his long slender fingers plucked at the Dobro, she wondered if he was singing to her and for her.

"I called you twice, earlier," he said now, sounding puzzled. "Didn't you get my messages?"

She had gotten his messages, of course. But she didn't want to tell him she'd been at her ex-husband's wedding when he called.

"My phone is kinda messed up," Annajane

said. "What message did you leave?"

"I said I love you, and I miss you," Shane said. That was how he'd been right from the start. So open and loving.

That first night, at the bar, she kept thinking it was late and she needed to leave, but she couldn't. At the break, the rest of the band went to the bar, where the women mobbed them, buying them drinks, laughing and flirting. Annajane, bored, was scrolling through e-mails on her phone when she heard the scrape of a chair. She looked up and it was the Dobro player.

He had a glass of white wine in his hand. "The bartender thought this was what you're drinking," he said.

She took the wine and asked him to sit down, and the smile that spread across his face was liquid and sweet, and his dimples deepened. And for a moment, the insane thought occurred to her — *Wouldn't this man make beautiful babies?*

He glanced toward the bar, where his bandmates were engaged in slamming back shooters and flirting with the women flocked around them. She looked, too, and saw a couple of the women staring daggers at her. He started to say something, stopped, started again, and then just grinned.

"What is it?" she asked.

"I can't think of a single thing to say to you that doesn't sound like a pickup line."

"Oh." She thought about it.

"You've probably heard every pickup line in the book, I bet," he said.

"Not really." She wasn't being coy. She'd never been much for the bar scene, even in college. And she honestly couldn't ever remember anybody even approaching her with a pickup line in a bar. She was pretty enough, she thought, but she just didn't attract that kind of attention.

"I find that hard to believe," he said. "My name's Shane, by the way."

"So I gathered, from your fan club," she said with a laugh. "I'm Annajane."

"That's a pretty name, Annajane," he said. "Kind of quaint, a little old-fashioned. Are you an old-fashioned girl?"

"I was named for my grandmothers," she said. "But no, I'm probably not all that old-fashioned."

"Are you a bluegrass fan?"

"Not really," she said. "But I like your music. You've got a beautiful voice."

"Thanks." When he smiled, the dimples were so deep she was tempted to see if she could poke a finger in one.

"I really do like your name," he said thoughtfully. "I guess I'm a sucker for double names. Good for songwriting."

"Do you write music?"

He shrugged. "I tinker with it. Bars like this, though, the audience wants the familiar.

You know, 'Rocky Top' and crap like that. How about you, what do you do for a living?"

She sipped her wine. "I work in marketing for a soft drink company."

"Coke?"

She laughed. "I wish. Nope. Quixie — you know it?"

"The quicker quencher, sure, practically mother's milk," he said. "Don't they make that somewhere around here?"

"Our headquarters are in Passcoe," she said. "So . . . if you know Quixie, you must be from the Carolinas, right?

"Gastonia," he said. "Went to Middle Tennessee, got an English degree, but decided I liked music better."

They heard chords of music coming from the stage, and when they looked up, saw that the band was getting ready to start playing again.

"Gotta go," he said, pushing his chair back. "Any chance you might stay for the next set?"

She looked at her watch, but it was a pretense. She knew she intended to stay.

Shane kept his eyes riveted to hers throughout the night. After the last song, as the last stragglers drifted out of the lounge, he came bounding up to her table, his Dobro case in hand, clearly delighted to still find her sitting there.

"How 'bout I buy us something to eat?" he asked.

They took her car and found a Waffle House out by the interchange, and Shane wolfed down a steak and eggs, with hash-browns, covered and smothered. She nibbled at a grilled cheese sandwich. At three o'clock, they were the only customers in the place. He'd told her his story; she'd given him a brief version of hers.

Annajane drove him back to the Holiday Inn. She parked by the door of the lounge. He made small talk, clearly not wanting to get out of the car. "It's late," she said finally. "If my mama wakes up, she'll think I've been kidnapped by aliens."

"I know." He had the Dobro case across his knees. He leaned in and brushed his lips across hers. "Will it sound like the worst pickup line in the world if I tell you I don't want you to go?"

"Try it," she suggested.

He took her face in his hands and kissed her, this time, a long, slow, deep kiss. He rested his forehead against hers. "I don't want you to go."

She felt her toes curl. "Hmm. Maybe try it again?"

He kissed her again. Even better. She gave into temptation and lightly touched one of the dimples with her fingertip. He caught it and kissed her hand, and drew him to her.

The next time she looked up, she giggled.

"What?" Shane was distracted.

She gestured at the Acura's windows. "We've fogged 'em up," she said happily. She hadn't been with a man since her divorce. She hadn't realized how long it had been until just that moment. And she hadn't realized how much she missed being touched, either.

He pulled her toward him again. "You know, we don't have to stay down here in this car. I've got a room here. Deluxe king, nonsmoking. Free Internet. Free cable. Free coffee. And there are a lot of windows there that we could be fogging up . . ."

Annajane sighed. "That sounds . . . nice. But remember how you asked me if I were an old-fashioned girl?"

"Yeah?"

"I guess I kinda am. I guess I'm not the kind of girl who picks up a musician at the Holiday Inn lounge and then goes to bed with him later that same night."

"Oh." He didn't bother to hide the disappointment in his voice. "You probably think I do this all the time. I swear, I don't. Maybe I did the first year the band was out on the road . . . but not anymore."

"I believe you," she said. She let her fingertips trail down her arm. "Tomorrow's Saturday. Well, okay, I guess today is Saturday. I go home to Passcoe on Sunday."

176

"We're only here one more night before we head up to Roanoke for a gig," Shane said. "Can you come back tomorrow, I mean, tonight?"

"Probably," she said lightly. "Maybe I could bring a toothbrush."

He grinned, and his dimples were deep enough to dive into. "I'll buy you one my ownself."

The weekend after that, she'd driven up to Roanoke, and two weeks after that, they'd met in Nashville, and then, when the band had a week off right after Christmas, she met him down in Jupiter Beach at his cousin's condo. At some point, she was startled to realize how different he was from any other man she'd known. Being with him was so easy, so effortless. He was the exact opposite of the driven, intense Mason Bayless. And that was a good thing, she was sure. On their last morning at the beach condo, she woke up and found Shane, his head propped on an elbow, gazing down at her.

"What's up?" she asked sleepily.

"I'm just thinking about how cool it's gonna be years and years from now when we tell our kids the story of how we met when I picked you up in a bar and I spent the next night at the Holden Beach Holiday Inn rollin' in my sweet baby's arms."

Kids? She'd deliberately told herself she was not getting that serious about Shane, that

177

they were just two adults enjoying getting to know each other. But all along she knew she was falling for him.

"When and if we have kids, as far as they will be concerned, we met at a church picnic," she informed him.

Two weeks later, the band was playing at a tiny club in Durham. She was sitting in the audience, sipping the glass of wine he'd sent over to her table, when the band swung into "Could I Have This Dance?" She'd been a little surprised, because it wasn't on their usual set list, but mild surprise had turned to shock and numbness when Shane stepped off the bandstand, made his way to her table, and slipped the sterling silver band on her left ring finger.

"Okay?" he'd whispered in her ear, with everybody in the whole club watching. She'd started to cry, and eventually, she'd nodded her head yes. And so they were engaged. Just like that.

It wasn't until she'd gotten back to Passcoe and unpacked her suitcase that Sunday night that the enormity of the situation struck her. She'd just agreed to spend the rest of her life with a man she'd only met three months earlier.

Every time she started to have reservations about the engagement, though, Shane managed to persuade her that she was doing the right thing. Even when she called him at three in the morning and woke him out of a sound sleep, he was ready to whisper sweet nothings.

"Why don't you come on down here and let me show you how much I'm missing you?" His laugh was low and provocative.

"Can't," she said, hoping she sounded regret she didn't quite feel. "I've got a million things to get wrapped up here. I'm not even packed yet."

"I could come up there and help," he offered. "You really don't have to do this all by yourself, you know."

He was amazing. So thoughtful. He loved her. She loved him, too. Didn't she?

"No way," she said quickly. "If you got a good look at how disorganized my life really is, you'd run the other way."

"Never," Shane said. "I'll take you any way I can get you, not that I believe there's anything disorganized about you. You're the most together person I've ever met."

"Not lately," Annajane said, rifling through the pages of the book she'd put on her nightstand. "Lately, I feel like my life is all falling apart at the seams. And no matter how hard I try, I can't seem to hold it together."

There was a silence at the other end of the line.

"Okay, I'm coming up there," Shane said. "So don't tell me not to. I can tell you're upset. You're stressed about the move and the new job, and you're not sleeping. You're not yourself."

She found the photo again. As she stared at it, the image blurred through her tears.

Who was that girl?

"I'm fine," she told Shane. "Really, I am. Guess I was just feeling overwhelmed. I packed a bunch of boxes tonight, before I called you. The kitchen's almost done, and I've started on the bedroom and my clothes. I'm warning you Shane, we might have to add on to the cabin before the wedding, just to make room for all my shoes."

"Done," he said. "I've already moved all my stuff into the closet in the guest bedroom."

"Shane! You know I've rented my own place. I've got a six-month lease."

"I still think it's ridiculous," he groused. "A waste of good money, when you could just as easily move in here right away."

Why didn't she just move in with Shane? Why was it so important to have her own place? Didn't she want to live with the man she loved?

"It's only six months," she said softly. "Just til the wedding."

"And that's another thing. I don't get why we can't just get married as soon as you get down here. Yeah, I'll be on the road some this summer, but so what? You can come with me. It'll be fun. An adventure."

She laughed. "I'm starting a new job!

180

Anyway, you forget I've seen how you live on the road. It's fine for you guys; you're used to piling four to a room, or sleeping in the van and living on warm beer and stale pretzels. But that's not me, Shane."

"We'll get our own hotel room," Shane said. "Like at Holden Beach. I don't care. Let's just get married. Right now. That's all I'm saying."

"We've already talked about this," she reminded him. "Remember? I want to be with you, I really do. But I need a little time, and a little space. Just six months. To transition. That's not so long, is it?"

"It's forever," he groused.

"How did the gig go?" she asked, wanting to change the subject. Shane loved to talk about his work. It was one of the things she admired about him, his unstinting enthusiasm for whatever went on in his life.

"It was awesome," he said. "This club has only been open a couple months. It was packed tonight, babe. They had to quit letting people in the door at ten, an hour before we went on! The energy was amazing. They want us to come back in June, and we'll be the headline act!"

"That's great," Annajane said.

"I've got an idea for a new song, too," Shane said. "About a girl with green eyes. And long legs."

"Anybody I know?"

"Only you," Shane said. "All my songs are about you now. Why can't you get down here tomorrow?"

"Hush," she said. "Go back to sleep."

He let out a long, extended yawn. "I'll call you tomorrow. Love you."

"Love you too," Annajane said.

Liar. Liar. Liar.

13

On Sunday morning, Annajane walked briskly down Main Street, turning three blocks down from her loft, onto Church Street. She passed Passcoe First United Methodist, Passcoe First Presbyterian, and the biggest church in town, First Baptist of Passcoe, with its imposing white columns and three-story marble-lined sanctuary.

It was early yet, not even eight o'clock, so the town's worshipers were still presumably at home, polishing off their bacon, grits, and eggs; pressing their dress shirts; or dabbing on a final bit of makeup. Because that's the kind of town Passcoe was, a nice southern town where nice southern men and women still wore suits and dresses to church on Sundays.

Two blocks past First Baptist, she finally came to the Quixie Beverage Company, which, in its own way, was just as much of a temple of worship as the real churches in town. The sprawling red brick complex even looked like a church from the front, with two-story columns and a peaked roofline. The building had been added onto so many times since Mason's great granddaddy founded the company in the 1920s, it now took up an entire block, fronting on Church Street and backing up to the railroad tracks.

Annajane skirted the front of the building, where a perky red-and-green-striped awning shaded a set of big plate-glass entry doors to the reception area. Instead, she walked around to the east side of the building, to the loading dock. A pair of boxy Quixie delivery trucks were parked at the dock, nose out, and she could hear the rattle of hand trucks and the soft murmur of voices as she climbed the worn wooden steps up to the dock.

"Hey, Annajane," called out a husky middle-aged man in a Quixie driver's uniform. He had a hand cart loaded with cases of Quixie poised at the open doors at the back of one of the trucks. "Thought you'd done moved off to Atlanta. What are you doin' round here on a Sunday?"

She'd known Troy Meeks since she and Pokey were kids playing hide-and-go-seek around the plant. He'd given them rides on his hand truck, bought their Girl Scout cookies, and turned a blind eye when they pilfered dented cans of Quixie to sell for a quarter apiece at school.

"Hey Troy," she said, giving the older man

a hug. She reached out and gave his stubbly gray crew cut an affectionate rub. "I'm not gone just yet. I've still got a bunch of stuff to tie up in the office. That's why I came in this morning. I can never get anything done with Davis popping in and out all day long, giving me orders and trying to boss me around. I just need a few hours of peace and quiet."

"It's a sure bet you won't catch Davis Bayless in here on a Sunday morning," Troy agreed. "Especially not the day after his brother got married." He gave her a knowing wink. "That musta been some party."

"Well, that's a funny story," Annajane said. "The wedding didn't exactly go off as planned."

His mouth gaped. "You're kidding me. What'd you do — trip the bride as she went up the aisle?"

She shook a mock finger at him. "Careful. Celia's management now, you know."

He grinned. "Are you serious? The wedding really didn't happen?"

"Nope," she said. "Sophie got sick — right as Celia was walking up the aisle. They had to call the wedding off and rush her to the hospital. She had an emergency appendectomy."

He shook his head. "Appendectomy! Poor little thing. Bet old Mason was fit to be tied."

"He was. We were all pretty worried about Sophie. But Dr. Kaufman says she'll be right as rain. I talked to the nurse at the hospital this morning, and she's awake and demanding ice cream, so that's a good sign."

"Called off the wedding," Troy repeated under his breath. "Ain't that something." He gave Annajane a cockeyed smile. "Maybe there's still time for you to snag the boss. Again."

Annajane blushed. "Sorry, Troy. That ship has sailed." She held up her left hand so he could see her ring. "Anyway, I'm engaged."

"Damn shame, too," he muttered.

The thick, sweet smell of cherry syrup hung heavy in the air of the quiet plant. Annajane passed only two more workers, which was worrisome. At one time not so long ago, the plant would have been humming, even on a springlike Sunday morning.

But times had changed. The economy had soured. People were fickle. Their tastes and preferences in soft drinks and soft drink flavorings had changed. Quixie had lost market share to the spate of "energy drinks" flooding the market. Even their demographic had changed, from young and upbeat to, well . . . not.

When she'd been in college, Quixie had been the mixer of choice at parties. She and her friends had drunk Quixie and Captain Morgan rum, Quixie and vodka, Quixie and Southern Comfort, even — she shuddered to think of it now — Quixie and natty lite.

Somehow, though, the Quixie brand had gotten stodgy. Davis had commissioned market studies and focus groups to seek the root of the problem, but the answers hadn't been encouraging. Quixie just wasn't cool. Not that they hadn't tried.

The company had spent millions on surveys and focus groups and ill-fated ad campaigns. They'd overhauled everything, from the original flavoring formula to the size, shape, and color of the bottles, cans, and packaging, to the look of the brand itself. But nothing worked.

Annajane pushed open the heavy metal double doors leading from the plant into the office building. She followed a narrow corridor past a slew of closed office doors before pausing in front of her own. ANNAJANE HUDGENS, ASST. V.P. MARKETING, said the plaque on her door. She slid the plaque out of the slot and dropped it an empty trash basket. By the end of the week, it would be Tracey's office, not hers.

She drew a spare key to her office from her pocket and unlocked the door. She flipped on the light and sighed at what she saw.

More cardboard boxes were scattered around the office. Stacks of books were piled on top of her desk, and even more stacks — of boxes, files, and miscellaneous papers — stood piled at precarious angles. There was a coatrack in the corner, and from it hung a couple of her old, threadbare sweaters, a Quixie Beverage Company red-and-green-striped driver's uniform shirt with her name embroidered on the breast pocket, and, yes, shrouded in an age-clouded plastic dry cleaners bag hung the dreaded Dixie the Pixie costume.

Annajane lifted a corner of the plastic bag and inspected the green felt tunic and red tights. Somebody — her mother, maybe? — had done a neat job of mending the rips from her Fourth of July fall all those years ago. She had a corresponding scar on her knee. You couldn't even tell — unless you looked really closely.

She smiled wryly and let the plastic drop. Old wounds. They faded, but they never really went away, did they?

No good worrying about that now, she decided, clearing a path to her desk. She sat down in front of her computer and plunged herself into her work.

Two hours later, she sat back in her chair and paused for a moment. The end-of-quarter sales figures she'd been scanning were depressing. Fountain sales, canned sales, liter bottle sales — all were down.

Her department was gearing up to work with supermarket chains around the region for an important summer promotion. The ad agency's art department had worked up sketches for the supermarket displays, but to Annajane they were uninspired and, worse, downright ugly.

She sighed and kneaded her forehead with her fingertips. Davis had already approved the sketches with an enthusiastic "looks great" scrawled in the margins. Annajane was only the second in command in marketing. The final okay was up to Davis — and Mason, to some extent. She had one foot out the door, so why should this matter to her?

It just did. She hated the idea of stores all over the region flooded with the tacky cardboard displays featuring a likeness of Quixie's new spokesman — a second-rate Nascar driver — holding the Quixie bottle. The colors were garish, the production quality mediocre, and the driver, Donnell Boggs, whom Annajane had met on his one and only stop in Passcoe for promotional purposes, was a skeezy drunk who'd instantly become Davis's new best friend.

She jotted some quick notes on a Post-it and attached it to the sketches before returning her attention to her e-mail.

A woman's voice echoed down the hallway, and Annajane looked up, startled.

Celia Wakefield's slightly nasal Midwestern accent was impossible to miss.

"No," she was saying to somebody. "No, we haven't discussed a new date yet. It just happened last night, for heaven's sake!"

Annajane felt the hair on the back of her neck prickle. Her office door was closed, but she found herself slumping down in her chair, just in case.

Celia's heels clicked on the linoleum hallway floor. She was coming closer, and apparently she was having a discussion on her cell phone. "No, Jerry," she said sharply. "You don't understand how things are done down here. It's not just a business to these people. We have to finesse this. It's a courtship, you know?"

"These people?" Was she referring to the Baylesses? And was Quixie the business under discussion?

Celia started to say something, but then she was quiet, probably listening to the unseen Jerry on the other end of the line.

"Mmm, actually, I think the younger brother is amenable. He's the middle child, and you know how they are. Starved for approval. I get the feeling he's interested in exploring his options."

Annajane sat up straight now. *Davis? Exploring his options? What the hell was going on here?*

Celia had passed Annajane's door now, and her voice was starting to fade. Annajane got up and pressed her ear to the door, feeling guilty even as she did so.

"Well, the sister is definitely *not* president of my fan club," Celia was saying.

190

You got that right, Annajane thought.

"Mmm-hmm, no, she doesn't participate directly, kids and all that. But yes, I think it's likely she does have a stake in the business. No, unfortunately, that's a bit tricky since she's best friends with Mason's ex."

Annajane bristled.

Celia laughed at something her caller said. "You don't even know the half of it," she drawled.

The footsteps receded, as did Celia's voice.

What the hell is she up to? Annajane wondered again.

She went back to her computer and tried to concentrate on the memo she was writing for Tracey, but her mind kept drifting back to the conversation she'd just overheard.

Ten months. That's how long it had taken Celia Wakefield to get her claws into first Quixie and then Mason Bayless. Knowing Celia as she did now, Annajane was only surprised that she hadn't managed it any faster.

Like everybody else in Passcoe, as well as at the company, Annajane had been thoroughly charmed by her first meeting with Celia.

Davis had been singing the praises of the hotshot management consultant he'd met on a business trip to Chicago for months.

"Mama actually met her first, if you can

believe it," he'd told Annajane at a meeting the day after he returned.

Sallie often tagged along with both her sons on business trips after Glenn's death. Not that she had much to do with the day-to-day operations of Quixie, but she'd made friends over the years with people in the soft drink business, and Annajane suspected she was eager to go along on the trips because it gave her a chance to get out of Passcoe, stay in the best hotels, catch up with old pals, and shop. Sallie Bayless was a world-class shopper.

"Mama was sitting in our suite, leafing through the program for the marketing meeting, and she got all excited when she saw that Celia Wakefield was on a panel about brand building," Davis said. "Turns out, she'd just bought a little dress for Sophie from a company called Gingerpeachy at some ritzy boutique up there and went crazy over them," Davis said. "Of course, Gingerpeachy is Celia's company. Or was, until she sold it. Sallie insisted on sitting in on Celia's panel, and she was so impressed, afterwards she invited Celia to meet us for dinner. I had drinks with her in the bar first, you know, just to see if she checked out."

Davis rolled his eyes dramatically. "Of course, I took all of this with a grain of salt. I mean, come on, what does Sallie know about brand building, or marketing? I tried to get out of it gracefully, but you know Sallie.

Damned if she didn't force me to go to dinner, and damned if she wasn't right. Wait until you meet this gal, Annajane. She's the real deal!"

"This is a woman who really understands branding," he told Annajane. "She built her own company from scratch — kids' clothing, starting from the time she was twenty-one years old, working as a sales clerk at a little boutique in the middle of nowhere. She was the designer, the manufacturer, the marketer — everything. Last year, she sold the company to a big retailer. Believe that? Ten million dollars! Guess she's gotten bored with the good life, because she's doing consulting work these days."

A few weeks later, Davis called her into his office and introduced her to Celia.

Annajane's first impression had been that this was the most exquisite creature she'd ever met. The chair she was sitting in seemed to swallow her whole. Even with five-inch stiletto heels on her lime-green pumps, she was barely a notch above five feet tall. Her blond hair was silvery against a deep tennis-player's tan, and her pale lavender suit and low-cut lime-green silk shell should have been too girly for business. But on Celia, it was perfection. She reminded Annajane of a hummingbird. The only thing missing was a tiny pair of wings.

"Annajane!" Celia had said, leaping up to

shake her hand. "Davis has told me so much about you. He says you're the heart and soul of the company. How can I lure you into going to lunch with me and sharing your insights on Quixie?"

Of course, Annajane had been flattered. Flattery was one of Celia's many talents. She was warm and bubbly, so easy to talk to. They'd had a hilarious lunch, laughing and talking about the quirks of working for a small-town family-owned company. Celia had seemed surprised to learn that Mason was Annajane's ex-husband.

"Really? And you still work for the company after all that? How do you stand it?"

Annajane winced now at how easily it had been for Celia to draw her into her confidences. For a few weeks, they'd been best buddies, sharing drinks, lunches, even a shopping trip to Charlotte.

Everybody, it seemed, loved Celia. Everybody except Pokey.

"She's a phony," Pokey said, after the first and only lunch date with Annajane and Celia. "If she's so rich from selling her own company, why is she piddling around with contract consulting work for Quixie?"

Secretly, Annajane wondered if Pokey's dislike of Celia wasn't just a case of good old-fashioned jealousy. With three small children to ride herd over, Pokey was out of the loop on lots of things. And Annajane and Celia

194

were seeing a lot of each other. But she kept that to herself.

Instead, she repeated what Celia told her about herself. "She's only thirty-two. I think the payout is probably over a number of years, and some of it's actually in stock she can't touch for a few years. She's too young to retire, and, anyway, she's one of these people who always have to be doing something. She loves a challenge. And you've got to admit, with the way things are going, we've got a big challenge on our hands at Quixie."

"She wants more than a job," Pokey warned. "You wait and see."

But before Annajane could come up with a good defense for Celia, the memos started.

Like Celia herself, they were charming and disarming initially, couched as questions at first, then as suggestions, and then, within a very short period of time, as directives and missives. Celia's range was broad — she was interested in anything and everything that happened at Quixie, and no detail was too small for her laserlike focus.

But it wasn't until she was on the receiving end of one of those memos — this one a coolly worded e-mail she received after filing an expense report following an out-of-town marketing association meeting — that Annajane realized just how lethal Celia's influence could be.

AJ: Don't you think it's excessive to bill the company for airfare, meals and a night at an expensive New York hotel when we both know these conferences are really more about gossip and personal networking than they are about Quixie business? — CW

Stunned, Annajane had fired back with a memo of her own, detailing the subject matter of each meeting she'd attended and its value to the company, and adding the fact that she'd spent the other two nights of the conference in an old friend's apartment, which cost the company nothing. And she'd ended her memo with one last observation.

CW: Obviously, I disagree with you about the value of these conferences. And by the way, didn't you meet Davis and Sallie at a conference just like this one? — Annajane.

After that, there were no more lunches or shopping trips. She had, she admitted to Pokey, finally seen Celia's true colors. And they weren't pretty.

But to everybody else at Quixie, especially Mason, Celia Wakefield was regarded as the second coming. The one time Annajane had dared complain to Mason about one of Celia's pointed memos to her, Mason worked himself into a righteous indignation.

She'd entered his office meekly and couched her objection as tactfully as possible, but he'd issued her a stinging and immediate rebuke. "Frankly, criticism of Celia, coming from you, seems kind of petty. She sees the big picture, Annajane, something we desperately need right now. She's done a great job of analyzing these types of things, and I have no intention of reversing her."

Annajane could see the matter was closed. She and Mason had managed to keep their relationship at the office on an even-keeled, professional level after their divorce, but during that brief meeting, she realized things had changed. Celia was making sure of that.

Not long after that, she noticed that Celia had been given her own parking space, with her name stenciled on the pavement, situated between Mason's and Davis's in the company lot. And not long after that, she'd seen Celia and Mason leaving for long lunches together. Soon, they were arriving at the office together on Monday mornings.

"He brought her to Sunday dinner at Mama's," Pokey reported. "You know how many women he's dated since you two split up — and he's never brought any of those women around the family. Hell, we never even met Sophie's mother. I've got a bad, bad feeling about this chick."

It wasn't long before Annajane came to realize just how astute Pokey's assessment of Celia was.

The day Celia and Davis presented her with plans for the upcoming summer promotion with the Donnell Boggs tie-in, a promotion she'd had no hand in at all, Annajane realized that Celia had quickly and stealthily cut her out of the decision-making loop in the marketing department. Before that day was out, Annajane had begun updating her résumé and quietly putting out feelers to find a new job. Her days at Quixie, she knew then, were numbered.

Still, the engagement announcement, just six weeks after her own engagement, had taken Annajane totally by surprise. And not, she would admit now, in a good way.

Celia Wakefield was not a woman to be trusted.

Annajane's cell phone rang, startling her badly. She groped on her desk to find and answer it.

"Hello," she whispered.

"Hey, Annajane." It was Mason, sounding . . . awkward.

"Hi," she said, already feeling guilty about eavesdropping on Celia.

"I'm over at the hospital, and Sophie's awake, and asking for you," Mason said. "I told her you're pretty busy what with the move and all, but . . ."

"I was just wrapping up some work, and then I'll be over," Annajane said hurriedly. "How's she feeling?"

"She's kinda pitiful," Mason admitted. "She's trying to be brave, poor kid, but she can't understand why it still hurts. I thought maybe you could take her mind off it."

"I'll stop on the way over and pick up a video we can watch together," Annajane said. "I've got her copy of *Milo and Otis* at my place. She never gets tired of seeing that."

"Great idea," Mason said, sounding relieved. "Should have thought of that myself."

Yes, Annajane thought to herself. *You should have. Or your fiancée should have — if she weren't so busy plotting something nefarious.*

Annajane got up from her desk and looked around the room with a sigh. She really should make a start on clearing out some of this old junk before leaving for the hospital. That wooden bookshelf nearest the door, for example. The bottom shelf held a row of dusty cardboard filing boxes that had been sitting there since she'd moved into the office eight years ago. As far as she knew, the boxes hadn't been touched for decades before that.

She grabbed the hand truck she'd borrowed from the plant and stacked three of the boxes on it. The cartons were unexpectedly heavy. A plume of dust arose as she lifted the lid of the carton on top, and she sneezed repeatedly. Inside the carton were stacks of age-browned file folders with fading but neatly typed labels. The top file was labeled COR-RESPONDENCE, 1972. Clearly, the boxes contained nothing anybody had needed or wanted in the past forty or so years.

Annajane maneuvered the unwieldy load of file cartons through the plant and out to the loading dock, where a large Dumpster was located. She grunted as she hefted the first box into the empty Dumpster. But when she bent to unload the second box, which had been somewhat crushed from the weight of the top box, its sides collapsed, spilling the contents onto the concrete surface of the loading dock.

"Dammit," she muttered, scooping up a load of papers.

Her mood changed when she saw the contents of the box. They were slick, full-color mechanicals of vintage Quixie advertisements.

The top ad had a vividly rendered illustration of Dixie, the Quixie Pixie, perched on the top of a Christmas tree, winking impishly and offering a bottle of Quixie to two pajama-clad children peeking around the corner of a living room that could have come straight out of a 1950s movie.

GO AHEAD, the ad's headline urged. SANTA WON'T MIND.

"Oh, wow," she breathed, looking closer. A notation on the bottom of the mechanical indicated that the ad had run in the December 1957 issue of *Look* magazine. The illustration was signed, in the corner, with familiar block lettering. She blinked and looked again, but the signature was still there. Norman Rockwell.

She had no idea the company had once hired the country's most famous illustrator for its ad campaigns.

Annajane looked at another mechanical. This one was for the June 1961 issue of *Saturday Evening Post* and showed Dixie again. The illustration had the mascot water-skiing behind a sleek speedboat driven by a pair of windswept but gorgeous bathing-suit-clad teenage girls. Both the girls held bottles of Quixie in their raised hands.

THE WATER'S FINE, the ad's headline said. BUT QUIXIE IS EVEN BETTER.

She fanned through the rest of the files. There were more mechanicals for Quixie ads over the ages, artists' sketches, and even memos about upcoming promotions.

One of the promotional pieces was a recipe booklet titled *Entertaining Ideas with Delicious and Nutritious Quixie.*

Delicious, yes, Annajane thought, but what demented marketer had dared to suggest that

Quixie was actually healthy?

And yet, the booklet, which Annajane surmised was '60s-era, offered more than a dozen recipes with accompanying color photographs for Quixie-inspired dishes, ranging from a Quixie-glazed Easter ham to an elaborate three-layer molded Quixie JELL-O "salad" to a Quixie-based fruit punch featuring a festive cherry and lime sherbet-accented frozen ice ring.

The recipe for Quixie baked beans was illustrated with a color photo of an immaculately coiffed housewife offering the gooey-looking brown concoction to a trio of eager children. The woman in the photo was definitely a dewy-eyed, probably not more than nineteen-year-old Sallie Bayless, although the children were young models, since Sallie's own children weren't even born yet.

"Mrs. Glendenning M. Bayless proudly serves her family healthful dishes from her personal recipe files," the photo's caption proclaimed.

That one gave Annajane a laugh. She'd eaten countless meals at her former mother-in-law's house, and never once had Sallie served anything as pedestrian as baked beans. Sallie Bayless would have slit her own throat before following a recipe that called for combining canned baked beans, bacon, Vienna sausages, pineapple tidbits, and, yes, a twelve-ounce bottle of Quixie.

Still, the box was a miniature treasure trove of the company's marketing history. She shuddered now to think how close she'd come to trashing all of it.

Annajane slid the ruined box off the hand truck and lifted the lid on the bottom box. So this was why her load had been so heavy! Inside she found a dozen old glass Quixie soda bottles, each of them different. Of course she'd glimpsed some of the same bottles in the glass display case in the company foyer, but they'd been there so long, she'd really never taken the time to examine them.

Most of the old bottles were either clear or the same pale green tint that was used in the current Quixie bottle. But the shape and silhouette and labels varied. One in particular drew her attention. She lifted it out and held it up to the sunlight.

The bottle was short and squat, an eight-ounce size, and its base bore concentric rings. On the label, the winking face of Dixie leaned out from the Q in the company name.

"Adorable," Annajane breathed, turning the bottle this way and that. At the same time she was admiring it, she realized that she was thirsty, parched, dying, actually, for an icy-cold glass of delicious, even *nutritious* Quixie cherry cola. Talk about a subliminal message.

Suddenly, she heard the loading dock door open behind her and the familiar tap of heels and that overly loud voice.

"Well, hey," she heard Celia say. "What on earth are you doing, Annajane?"

Reflexively, Annajane shoved the top on the file box.

"Just cleaning out my office," she said, struggling to her feet.

"I'm so glad you're doing that!" Celia exclaimed. "I promised Tracey we'd get the office spiffed up before she moves in, but the last time I peeked in there, I realized we'll have a lot of work to do before the painters can come." She favored Annajane with one of her twinkly smiles. "I realize you've still got another week to work, but that's really just a technicality. I was hoping you'd get the place emptied out a little early. I know Davis wouldn't mind if you quit a few days earlier."

In other words, Annajane thought, *"Here's your hat, what's your hurry?"*

Annajane forced herself to return something like a smile, without Celia's phony wattage. "That's very sweet of you, but I wouldn't dream of taking off work until I get every last loose end tied up. And I've still got lots I need to accomplish, especially with the summer sales promotion."

In other words, back off, bitch. I'll leave when I'm good and ready.

"Well," Celia said reluctantly. "I guess you've got a better grasp of those kind of nitty-gritty details than me. Mason and Davis really want me focused more on the big-picture stuff."

Like selling off the company? Annajane wondered.

Annajane pointed at the cartons on the loading dock. "While I was emptying boxes I did find some interesting old files and old bottles I think Mason might want to keep."

Celia looked as fresh as a daisy. She wore a pale gray-blue sleeveless sheath that showed off her tanned arms, a chunky silver chain necklace, matching earrings, and gray-blue kitten-heel mules that brought her up to just about chin level with Annajane.

"Throw it all out," Celia said, waving a hand in the direction of the Dumpster. "I swear, this place has mountains of old crap that these people have been hanging onto since God knows when. And don't even get me started with Cherry Hill. Do you know that Sallie told me she actually still has all of Pokey's old baby dresses? What is it with you Southerners? Doesn't anybody ever throw anything away down here? Don't even bother Mason with that junk, please. He's got enough to worry about these days."

He sure as hell does, Annajane thought.

Instead, she gave Celia a pleasant smile. "I've thrown out most of it, but if it's all the same to you, I think I'll just box up some of the stuff and take it home myself. Sort of a

205

memento from my time with Quixie, you know?"

"Really?" Celia said, cocking her head and crossing her arms. She looked Annajane up and down and shook her head. "I wouldn't have thought you'd be sentimental about something like your ex-husband's family's business. But then, I can't pretend to understand much about your arrangement, which even you have to admit is pretty unusual."

So now the claws come out, Annajane thought. *Mee-owwww.*

"I was born in Passcoe, and my daddy and my stepfather both worked for the company. And Mason and I had a life together," Annajane said finally. "Quixie was an important part of that, even after the marriage was over. Some of our times were good, some of 'em not so good. Just because I'm moving away doesn't mean I want to forget all of it."

"Help yourself, then," Celia said. She stepped daintily over the pile of advertisements.

14

"Look who I brought!" Annajane announced when she walked into Sophie's hospital room. She held up the DVD so Sophie could see it.

"Milo and Otis!" the little girl cried.

Annajane brushed a kiss on Sophie's forehead and looked over at Mason, who was sitting in a chair at his daughter's bedside. "Is she being a good patient?"

"She's an awesome patient," Mason said, standing. "She's letting the nurses take her temperature and pulse and check her incision, and she just had a little Jell-O for lunch. Here," he said, gesturing toward the chair he'd just vacated. "Have a seat and I'll put in the movie."

As he was fiddling with the controls for the DVD player, the hospital room door opened.

"Aunt Pokey!" Sophie said. "We're gonna watch *Milo and Otis.*"

"Thank Gawwwd," Pokey said dramatically, dropping a large pink beribboned gift bag on Sophie's bed tray. "I haven't seen *Milo and*

Otis for hours and hours."

Sophie was tearing the tissue and ribbon from the gift bag. She held up the slightly dingy pink plastic purse that was her most treasured possession. "My pocketbook!" she exclaimed. She unsnapped the catch and took a quick peek at the contents.

"You left it in my car," Pokey volunteered. "I threw out the chicken nuggets because they were getting a little, um, stinky. But you can keep everything else."

Pokey looked over her niece's head to Mason. "She had one of my lipsticks, the baby's silver teething ring, some beer-can pop tabs, a key that I don't recognize, and an empty Altoids tin."

"Treasures," Sophie said, tucking the pocketbook under her blanket. She dove back into the gift bag, exploring the rest of her loot. "New crayons!" she exclaimed, holding up a box of sixty-four Crayolas.

"And some coloring books. Pocahontas, Little Mermaid, Sleeping Beauty."

Mason picked up one of the books and laughed. "How did Spider Man get in here with all these Disney princesses?"

"That's a gift from those brutish boy cousins of hers," Pokey said. "They seem to feel that Little Mermaid is strictly sissy stuff."

"Can you stay for a while?" Mason asked his sister quietly. "Letha's insisting on spending the night in the room with Sophie, but I sent her home to get a shower and some rest. I've got some stuff I need to do at the office. I'll be back in an hour."

"Why not?" Pokey said. "Pete took the boys out to ride around on the ATV around the lake. They won't be home for hours and hours. With any luck," she added, with a wink to her niece.

"Now it's just us girls," Pokey said, perching on the side of the hospital bed. "I love movie night with the girls. Think the nurses would make us popcorn if we ring that buzzer of yours, Sophie?"

"I can only have Jell-O. And apple juice," Sophie reported sadly.

"Never mind," Annajane said. "We'll have popcorn and Milk Duds next time for girls' movie night. And Quixie, of course."

"When?" Sophie asked, not missing a beat.

Pokey looked at her best friend and raised one eyebrow. "Yes. When, Annajane? Soon?"

"Pretty soon," Annajane amended. "Maybe Aunt Pokey will bring you to Atlanta to visit me after I move, Sophie. And we can have a whole girls' movie weekend."

"I don't want you to move to Atlanta," Sophie said plaintively.

"Me neither," Pokey added.

"Thanks," Annajane said, rolling her eyes. "Let's just watch the movie now, okay? We'll worry about coming attractions later on."

Ninety minutes later, with Otis and Milo

trotting bravely across country, while Sophie snored softly, Pokey eased off the bed, stood, and stretched.

She glanced at her watch. "Ugh. This is what I hate about being pregnant. I'm always hungry. Have you had lunch?"

"I could eat," Annajane admitted. She moved over to the bed and smoothed a strand of Sophie's hair behind her ear. "Do you think we should leave her like this?"

"Mason should be back soon," Pokey said. "Anyway, she'll probably sleep for at least another hour after that last dose of pain meds."

They were getting ready to slip out of the room when the door swung open and Celia stepped inside. She held a huge stuffed pink rabbit under one arm and a plastic-wrapped slab of wedding cake in one hand, with a bobbing bouquet of balloons in the other.

"Oh," Celia said, taking a half step backward when she saw Annajane and Pokey. "Oh. Hi."

"We were just leaving," Pokey said, taking Annajane by the elbow and steering her toward the doorway.

"Where's Mason?" Celia called.

"Isn't he with you?" Pokey asked innocently. "He left here nearly two hours ago."

Celia frowned and put the bunny, cake, and balloons on the table by Sophie's bed. "He was supposed to meet me here."

"You know Mason," Pokey said with a shrug.

Outside, in the hallway, Annajane gave Pokey a stern look. "You know he's just out running errands. Are you trying to start trouble between Mason and Celia?"

"Yes," Pokey said. "I am. It was only by an act of God that they didn't get married yesterday. So now, I aim to do everything I can to get this wedding completely called off. Forever."

"You're crazy," Annajane said, walking as fast as she could through the hospital corridor. "And it won't do any good. By now you know Celia. She's unstoppable. She gets what she wants. And she wants Mason."

"Tough shit," Pokey said, trotting along beside Annajane. "How long have you known me?"

"Too long," Annajane muttered.

"How long?"

"Going on thirty years, God help me," Annajane said.

"Do you remember Toni? With an I?"

Annajane wrinkled her brow, trying to remember anybody from their shared past named Toni.

"I give up. Who was Toni?"

"Toni the Pony," Pokey prompted. "When we were ten?"

"Ohhhh, that Toni," Annajane said. "Poor old thing. How old did she live to be?"

"She was seventeen when she just laid down in the pasture and went to sleep," Pokey said proudly.

"And how does Toni the Pony have anything to do for your loathing of your future sister-in-law?" Annajane asked.

They'd left the hospital and were in the parking lot, headed, by unspoken mutual agreement, for Pokey's Land Rover.

"Do you remember how Toni came to live at Cherry Hill?" Pokey asked, sliding into the front seat of the unlocked car.

"You wanted a pony. Your daddy bought you a pony. That's how things usually worked in the life of Pokey Bayless," Annajane said.

"Not just any pony. I wanted Toni. I guess you've forgotten. Mama hired some company that had pony rides to come out to Cherry Hill for my tenth birthday. Remember, we had the cowgirl theme?"

Annajane laughed. "I just found my monogrammed cowboy hat and personalized cap pistol when I was packing stuff last week. And I still didn't throw them out, for some reason that escapes me right now. Your mama did throw some amazing birthday parties, that's for sure."

"The company brought four ponies to my party. And Toni was just . . . pathetic. She was so skinny, I wouldn't let anybody get on to ride her. She had sores on her neck, and her eyes were all runny. I begged Mama to

212

get Daddy to buy her for me, but Mama wouldn't even consider it. She pointed out that Toni was about half-dead."

"So you went to your daddy."

"Exactly," Pokey said, nodding. "Daddy agreed with Mama. Said I already had a dog and a cat and a lizard, and we didn't even have a place to keep a pony, which was ridiculous, because we totally had a fenced-in pasture and the old dairy barn out at Grand-dad's farm."

"It's coming back to me now," Annajane said. "You pitched a fit and didn't quit."

"Toni would have died!" Pokey said. "She was sick, and those awful people treated their animals like crap. I begged and I pleaded. I got that woman's phone number and called her up and told her I was gonna report her to the police for being mean to animals."

"You were ten," Annajane said, marveling at the memory. "How on earth?"

"I just knew I was the only person who could save Toni. I told Mama I would never ask for anything else the rest of my life. I prayed every night that they would buy Toni for me. I went on a hunger strike, refusing to eat."

"Of course you ate when they weren't looking," Annajane reminded her.

"But not dinner," Pokey said. "I kept it up for a whole week, pestering and whining and carrying on, until I finally wore Daddy out and he bought Toni just to shut me up."

"You got your way," Annajane agreed. "So that's the moral of this story?"

"Toni came to live in a stall I fixed up for her at the farm. We got the vet to see her, and she got healthy and fat and happy, and I rode her every day until I got too tall to ride her without my feet dragging on the ground. So Toni lived out a long and happy life. And that, my friend, is the moral of this story. Never underestimate the power of Pokey Bayless Riggs, especially when it involves something or somebody she loves."

"Hmm," Annajane said. "You know I am your biggest fan and best friend for life, right? But you may have met your match with Celia."

Pokey whipped the Land Rover into the parking lot at the only restaurant in Passcoe that was open on Sunday. The Smokey Pig. She put the car in park and turned to give Annajane an appraising look. "You know something you're not telling me?"

Annajane shrugged. "I was in my office this morning. At Quixie. Trying to get some last-minute memos and reports out. I had my door closed, but I could hear her as she was walking down the hallway. You know how loud her voice is."

"Celia?"

"Yeah. She was talking to somebody on her cell."

"About?"

"I only heard one side of the conversation," Annajane admitted. "She was telling somebody named Jerry that they had to go slow — because these people's business was their life."

"People — as in us?"

"That's what I assumed," Annajane said. "Look, I don't really know what they were discussing."

"But you have an idea. Let's hear it."

"She talked about Davis — and how since he's the middle child, he always thinks he has something to prove to the world."

"Ain't that the truth," Pokey said under her breath.

"And that he was in favor of whatever Celia and her pal were discussing — because he wants to spread his wings, because he has bigger plans for himself. And she said she thought Davis was the key to the deal."

"Good old Davis," Pokey said. "Always scheming something. What else?"

Annajane laughed. "She said it might be tricky because the younger sister — you — didn't really like her very much, but that you probably have a substantial ownership interest in the company."

"Quixie!" Pokey exclaimed. "You think she was talking to this guy about trying to sell Quixie?"

"I don't know," Annajane said. "Maybe?"

"Son of a bitch," Pokey said slowly. "What else did you hear?"

"Nothing. She walked on past my office, and then my phone rang, and it was Mason asking if I was going to come to the hospital because Sophie was asking for me."

It was another beautiful spring day, so they found a wooden picnic table on the patio and placed orders for two Smokey specials — sliced pork, cole slaw, and potato salad. The waitress brought them jelly jars full of sweet iced tea, and they waved and greeted neighbors and acquaintances.

"We have got to stop Celia," Pokey said, leaning across the table to keep from being overheard.

"Stop her from what? We don't even know that she's up to anything," Annajane pointed out.

"First, we stop her from marrying my brother. Then, we stop her from whatever nefarious other plot she's scheming in that adorable little blond head of hers," Pokey said with a scowl. "This is war."

"We don't even know what she's up to."

"So we'll figure it out," Pokey said. "You're smart and I'm conniving. Are you in, or are you out?"

Annajane took a long sip of her iced tea. She plucked a package of Town House crackers from the basket on the table and picked nervously at the cellophane wrapper.

"I care about Quixie," she said finally. "And I care about you and the family, really I do. Especially Sophie. But let's be honest here. I don't actually have a dog in this hunt."

"You admitted to me yesterday that you still have feelings for Mason," Pokey protested.

Annajane sighed loudly. "I should have kept my big fat mouth shut."

"But you didn't. Anyway, you didn't have to tell me. It's written all over your face. You're still in love with Mason. And you still work for Quixie."

"Only until Friday. Although Celia suggested earlier I should get the hell out right away because she's having my office painted for my successor."

"And you said?"

Annajane gave her a conspiratorial grin. "That I couldn't possibly vacate the premises that early."

"Good for you," Pokey said. "Until Friday, you're still on the company payroll, so you actually do have a dog in this hunt. If Celia is plotting to take over the company or sell it off to the highest bidder, or whatever, this is an emergency. You have to help."

"You're being overly dramatic," Annajane said. "Maybe Celia was talking about something else entirely. I only heard a few sentence fragments, and we can't be sure . . ."

"Hey!" Pokey said, interrupting. "Oh my God." She held her hand over her heart, as though she were having palpitations. "I just realized we've both overlooked one incredibly important fact."

"That you can save a pony's life by nagging your parents?"

"No," Pokey said, a slow smile spreading across her round pink face. "I think we're both forgetting how much my daddy loved you."

"I'm not forgetting that," Annajane said. "Your daddy was always wonderful to me. Treated me like I was his own daughter."

"He sure did," Pokey agreed, nodding her head for emphasis. "He loved you so much he gave you your own stock in the company as a wedding gift, didn't he?"

Annajane's mouth fell open. "You're right. I had forgotten. Five hundred shares. He drove over to my mama's house the morning of the wedding. He wouldn't come inside, but I went out on the porch and he handed me an envelope, and kissed me on the cheek and told me I'd made him a very happy man. I didn't even know what a stock certificate looked like before that."

"You never gave the stock back, right? Not in the divorce or anything, right?"

"I still have it," Annajane said, sitting back in her chair. "I hadn't thought about it in ages. And I bet Mason hasn't either."

"So there's a chance Celia doesn't know you own stock in Quixie," Pokey said.

"It's just five hundred shares," Annajane pointed out. "A drop in the bucket compared to what you all own."

"True," Pokey said. "Still, down the line, that could be important. We won't know until Mr. Thomas meets with us about that stupid trust agreement. Right now, we've got to figure out what Celia is up to. And then we have to get Mason to open his eyes and see her for the scheming, manipulative little bitch that she is. And get him to realize he still loves you."

"In a week," Annajane said. "No problem. Easy. Peasy. We should be able to get that done by Monday lunchtime."

"We need to do some research on Celia," Pokey went on, ignoring Annajane. She reached into her pocketbook and brought out a pen. "What was the name of her company?"

"Gingerpeachy," Annajane said.

Pokey was making notes on the back of her paper placemat. "And it sold to who?"

"I think the company is called Baby Brands," Annajane said. "I guess I could look up the announcement of the deal on the Internet."

"Do that," Pokey said, scribbling. She put down her pen. "Who do we know that might know something we can use against Celia?"

"I don't know anybody," Annajane said. "She's not from around here, didn't go to school in the South. This is impossible.

Celia's from a whole different world from us."

"Don't be such a defeatist," Pokey scolded. "Come on, think, Annajane, dammit."

"I think Celia is from Nebraska," Annajane said. "Do we know anybody in Nebraska?"

"We don't know anybody who even knows where Nebraska is, probably," Pokey said. "But I'll google Celia's name, just in case. Who knows? Maybe she's a wanted murderess. In the meantime, one of my sorority sisters is a buyer for Belk's. Maybe she'd know somebody who knows somebody. I'll give her a call."

"It's too bad we can't ask Davis what he knows about all this," Annajane said.

"Ha! He's the one we have to thank for bringing that pit viper into the family bosom in the first place," Pokey said. "Davis thinks Celia is 'awesome.'" She made finger quote marks.

"And you can't really ask Mason any questions about Celia," Annajane said. "What about your mama?"

Pokey toyed with a forkful of coleslaw. "Are you kidding? Celia's the daughter Sallie never had! Let's see. She's beautiful and skinny, plays tennis and golf, always looks perfect, and she's got an adding machine instead of a soul. Yup, Celia's everything I'm not. Mama's even giving her bridge lessons. Plus, she sucks up to Sallie every chance she gets. It's revolting."

"Hey," Annajane said sharply. "You're beautiful. Inside and out. You're a great wife, friend, mother, sister. You're what Celia will never be."

Pokey blew her a kiss. "Back atya."

"How do you think Sallie would feel about the company being sold, or moved, or whatever?"

"Good question," Pokey said. "If Daddy were still alive, the answer would be a big 'hell no!' "

"But he's not."

"I know," Pokey said. "She's always talked about Quixie being our family legacy. But if this were something Mason wanted, or if Davis convinced her it was a good idea, she might just go along with it."

"But it's not something you'd agree to, right?"

Pokey stared at her best friend. "Not in a million years. Not for a billion dollars. My brothers may think the grass is greener someplace else, but I don't. Passcoe is home. We were raised here. I intend to raise my own children here. And I don't intend to let anybody change that. Not without putting up a hell of a fight."

"That's what I thought," Annajane said, smiling.

"And what about you?" Pokey asked.

"You're supposed to be leaving town Friday. That's what you keep telling me."

"I'd hate to see anything happen to Quixie," Annajane said, trying to choose her words carefully. "If the company got sold, or moved, or swallowed up by a bigger company, it could be devastating to Passcoe. I'm like you. No matter where I go or what I do, this is my hometown. And Quixie is a huge part of that. It's a part of me and who I am and what I've been doing for the past eight years. Yeah, I know it's just cherry soda. But I don't want to see Quixie get swallowed up or closed down. I can't promise anything, but I can make some phone calls, and ask around. I want to find out what Celia's up to."

"And if she's up to what we suspect?"

"I don't know," Annajane said.

"Have you talked to Shane? Did you tell him about Mason's wedding?"

"We talked late last night," Annajane said. "I didn't mention the wedding. Didn't think it was important. Not to Shane, anyway."

"I see," Pokey said.

"No you don't," Annajane said with a moan. "This is all just a big mess. And I don't know how to fix it. He wants me to move in with him, Pokey. As soon as I get to Atlanta. And he doesn't see why we should wait til fall to get married. I tried to explain to him, everything is all happening so fast. I love him, but I want it to slow down. Just a little."

"Are you sure that's all it is?" Pokey asked.

"Yes. No. I can't explain how I feel. Something's just . . . making me want to hold back. Maybe I'm just gun-shy about marriage, after what happened with Mason."

"No," Pokey insisted. "You are gun-shy because you don't really love Shane. You're still in love with Mason. And you're scared to death to admit that Shane is rebound guy."

"Oh Gawwwd," Annajane said, burying her head in her hands. "You can't be right."

"But what if I am?" Pokey asked.

15

Sophie's eyelids fluttered. She yawned widely and looked around the room.

"You're awake," Celia said brightly. "Did you have a nice rest?"

"Where did Annajane and Aunt Pokey go?" Sophie demanded. "We were watching *Milo and Otis.*"

"You were sleeping, and they had to leave," Celia said. "But look what I brought you!" She propped the huge stuffed bunny on the pillow next to Sophie.

"Thank you very much," Sophie said politely, clutching the teddy bear the nurse had given her the night before and ignoring the bunny.

"You're welcome," Celia said. She whisked the plastic off the plate of wedding cake she'd placed on Sophie's dinner tray. "And look at this beautiful cake I brought you. It's our wedding cake!"

"It's pretty," Sophie said.

"Shall I get you a fork?" Celia asked. "We

can ring the nurse and get her to bring one. And maybe some nice cold milk."

"No," Sophie said, shaking her head. "I'm only 'lowed to have Jell-O. And apple juice."

Celia laughed. "Who told you that?"

"Daddy."

"Oh, well, daddies don't know everything," Sophie winced as Celia's tinkly laugh filled the room. Mason pushed through the door. "What's this?" he said, trying to sound stern. "Since when don't daddies know everything?"

"I was just about to tell Sophie it wouldn't hurt for her to have a little piece of our wedding cake and some milk," Celia explained, snaking her arm around Mason's waist.

"She actually isn't allowed to have something like that," Mason said.

"See!" Sophie smirked.

"Sophie . . ." Mason said, trying to look stern. "That's not nice. Celia didn't know the doctor doesn't want you having much in the way of real food just yet — this soon after surgery."

"Oh," Celia said. "Well, of course. In that case, we'll just freeze some cake for her, and she can have it later, after she comes home from the hospital."

"I don't like wedding cake," Sophie said stubbornly.

Celia cocked her head and considered the little girl. "How do you know? I'll bet you've never even tasted wedding cake."

"Have too!" Sophie shouted vehemently. "Have too, have too, have too."

"All right," Celia said with a note of resignation. "If you say so, that's fine."

"She was a flower girl at my cousin's wedding last summer," Mason said. He gave Sophie another stern look. "But that is no way to talk to Celia. I'd like you to tell her you're sorry for being rude."

"I'm sorry for being rude," Sophie said. She pulled the sheet up until it completely covered her head. Her voice was muffled. "Now go away."

Celia shrugged and reached for her pocketbook. She patted Sophie's sheet-covered knee. "All right, lamb-chop. I'm going now. Feel better fast so we can bring you home!"

Mason shook his head. "I'll talk to her," he said in a low voice. "She's not herself."

Celia arched one eyebrow. "If you say so."

"I'll call you later," Mason said, kissing her cheek.

"Tell Celia good-bye, Sophie," Mason said.

"Good-bye, Sophie," the little girl singsonged.

Mason was sitting in the living room, reviewing a memo about maintenance costs for the Quixie truck fleet when he heard a key turn in the front door.

Celia bumped the door open with her hip.

226

She was carrying a large sack of groceries and had an overnight bag slung over her shoulder.

"Let me get that," Mason said, jumping up to take the packages from her. He kissed her cheek and glanced at the contents of the sack. "What's all this?"

"Dinner for two," Celia said, heading for the kitchen. "You haven't eaten already, have you?"

"Uh, no," he said, following her into the kitchen and hoping she wouldn't find the greasy brown paper takeout bag from the Smokey Pig. "I was waiting to see what you wanted to do."

He put the groceries down on the kitchen counter. Celia wound her arms around his neck. "I just want to spend a quiet evening all alone with my man tonight. I want to cook him a gorgeous dinner, and drink some gorgeous wine, and later on, maybe show him just what he missed out on last night."

"You mean like a wedding? Hey, it's gonna happen. We just have to get Sophie . . ."

Celia gave him a coy smile. She unzipped the overnight bag and presented, with a flourish, a filmy black scrap of fabric, only slightly larger than a handkerchief. She held it up to her torso.

"I mean like a wedding night. I thought since you didn't get to see this last night, maybe we'd have a showing tonight."

Celia kissed him, and he kissed her back, and she pressed herself tightly against him, and his body responded in a predictable way.

"Mmm," Celia purred. But she pulled away. "Now don't try to distract me," she said, wagging a finger at him, as though he'd been a naughty schoolboy. "I have to get this dinner going."

Mason leaned back against the counter. "Need me to do anything?"

"Not really," Celia said. "I thought we'd just have a big, juicy pan-seared steak and some baked potatoes and garlic-creamed spinach. I looked up the recipe from that steak house in Charleston that you love. Oh, and a salad."

Celia removed a head of romaine from a plastic bag and rinsed it under the faucet.

"Mase?"

"Hmm?" He was staring out the kitchen window at a robin hopping around on the grass outside. He'd talked about putting in a garden out there. It was nice and sunny, but Celia didn't want the lawn disturbed, and, anyway, she'd informed him that tomato cages and pepper plants looked "trashy."

She hesitated. "I had a call from an old friend last week. I think maybe you might have met him around? Jerry Kelso?"

Maybe if he put the tomato plants in some nice wooden planter boxes or something? That wouldn't look trashy, right?

"Kelso?" He frowned. "The president of Jax Snax? You know him?"

"Davis introduced us at a marketing thing in Houston a few months ago."

Jerry Kelso was a name that had been on Mason's mind for weeks. Ever since Kelso requested a confidential meeting six weeks earlier. He hadn't said anything to anybody about the meeting, and was hoping that might be the end of the issue. But apparently, it wasn't going to be.

"Oh, yeah," Mason said. "Now I remember the name. What's up with Kelso? He trying to recruit you away from Quixie?"

She laughed the tinkly laugh, and it sent a shiver down his spine, as though someone had walked over Mason's grave. What was up with that?

"As if I'd leave Quixie. Or you."

"As if," Mason agreed.

"Did you know Jax Snax is the second largest packaged chip and cookie baker in the Eastern U.S.?" Celia asked.

"I knew they were big, but not that big," Mason said, wondering why they were having this discussion.

"They just bought out Cousin Ruth's Old-Tyme Chips and Pretzels, that company out of Knoxville," Celia informed him. "You've seen their stores; they're in all the malls."

"Yeah, maybe I read about that somewhere in one of the trade magazines," Mason said, trying to sound noncommital. "Didn't they buy another company at around the same time?"

Pole beans would be good. He could make tepees from bamboo for them to climb on. Pole beans weren't trashy looking, were they?

"Monster Cookie," Celia said. "They sell those enormous chocolate chip and peanut butter cookies you see in those jars at the convenience stores."

"That's the one," Mason agreed. "Looks like Jax is on a buying binge, huh?" He was mentally surveying that scraggly patch of lawn outside the kitchen window. Maybe he'd take a ride over to the garden center next weekend; if the weather stayed decent, he could put in a garden by Good Friday, which was when his granddaddy always planted.

Just how well did Celia know Jerry Kelso?

"A huge Dutch grocery conglomerate just bought a big chunk of Jax," Celia said. "They're pretty flush with cash right now. Jerry was saying they'd really love to add a soft drink company to their business mix. You know — Pepsi and Frito-Lay are the same company, so it makes sense."

That got his attention. "You've been discussing selling Quixie with Jerry Kelso?"

"No," Celia said hurriedly. "Of course not. Jerry just mentioned it. So I thought it would be worth mentioning to you. I mean, with Jax's saturation of the chip market — especially in convenience stores, where we're trying to grow Quixie, I thought it was an interesting idea. There's the potential for amazing synchronicity. That's all."

"Synchronicity, my ass," Mason said, his tone sour. "They'd like to gobble us up, spit us out."

"It's just something to think about. Don't get yourself all worked up," Celia said, wrapping her arms around his waist. "I don't want us to talk about business tonight. It's our wedding night, remember? Forget I even mentioned it."

"I will," he assured her. "Quixie is not for sale."

She changed the subject in a hurry. "I saved some of your chocolate groom cake from the wedding. It seemed like such a shame to throw it out. I thought we'd have it for dessert."

"Fine," Mason said, leaning back against the counter. "Sorry I jumped on you. Need me to do anything?"

"Not a thing," Celia said, unwrapping the steaks. "I have everything completely under control."

"As always," Mason said. He regretted it the minute the words were out of his mouth.

She wheeled around to face him with a mock pout. "What exactly is that supposed to mean?"

"Nothing," Mason said. "It's a compliment.

You're the most organized, efficient woman I've ever met."

She frowned, and a deep crease appeared between her eyebrows. "Honey, it doesn't exactly sound like a compliment to me. You make it sound like I'm some kind of control freak or something."

"Not at all," Mason said. "Look, let's not fight, okay?"

Celia centered the romaine on a cutting board and began whacking at it with a large sharp knife. "This isn't a fight," she said, slamming the knife's edge against the hapless romaine. "It's a constructive conversation. If we're going to make this marriage work, we have to get things out in the open, Mason. So, I need you to know that it hurts me when you make derogatory comments about me." She took another whack at the lettuce, sending bits of it flying.

"I'm sorry," Mason said, picking a piece of romaine from his eyebrow. "I don't want to hurt you."

"See?" she said brightly. "Communication. It's the key to everything."

"Right," he said, feeling his jaw muscle twitch.

She sighed dramatically. "Sweetheart, while we're on the topic, I really think we need to talk about Sophie, and the way she spoke to me today, at the hospital. She treats me as though I'm the wicked stepmother — and you know I've gone out of my way to treat her like my own child."

Mason winced, and his jaw twitched again. Twice. "She's just a little girl, Celia. And remember, she just had surgery."

"I know, poor little angel. I just think you need to be a little stricter with her. Or let me deal with her, when it's an issue that affects me." She gave that little laugh again. "Honestly, I know everybody means well, but between you and Pokey and Annajane, you've all managed to spoil the child rotten."

"Spoiled?" One of his dark eyebrows shot upward. "Sophie's a nice, normal little kid. Somedays she acts out, cuts up. But that doesn't make her spoiled."

Celia began scooping the lettuce into a wooden bowl. "Look. I get that she feels threatened by me. I mean, Sophie's been daddy's girl her whole life, and she's had you all to herself. Until I came along and changed everything. I totally understand that. But I need you to back me up when it comes to disciplining her."

"Let me get this straight," Mason said, his fists clamped tight on the countertop. "You're calling Sophie spoiled and me spineless? Is this your idea of a constructive conversation?

"No!" Celia cried. "Oh, I'm just no good at this. You know I adore Sophie. But I think she'd be happier with some guidelines. I want her to see me as an equal in her parenting.

Mason, I'm sorry. I shouldn't have said anything at all. Never mind. I don't want our nice evening spoiled."

Celia gathered up the discarded steak wrappings and lettuce bits. She flipped the trash can lid to dump them in and spied the large Smokey Pig takeout bag. She held the bag up for Mason to see. "What's this?"

"Lunch?"

"Mason!" She dropped the bag back into the trash and put her hands on her hips. "You've already eaten dinner, haven't you? Why didn't you say something?"

"More like a late lunch," Mason protested. "But it was hardly anything. I'm still starved."

"You're just trying to humor me," Celia said. She dumped the bag and food scraps into the trash with a huge, martyred sigh. "Never mind. I'll just fix myself a salad. Will you still want dessert?"

"I had lunch hours and hours ago," Mason said. "Besides, you haven't eaten, have you? Come on, let's fix dinner together." He picked up the steaks. "You want me to grill these?"

"No," Celia said petulantly. "It'll take too long for the coals to get ready. I'll just pan sauté them." She grabbed a skillet from the pot rack hanging over the kitchen island and dropped it onto the range.

Mason took a step backward. "I'll open some wine. White, right?"

"Never mind the wine." Celia drizzled olive oil into the pan and turned on the burner. "I'm getting one of my stress headaches. The last thing I need now is wine."

But wine was what he really, really needed right now, especially if she was getting one of her headaches. He opened a bottle of burgundy and poured a hefty serving into one of the fancy ultrathin Riedel wineglasses they'd gotten as a wedding gift. At the last moment, the lip of the wine bottle clinked against the goblet. *Ching.* A wedge-shaped chunk of glass fell neatly onto the countertop.

"Damn," Mason said. He opened the cupboard and reached for his favorite cut-glass old-fashioned tumbler and transferred the burgundy out of the ruined Riedel.

Before he could stop her, Celia swept the wine glass into the trash. "It's all right," she said. "I can always order more from the store in Charlotte."

"Sorry," Mason said under his breath. "I'm gonna get out of your hair now. Call me if you need me to do something." He picked up his wineglass and retreated to the study.

But not a lot of studying got done. He made notes on the margins of the reports, began working on a draft of a memo to Davis, and read more e-mails, but from the clatter of pots and pans and the slam of cupboard doors coming from the kitchen, he could tell things were not going well.

He googled Jax Snax on his computer and was amazed by the number of hits his search brought up. Jax had been on a shopping binge for sure. Just within the past year, in addition to the cookie company and potato chip outfit Celia told him about, Jaz had bought up a family-owned soft-pretzel baker out of Pennsylvania called Dutch Uncle and a popcorn outfit from Iowa called Poppinz'. As he scrolled down the list of stories mentioning Jax Snax, he spied a reference from *Beverage World* that was only two months old. He clicked on the citation and read with alarm.

Jax Snax CEO Jerry Kelso confirmed that his company is on the hunt for a small-to-average-sized regional soft drink bottler to add to their mix of businesses. "We've got the expertise, the distribution channels and the proven success story in the convenience food business," he said in a recent interview. "We're looking at several options right now, including one novelty soft drink bottler in the Carolinas that we think could be ripe for the picking."

Mason slapped the cover of his laptop. "Celia," he hollered.

She didn't answer. She was still out in the kitchen banging pots and pans around. He didn't get the big deal about dinner. He didn't get her compulsion to prove to him that she could cook. There were restaurants in Passcoe, not a lot, but enough that they'd never starve. They belonged to the country club and could eat there any night except Mondays, when the club was closed, and, anyway, he was a pretty decent cook himself. He'd fended for himself all those years after he and Annajane broke up, hadn't he?

"Damn!"

He looked up to see Celia standing in the doorway, holding her cell phone and looking supremely pissed off.

"Something wrong?"

"Your mother just called," Celia said. "It's my aunt Eleanor. She was napping in her room, and Sallie went to check on her, and according to your mother, there's something wrong with Aunt Eleanor's breathing."

Mason stood up abruptly. "Do we need to get a doctor? Take her to the hospital?"

"Who knows?" Celia said. "She's in her nineties. I don't know why she insisted on coming down here all alone for the wedding if her health is this precarious. I could just strangle my cousin Mallery for putting her on the plane."

Mason reached for his car keys. "Come on. I'll drive you over to Cherry Hill. We can call Max Kaufman, and if need be, he can come over and check out the old girl."

"I don't want to bother you," Celia said.

She had her pocketbook over her shoulder and her car keys in hand. "It's probably nothing. I'll call you if I need you."

"What about your dinner?" Mason asked. "Can I just put it in foil or something for later?"

She glanced in the direction of the kitchen, her lips pursed. "I'm sorry, darling. Just pitch it out."

16

Mason exhaled slowly. Was Celia upset with him? She was usually so sweet and accommodating. What had gotten into her lately? She'd left in a huff. If she'd stayed, he would have had it out with her over this Jax Snax thing. She knew more about the subject than she'd told him. This was no casual bit of gossip. Celia didn't do casual. Maybe she just thought it best to alert him to the fact that they were being checked out by another company. No harm, no foul, right?

He should feel bad about their dinner, he knew. After all, her wedding had been spoiled, and her prospective stepdaughter was being a little bit of a pill, and now her great-aunt might be sick. Really sick.

Upon reflection, he realized he didn't actually feel bad at all. Probably this made him a terrible person, certainly a terrible husband-to-be. He should call and apologize, at least drive over to his mother's house and insist on helping her take care of her aunt, or *some-*

thing. But right now he really just wanted to do what he wanted to do. And hadn't she just called him spineless and his daughter spoiled, in a roundabout kind of way?

So he strolled out to the garage, found his golf clubs and some whiffle balls, and went out to the side yard, to that scruffy future garden plot. For an hour or so, he practiced putting because his short game sucked. He didn't think about postponed weddings, or pissed-off brides, or why he seemed to take such perverted pleasure in pissing off his bride to be. But he did feel something, unease, maybe, about the fact that he was actually feeling relieved that Celia's big night with him was probably not going to happen. He was a totally shitty husband-to-be, for sure.

After he'd worked on his putting, it was still daylight, and there was still at least another hour of warm, buttery sunshine left. Without giving it much thought, he got in his car and drove over to the bottling plant. He let himself into the garage, found a clean rag, and dusted a film of thick yellow pollen off the red Chevelle. Had it been that long since he'd driven the fun car? He got in and fired her up, doing a silent fist-pump when the engine throbbed to life. He put the top down and carefully backed it out of the garage.

Ten minutes later, he was tooling around Passcoe, seeing the sights, tooting his horn at anybody and everybody he recognized. He felt really, really good. But, and this surprised him, maybe a little lonely.

What he needed was a passenger. Somebody who could share his appreciation for just how cool it was to drive around on a beautiful spring evening with the top down. He reached for his phone, and without giving it much thought, tapped the icon for Annajane's cell.

Wrong. He disconnected before her phone could even ring. He drove another block and reconsidered. Why the hell not? It was just a car ride, for God's sake. He tapped the icon again, and at the next block, swung the Chevelle back in the direction of her loft. All she could say was no, right?

Annajane's cellphone rang once. The screen lit up, and she saw that it was Mason calling, but he'd disconnected before she answered.

She held the phone in her hand and stared at it. Should she call him back? Act as though she didn't know he'd called? She felt like a stupid teenager. She started remembering all the Friday nights she'd spent, staring at the phone, fantasizing about picking up the phone and hearing Mason's voice on the other end of the line. She remembered the sleepovers at Pokey's house and how she'd sneak into his empty room when the rest of the household was asleep, studying his books, his bed, the football and baseball trophies casually lined up on the shelves. She remembered the notebooks she'd filled in high school, practicing her signature: Mrs. Mason Bayless, written in stupid, girly flourishes. While she was remembering all the things she missed about being a stupid teenager, the phone rang. Mason, again. She let it ring three times and then answered.

"Hey, Annajane," he said.

"Hey, Mason." She felt herself blushing with pleasure. "How's Sophie?"

"She's good. Sleeping. So, there's something I was wondering about. We're okay, right?"

"Okay?"

"You know. As friends. We've been through some stuff together. Good and bad."

Annajane laughed ruefully. "That's the understatement of the year. But yeah. I'd say we're okay now. Mind if I ask why you're asking?"

There was a long pause at the other end of the line. "I don't know. This is just so weird. I guess I'm sad that you're leaving town. Leaving the company."

"That's sweet. But you've known for months that I was leaving the company and moving to Atlanta. And getting remarried," she reminded him.

"Yeah, but none of that seemed real until today. I went by your office at the plant, and

I saw all the moving boxes and stuff."

"It's real. I've sold the loft. I'm finishing up packing right now," she lied. "Friday's my last day."

"I wish you'd stay," he blurted out.

Annajane held up the phone and stared at it. *Who was this guy? Were they really having this conversation? Mason had never once expressed any regrets about her leaving — not him, and not the company. No regrets, that's what he'd always told her in the past.*

"Staying is not a good idea," Annajane said. "Not for me. It probably wasn't a good idea for me to stay in town after we split."

"I don't know why you say that. I mean, yeah, it was a little awkward at times, but I think we managed to keep things on a pretty professional level. You don't think we could keep that going?"

No, she wanted to scream. *We cannot keep things going while you're married to Celia, because I want to throw up whenever I see you two together. We cannot keep things professional because I cannot keep telling myself I'm over you when I'm pretty sure I'm not over you.*

"This isn't about any of that," she said finally. "It's not about you and me, Mason. That's over. This is about me getting a great job offer and really challenging myself. It's about me starting a new life with Shane. Maybe even starting a family. I think it's time, and I think I deserve some happiness. You should be happy for me. I'm happy for you."

Liar, liar, pants on fire.

She heard him inhale and then exhale. "Hey," Mason said. "You're not doing this because you're pregnant, right?"

That's when she disconnected the phone and tossed it onto the sofa. Annajane stomped into the sleek galley kitchen and, spying the bottle of Maker's Mark she'd left on the counter Saturday morning, poured herself two fingers of bourbon, which she drank, straight up. She heard her phone buzzing from its resting place among the sofa cushions. It stopped buzzing. She poured a little more bourbon in the glass and, not wanting to become a sloppy drunk, thoughtfully added some ice cubes to the glass, forcing herself to sip slowly while the phone buzzed softly in the other room.

17

Mason banged his head on the Chevelle's steering wheel. Once, twice, three times. He needed to knock some sense into his own skull. What the hell was wrong with him? Had he really just suggested that Annajane was only getting married because she was knocked up? He massaged his forehead and tried to call her again. Of course she wasn't answering. He looked up at the second floor of her building. The lights were on. He redialed. Nothing.

He should go home, he knew, but he didn't feel like being alone, and he couldn't leave things with Annajane like this. He got out of the Chevelle, squared his shoulders and approached the inset entranceway to her loft apartment. The real estate listing sign had a cheery SOLD! placard attached. He scowled at it and pressed the intercom buzzer. Once, twice, three times.

He looked up and down the street. It was deserted. Sunday night in Passcoe. You could have fired a cannon down the middle of the street and not hit anybody. He put his finger on the intercom buzzer and left it there.

"What?" Her voice sounded tinny, but unmistakably pissed.

"I'm sorry," he said. "Really. Can I come up? I really need to talk to you in person. To apologize."

"No. Go away."

"Annajane?"

Silence.

He leaned his back against the faded gray brick wall and considered his next move. He was feeling desperate, not an emotion he was used to, especially when it came to women. Come to think of it, the last time he'd felt this shitty, this desperate, was when Annajane left him for good.

Mason rang the intercom buzzer again.

Her voice came on. "What?"

"Please let me come up," he said, enunciating each word. "Just let me apologize in person, and then I promise not to bother you again."

"All right," she said finally. "Let's get this over with."

She heard his footsteps echoing in the stairwell. He knocked once. Annajane unlocked the door and looked Mason straight in the eye. "You're a pig," she said stonily. "And for

your information, no, I am not pregnant. Asshole."

"You're right, I am a pig," he agreed. "A
swine."

He stepped inside the loft and looked
around. "This is really nice," he said, sounding surprised. "I've never been in one of these
places."

"Walk around. Enjoy the view. Because I'm
outta here come Friday," she said, trying her
best to sound mean. Why was it so difficult
to be mean to Mason, even when he was being such a monumental jerk?

"You told me you were all packed," he said
pointedly, gesturing around the decidedly
not-packed-up room.

"I lied," she said. "So sue me."

"Can I sit down?"

"Whatever."

"Here?" He pointed at the sofa, which was
covered with stuff.

She moved a stack of books from the sofa
and gestured for him to sit, but she stayed
standing, arms crossed defiantly. What she
needed now was a position of power. "You
were saying?"

"I needed to tell you face-to-face. What I
said to you was inexcusable," Mason said,
sounding miserable. "I'm sorry, Annajane. I
don't know why I'm being such an asshole,
when all I really wanted to do was say I'm
gonna miss you. And not just because you're

great at your job and I'm worried about what's gonna happen at Quixie without you. Sophie and I are gonna miss you, Annajane."

He looked up and gave her that dopey sad-dog look of his.

She returned his look with steely resolve not to get sucked into the charm that somehow managed to ooze from every pore of his body with absolutely no effort on his part.

"Thank you," she said tartly. "I'm sure the company will survive without me. I hate the idea of not being around Sophie, but Pokey has promised to send me lots of pictures. Was there anything else?"

"Well, I did have an idea. But probably you don't want to hear it now. Because I'm such a major dickhead and everything."

Momentarily putting aside the need for power, she perched on the edge of the arm-chair opposite his. "I'm listening."

"It's a gorgeous evening," Mason said. "I actually came over here to ask you to come out and go for a spin in the Chevelle with me. Would you even consider that? For old time's sake?"

She felt her heart thudding in her chest. The memories came rolling over her like a tidal wave. The two of them, riding through the night in the fun car, top down, headed for the beach, back to their lake cottage, or even just to the Dairy Dog for soft-serve ice cream. Anywhere at all. Against her will, she felt the corners of her lips tilting into something like a smile.

"Annajane? Is that a yes?"

She sighed, and tried to force herself to think about reality. Those golden memories of hers were just that. Memories. Tricky and totally unreliable. They should be packed away like all the books and old clothes she'd bagged up for giveaway to the Goodwill. From now on, she was going to live in the here and the now. Right?

"I don't know if that's such a good idea."

"Why not?"

"What would Celia think?" She deliberately avoided the question of what Shane might think.

He shrugged. "I don't know. Maybe I don't care."

She raised one eyebrow. "Really?"

He stood up and walked over to look out the window onto the street. It was dusk, and the street lights were just winking to life.

"What is this about, exactly?" she asked, afraid to hear his answer.

"Does it have to be about anything? It's a gorgeous night. We're old, old friends. Can't you just come out and go for a ride with me? Just for the hell of it. I swear I'll be nice."

Annajane felt herself caving. What would be the harm in going for a ride on a beautiful spring night with an old friend? Old lover. Old husband. Whatever. She looked down at herself. She was dressed in tattered jeans with the knees ripped out, an old oversized Atlanta Braves jersey, and a pair of red Chuck Taylor high-tops. Her hair was pulled back in a headband. "I'm not really dressed to go out."

He turned and smiled. "You look fine. Great, actually. Do I recognize that jersey?"

She blushed. Why had she hung onto this ratty old shirt? In fact, it was his jersey, as he well knew. His lucky jersey, he'd called it.

The first spring after they'd gotten engaged they'd driven down to Atlanta for the Braves home opener. Mason bought her a sun visor and himself a jersey at the game, but their team had lost steam early, and by the seventh-inning stretch, with the Braves losing eight to zip, they'd left, returning to their cheap hotel not far from the stadium, telling themselves they'd watch the end of the game back in their room. It never happened. At his request, she'd modeled his jersey for him, doing a slow striptease while Mason did his own X-rated play by play of her performance. For the rest of that summer, she'd worn the jersey for him every time they made love. His lucky jersey had nothing to do with baseball and everything to do with sex.

She should burn the jersey.

Yeah. Right.

Mason obviously sensed her indecision.

He held up the car keys and jingled them tantalizingly. "I'm parked outside. C'mon,

Annajane, for once, don't overthink things. Let's just go for a ride, can we?"

"What the hell," she said finally. She had all week to pack. It was, as Mason had said, a gorgeous night out. She shoved her phone in her pocket, grabbed her keys, and walked right out the door, with Mason following closely on her heels. She closed and locked the door in a hurry, before she could, as he'd put it, overthink things.

Annajane swept a film of cobwebs from the dashboard. "Wow," she said. "When was the last time you drove this thing?"

Mason turned off Main Street and onto Seventh, rolling past Willard's Feed and Seed, the Family Dollar Store, and a couple of boarded-up storefronts.

Seeing the vacant buildings made him sad. He could remember the name of every single business on that street. His father traded at Passcoe Hardware, and his mother always bought their school shoes at Fashion Shoe Shop, which she'd said was a joke, because the owners had zero sense of fashion. Cline Drugs was still hanging in there, but the soda fountain at the back was closed, and the last time he'd been in the store, the shelves looked more like a museum than a functioning store. His family had made a point of doing business at those stores because the owners were neighbors and friends. Passcoe was hurting, just the way Quixie was hurting. He hated to think about what would happen if Quixie left town.

"Mason?" Annajane snapped her fingers in front of his face. "Anybody home?"

"Sorry," he said, returning to the here and now. "I haven't driven the old girl for a few months," he admitted. "I've been pretty busy at work. And Celia hates this car. She refuses to ride in it. So I've been keeping it in the garage at the plant."

"But you used to love this car," Annajane said. "What's to hate about a classic convertible?"

"She says it's a pimp car," Mason said. "And as she points out, it doesn't even have air-conditioning."

"Hmm," Annajane said. She slung an arm on the open window and leaned back into the headrest. "So, where are we headed?"

"I thought we'd ride out to the farm," Mason said.

Cherry Hill Farms wasn't a real farm anymore, and hadn't been since Sallie's father, Sam Woodrow, passed away in the 1980s and the family had sold off the last of his cattle and horses. The last Annajane had heard, the old farmhouse was being used as hay storage for the tenant farmer's cows.

"That sounds nice," she said.

Mason slid a cassette into the tape deck

and "Walk This Way" blasted out of the speakers.

"Mötley Crüe?" Annajane rolled her eyes.

"Aerosmith!" Mason said, chastising her for her rock ignorance. "Root around under the seat there and find something else if you don't like it," Mason said, secretly disappointed in her musical taste.

"I like Aerosmith sometimes. Just not tonight. Have you got anything . . . mellower?"

Mason reached over the backseat and found a battered leather box that he plopped in her lap. "Here. Pick your own damn music."

Annajane opened the box gingerly. "Okay, let's see what you've got. Wow, this is like a for-real time machine. Led Zeppelin, Santana, Blue Öyster Cult. Were you even born when these guys started playing?"

"Those bands, madam, are rock classics," he said. "Ageless and timeless."

She held up a tape with a bright purple case. "John Denver. Really?"

He snatched the tape out of her hand and stowed it safely under his seat. "That's Sophie's. I think she saw him on an old *Sesame Street* rerun."

Annajane laughed. "I can't hate her for that. C'mon, give it back. Tonight's perfect for John Denver cheese. A little 'Sunshine on My Shoulder' maybe. Or some 'Rocky Mountain High'?"

"Nope," he shook his head. "You've hurt my feelings. I'm afraid you'll have to find your own mood music."

She leafed idly through the tapes, pausing to look out at the deep green countryside flashing by.

"Maybe later," she said. She threw her head back and enjoyed the feel of the wind whipping through her hair.

But she couldn't shake the need to know what had brought about Mason's unexpected visit. And she desperately wanted to know what had happened between the happy couple. She stole a sideways glance at Mason. He looked as happy and relaxed, as unguarded, as she'd seen him in years. And years.

"What's going on between you and Celia? Not that it's any of my business."

Mason shrugged. "Nothing really. She was annoyed that I ate a late lunch, and then she was annoyed because I broke one of our wedding-present wineglasses. I think I kinda wrecked her plans for our big evening together."

"Where is she now?"

He laughed. "At my mom's. Her aunt had some kind of spell, and you know Sallie. She's not exactly Nurse Nancy. She called and issued a summons, and of course Celia went."

"Nobody, not even Celia, ignores a summons from Sallie Bayless," Annajane agreed.

Mason laughed. He'd forgotten how easy Annajane was to be around. Effortless. With Annajane there was no subterfuge, no hidden messages. She was as open and real as . . . well, he didn't know. Just easy, that's all.

How the hell had things gotten so complicated, so quickly, with Celia? He felt like he was treading on broken glass every time they were together lately.

"Let me ask you something," he said. "Do you think I spoil Sophie?"

Wow, Annajane wondered. *Where was this coming from?*

"Spoil?" She repeated the question, stalling for time. "I don't know. I don't think so, but I'm probably biased. Sophie's . . . she's special, you know? She was so tiny, and so needy, when you first brought her home. I guess maybe some people might say you went a little overboard. But she's your daughter! And she is the sweetest, smartest, most loving little girl in the world. She doesn't ask for a lot. And it's not like she really plays you or manipulates you."

Mason was nodding thoughtfully as she spoke, so Annajane took a deep breath and asked a question of her own.

"Does Celia think Sophie's spoiled?"

"She thinks I should be firmer with her," Mason said. "Sophie was kind of rude to Celia today at the hospital. You know, pulling her covers over her head, not talking to her, that kind of thing. Kid stuff, really. But it really got under Celia's skin."

Annajane was tempted to fire off something clever or flippant about evil stepmothers. But something made her hold back.

Sophie's only five, but she's no dummy. She could tell Celia was trying to buy her off. And she can spot a phony, even if her clueless daddy can't. Tread cautiously here. Think before you open your mouth.

"Well," Annajane said finally. "Discipline and rules and politeness, those are things every child needs. It's not like Sophie to be rude. Maybe that's something you and Celia are going to have to work on together."

Mason nodded. "Yeah, probably you're right. Guess I shouldn't be so touchy, huh? Anyway, it's too nice a night to get into all this heavy stuff. We'll work it out. Eventually."

Hope not, Annajane thought.

18

When they got to the turnoff for the farm, Mason swung the car easily into the graveled drive. Lights glowed from within the old white-painted farmhouse, and a battered pickup was parked in the shade of the tin-roofed shed that had once sheltered tractors.

"Somebody's living here?" Annajane asked.

"You remember Grady Witherspoon? Maybe not. He was a little older than me. Went in the navy right out of high school, and I guess they've lived all over the world. He and his wife moved back last year. They're renting the place. He's planted one of the old cornfields, gonna be selling organic vegetables to some of the fancy restaurants over at Pinehurst. At least that's the plan."

The Chevelle bumped along over the rutted dirt road that skirted an old pasture gone to weeds. Waist-high pine-tree saplings lined the rusty barbed wire fence. More than once, the high-beam headlights caught a deer bounding gracefully across the path, and junebugs and moths seemed to float in the still, cool air. Finally, Mason pulled the car alongside a weathered outbuilding.

"What is this place?" Annajane asked, half-rising from the seat to get a better look. It had been years and years since she'd visited the farm.

"It's the old corncrib," Mason said. "It's about to fall in, along with the rest of the buildings out here. Davis and I used to bring sleeping bags and camp out here back in the days when we deer hunted together. We thought we were Daniel Boone and Davy Crockett."

He cut the engine and they let the quiet settle over them. It was a country kind of quiet, lush and deep and green, Annajane thought, with cicadas sawing away and the hooting of an owl echoing from a nearby treetop.

"Do you and Davis still hunt together?" Annajane asked, shivering involuntarily at the sound of the owl.

"No," he said, and she thought she detected a note of regret in his voice. "The only deer he's chasing these days are the kind spelled d-e-a-r. We actually don't do much of anything together anymore, except bicker."

"About the company?"

"That, and other stuff," Mason said. "Lately, I look at him and have to wonder how we could be so completely different and yet come from the same set of parents."

"Davis definitely marches to his own tune," Annajane said, trying to be diplomatic.

"That's part of the problem," Mason said darkly. "We're supposed to be running a family business. I keep trying to remind him of that, but it doesn't do much good. If he had his way, Quixie would be a division of some giant chemical company, and he'd be sitting in a penthouse office in Manhattan. But that wasn't my grandfather's vision for the company, and it sure wasn't Dad's. Nor mine. Jax Snax, my ass."

"Jax Snax?" she asked. "The potato chip company?"

"You won't say anything to anybody, right?"

"Of course not."

He cleared his throat. "They're making noises about buying a controlling interest in Quixie. Nothing formal yet, just talk. But some numbers have been floated. The people I've talked to say it's a decent offer. Not great, but decent, considering our recent sales slide."

She wondered if she should disclose the conversation she'd overheard Celia having earlier at the plant. Did Mason know his bride to be was in cahoots with his baby brother?

"Would you sell?" Annajane asked.

"It's kind of a moot point right now," Mason said. "You know Dad's biggest fear was that after his death the company might get broken up or sold off. He'd seen it happen to other family-owned companies, seen the kinds of feuds that erupted between siblings, and he was bound and determined it wouldn't happen to Quixie. Or to us. Which is why he put the company ownership in an irrevocable trust that would prohibit any discussion of a sale until after he'd been gone for five years."

Annajane raised an eyebrow. "I didn't know that."

"The rest of the estate was settled after Dad died," Mason said. "That part was pretty cut and dried. He left Cherry Hill to Mama, and Davis and Pokey and I got what we got. But none of us realized, until we met with Norris Thomas, Dad's lawyer, that he'd left it so that Quixie couldn't be sold. Not only that, he instructed Norris that the exact details of the trust couldn't be disclosed for five years."

"It's been more than five years now," Annajane pointed out.

"The clock on the trust didn't start ticking until April fifteenth, which was when the will was probated," Mason said.

"What's that mean for Quixie?" Annajane asked.

"In the short term, it means no sale," Mason said. "After that, we don't really know. Norris told me himself that Davis has been pestering him about the trust for a couple months now — probably ever since the Jax Snax people started talking about a deal. Davis even threatened to sue to get the trust arrangement revealed early, but Norris is a stubborn old bastard. He's sitting tight. He says he'll meet with all of us next week — on the fifteenth, and not a day before."

"Why all the secrecy?" Annajane asked, studying Mason's face for any clues. "I mean, your dad always said he was leaving the company to you kids, right? So I don't understand why he'd make y'all wait five years to find out exactly how everything would play out."

"You knew Dad. He was a poker player his entire life. He always liked to play his cards close to his chest. And to tell you the truth, I think he probably liked the idea of controlling us from beyond the grave."

"And your mama doesn't know what's in the trust agreement either?" Annajane asked.

"Nope. She swears she can't get Norris to tell her a thing. And believe me, she's tried everything up to and including bribery and death threats."

Annajane grinned. "How's that sitting with Sallie?"

"She's been pissed about it for five years," Mason admitted. "But there's not a damned thing any of us can do about it."

"I guess selling the company would mean a lot of money," Annajane said.

"That's why Davis is so fired up. A sale would make us all rich."

She coughed politely. "Pardon me for stating the obvious, but you're already rich."

"Moderately wealthy," Mason corrected her, laughing at himself. "On paper, anyway. Don't forget, Dad took on a lot of debt when he bought that land in Fayetteville. That's what Mama would prefer we be called. But Davis definitely would prefer to be rich. Filthy, stinking rich."

"What *does* Sallie think of all this?" Annajane asked.

"She's playing it cool. She says she'll listen to any offer. But she's gonna have to hop off the fence pretty soon. The Jax offer is looking like a reality, and if our costs keep rising and our sales keep sinking the way they have been, they may cut their price, or just go away for good."

"Would that be a bad thing?"

"We can't keep going the way we have been," Mason said. "We've been in a holding pattern since Dad died. Maybe it's my fault. I'll admit I've been reluctant to make any drastic changes."

He lowered his voice. "Not long before he died, Dad hired a food chemist to come up with some new flavors of Quixie. To extend the brand. He'd tasted and liked the key lime and pomegranate, but hated the peach soda. He'd pretty much made up his mind to do it

262

— roll out one new flavor a year. But then he had the heart attack and died."

"So you put the plans on hold," Annajane said. "Probably wise, given the economy."

"Maybe," Mason said, sounding dubious. "Or maybe I'm just chicken. I keep worrying, what if I screw it up? And then I start second-guessing myself. That's no kind of leadership. Something has to give. That's all I know for sure."

He turned and gave her a half smile. "But none of this is your problem. In a way, I envy you. You can just walk away and start over. Do your job, cash your paycheck, clock out on Friday, and forget about it until Monday."

"Theoretically," Annajane said.

"Yeah," he agreed. "I guess maybe you'll never be a wage slave. You care too much about stuff."

"Way too much."

He yawned and stretched and slipped his arm easily along the back of the seat.

"Sophie is gonna miss you like crazy when you move," he said, deliberately changing the subject.

Annajane felt a sharp stab of sadness. "Leaving her is the hardest thing about making this move," she said. "God, I'm going to miss her. More than you know. Do you think Celia would let her come and visit me in Atlanta? Maybe with Pokey? I really can't stand the idea of not having her in my life."

"I don't think she'd have a problem with that," Mason said. "More importantly, I wouldn't have a problem with it. You're family to her. Always will be, if I have any say in the matter. Which I will."

"Thank you for that," she said earnestly. "I mean it. I guess it's weird to fall in love with your ex-husband's child. I didn't mean to, but not loving Sophie? That would be impossible."

They heard the owl hooting again, and Mason craned his neck to try to figure out where the bird might be perched.

"What about Shane?" he said, trying to sound casual. "How do you think he'd be with having your ex's kid hanging around?"

"I've told him how much Sophie means to me," Annajane said. "Shane loves children. And he doesn't have a jealous bone in his body. Anyway, he'll be traveling most of the summer."

"So . . ." Mason strung the word into two syllables. "You've set the wedding date?"

"Not exactly," Annajane said. "Shane wants to get married right away, but I'd really like to get settled in first. You know, new apartment, new job, new town. It's a lot, you know?"

"You're not moving in with him?" Mason sounded surprised.

"Why do people keep asking me that?" Annajane snapped. "Why do I have to live with him? Just because we're engaged? Do I have something to prove?"

"Not to me," Mason said quickly. "Seems to me you just met the guy. Why rush? In fact, I'd say you definitely should not live together."

"You and Celia have been living together for months," she pointed out.

"That's different."

"How?"

"I don't know," he sounded impatient. "It's not like I planned for Celia to move in with me. It just sort of happened. She left some clothes at my house, and then the place she was renting at first was so far from the office . . . Are you going to get mad at me if I tell you I don't think you're that kind of girl?"

Annajane smiled to herself in the dark, turning away from Mason so he couldn't see her reaction.

"I won't get mad if you mean that as some kind of twisted compliment."

"I do!" Mason said. "Of course it's a compliment. You act like I never say anything nice to you."

"Do you?" She swiveled around on the leather seat to face him.

He sighed. "Don't I?"

"No," she said decisively. "You haven't said anything, well, nice to me, in a personal way, in a really long time. You say things at work like, 'good job' or 'great idea.' Sometimes you copy me on an e-mail with a thumbs-up emoticon. But that's not really a compliment, Mason."

He nodded slowly and took a deep breath. "Okay. Maybe I'm just *thinking* the compliments. And I got out of the habit of saying them out loud." He paused. "Or maybe I got worried about what other people would say if I, you know, paid you special attention."

"People? Or Celia?"

"Celia," he said.

"Why would Celia care if you're nice to me? I'm certainly no threat to her."

Mason rolled his eyes. "That's not what she thinks."

Annajane had to think about that for a minute.

"Jeez," Mason said. "This is getting pretty heavy here. I think I could use a drink." He pointed at the dashboard in front of her. "See if my flask is still in there, would you?"

How like him, she thought, to want to distract her once things got uncomfortably personal. She thumbed the latch of the glove box, and its contents slid onto the floorboard. She rooted around in the heap: some gas station receipts, a messily folded map, some old cassette tapes, and, finally, a handsome chased-silver flask with its characteristic inverted shape molded to fit in a gentleman's hip pocket.

"Here it is," she said, holding it up. She

unscrewed the cap and sniffed.

"You still drink Maker's Mark?" she asked, referring to the brand of whiskey he'd favored during their marriage.

"It's Blanton's these days," Mason said. "Celia introduced me to it. Try it out."

She took a deep drink of the warm whiskey, letting it glide slowly down her throat.

"Pretty good," she said reluctantly, before handing it over.

Mason sipped, nodded, and then drank deeply, wiping his mouth with the back of his hand.

"You and Celia were thick as thieves when she first came to Passcoe. But something happened. You really just don't like her now, do you?"

Instead of answering, Annajane took the flask and helped herself to another gulp of the amber liquid.

"Not much," she said, grateful for the courage the whiskey afforded. "But be fair. What do you think she thinks of me?"

"Pass that back," Mason instructed. He drank again.

"She thinks it's pretty weird that you'd hang around and work for me, for Quixie, that is, after we split up."

Annajane laid her head back against the cool leather of the headrest. "I guess a lot of people would agree with her. It certainly has inspired a lot of discussion around Passcoe."

"Who cares?" Mason asked. "Why can't people mind their own business? You're great at what you do. You're a huge asset to the company. In fact, I still can't quite figure out why you're leaving. You know, aside from the Shane thing."

She reached over and took the flask and drained it in one long swallow. She put the empty flask on the floor and picked up one of the cassette tapes, squinting to see what it was. In the moonlight, she thought the handwriting on the white plastic case looked familiar. It was her own.

Surprised, Annajane held it up for him to see. "Is this what I think it is?"

"What? It's just an old tape. I forgot it was in there."

But you don't keep it with the other tapes. You keep it hidden in the glove box.

Silently, she reached past him and turned the key in the ignition. The headlights winked on, and she slotted the cassette into the tape deck. He switched the headlights off.

Journey's "Faithfully" floated out of the speakers.

She turned to him in surprise. "This is the mix tape I made you all those years ago."

He shrugged it off. "It was a good tape."

She listened to the song and felt the whiskey warm in her belly, and she was aware of a sort of bittersweet longing, only dimly remembered, but now, achingly awful in its power.

Annajane turned up the volume. The song drowned out the cicadas, and the chorus of spring peepers coming from a nearby farm pond, and even the bass line of the invisible barn owl, floating from the treetop.

"You really can't figure out why I'm leaving, Mason? Are you that dense?" She turned in the seat to face him, to see if she could tell what he was thinking.

He bristled. "You're leaving because of Celia? Look, I know you've been unhappy with some of her decisions. And maybe Davis did let her undercut your position in marketing. You know Davis. He can be a bulldozer. But if you'd just come to me, and told me you were unhappy with the way things were going . . ."

His voice trailed off. His arm slid down, and his fingertips rested rightly on her shoulder.

She felt her breath catch. Just the barest brush of a touch and she was already dizzy with the sensation.

"I didn't think it would make a difference," Annajane said quietly. "Clearly, you two were getting . . . involved."

"Were we?"

"You came about five minutes away from getting married to her yesterday," Annajane pointed out.

"Yeah," his voice trailed off and he looked out into the darkness. "I'm really not sure exactly how that happened, to tell you the truth."

"You're telling me it was all Celia's idea — to get married?"

"No," Mason said. "I wouldn't exactly say that."

"What would you say? Exactly. Come on, Mason. Tell me what's going on here. Give me a clue, can you?"

His hand brushed her cheek. "I'd say I must have been out of my friggin' mind to let things get that far. Yesterday? It all seems so surreal now. I was standing there on the altar, and I saw Sophie walking towards me, and it was like I was in some kind of fog. Then that harp music started to play, and all of a sudden, here comes Celia in that damned white dress. I knew I should have been thinking about her, and how great she looked, and how glad I was. All that stuff. But then I saw you sitting in the pew, right beside Pokey. In your green dress. All I could think was — how did Annajane get in that pew? Why isn't she walking up the aisle, toward me? What happened? What the *hell* happened to us?"

Mason cupped his hand around her chin and stroked her cheek with his thumb.

She was barely aware of the small voice in her head, like an insistent, blinking red warning signal. *Turn back. Turn back.*

But she couldn't have turned back if she wanted to. She was as drawn to Mason Bayless now as she had been as a teenager all those years ago. The red blinking faded in the dark and she was only aware of his nearness and her need.

"My God, Annajane," he whispered. "What's going on? Why can't I let go of you?"

He didn't wait for an answer, which was good, because there was no answer. He leaned in. His whiskey-scented breath tickled her ear. His lips brushed her cheek.

What was she doing? She didn't care. *Don't overthink. It all feels right.*

Just like that, they kissed. So sweet, so slow. Her body had never forgotten his. Her arms went around his neck, his fingers twined naturally through her hair, and she felt a roaring in her ears. Mason pulled her closer, and she willingly went.

His kisses were hot, urgent, relentless. His hands slid down her back, and beneath the fabric of the baseball jersey. His lucky jersey. Effortlessly, he worked his fingers under the band of her bra, finding her breasts, caressing them. His head bent, and he effortlessly pulled the shirt over her head.

The night air came as a thrilling shock to her bare skin. Mason pulled her onto his lap, and she started to giggle at the sense memory of the steering wheel pressing against her back, but the giggle was supplanted by a gasp when his lips found her right nipple.

"Hey!" It was a man's voice, coming from only inches away. Next came the sound of heavy metal clinking against the driver's side door.

Annajane jumped. A beam of bright yellow light blinded her momentarily.

"What the hell?"

She dove off Mason's lap, scrambled onto her side of the front seat, grabbed desperately for the shirt, which seemed to have been swallowed up in the bowels of the Chevelle's floorboard. The glare was unblinking, unforgiving. She squeezed her eyes shut.

"Mason? Mason Bayless? Is that you? How the heck are you?"

The tape was abruptly shut off. The sudden quiet was deafening.

"It's me, Grady," Mason drawled. "How 'bout turning off that flashlight, and giving the lady here a little privacy, huh, buddy?"

Annajane did not dare lift her head. Mercifully, the light was snapped off, and she somehow managed to pull the shirt over her head with trembling hands.

In her mind, the red blinking light had transformed itself into neon foot-high letters flashing out *Damn. Damn. Damn.* And then the words morphed into something worse. *Cheater. Cheater. Cheater.*

"Maybe you could put the shotgun away now too, huh?" Mason said.

Shotgun? Why not kill me now? Annajane thought. *Put me out of my misery.*

She inched as far away from Mason as she could get, keeping her face averted from their clueless interloper.

"Sorry about that, Mason," Grady Witherspoon said with a chuckle. "Gail heard music coming from down here, so I came out to investigate. Since the weather turned warm, we've had kids coming out here, drinking, smoking dope, raising hell. I wouldn't care that much, but last week somebody went ripping through my patch of spring greens, mashed everything flat. Kale, radicchio, arugula. Total loss. You believe that? The gun ain't even loaded. I just wanna scare the little pissants off before they do any more damage."

"Totally understandable," Mason said easily. "I apologize for the disturbance. My bad. We'll just be going now."

But before he could start the Chevelle's engine, Grady Witherspoon craned his neck, walking all the way around the car until he stood just inches from Annajane.

"Don't I know you?" he asked, studying her face with interest. He snapped his fingers. "I got it! Annajane. Annajane Hudgens, right? My little sister used to babysit you when you were just a kid."

She thought her head would explode from shame.

"Hello," she said weakly, wishing the earth would open and swallow her whole.

Finally, Mason started the car. Grady Witherspoon gave them a friendly wave. "Bye now. Tell your mama I said hey, Mason, will you?"

Mason threw the car in reverse. "I'll sure do that."

19

Mason finally glanced over at her once they were back on the paved road. "You okay?"

Annajane buried her face in her hands. "No."

"Hey," he said softly, reaching for her hand. "It was just a kiss. Kinda embarrassing that Grady walked up and surprised us like that. But it was a long, long time coming. I'm not sorry it happened. Only sorry that we had to stop."

Annajane jerked her hand away from his. "We *do* have to stop! What we just did was not okay. It's called cheating. And I won't do it. I can't. You're engaged to another woman. I'm engaged to Shane."

"Allll right," Mason said slowly. "Take it easy. Don't get so worked up. You're getting way ahead of yourself here. Look, Annajane, maybe this, what just happened back there, it was inevitable. Maybe it's time we stopped avoiding each other and start thinking about us. Like we used to be."

Annajane felt her phone vibrating in her pocket. She took it out and glanced at the readout. It was Shane. Talk about timing. She let the call roll over to her voice mail and tried to think rationally about her situation.

She was suffused with shame and guilt and, yes, desperate happiness. Ten minutes ago, she'd been weak and willful. If Grady Witherspoon hadn't arrived when he had, she would have willingly climbed into the backseat with Mason. Her hormones had betrayed her, and she'd betrayed Shane. How could she hurt Shane the way Mason hurt her all those years ago?

"There is no us," Annajane said.

Mason looked at her incredulously. "You're telling me you didn't enjoy what happened back there at the farm? That it means nothing to you?"

"Yes," Annajane said. "That's what I am telling you."

"You've got a funny way of showing it," Mason muttered.

"That's not the point," Annajane said, feeling wretched. "What we just did . . . that was bad . . . it wasn't right. You were mad at Celia, and I was, I don't know, I guess, maybe just feeling vulnerable and sentimental. For the way we used to be. What happened back there, it was just . . . revenge. And horniness."

"What?" he exclaimed, nearly swerving off

276

the road.

"We have no right to be alone together like this," she continued. "I admit, I still have . . . feelings for you. I guess I always will. But there was a reason we split up. It was ugly and awful. We patched things up, yes, and figured out how to go on with our lives, separately, but I can't pretend, Mason. Our divorce nearly killed me."

Mason's hands gripped the steering wheel so tightly his knuckles turned white. "If you'll recall, I never wanted the divorce. That was your idea. I just gave you what you wanted."

Annajane felt the bile rising in her throat, all the old pain stirred up again. "What I wanted was a marriage based on honesty, but that's beside the point now. And it's been so damned hard to make myself give up and move past all that, to move forward. But the things that ended our marriage were real. And as much as I care about you, I can't go through all that again. There's no going back."

"Annajane," he started, then stopped, shook his head. "Maybe you're right. Maybe nothing has changed. You didn't trust me then; you won't trust me now."

"You cheated," she exclaimed. "And maybe I could have gotten past that, if you'd just told me the truth."

"I did tell the truth," Mason said through gritted teeth. "I never, ever cheated on you.

You talk about honesty, but if you were honest with yourself, you'd admit you had some responsibility, too, for our breakup. The first time things didn't go your way, you just took off and ran home to your mama. Who I'm sure helped you figure out what a crappy husband I was. Marriage is a two-way street, you know. You talk about trust, but you never did trust me."

The headlights of an oncoming car lit up Mason's face — his jaw was clenched, his eyes unblinking. She'd seen that look before, and it harkened back to the bad old days when their marriage had come unraveled. What had she been thinking? The answer, of course, was that she'd done just what he'd urged her to do — she hadn't thought at all.

"You're right," she said finally. "It wasn't all you. There's a reason we're not together anymore. We were just too different then. And now the gulf has only widened. It's idiotic to think we could make it work again. It's just too late. I'm sorry, Mason. For everything. Then and now."

"Unbelievable," he muttered. "All this fuss over a damned kiss."

The silence was overwhelming. He punched the button on the tape deck, forgetting what they'd been listening to earlier in the evening. When their song came on, he silently cursed and punched the stop button.

The ride back to town was interminable.

Finally, Mason pulled the car up to the curb in front of her loft. He left the motor running and didn't bother to come around and open her door. She'd barely closed the door before he gunned the Chevelle's engine and screeched away down the dark street.

20

Celia dropped her bag and water bottle on the bench outside the tennis court. She sat down and squinted up at the Monday morning sky. Puffy white clouds floated overhead, and the temperature was already warming up. She unzipped her hot pink Nike jacket and bent down to retie one of her shoes. What with all the wedding planning and hoopla, she hadn't played tennis in weeks. It would feel good to get out on the courts and work up a sweat.

"Well, Celia!" Bonnie Kelsey dropped down beside her on the bench. She cocked her head to the side and gave her an odd look. Bonnie swiveled her legs until their knees were touching, and she took Celia's hand and squeezed it.

"Are you all right?" she whispered, looking around to make sure they couldn't be overheard. They were early though, and DeeDee and Jenn, their opponents, hadn't yet shown up.

"I'm fine," Celia said. "Sophie's fine, too. They may even let her come home today."

"Oh yes, well that's a blessing," Bonnie said. "But, well, I meant, how are you? I'm actually surprised you came this morning. You can talk to me, you know. I'm totally discreet."

"Why would I cancel our doubles match?" Celia asked, puzzled.

"Oh, no reason," Bonnie said. She patted Celia's knee. "You're such a trouper. That's what I love about you, Celia. Such a positive outlook on life."

"Bonnie," Celia said, a note of warning coming into her voice. "I have no idea what you're getting at. So you might just as well tell me."

Her tennis partner had the grace to blush and look away. "I'm not one to spread gossip," she said, fiddling with the clasp of her tennis bracelet.

As if, Celia thought. She'd met Bonnie Kelsey and her dippy husband, Matthew, at a cocktail party at the country club the week after she'd arrived in Passcoe, and after three margaritas and two trips to the lady's room in the space of three hours, she'd gotten filled in on the sexual and social history of every single person in the room. Sex, lies, and innuendo were the coin of the realm in the small world of Bonnie Kelsey.

"I know that," Celia said, trying to sound

reassuring. "But if it's something that con-
cerns me, don't you think I should be made
aware of it?"

Bonnie bit her lip as though trying to make
up her mind.

Tell it, sister, Celia thought. *Before I have to
choke it out of you.*

"I'm sure there's a logical explanation for
all of this," Bonnie started. "Or maybe the
person who told it to me got the names
mixed up. Although usually, this person is
pretty reliable. And the parties involved *do*
have a history . . ."

"Please just tell me, for God's sake," Celia
said through clenched teeth.

"And you're sure you won't get upset?"
Bonnie asked.

Celia's hand was just itching to reach out
and yank the bitch's ponytail as hard as she
could.

"I'll be fine," Celia said, trying to sound
soothing. "It's always better to know than
wonder, right?"

"Riiight," Bonnie said.

"The way I heard it," she said hurriedly,
"was that Grady Witherspoon — I guess you
don't know him — he doesn't really run in
our circles? Anyway, he's retired from the
service, the navy, I think, and moved back to
town and he's renting Miss Sallie's daddy's
farm. He and Gail have fixed up the old
homeplace really cute, I hear . . ."

"Bonnie?" Celia said, about out of patience. "How does this affect me?"

"Right. As I was saying, apparently Grady and Gail were watching television last night; it was after dark, and they heard music coming from the field down by the old corncrib. And he's had a lot of trouble with the local kids going down there and doing drugs and vandalizing things and so forth. So he got his shotgun and a flashlight and walked down there to check it out. And when he got down there he saw this big old shiny red convertible, and there were two people in it, and they were, uh, well . . ."

Shiny red convertible? As in that horrible old car of Mason's? The one Sophie called his fun car? What was it, a Camaro, or a Mustang, something like that?

Celia tried to keep her composure. "What were the couple doing, Bonnie? And who were they?"

Bonnie clutched both Celia's hands in hers. "Oh honey," she said, her pale blue eyes brimming with tears. "It was Mason. And Annajane Hudgens. And according to Grady, who I believe, because he is a decorated veteran after all, he caught the two of them. In the act."

"In the act?" Celia needed to be absolutely sure she understood exactly what Bonnie considered the act to be.

Bonnie nodded her head vigorously.

"As in?" Celia prompted, wishing Bonnie would let go of her hands.

"You know," Bonnie whispered. "It. They were naked and they were doing it." She lowered her voice again, just to make sure Celia comprehended. "F-U-C-K-I-N-G."

Somehow, Celia managed to keep her composure. But her mind was whirling, going a thousand miles an hour.

The son of a bitch! She should have known something was up between him and Annajane. She'd seen his face at the wedding — just for a moment — right before Sophie got sick — he'd had that awful deer-in-the-headlights look. She'd chalked it up to nerves at the time. But then afterward, when Annajane had commandeered her spot in the ambulance, conned Mason into driving her home from the hospital, Celia should have put a stop to things right then and there. She should have seen that Annajane was still carrying a pathetic torch for Mason.

But she'd had no reason to doubt Mason's faithfulness. He was honest to a fault, disgustingly loyal. Look at the way he kept resisting Jerry Kelso's perfectly acceptable offers for Quixie. The man just loved a lost cause. She would have to do something about Annajane Hudgens, and she would have to work fast. In the meantime, she needed to throw some water on this particularly volatile piece of gossip.

"Mason and Annajane?" she heard herself say, with a careless laugh. "Are you serious, Bonnie?"

Bonnie looked at her as if she'd just sprouted another head.

"That's the silliest thing I've ever heard," Celia said. "I don't know this Grady person, Bonnie, but I can tell you right now he needs to get himself some new glasses. Mason positively could not have been out in some cornfield doing the deed with Annajane last night. Because he was right there at home with me last night, and I don't like to be indelicate, but honey, for all intents and purposes, it *was* our wedding night. I fixed the two of us an intimate little dinner, and then I modeled that little black lace number — you remember the one Jessica Satterthwaite gave me at the lingerie shower?"

Bonnie, the stupid cow, just nodded her head, wanting desperately to believe her story.

Celia rolled her eyes heavenward. "Well, I hate to think what she spent on it, because Mason took one look at that thing and he was like a man possessed." She gave a self-conscious little giggle.

"I made the mistake of modeling it in the kitchen." She rubbed her backside for effect. "All I can say is, thank heaven for throw rugs."

Bonnie's eyes widened. "You did it on the kitchen floor?"

"The kitchen floor, the living room sofa, the recliner in his study," she giggled again. "I think we figured out a new position that La-Z-Boy definitely wouldn't approve of. And that was just the first floor."

"But," Bonnie sputtered. "That red convertible. The old Chevelle. There's no mistaking it. Everybody in town knows that car. Mason's daddy gave it to him for his twenty-first birthday."

"Well that explains it," Celia said. "Mason keeps the convertible in the garage at the plant, and he leaves the keys under the floor mat. Anybody who works at the plant could have decided to borrow it. Anybody at all. Who knows, maybe your farmer friend mistook Davis for Mason?" She raised an eyebrow, daring Bonnie to contradict her. "Everybody knows what a wild hare Davis is."

"That's true," Bonnie agreed. "Davis does have a reputation."

Celia spotted their doubles opponents walking toward them, racquets slung over their shoulders. "Here come the girls," she said. "Let's forget all this nonsense and play some tennis, all right?"

DeeDee and Jenn never knew what hit them. Celia's typically restrained brand of country club tennis was abandoned. She proceeded to mop up the courts with the other two women with an unexpected combination of killer serves and slashing backhands. She made suicide dives for impossible shots, played the net, and roamed the back court, rifling volleys right back in the other women's teeth. The final score was brutal: six-one, six-love.

The putting green at the club was deserted this early on a weekday morning, which was good, because he was in no mood for company. He had a lot to think about. Mason heard the muted toot on his cell phone, letting him know he had an incoming text message. He laid his putter down on the green, took the phone from the pocket of his golf slacks, glanced down at the readout panel, and saw that the text was from Celia.

WE NEED TO TALK. NOW!!!

He felt his gut twist with dread. So she'd heard already. He shouldn't have been surprised. He looked down at the cell, knowing that modern etiquette, not to mention common decency, decried the idea of breaking an engagement with a text, but secretly wishing the deed could be done with just a few taps of the keyboard on his BlackBerry. He knew better, of course.

He removed his golf glove and tapped his reply.

287

Mason let himself in the kitchen door, warily peering around the corner to see if the coast was clear. His heart sank at the sight of Celia, seated at the kitchen island. Her face was pale and tear-streaked, her eyes red-rimmed.

"Hi," he said, setting his golf bag down in a corner. He was looking for a neutral opener, an icebreaker. What he came up with was admittedly lame. "How's your aunt feeling?"

"My aunt?" She raised one eyebrow. "You're telling me you care how my aunt is feeling? How about me? How do you think I'm feeling?" Her voice rose to something approaching a shriek, or the closest he'd ever heard Celia come to a shriek.

"Celia, look . . . I'm sorry . . ."

"Do you realize that you have humiliated me in front of this entire town?" she asked, her voice just barely above a whisper now. "I showed up at the club this morning for my doubles match with Bonnie Kelsey, and I'd hardly gotten my racket out of my bag before she pulled me aside, and with this look of pity on her face, *which I will never forget,* actually suggested that, considering the emotional pain I must be in, we might want to forfeit the match."

So, Mason thought dully, it had been Bonnie. He might have guessed the delight she would have taken in sharing the news with Celia.

"I don't know what to say . . ."

She opened her eyes wide. "Tell me it's not true. Tell me you were not with Annajane last night. In a cornfield. Tell me it's all just a hideous lie." Her lower lip trembled and her huge eyes filled with tears. "Please tell me that, Mason. *Please?*"

"Christ," he swore quietly. "It's not true. Well, not exactly."

She held out her hand, like a school traffic-crossing guard. "Stop!" she cried. "Whatever is going on between you and Annajane, if you love me, you'll stop seeing her. For God's sake, Mason, last night was supposed to be our wedding night. What were you thinking?"

He said the first thing that came to mind. The truth. "I guess I wasn't thinking at all. After you left, I went out for a drive in the Chevelle, and things just kind of happened."

"Happened?" She was weeping again, with her head down on the counter, her petite body jerking with every sob. She raised her head. "You just happened to find yourself in a car in a cornfield with your ex-wife, naked? How does that just happen?"

"Nobody was naked!" he said. The thing of it was, he really couldn't explain how any of the previous night had happened. In fact, this morning, when he'd thought about it, he couldn't say with any certainty that it hadn't all been just a whiskey dream. One thing he did know was, he had to find a way to make things right. With Celia, and with Annajane.

"I still care about Annajane," he said finally. "I'm sorry. I guess I just never really got over her."

There. He'd done it. Said it out loud. He felt better. For about five seconds.

Celia's shoulders slumped and she dropped her chin to her chest, as though somebody had knocked the wind out of her body. "Why did you ask me to marry you in the first place?" she asked, her lower lip starting that trembly thing all over again. "If you still had a crush on her? Didn't you ever love me? Even a little?"

"I don't know," he said miserably. "It just kind of happened. I mean, you and I were spending a lot of time together, business lunches turned into dinners, and we had some fun, and the next thing I know, you're moving in with me, and then, all of a sudden, we're engaged."

"What?" she cried. "Are you saying I railroaded you? That the engagement was all *my* idea?"

Yes, actually, now that he thought about it, the engagement was definitely her idea.

"No," he lied. "That's not what I'm saying at all."

"Then what are you saying?"

He sighed. This was not going well. He'd

turned the whole situation over in his mind on the way back to the house, and he'd mapped out a compassionate, logical discussion with Celia. He would tell her about Annajane, and she would be hurt at first, but then, being the practical, logical girl she was, she would shed a few tears and then allow him a graceful exit from this whole marriage thing. But so far, Celia wasn't playing fair. She'd turned on the tear tap, full throttle. It was brutal, is what it was.

"I'm just saying," he started. "Somehow, things spun out of control. I thought I was in love with you. I mean, probably I was. Kind of. At some point, I knew I should man up and tell you how I felt, but then, once you started planning the wedding, it kept getting bigger and more elaborate. And then, there was the country club, and the harpist from Atlanta, and that enormous damned cake, and your aunt was flying in . . . I just couldn't . . . I didn't want to disappoint you."

Celia looked like she'd been slapped across the face. "So this is all my fault? Because I wanted a nice wedding day? A day I would have been able to remember my whole life?"

"It's nobody's fault," Mason said wearily. "It just is. Look, I never, ever meant to hurt you, but knowing how I feel about Annajane, how conflicted I am, well, I can understand that you'd want to call off the wedding for good now. Nobody could blame you after the heel I've been."

"Call it off?" Her face crumpled. "For good?"

"It might be for the best," he said, feeling like more of a heel than ever. "We're just too different. We want different things. I mean, you hate my car, and you don't really like living in a small town like Passcoe, and you hate my sister, well, okay, I guess she's the one who hates you, but you know you never really warmed up to Pokey . . ."

He was babbling, and he wasn't normally a babbler. But then he'd never been in a situation like this before, so really, who could blame him?

Mason laid a tender, caring hand on Celia's arm. "Celia, I know this is pretty rotten right now, but believe me, eventually, you'll agree it's all for the best that we didn't go through with the wedding. It never would have worked out."

Celia pushed his hand away and ran from the room. She threw herself onto the sofa in the den, burying her face in the cushions.

Things were happening too fast. She had to step back and regroup. Call off the wedding? Just because she and Mason had a little tiff and he'd gotten sloppy drunk and sentimental and ended up giving his pathetic ex-wife a pity fuck? Oh, no. This was not happening. She would not allow this to happen. Mason was hers, and she would not give him up without a fight. She had a plan, a whole new life plotted for herself, and she'd be damned if she'd give it up now and end up like her wretched, welfare-cheating, coupon-clipping, snot-dripping coven of sisters back in Nebraska. But how to win Mason back, when he was convinced he still carried a torch for somebody else?

She knew Mason, better than he knew himself. Knew what mattered to him. Honor. Loyalty. Fidelity. Family. Doing the right thing. It was what he lived for.

Mason trudged stoically into the den. Just when he'd convinced himself that they were almost through with this unending agony, things seemed to go from bad to worse. Probably he should just shut up and leave and let her cry it out. But maybe not.

He sat on the sofa and rubbed her back. "Heey," he said softly. "I'm so sorry."

She turned and looked up at him and her face softened. "I knew it," she whispered. "In my heart, I knew this wedding, this marriage was too good to be true. I knew somebody like you could never really fall in love with somebody like me."

Even with tears streaming down her face, Mason thought, Celia still managed to look stunning. Her hair wasn't mussed, her nose wasn't running, and her makeup wasn't streaking. It was the damnedest thing.

"I just thought if I wanted it enough, I could make it happen," she said sadly. "And we came so close."

He felt like a heel. Like a jerk. Like a dickhead.

"This isn't your fault," he said, kneeling down awkwardly on the floor beside the sofa so his face would be level with hers. "Don't blame yourself."

Celia sniffed loudly. "No. It's me. I try too hard. I always have. I don't know. Maybe because my folks moved around so much when I was a kid, and because I was an only child, I always thought if I were nice and friendly, and tried to be everything for everybody, they would like me. And I thought if I worked really hard, harder than anybody else, I'd be a success. When I came to Passcoe, I thought it would be just another short-term thing. I'd sold my company; I didn't have anything to prove. But then I met you and . . . fell in love."

She sat up and dabbed at her face with the hem of her tennis top. "I didn't mean to. I'm so stupid. So naive. I really thought we could do something together. With Quixie. That we could build a life together."

"I thought so, too," Mason admitted. He sat on the sofa beside her, took her hand, and squeezed it. "That's what I wanted for us."

Celia tried to smile. "I don't blame you for

294

wanting Annajane instead of me." More tears welled in her eyes. "She's sweet, and you've known her forever. I just wish you'd figured out things between you sooner. Before I came here and fell in love with you, and Sophie and your mom . . . oh God. Sallie has just been so wonderful. Like my own mom, if she'd still been alive."

Oh, Christ, Mason thought. Sallie. She adored Celia. What would she say about this bizarre turn of events? His temples were starting to throb. What the hell had he gone and done?

Now Celia was patting his knee, trying to make him feel better, which actually made him feel much worse.

"Don't worry," she said, her voice wobbly. "I'm not going to make any more of a scene. I'm sorry I carried on. I don't know what's come over me. I guess maybe it's my hormones."

"You had every right to make a scene," Mason said. "And if you want to hit me or something, I'll go out to the garage and get you a wrench. Or a tire iron."

"If I thought it would change anything, I still might," Celia said. She slumped back against the sofa cushions.

"You don't hate me?" Mason asked cautiously.

"No," she sighed. "Maybe I should, but I don't."

"If it makes you feel any better, Annajane doesn't actually want me back," Mason said glumly.

Celia fixed her huge, luminous eyes on his. "She doesn't?"

"No. She said it was all a mistake. That she really loves this Shane guy. She thinks we were both just . . . confused."

"Mason," Celia gripped his shoulder with her fingertips, her nails digging into his flesh. "Is . . . is what Bonnie Kelsey said, is it true? Were you two having sex?"

"No!" Mason said. "It was just stupid teen-age stuff."

"You say Annajane doesn't want you back. But what about you? What do you want?"

"God, I don't know anything." He looked over at her. "Except that I don't want to hurt you any more than I already have. I am truly sorry I've screwed everything up so badly."

"What about us?" She leaned her head on his shoulder. "What happens with us? With all our plans?"

There is no us, Annajane had told him only a few hours ago. *She'd been very clear about that. No going back. What was that saying? Love the one you're with?*

He turned and, with his fingertip, wiped away one last lingering tear as it rolled down her cheek. "I don't know, maybe just step back and really figure out what we both want. Take things a little slower this time. We can still be friends, right?"

"Friends?" her laugh was shaky.

"Well, really good friends," Mason said. "I still care about you, Celia."

She grabbed his hand. "Do you mean that, Mason? It's really over with Annajane?"

His face darkened. "It really is."

"Thank God," she said fervently. "Because there's something else. I didn't want to tell you like this. I was waiting until after the wedding. I didn't know how you'd feel about it, but Mason, I just can't keep it from you anymore."

Somehow, he knew what she was going to say before the words were out of her mouth. A sense of dread washed over him.

"I'm pregnant," Celia said. "Mason, we're pregnant."

21

When he was eight years old, he and his friend Stevie Heckart stole a package of firecrackers and a box of kitchen matches from Stevie's older brother. They rode their bikes out to Hideaway Lake and took the firecrackers out onto the dock. It was winter and nobody was around. For a while they amused themselves by lighting firecrackers and flinging them into the lake. But then boredom set in and they began looking for a bigger thrill, a bigger bang. They found a rusty coffee can full of nails in the tin-roofed boathouse. They dumped out the nails and put an entire package of the firecrackers in the can and lit it. The ensuing explosion left him numb and deaf for several minutes, with only a vibrating ringing in his ears.

That was how Mason felt after hearing that Celia was pregnant. It was as if the words she'd uttered had been spoken from the bottom of a well, through a wall of water.

She grabbed his arm. "Say something,

please. Tell me you're as happy as I am. Because I'm, well, I'm delirious. I'll finally have a family of my own now."

Too stunned to speak, he simply stared.

"Mason?" She grabbed his arm and shook it.

"I thought you were on birth control," he said, when his brain started to thaw.

"I was using birth control," she said. "The patch. But apparently, sometimes things can happen. Remember that upper-respiratory infection I had this past winter? I took antibiotics? They can counteract birth control. And I guess they did. Because here I am . . . pregnant!"

"But . . . when? I mean, we haven't even really been together . . . like that, since you started planning the wedding."

She wrapped her arms around his neck and kissed him. "I know. Which was another reason I was so upset that my plans for last night were ruined. It's been soooo long. But I promise, I'm going to make it up to you tonight." She laid her head on his shoulder and looked up at him from beneath her uncannily luxurious eyelashes.

He continued to stare at her. "How long, exactly? I mean, if you know."

"The ides of March," she said, snuggling against his chest. "I'm due in December. Just think, a Christmas baby."

He looked at her carefully. She didn't look

pregnant. She was wearing tight jeans and some kind of stretchy top and her belly was as flat as the palm of his hand. When Pokey was pregnant, she swore you could tell the minute her egg latched onto a sperm. But Celia seemed to be saying she was at least six weeks pregnant and she was no bigger around than a twig. "And you're sure? I mean, have you seen a doctor or something?"

"Of course I'm sure," Celia said smoothly. "I took two of those home pregnancy tests. Plus I saw a doctor in Charlotte the last time I was there."

"Oh," Mason said. He buried his head in his hands. He got to his feet unsteadily. "Excuse me," he said, ever the southern gentleman. He hurried into the powder room and closed the door firmly.

"We have to talk," Mason said, when he finally emerged from the powder room, pale and grim-faced. While he'd been retching, she'd moved into the kitchen, washed her face, and combed her hair. She looked radiant, if that was possible.

"Yes," Celia said, nodding eagerly. "I agree."

He went to the liquor cupboard, pulled out a bottle of bourbon, poured three fingers into a water glass, and downed it in one swallow.

Celia had never seen Mason drink this early in the day. She slid onto one of the leather barstools at the kitchen counter. But Mason remained standing, his backbone ramrod straight.

"There's no easy way to say this," Mason started. "The thing is, even before, well, the thing with Annajane, I guess I'd started to realize maybe we should rethink getting married."

One large tear rolled down Celia's cheek. She turned her head and brushed it away with the back of her hand.

"I'm sorry," Mason said. His shoulders slumped. "I just don't love you. I thought I did, but I don't. You deserve better than that. Marrying me would be the biggest mistake of your life, Celia."

"But, the baby," she whispered, fighting back the tears. "Our family . . ."

He sighed. "I can't lie. The baby complicates things. You said December?"

Celia nodded.

He looked out the kitchen window. A baby. His own flesh and blood. How could he have been so careless? And not just about that. How could he have let his marriage to Annajane dissolve, without a fight? How could he have let the business deteriorate to the point that it was at risk? How could he get himself engaged to a woman he didn't really want to marry? Had he been asleep for the past five years? What would his old man think of the way he'd screwed things up?

"I will, of course, take care of you and the

baby," he started to say. "Financially, emotionally, whatever. You'll never want for anything."

Celia was uncharacteristically quiet.

"You don't still want to get married, do you?" he heard himself ask.

She shrugged. "I don't want to force you to marry me." She sniffled a little. "But I never thought I'd be an unwed mother!" And then she was crying again. Loud, gasping sobs. He put a hand on her arm, and she shook it off angrily, refusing to be comforted. "Just leave me alone," she said.

22

Annajane couldn't sleep. She was haunted by the consequences of her actions. By six that morning, she'd decided on a course of action. She had to go to Shane, tell him what she'd done, and ask for his forgiveness.

She threw some clothes into an overnight bag and text-messaged Davis.

"Won't be coming in today. Maybe not tomorrow either. Sorry."

Celia, she thought wryly, would be delighted.

It was a six-hour drive to Atlanta. She welcomed the quiet, the chance to think, the absence of distraction. She watched the sun come up over an emerald-green pasture dotted with horses and an old sway-backed mule and, finally, at eight, gave herself permission to stop at a Bojangles' north of Greenville, South Carolina, for coffee, a biscuit, and a bathroom break.

The restaurant was busy, with construction workers picking up bags of chicken biscuits, office workers lined up in their cars at the drive-through, and two long tables of elderly men who were obviously members of an unofficial coffee klatch.

Her cell phone rang as she was getting back into her car. She glanced at it warily, praying it wasn't Mason, grateful it was only his sister, Pokey.

"Hey," she said.

"Oh my God!" Pokey breathed. "OhmyGodOhmyGod. I can't believe you did not call me."

"I was going to," Annajane said. "But I left at six. I figured you'd probably still be asleep."

"Left where?" Pokey asked, her voice rising with excitement. "Are you telling me you actually spent the night with him? That is the best news I've had in months. Years maybe."

"Spent the night with who? What are you talking about?" But Annajane had a sinking feeling she knew exactly what her best friend was talking about.

"You. And Mason. Last night. Doing the wild thing out at the farm. In the Chevelle."

"Oh, no," Annajane moaned. "This cannot be happening."

"Oh, yes," Pokey crowed. "Believe it."

"Where did you hear it?"

"What's important is who I didn't hear it from," Pokey said. "You! How could you?"

"This is not exactly my finest moment," Annajane said dully. "How did you hear, anyway? Surely not Mason . . ."

"My brother? Be serious!" Pokey said, laughing. "Of course I didn't hear it from him. I did call him right before I called you, but he's not answering his phone, the jerk."

"Then who?" Annajane asked, bewildered. Her face was in flames. "It's only eight o'clock in the morning. How on earth . . . ?"

"Oh, honey," Pokey drawled dramatically. "It's gone viral. You know I walk every morning on the high school track at seven with Vera Hardy, and she was just agog over the news. And then on my way home, I stopped to get milk and cereal and juice boxes at Harris Teeter, and Bonnie Kelsey, that bitch, stopped me by the Pop-Tarts and wanted to know what was going on with you two. Don't worry, though, I played dumb . . ."

"I'm having a nightmare," Annajane said.

They heard a faint beeping on the line.

"Oops," Pokey said. "That's Pete. I'll call you back."

Ten minutes later, she called back. "Pete wants to know if you two could reschedule the wedding before he has to return his tux to the rental place," Pokey reported. "Save him a hundred bucks."

"Not funny," Annajane said. "Did you have to tell him?"

"I *didn't* tell him," Pokey said. "He already knew."

"How?"

"Kiwanis breakfast meeting," Pokey said succinctly. "You know those men gossip like a bunch of old biddies."

"The whole Kiwanis Club knows?" Annajane felt fine beads of perspiration forming on her upper lip and forehead.

"Rotary, too, apparently," Pokey added. "Pete said Davis called him this morning, about to split a gut over it. Davis told Pete he's furious at Mason for disgracing the family, if you can believe it. Talk about the pot calling the kettle black."

"Davis knows?" Annajane felt a stabbing pain in her abdomen.

More faint beeps.

"Oh, Lord, that's Mama," Pokey said. "I've gotta take this. You know if I don't pick up on the second ring she'll pout for days and days."

Please, please, please, Annajane prayed. *Please don't let Sallie have heard. Anything but that. Please.*

But apparently the gods were deaf to her pleas.

"Mama knows," Pokey said, calling back ten minutes later.

"Davis told her?"

"Afraid not," Pokey said. "She heard it at altar guild this morning."

"What all did she say?" Annajane asked, dread in her heart.

"Don't ask," Pokey said darkly.

"I just don't understand how this got out so fast, and so far," Annajane cried. "Mason would never have said anything to anybody, and I for sure didn't."

"Well, that's easy," Pokey said. "Grady Witherspoon! If you wanted to keep your affair with your ex-husband secret, you should have picked a more private place than the farm."

"We are not having an affair! It was a kiss. One stinking kiss."

"That's not how I heard it," Pokey said. "Pete said Watson Bates saw Grady at the feed and seed this morning. Watson told Pete he heard the two of you were going at it buck nekkid in the backseat of the Chevelle."

"It was the front seat!" Annajane objected. "And we were not naked."

"Were you fully dressed?" Pokey asked.

"None of your business."

"Half-dressed?"

"It doesn't matter now," Annajane said, biting her lip. "The truth doesn't matter, because all of Passcoe is now firmly convinced I was having sex with Mason Bayless last night. So that's it. I can never show my face there again. Thank God my loft is already sold. You're gonna have to finish up my packing for me."

"Come back from where? You never did tell me where you are right now."

"I'm going to Atlanta," Annajane said. "I

need to talk to Shane."

"To tell him it's over between you?" Pokey said hopefully.

"To confess my sins and ask forgiveness," Annajane said.

"Bad idea. Terrible idea," Pokey said. "Clearly, something, even if it wasn't full-blown, buck-nekkid car sex, is going on between you and my brother. You need to turn around and come back here and get it all sorted out. And then take another ride in the Chevelle to finish off what y'all started last night. Hopefully to a motel or somewhere twenty miles away from the prying eyes of Grady Witherspoon."

Annajane's phone beeped again. "I'm gonna let you get this," she told Pokey. "But please, don't bother calling me back with any more reports of who said what. I can't take any more."

23

Shane's faded blue Aerostar van was parked in front of the cabin. A beat-up bicycle leaned against the concrete-block foundation, and his yellow lab, Wyley, barked once as she pulled the car under the shade of a huge old dogwood with fading pink blooms.

A minute later, Shane stood on the porch, his face alight with pleasure.

"Hey!" he called, grinning. "Awesome!"

Annajane ran from the car and threw herself into his arms. "I've missed you," she whispered into his neck. "I just had to come to remind myself why."

"I'm glad," Shane said, patting her back reassuringly. "Totally."

He rubbed his cheek on hers, the dark stubble scraping against her skin. He was dressed in rumpled khakis and a faded Doc Watson T-shirt, and his feet were bare.

He pulled back a little. "But I wish you'd called to let me know you were on your way. The place is a wreck. They guys and I have been pulling all-nighters, working on stuff for the tour."

"Who cares?" Annajane said. Wyley bumped up against her leg, nudging her hand with his muzzle until she relented and leaned down to scratch his ears.

"See? We're both glad to see you," Shane said.

He retrieved her overnight bag from the car, and they walked inside arm in arm. The cabin was essentially two rooms: a combined living and dining room with a small kitchen L, and a tiny bedroom with adjoining bath.

It didn't look like it had been cleaned since the last time Annajane was there a month earlier.

Newspapers and books littered the floor and tabletops. A guitar and a Dobro were leaned up against the soot-blackened brick fireplace, and the leather sofa and matching armchair were coated in a fine layer of yellow dog hair. The coffee table in front of the sofa held an open laptop computer, a cereal box, and an empty plastic milk jug. Music wafted from a pair of enormous old stereo speakers that served as Shane's end tables.

The tiny kitchen counter and sink held an array of dirty dishes, and the trash can overflowed with beer bottles and pizza boxes.

Annajane wrinkled her nose. "You really do need a woman's touch."

"That's what I've been telling you," he said.

"I'm sorry you had to see the place like this, but the guys and I have been working on new material," Shane said. "Wait til you hear."

He swept the newspapers off the sofa and pulled her down beside him. "We've got almost enough material for a new album." He tapped some keys of the lapboard and turned up the sound.

Banjos and fiddle music and a harmonica and three voices, combined in high harmony, with lyrics about pleasing and sneezing, and summer and bummer.

"Nice," Annajane said, nodding her head to the beat. "What's it called?"

Shane beamed. "Ragweed Rag. I mean, this is just kinda the first pass. Corey wants me to finesse the lyrics some. I'm kinda worried about the bass line. What do you think? Too clunky?"

Without waiting for a response, he started the song over again.

"It's good," Annajane said. "But you know I don't know that much about bluegrass . . ."

"You'll learn," he said, squeezing her knee. "Let me play you the song we were working on last night. Okay?"

"Actually," Annajane said, catching his hand, "there's something important I need to talk to you about. It's why I came down here today."

"Sure," Shane said, still tapping at the computer's keyboard. "Hang on just a sec, can you? Corey just IM'ed me. He's got an idea for the melody for the bridge for one of the new songs." He grabbed his Dobro and started to strum, nodding and pausing.

She got up and wandered into the kitchen and began putting it to rights without giving it much thought. The space was too tiny for a dishwasher, so she ran a sink full of hot soapy water and scrubbed and rinsed and dried virtually every dish, spoon, or fork Shane owned. When the dishes were dried and put away in the one tiny cupboard, she bagged up the trash and took it outside to the garbage can, which was also overflowing with what looked like a month's worth of bagged-up trash.

The bedroom was a disaster. A plastic laundry basket erupted with dirty clothing. The bedding was a tangled knot of threadbare sheets with a worn green sleeping bag stretched across them. And frankly, she thought, the place smelled like a swamp.

"Ugh." She tugged at the window, finally forcing it upward. But the window had no screen, and a fine film of yellow pollen drifted inside. She sneezed but left it open. With a singular motion, she swept all the bed linens into the laundry basket, took them out to the tiny mud porch at the back of the cabin, and unceremoniously dumped everything into the washing machine.

She would not, she decided, be spending

the night at the cabin tonight. She would have to find a tactful way to suggest that a night at a nice motel would be just the thing to reignite their romance.

When she'd done all she could in the way of housekeeping, Annajane rejoined him.

Shane was still noodling around on the Dobro, but now he was talking on his cell to one of his bandmates. She recognized that he was in what he liked to call his "groove," and with a shrug, she found a weather-beaten broom and gave the entire house a thorough sweep.

"You don't have to do that, baby," Shane said, glancing up from his playing. He slapped the sofa cushion next to his. "Come sit down. I'll get that later. Didn't you say you needed to talk to me about something?"

"Okay," Annajane said, feeling a lump in the pit of her stomach. *Just tell him,* she thought. *Don't be a chickenshit. Get the truth out in the open, and everything will be all right.*

She sank down onto the sofa and turned to face him. "First off," she said nervously. "I don't want there to be any lies between us. Remember when we first started seeing each other, the promise we made to each other?"

"Right," he said. "No lies. It's the foundation of our relationship."

"Okay, well, the thing is, some stuff has come up with Mason."

"Your ex? Didn't he just get remarried, like, yesterday?"

She took a deep breath. "He was supposed to get married on Saturday, but his little girl got sick right in the middle of the ceremony, so they had to postpone it."

"I'm sorry," Shane said. "Is the kid okay?"

"She had an emergency appendectomy," Annajane said. "She'll be fine. Mason, on the other hand, may not be getting remarried after all."

Shane frowned. "How come?"

"It's a long story," Annajane said. "Celia's all wrong for him, but he's just figuring that out. Better now than later, I guess, huh?"

"Better now than later," Shane said, nodding solemnly.

"Uh, well, then we went out for a long drive together last night," Annajane continued. "And he had a flask of bourbon in his glove box, and I found an old mix tape I made him, from years ago, and I don't know, it might have been the combination of the bourbon and Journey, but I . . ."

"Wait!" Shane interrupted. His eyes were aglow. He grabbed up the laptop and started typing like a fiend.

"Better late than never," he said, humming. "It's genius! That's the bridge lyric, the one we've been trying to nail down all week!"

Now he grabbed the Dobro and started picking. "Better late than never," he sang in a high, nasal twang. "You never promised me foreverrrrr."

314

He leaned over and kissed Annajane's nose. "Keep talking, babe. It's all golden. You're my muse. Just tell me what's on your mind, it's like you're opening up my creative floodgates here."

Annajane started over. "One minute we were listening to Journey, and the next minute, Mason was kissing me, and I was kissing him back . . ."

"Journey? Seriously?" Shane put down the Dobro and frowned. "I'm starting to question your musical judgement."

"I *like* Journey," Annajane said. "Or I did at the time. But that's really not the point. The point is, my ex kissed me, and I kissed him back." She sat back and waited for the realization to hit him.

"I see," Shane said. His face was solemn. "Did you say you'd been drinking?"

"Bourbon," Annajane confirmed.

"Alcohol can cloud anybody's judgment," Shane said. "Sometimes I have a few brews with the guys and the next thing I know, I'm watching old Guns N' Roses videos on YouTube and shooting squirrels with a BB gun."

Annajane reached over and gently took the Dobro from her fiancé.

"I don't think you get what I'm telling you here, Shane," she said. "I was alone out in the country with Mason. I willingly went with him. Yes, I was drinking a little bourbon, but to be perfectly honest with you — and I do want to be honest with you — I sort of knew he was going to kiss me before it happened. And I didn't fight him off. In fact, I enjoyed it."

"Jesus, Annajane." His face fell, and she felt as though she'd slapped him.

"I know. I feel horrible," she said. And she did.

Wyley looked from Shane to Annajane. The dog whined and licked Shane's hand, and Shane scratched his ears absentmindedly.

He looked down at the floor, and then, with hopefulness, at Annajane. "So, it was an of-the-moment kind of thing, right? Not something you'd do again, right?"

"Not if I was thinking rationally," Annajane said.

"And when you're thinking rationally?" Shane asked, taking both her hands in his.

"I know it will never work for Mason and me. There were too many issues when we were married before that never got resolved. I'm done with all that."

"You're sure? Really?"

She took a deep breath and let it out slowly. Her pulse was racing, and she could feel her heart hammering in her chest. Finally, fighting back tears, she nodded.

"Okay then," Shane said. He leaned his forehead and rested it against hers. "You had me worried there for a minute, babe, showing up like that, out of the blue." He kissed her. "It's forgotten. Right?"

"Riiigghhht," she said.

As if, she thought.

"I trust you totally," he told her. "What we have together, it transcends petty jealousy. In a week, you'll be down here, we'll be together, and Mason whatshisname will be ancient history."

And that's what she wanted to believe. She would have given anything to believe it. But no matter what she did or where she went, she knew Mason would never be history. Not completely.

He stood up, stretched, and yawned. "Wow, I've been so busy, I totally forgot to eat today. So, what's your plan? Wanna get some lunch or something? We're meeting over at Rob's house at two for rehearsal, but there's still time for us to run up to the sandwich joint at the shopping center and grab something before I take off."

She was staring at Shane now, who was standing there, his hand resting lightly on her shoulder, so trusting, so willing to forgive what he considered her minor transgression. She thought of the qualities that had drawn her to him the first time they'd met in Holden Beach.

Shane had no inkling it wasn't cool to call a girl five minutes after she'd driven away from him, and that was part of his charm. He didn't care about cool. He cared about her. The next time they met, in Roanoke, he'd gone to a supermarket and bought pink roses and had them delivered to her table in the club where he was playing. And the next time he was in North Carolina, he called, and even though he was playing in a bar halfway across the state, he drove the three hours over and back just to take her to dinner before he had to drive back and play a late-night set.

He sent her sweet, funny e-mails, links to his music and the band's Web site. He started, but never finished, writing a song called "Annajane in the Morning." The band was a regional success. Shane made enough money to do what he loved to do — making music, hanging with his friends, traveling around in his van with his dog, and then coming home to his little cabin.

The life was enough for him, she thought, and he was blessed that he thought so. The problem was, she saw now, it wouldn't be enough for her. Shane wanted her, she knew. But he didn't really need her. His life was just the right size, just as it was.

She'd been spouting off about honesty — both to Mason and Shane. But if she was being really honest with herself, she knew there was a reason she'd resisted moving in here or setting a date for their wedding.

"Annajane?" Shane was standing at the door, his Dobro in his hand. "Ready to go?"

She covertly twisted the plain ring from her left hand and looked around the room one last time.

"Shane?" He turned to her, and when he saw the somber look on her face, his beautiful, sunny smile clouded over, and then disappeared.

"It's over, isn't it?" he asked, leaning up against the doorjamb. "You're never moving in here; we're never getting married. God. I am so damned dense. That's what you really came to tell me, wasn't it?"

"No," she said, walking toward him. "I mean, I thought I came here to convince myself that you're what I want. To remind myself how lucky I am to have your love. And I know, I must be the luckiest girl in this state. But as much as I want this to work, I just don't think it will."

"We could make it work!" Shane exclaimed. "Once you're living closer, away from all that drama back in Passcoe, things will be different. We'll make them different. If you need some time and space, I get that. You can have all of it you want. Just as long as you stay in my life. Okay?" He reached out, took her hand, and kissed it.

"Your ring?" he asked, dropping her hand.

She dug it out of her pocket, put it in his palm, and gently closed his fingers over it. "I messed up my last marriage. Gave up and ran off when things got bad. It was easier to blame him, his mama, my mama, everybody but myself. But now I've got to stop running. I've got to figure out what I want from life."

"Mason?" His mouth twisted as he said the name.

"I honestly don't know," she said. "He's got a lot of his own stuff to figure out. Right now, I think I'll just concentrate on fixing me."

"You're fine the way you are," Shane said.

"No, I'm not," Annajane said. She picked up her overnight bag and slung it over her shoulder and gave Wyley a final head scratch. "But I'm gonna be."

24

Farnham-Capheart's offices were on the seventh floor of a midsized office tower in midtown Atlanta. Annajane parked in the underground garage and took the elevator to the marble-floored lobby. As she passed a small sandwich shop, her growling stomach reminded her of the breakfast and lunch she'd skipped.

A trio of women, dressed in chic dark suits and heels, stepped out of the elevator as she stepped in. She looked down, ruefully, at her own attire: black slacks, a pale pink ruffled cotton blouse, and quilted black ballet flats. When she'd fled Passcoe before dawn that morning, she hadn't stopped to think about what clothes she'd need. She brushed some dog hair from her slacks, reached in her pocketbook, and brought out a simple pair of pearl earrings and fastened them to her ears.

This would have to do for now, but she'd certainly have to step up her game, fashion-wise, once she started work at the ad agency.

Back in Passcoe, she'd dressed much more casually for work, even wearing jeans on Fridays in the summer. Clearly, that wouldn't work in Atlanta. She was in the big leagues now. And, she reflected ruefully, she was single again. Probably destined to stay that way, too.

When she arrived at the agency's office suite, she had to wait a moment for her new boss, Joe Farnham, to meet her in the reception area.

"Annajane?" he said, looking a little flustered. "Aren't you still working in Passcoe?"

"I came into town this morning on the spur of the moment," she said. "Just thought I'd drop by and chat for a minute before I head back home to finish up my packing."

"Come on back to my office," Joe said, guiding her by the elbow. "I guess it's just as well you're here."

When he was seated at his desk with his office door closed and with Annajane sitting across from him, Joe Capheart pulled a foil-wrapped roll of antacids from a desk drawer. He popped one in his mouth and silently handed one across to her.

Her stomach fluttered. News was coming, and it wasn't gonna be good.

"I take it you haven't talked to Davis today?" he asked, frowning.

"Uh, no," she said. "It's been a pretty crazy weekend at home. I left super-early this morning and haven't had a chance to talk to Davis."

"You're gonna want to," Joe said. He chewed the antacid silently and stared out the window. "They've put me in a hell of an awkward position here. Not to mention all the other repercussions."

"What's going on?" Annajane said, trying not to sound alarmed.

"The long and the short of it is, Quixie has pulled their account."

She chewed the antacid furiously for a moment, while she let the news settle in. "Since when?" she asked, when she could speak again. "That's crazy. I talked to Mason yesterday, and he didn't say anything like that."

"Davis e-mailed me about fifteen minutes ago," Joe said glumly. "I haven't even told the rest of the partners yet. An e-mail — you believe that? After all the years the agency's done business with them?"

"Did he give you a reason?" Annajane asked, still dumbfounded. "I mean, Joe, I was just in the office yesterday, going over the new summer promotion plans. Davis had signed off on all of it."

"This came from out of the blue! As far as I knew, we were golden," Joe said. "Thirty years we've been working on the Quixie account. I was just a junior copywriter when Glenn Bayless hired us, and Davis, the little prick — excuse my language, Annajane — was barely potty-trained. All his e-mail today said was that there were some new developments in the company's ownership. Do you have any idea what that's supposed to mean?"

She felt a chill go down her spine. "All I know is that Jax Snax has indicated they're going to tender an offer to buy Quixie. Mason is totally opposed to a sale. And so is his sister. But Davis has been actively agitating for it."

"What about Sallie?" Joe asked urgently.

"According to Mason, she's been on the fence."

Joe crumpled up a piece of paper and tossed it into the trash. "Sounds to me like maybe she fell off that fence."

Annajane took a deep breath. "What does this mean for the agency?"

"It's a huge punch in the gut, of course," Joe said. "Quixie was one of our biggest accounts. I'm gonna try and talk to Davis, and Mason, if I can. But if we don't retain that account, well, that changes everything."

"Including my hire?" She kept her tone deliberately neutral, calm.

"I'm afraid so," Joe said. "We'll still pay for your moving expenses, of course, and any other out-of-pocket expenses you've incurred, but without the Quixie account, we'll have to do some major reshuffling around here."

"I see," Annajane said. She stood up and

held out a hand to Joe Farnham. "Well, thanks, I guess."

"Son of a bitch!" he growled. "This isn't right. It just isn't. I wish there was something more I could do. We were all really looking forward to having you join the team, Annajane. I told Davis, right before we offered you the position, he'd be crazy to let you walk away."

Annajane turned, startled. "You talked to Davis about hiring me? Not Mason?"

Joe shrugged. "It was Davis's idea. I mean, if I'd known you were thinking of leaving Quixie, I'd have snapped you up in a minute anyway, but yeah, he mentioned in passing that he thought you'd be uncomfortable staying at the company after Mason got serious with that consultant of theirs."

"Celia," she said. "Her name is Celia." And her grimy mitts were all over this little maneuver, Annajane thought.

As much as she dreaded going back home, Annajane knew she had no choice. Celia had laid down the gauntlet, and it was too late now to back away from a fight. Before leaving Capheart's parking lot, she called the leasing office for the apartment she'd rented to let them know she wouldn't be moving in after all, and got the not-unexpected news that she would be forfeiting the first and last month's rent that she'd already paid.

She called Pokey as soon as she'd cleared Atlanta traffic and was back on the interstate, headed to Passcoe. "What's going on up there?" she demanded.

"Let's see. Where do you want me to start?" Pokey said. "I think the right rear tire on my Range Rover has a nail in it. Petey has a weird rash all over his body; and Clayton has decided he does not want to be potty-trained, which means he might still be in Pull-Ups in junior high; and, oh yeah, Mama announced a little while ago that she's just fine with selling Quixie to some outfit in Tenafly, New Jersey, that makes jalapeño cheese–stuffed microwaveable tater tots."

"Oh, God," Annajane moaned. "How? Why?"

A loud scream pierced the air from the other end of the phone.

"Hang on a second, will ya?"

Annajane heard the sounds of footsteps, and then the sound of water flushing, and then childish shrieks. "Denning Riggs!" Pokey yelled. "Do not dunk your little brother in the toilet. I don't care if he does smell like poopie. No! I mean it. Put him down this instant."

Pokey came back on the line and sighed. "What was I thinking having all these kids? One more is gonna put me in an early grave."

"You love it," Annajane said, laughing

despite the seriousness of the current situation.

"As I was saying, it seems that my darling brother Davis has somehow managed to pull another fast one on us," Pokey said. "And I'll just bet the formidable Celia has been bending Mama's ear, too. She's spent a lot of time over at Cherry Hill these past few weeks, in the guise of making wedding plans, sucking up to Mama."

"So that's it for Quixie? It's a done deal?" Annajane asked.

"Not quite yet," Pokey said. "Mama claims she doesn't want to do anything unless all of us are one hundred percent on board."

"Well, that's something," Annajane said. "Have you talked to Mason about any of this?"

"Not yet," Pokey said. "The shit literally just hit the fan. I've called the office and left a message with Voncile to have him call me, and I left him a voice mail on his cell, but I'm sure he's up to his ass in alligators right now. And speaking of which, how did Shane handle your true confession?"

"He said the right thing for all the wrong reasons. I'm more messed up now than I've ever been."

"You're gonna have to spell this out for me, hon," Pokey said. "I've got baby brain already."

"We're not getting married," Annajane said.

"I broke it off with Shane."

"Yippee! I mean, oh, that's too bad," Pokey said. "You sound pretty okay though."

"Definitely not okay. Shell-shocked," Annajane corrected. "But that's not all. I'm having a hell of a morning my ownself. After I left the cabin I went to see my new boss, Joe, at Farnham-Capheart. Who greeted me with the news that I don't have a job there after all, because Davis e-mailed him this morning that Quixie is pulling the account from the agency."

"Shut up."

"It's true. Joe was just as shocked as I was. He'd literally just gotten the news. Since Quixie was one of the agency's biggest accounts, it's a huge blow for them. And since the Quixie account was going to be mine, I am now, officially redundant."

"Can Davis do that?" Pokey asked. "I mean, Farnham-Capheart has been the company's ad agency since forever."

"He can and he did," Annajane said succinctly. "Although I have an idea this is a plot he probably hatched with Celia's assistance. Joe let it slip that Davis was the one who suggested they hire me — since I was probably going to want to leave the company anyway once Celia was in the picture."

"That conniving little slut," Pokey said. "I'd like to rip her arms off and beat her to death with 'em."

"And I'd help," Annajane said. "Except, knowing her, she'd just grow a second set of appendages."

"What are you gonna do now?" Pokey asked.

"You mean now that I'm both jobless and homeless? We close on the loft sale on Thursday, and I've got to be out of there by Friday at five. Of that I'm certain. As for the rest of it, who knows? I guess I'll start polishing my résumé, for a starter. Celia made it very plain when I saw her at the plant yesterday that she plans to install Tracey, the new girl, in my old office any second. She even suggested I didn't need to finish out this week. Of course, I lied and told her I had some very important business to finish up first. I just didn't tell her the business I needed to finish was her."

"Good for you," Pokey said. "Anything you want to do, count me in. Anything else?"

"Yeah. Back to Celia. Let's get back to destroying Celia. Did you ever ask your friend at Belk's about her?"

"I'd forgotten," Pokey said. "But I'll call her right now. Or right after I get these hellions down for their naps."

25

Mason felt his neck and shoulder muscles tighten as soon as he drove through the wrought-iron gates at Cherry Hill. The smell of freshly mown grass wafted through the open windows of his car, and small birds and large yellow butterflies hovered over the splashy ribbons of pink, white, and purple azaleas that lined the long drive, but he was too distracted to enjoy the sights of a beautiful spring day.

The message Sallie had left on his phone was brief and succinct. "Son, I need to see you this morning. I'll be at home until noon."

He massaged his temples with his fingertips. His mother's agenda could have any number of unpleasant items.

Mason parked his car and trudged slowly up the front steps of the Greek Revival house. The white paint gleamed in the sunshine. He paused at the front door. Normally, he just walked inside and announced himself. After all, this was his family home. He'd lived here right up until shortly before he and Annajane married and had moved back here, briefly, after their split. But somehow, today felt different. He was poised to ring the doorbell when the door opened and his mother greeted him, her voice decidedly cool.

"Since when do you ring the doorbell here?" she demanded, offering her cheek to be kissed.

He kissed her lightly, inhaling the familiar scents, hairspray, Chanel Number Five, and yes, cigarettes with an after-note of cinnamon-flavored chewing gum. His mother had been a closet smoker for as long as he could remember. You'd walk into a room at the house, and there she'd be, guiltily fanning the smoke out opened windows or spritzing the air with room freshener.

He followed her into the high-ceilinged entry hall, and her heels clicked on the black-and-white marble-tiled floor. "You look nice," he said, hoping to establish détente. Her hair had been freshly done and she wore a yellow silk pantsuit and a gleaming gold-link necklace and matching earrings.

"I had altar guild this morning," she said, leading him into the study. She sat down behind the dainty walnut French provincial desk she'd installed there in the place of his father's massive oak desk. "And I can tell you it wasn't a very pleasant experience, walking into a room full of buzzing women, all of whom fell silent the moment I entered. And what do you suppose they were talking about?"

Mason stayed standing. "Is that why you asked me over here? Because of a bunch of gossipy old biddies?" He turned and headed for the door. "You'll have to excuse me, Mama. I've got a business to run."

"I'd like you to stay," Sallie said. Her voice was steady. She seldom raised it, because she seldom had to. All her life, Sallie Bayless had been a force with which to reckon.

He slouched down into the pale blue damask wing chair facing the desk and instantly felt like a schoolboy called into the principal's office.

His mother fidgeted with a pen on the desktop, rolling it back and forth beneath her fingertips.

"Is it true?" she said finally. "You . . . and Annajane? Really, Mason, I can't imagine what you were thinking. Or doing? And out at the farm?"

"I don't know what you've heard," Mason said. "But I doubt much of it is true. Anyway, I don't care to discuss my personal life with you. Or the rest of Passcoe."

"Your personal life, and the way you conduct it, reflects on your entire family. And on Quixie," Sallie reminded him. "So when you and your *ex-wife* go cavorting around out in a public place, of course it's going to be talked about." She shook her head.

"If Celia decides to take you back, it will be a miracle. She should be nominated for sainthood."

Mason felt the muscle in his jaw twitch.

"And yes, I know about the baby," she added.

He jumped to his feet. "That's it. I'm thirty-nine years old. I'm a little too old to have my mother slap my hand."

"And what a shame," Sallie said. "I should have slapped your hand — and your fanny — much more frequently than I did when you were a boy. Maybe if I had, we wouldn't be having this conversation."

"We *aren't* having this conversation," Mason said. "I'm leaving now."

"Before you go rushing off, you should know that Celia didn't volunteer the information about her pregnancy," Sallie said. "I called her just a few minutes ago, and I could tell by the sound of her voice that she'd been crying. Still was crying, poor thing. She didn't want to tell me what had happened, but I persuaded her she needed a friendly shoulder. Mason, Celia doesn't have any family to speak of, except her poor old aunt. We're her family now."

"Lucky Celia," Mason said, not bothering to hide the sarcasm. He glanced down at his watch. "I have to go, Mama. Sophie gets out of the hospital this afternoon, and I haven't even made it into the office yet."

"Mason!" Sallie said, with just a hint of sharpness. "I want all this nonsense stopped. You are engaged to be married to a wonderful, intelligent woman, who will be an asset to this family and our company. You need to remember that and stay away from Annajane Hudgens. Especially now that Celia is carrying your child."

She gave another shake of the head. "I didn't say a word when you brought Sophie home, did I? We welcomed her into our family and treated her just the same as Pokey's children. We all adore Sophie. But Mason, one illegitimate child is the limit! You simply cannot walk away from Celia."

"I never intended to walk away from her," Mason said, his voice dangerously calm. "But Celia and I are the only ones who can make the decision to get married. I won't be pressured, Mama. Not by you or her."

"Why on earth would you hesitate to marry Celia?" Sallie demanded. "Please explain it to me, because I just don't understand what your problem is."

"I'm not in love with Celia," Mason said. "That's the problem, in a nutshell."

"Love? Don't be ridiculous. As you've already pointed out, you're thirty-nine years old, Mason. You tried marrying for love once. How did that work out for you?" She arched one eyebrow as a dare.

His neck began to flush red.

"You see?" Sallie went on. "Annajane was all wrong for you. I know you think it's snobbish to say so, but it's the truth. There's a reason these kinds of marriages never work out. Ruth Hudgens is little more than white trash. Annajane's real father was a high school dropout, and Leonard, bless his heart, never was the sharpest knife in the drawer. I'll give her credit for this: Annajane was always determined to marry up. And she succeeded in that, even though the two of you had nothing in common. But Celia is different. She's perfect for you. She's clever, she's ambitious, a hard worker, and she sees the big picture. It's a brilliant match. It will be a horrible tragedy for you and Quixie if you let this girl get away from you."

"A brilliant match?" Mason repeated. "What did you do, Mama? Set up an Excel spreadsheet with all the attributes of a corporate wife, and then set out to find her?"

"No," she shot back, "but if I had, I couldn't have done better than Celia. Nor could you." She leaned across the desk, her dark eyes snapping with intensity. "Mason, your daddy and I did not raise you to shirk your responsibilities. You have got to marry Celia and be a father to her child. And the sooner you do, the better. Celia's not going to wait around for you forever, you know. If you don't marry her, she'll surely leave Passcoe, and take my grandchild with her. Is that what you want?"

Mason winced involuntarily, and Sallie saw that her last remark had hit home.

Sallie opened the drawer in the desk and slid out an opened pack of cigarettes, an engraved silver lighter, and a heavy cut-crystal ashtray. She closed the drawer, lit the cigarette, then sat back in her chair and inhaled deeply.

Mason stared. He'd never actually seen his mother smoke. She saw him watching her, and she smiled, tilted her head back, and blew a perfect smoke ring.

"What? You think I'm too old to be misbehaving?" She held the cigarette at eye level for a moment, then tapped the end neatly into the ashtray.

"Did you ever smoke in front of Dad?" Mason asked.

"Of course not," Sallie said. "And don't change the subject. We're not talking about my marriage; we're talking about yours."

"No, we are not," Mason said. "Was there anything else, or can I go back to work now?"

"Just one other thing," Sallie said. "We'll find out the final disposition of the estate when we meet with Norris Thomas next week, but I think we can pretty much anticipate how Glenn will have divided up the company. In the meantime, I want you to give serious consideration to the offer from Jax Snax."

He started to protest, but she waved him off.

"Your father is dead, Mason," Sallie said. "I know he had some sentimental notion about keeping the company in the family, but five years have passed, and the state of the economy has changed, drastically, and not for the better. Glenn could not have anticipated the way our costs have escalated while our sales have dropped. And if you won't consider it in light of your own best interests, think about me. You and your brother are young enough to go out and start new businesses. On the other hand, I'm a widow. If Quixie fails, what am I left with? This house? It's a damned mausoleum. Do you have any idea of what it costs in maintenance? Seven bedrooms, five bathrooms? For a woman who lives alone? The pool needs to be relined, the tennis court needs resurfacing, and my heat and air man tells me we barely have enough BTUs to cool the living and dining room. I need a whole new system, dual heat pumps, the works. Twenty-five thousand dollars! I'd sell it in a minute, but to who? We're the only people in this town with any *real* money."

Mason looked around the study and tried to see it through his mother's eyes. There was a somewhat threadbare oriental rug on the wide-planked wood floor. The heavy linen drapes that hung at the windows had been there as long as he could remember. An oil portrait of his grandmother Bayless hung over the fireplace. He'd never once considered that Sallie might have come to resent the family homeplace. But clearly, she had.

"Now," Sallie went on. "I've talked to several people in the industry, and they assure me that the Jax offer is a good one, probably the best we'll ever get."

"I disagree," Mason said. "We should hold onto Quxie. It is what Dad wanted. That's why he put that five-year moratorium on a sale. We've had challenges, I know, but I really believe we can turn things around now, especially if we expand our brand with the new drinks Dad was considering. I won't support you on a sale, Mama. And neither will Pokey."

She took another drag on the cigarette. He found it fascinating and unsettling to watch a parent indulge in such a taboo. It felt like watching Santa Claus read a copy of *Hustler.* Unseemly.

"Davis is in favor of it," Sallie said. And Celia knows it's for the best, too. You should try listening to her, Mason. She has a really fine head for business, you know. Don't discount her just because she's a woman."

He stood up. "If we're done here, I need to go pick up Sophie."

"Oh yes," Sallie said, stubbing out her cigarette and stashing the still-smouldering ashtray back in her desk drawer. "Poor little

Sophie. I have some ice cream for her, out in the kitchen."

She came around from behind the desk and gave her son an awkward hug. "Think about what I've said today, Mason, will you? Patch things up with Celia, and let's get this wedding rescheduled." She gave his cheek a pat that was very nearly a slap. "And whatever you do, stay away from Annajane Hudgens."

26

When he finally made it into the office, Mason found a thick pile of phone-message slips and an endless stream of e-mails. He was exhausted, guilt-wracked, and pissed off at Annajane Hudgens, whom he blamed for plunging his usually well-ordered life into a maelstrom of doubt and indecision. He was clicking his way through the e-mails, when he came to a long one from Joe Farnham, expressing his regret about the termination of the Quixie account and wishing the family well, that set his blood boiling. He called Farnham and had a brief conversation with the ad-man. As soon as he hung up, he stormed into Davis's office without knocking, slamming the door closed behind him.

"Hey, bro," Davis was dressed in his customary custom-tailored suit, heavily starched white dress shirt, and an expensive Italian knit tie. He was on the phone.

"We need to talk," Mason said, and he felt his jaw muscle twitch. He glanced at Davis's computer screen — and saw what looked like a page of real estate listings. Davis quickly tapped the mouse and the Quixie logo appeared on his screen saver.

"Hang on a minute, can you?" Davis said, covering the phone with his hand. He gestured toward the wingback chair in front of his desk.

"Look, I'll get back to you on that," he said and hung up. He swiveled his chair around and gave his brother a searching look.

"Dude," Davis said, with a merry chortle. "I hear you had yourself quite a night last night. So. You and ole Annajane out at the farm, scaring the livestock. Congratulations, buddy. Didn't know you had it in you."

Mason clenched the sides of the chair with both hands. "Shut the fuck up," he said fiercely. "I mean it, Davis."

"Okay," Davis said, shrugging. "Don't get so bent out of shape. I was just messin' with you."

"You've been messing with a lot of people lately, haven't you, Davis?" Mason said. "I just got an e-mail from Joe Farnham. He tells me you've terminated our account with them?"

"Well, hey-yullllll," Davis drawled. "You know, it's just one of those things. If we do this deal with Jax Snax, they've got their own in-house agency. And I know you've been on a cost-cutting tear, so it seemed to me that now was the time to cut Capheart loose. We've got the summer promotion plans, and it's no biggie for me to cherry-pick the best parts . . ."

"It is not just one of those things," Mason said. "We've been working with Farnham-Capheart for years. They've done a good job for us. More importantly, this Jax thing you keep harping about is not a done deal. You know damned well we don't have any idea of how Dad's trust arrangement is going to shake out. For all we know, he may have left Quixie to the Humane Society."

Davis's eyes shifted nervously. "The old man wouldn't have done anything like that. Anyway, we'll know by next week. I'm just trying to make sure we've got all our ducks in a row once we do know how it shakes out."

"I am not going to let this company be sold, Davis," Mason said quietly. "Not without a fight. I know we've had some philosophical differences in the past, and we've managed to work things out, but this time, I'm not backing down. Our great-grandfather started this business. He and Granddad and Dad managed to keep it afloat during the Depression and the war years. They fought off Coke and Pepsi and half a dozen other companies that tried to put us out of business. But if Kelso and his bunch get their hands on Quixie, you know as well as I do that they won't leave us alone. I've seen how they operate. They don't want us — not the physical us. They just want our brand and our market share. Oh yeah, they'll make promises about keeping things just the way they are, but that's a bunch of bullshit. They'll write us a big check and then show us the door. They'll shut the plant down, ship the equipment somewhere else, and throw everybody in town out of work. Everybody but the Baylesses."

"You got something against making money?" Davis asked. "Or do you just enjoy the idea of being the last noble Bayless to run Quixie — right into the ground? Because that's where it's headed, big brother. Get your head out of your ass! Take a look at what's happening in the business."

"We can turn it around," Mason said stubbornly. "The new flavors, the focus groups loved 'em. And we need some fresh ideas, but we've got a good product . . ."

"I'm telling you it's too late," Davis said, half-shouting. "The brand extensions you're talking about will cost millions. We'd have to retool the plant, add extra capacity, and God knows what all. And I'm tired of flushing good money after bad. If you don't believe me, talk to Celia! She'll tell you the truth. The smart money is on Jax. We make the deal, get 'em to sign an iron-clad agreement not to move the company — at least for four or five years. Maybe milk the state for some tax incentives to stick around . . ."

The muscle in Mason's jaw twitched as though it had been touched with a live wire. "We are *not* going to hold this state ransom and hang around for a government handout just to turn around and double-cross them. That's not how Baylesses do business."

"The hell you say." Davis was leaning back in his leather chair. He clicked his mouse and his computer screen was again filled with color photographs of real estate listings. He swiveled the monitor so Mason could get a look.

"You see this? That's a four-bedroom house on Figure Eight Island." He tapped the screen with his forefinger. "The lot alone cost a million, three, and I know the owner spent another million and a half building the damned thing. Then he lost his ass in the speculative real estate market. Guy is hurtin' big-time. Now, he's begging me to buy it — fully furnished — including a thirty-five-foot Grady-White. I just put an option on it. Eight hundred thousand. You believe that?"

Mason felt his stomach churn. His brother relished the idea of feasting on another man's disaster. "You could buy that house and boat right now, without taking a dime out of Quixie," he pointed out. "You've got the money. Nothin's stopping you."

Davis leaned across his desk. Beneath the tan, a network of fine red veins threaded across his high cheekbones. "Quixie is stop-

344

ping me," he said. "Floggin' this dead horse takes up all my time and energy. But now I'm done."

He laid his palms flat down on the desktop. "And before you start in on lecturing me about family duty and all that bullshit, you need to know that I am not the only one in favor of this sale. I know Pokey's dead-set against it, but hell, Pete's got plenty of money, and anyway, our baby sister don't know squat about cherry soda."

He glanced over at a glamorous silver-framed photo of Sallie that rested at the edge of his desk. She'd had the portrait done only a year ago, not long after she'd made a trip to Florida that had been billed as a winter vacation, but which they all knew was for a skillfully done face-lift.

"I wasn't gonna get into this right now, but you need to know that Mama is ready for this deal to happen. She's not getting any younger. She wants to get out and enjoy her life while she still can. And if you let this company go to hell, out of your own stubborn pride, that's on you, buddy."

He pointed at the monitor with the photo of the beach house. "This summer, when you're messin' around out at that broken-down old boathouse and cottage out at Hideaway — that's where I'm gonna be spending my time. Ocean views on one side, views of the sound on the other."

Mason shook his head. "I went to see Mama this morning. You've been telling her all kind of lies about what'll happen to the company if we don't sell, haven't you, Davis? Scaring her, making her think she'll be a penniless widow?"

His younger brother gave a nonchalant shrug. "Mama's a grown woman with plenty of business sense, Mason. She can see the handwriting on the wall without a flashlight."

"I'm done here," Mason said tersely as he stood to go. "Anyway, I didn't come in here to debate the merits of Jax Snax. What I did come in here to talk about is Quixie. Here and now. Today. I've tried to stay out of your side of the business, but I can't do it this time. I called Joe Farnham after I got his e-mail this morning. He told me losing the account meant he couldn't hire Annajane. Was that your intention? Making sure she wouldn't have a job? What the hell has she ever done to you?"

"Nothing," Davis said. "I'm okay with Annajane. How was I supposed to know he'd let her go? I'm not privy to their internal workings."

"You need to fix this, Davis," Mason said, glaring at his younger brother. "Nobody knows the company history as well as Annajane or understands our market like she does. Rehire her, or I will. Firing Capheart is one of the stupidest damned moves you've ever

346

made. And you've made some pretty stupid decisions in your life."

"You're calling me stupid?" Davis leaned forward. "Take a look at yourself, big brother. I'm not the one lettin' my gorgeous fiancée sleep at Mama's house while I'm out fuckin' my ex-wife in a cornfield."

Mason felt the blood rushing to his head. He stood very still. He jammed his hands into his pockets to keep from slugging his brother.

"I'll call Annajane and let her know she's been rehired," he told Davis. "In the meantime, we need to concentrate on running Quixie, the best way we know how." He turned and stalked out of the room.

27

NOW ENTERING PASSCOE, N.C. HOME OF QUIXIE BEVERAGE COMPANY SINCE 1922. Annajane slowed the car as she passed the city limits sign.

Funny, she'd never really noticed the tasteful green and red billboard before. If Jax Snax managed to gobble up Quixie in the proposed merger, would the town fathers leave the sign standing? The real question, of course, was whether there would be anything left of the town if Quixie got sold.

She'd seen too many other small towns around the state decimated after the departure of textile mills, furniture manufacturers, and yes, even the much-maligned big tobacco. The sight of those abandoned buildings, with their weed-strewn properties; ghostly, boarded-up windows; and forlorn FOR SALE signs never failed to send a shiver up her spine.

They didn't cure cancer or promote world peace at Quixie. They just made fizzy soft drinks. But their product made people happy.

Mason might fret about shrinking market share, but one thing did not change. Their customers felt intense loyalty to a soft drink that had been around for more than ninety years. Quixie employed three hundred people in Passcoe, which made it the county's biggest employer. Quixie, and by extension the Bayless family, had provided most of the funding for Memorial Park, the high school football stadium, and the obstetric wing of the hospital. Quixie and its employees were always the biggest contributors to the local United Way fund, and, of course, their taxes kept county roads paved and libraries and schools funded.

Annajane ran her tongue over her now-straight teeth. As the child of a longtime Quixie employee, the company's health plan had paid for her orthodontia, and Leonard's company-sponsored savings plan had sent her to college.

Quixie, she vowed, could not just up and leave. She might not have a home or a job or a future here, but she couldn't let all of this go. Not without a fight.

Her cell phone rang and she recognized the number on the readout as her real estate agent's.

"Annajane, hey," Susan Peters said. "I'm so glad I caught you."

"Please don't tell me you have bad news,"

Annajane said. "I've already had enough to-day."

"Not exactly bad news," Susan said. "But news. We need to move up the closing on your loft to Wednesday. So you'll get your money two days early. Hooray, right?"

"But that's the day after tomorrow. I'm not even done packing."

"Sorry," Susan said. "Your buyer has to leave the country on business Friday, and Wednesday is the only day we can get it scheduled with the lender and the closing attorneys. So it's Wednesday or nothing."

"I won't have to move until Friday though, right?"

"Uh, no. You'll need to be out of there by noon Wednesday, so she can get moved in before she leaves on Friday."

"Susan!" Annajane said, with a moan. "You don't know what you're asking. I just found out today my job in Atlanta fell through. I don't have any place to move to."

"Can't you just move in with your fiancé?"

"Probably not, since we're no longer engaged," Annajane said.

"Oh. Wow. You are having a run of crappy news," Susan said. "Well, look on the bright side. You're making out like a bandit on the sale of the loft. You can afford to buy something really nice now. I've got a darling 1940s cottage over on Mimosa Street. It's a three-bedroom, two-bath, on a huge lot, with tons of potential. You could pick it up for a steal, and have lots of money left over for the restoration."

"Restoration?"

"It's what we real estate professionals call 'a handyman's special.' You know, it'll need a new roof, plumbing, electrical, heat and air, a new kitchen, like that. I can show it to you today, if you want, and if you love it, which I think you will, we can write up an offer by tonight."

"Whoa!" Annajane said. "I'm still processing the news that I'll be homeless in two days. Look. I can't wrap my mind around this right now. I'll have to call you back, okay?"

"Okay, but remember, closing is now at 9 A.M. Wednesday. And you really do have to be out of the loft completely by noon. Call me if you want to see Mimosa Street."

Annajane dropped her phone into her open pocketbook with a sigh. This day was one that would go down on record as one of the worst in her life. Ever.

She slowed the car at the intersection of the county road and the street that led to Mason's house. She would deal with her broken engagement, the job situation, and the moved-up closing later. What she needed now was a little cheering up. Sophie would be home from the hospital by now. Impulsively, she made the turn, and hoped all the turmoil at the office meant she could visit the little girl without encountering Mason. Or Celia.

Sophie's nanny, Letha, gave Annajane a quick hug. "She's been asking about you since we got home," Letha said. "Her daddy told her you'd gone out of town, and she sure didn't like hearing that!"

She found Sophie propped up on the leather sofa in Mason's study, sipping from a glass bottle of Quixie and watching *The Little Mermaid* video. The little girl's pallor was gone, and she was giggling as Sebastian the lobster capered around on the colorful flat-screened television.

"Annajane!" Sophie cried, spotting her. "You came back."

"I did," Annajane agreed, sitting gingerly on the edge of the tufted ottoman that served as a coffee table. She reached over and adjusted Sophie's sparkly pink glasses, then ruffled her hair. "Are you glad to be home?"

"Yeah. The nurses were nice, but Letha is nicer."

"Lots nicer. And you're feeling better, I hear?"

As an answer, Sophie pulled up her pajama top and pointed at her abdomen. A small square of gauze covered her incision. "I'm gonna have a scar," she said proudly. "Nobody else in my whole school has a scar like me."

Annajane laughed. She stuck out her leg and rolled up her pant leg to her knee. "I've got a scar, too," she said.

Clearly intrigued, Sophie ran her finger over the faint strip of puckered flesh and shivered. "Did you have to go in an ambulance and have an operation at the hospital?"

"Nope. My scar isn't anywhere near as cool as yours."

"How'd you get it?"

"It was a long time ago," Annajane said. "I was dressed up in the Dixie the Pixie costume. You remember that from my office, right?"

"Uh-huh."

"Well. I was marching in the Fourth of July parade, and I had a cart full of Quixie to give away to people watching the parade, but then these bad boys ganged up on me, and they stole my cart."

"Oh no." Sophie's eyes widened. "What did you do?"

"I tried to chase after them, to get the cart back," Annajane reported. "But I had on that big goofy pixie head, and I couldn't see very well, and then I was also wearing those silly shoes that were five sizes too big, and I tripped! And that's how I banged up my knee and got this scar."

"You left out the part about how I rode up in the fun car and saved you."

Mason. She hadn't even heard him come

into the room.

Annajane didn't turn around. "Actually, I saved myself. But your daddy did give me a ride home that day."

"Don't forget I bought you a hot dog and some potato chips," Mason said. He walked over to the sofa and dropped a kiss on the little girl's head. He held up a white paper sack. "Guess what's in here?"

"Ice cream!" Sophie exclaimed.

Mason pulled a round cardboard tub from the bag. "Your grandmother sent this over. Strawberry shortcake ice cream. Want some?"

Sophie nodded vigorously, sending the pigtails on either side of her face wagging.

"I'll fix it," Annajane volunteered, taking the bag from Mason.

She was out in the kitchen, scooping ice cream into bowls, when Mason strolled into the kitchen. "I'll just fix this for you guys, and then I'll take off," Annajane said.

He leaned with his back against the counter and crossed his arms over his chest, surveying her with studied indifference.

Tell her about the baby, he thought. *Tell her so she can cut and run. Do it now.* But he couldn't. Not tonight.

"Wanna share any news with me?" he asked.

Annajane gave him a backward glance. "Pokey told you I broke up with Shane, right?"

"She mentioned it. I'm sorry, Annajane.

354

So, he didn't take the news of our, uh, encounter well?"

"He didn't take it the way I anticipated," she said, avoiding all the messy details. "As it turns out, it's been a day full of unpleasant surprises."

Mason took her by the shoulders and turned her around to face him. "First things first. I want you to know that I had no idea Davis was going to fire our ad agency, effectively rendering you unemployed. He didn't bother to inform me until it was a done deal."

"What was he thinking?" Annajane asked.

"I have no idea," Mason said with a scowl. "We're basically only communicating by e-mail these days. But that's going to change pretty shortly. In fact, a lot of things are fixing to change."

"You met with Sallie?"

"Yes," Mason affirmed. "We had a fairly long, frank discussion about a lot of stuff. She's still not totally convinced the family should keep Quixie, but that's sort of a moot point at the moment."

Annajane looked over at the bowl of ice cream she'd just scooped out. "Sounds like this could be a long story. So let me just take this in to Sophie before it melts, and I'll be right back."

Annajane came back into the kitchen. "You

355

were saying?"

"My brother and I can't keep working at cross-purposes," Mason said. "It's hurting the company, and it's hurting the family. We managed to hammer out a short-term agreement this morning." He took a deep breath and looked directly at Annajane.

"I told Davis we have to find a way to get you not to leave the company." He clamped his hand over hers. "We need you, Annajane. Need your talent, your energy, your commitment. Davis and I don't agree on much, but it turns out we do agree about that. What do you say? Will you come back?"

She stared down at their hands and sighed.

"Please?" Mason's face looked haunted.

Annajane looked away, struggling to find the right answer, for the right reasons.

"I'm all done." Sophie stood in the kitchen doorway, her tousled blond curls backlit by the sun streaming through the windows. Her pink pocketbook was slung across her chest, bandolier-style. She padded barefoot into the kitchen and carefully placed her bowl on the table where Mason and Annajane were sitting. Without a word, she slid onto Mason's lap.

"Whatcha doing?" Sophie asked, glancing down at the intertwined hands on the tabletop.

Annajane snatched her hand away from Mason's, but she could feel herself blushing.

"I'm trying to talk Annajane into changing her mind about moving away," Mason said.

"Letha says it's a damned shame Annajane got chased outta town by that lil' hussy," Sophie said brightly.

Mason choked. "I'm going to have to have a talk with Letha about little pitchers having big ears."

Sophie cocked her head and regarded Annajane somberly. "Will you stay, pretty please?"

"I'm not sure," Annajane said. "I have a lot to think about."

"Like what?"

"For one thing, I don't have a job anymore," Annajane said, keeping her tone light.

"You can have your old job back," Mason offered.

"Yay!" Sophie clapped her hands in delight.

"Also, I don't have anyplace to live. My loft is sold, and I have to move out by the day after tomorrow," Annajane said.

"Since when?" Mason asked.

"My real estate agent called right as I was driving into town," Annajane said. "The closing had to be moved up to Wednesday, which means I have to be totally moved out of the loft by noon that day."

"You could come live with us!" Sophie said delightedly. "Right, daddy?"

Mason coughed politely. "I think Annajane probably wants a place of her own, Soph."

357

"Letha told Aunt Pokey that Daddy and Celia had a big ole fight, and now Celia is gone for sure, thank you, Sweet Baby Jesus," Sophie reported, mimicking Letha's slow southern accent with deadly accuracy. "So now, Annajane could sleep in your room, couldn't you, Annajane?"

Mason coughed so violently his face turned purple and tears streamed down his face. Annajane couldn't help herself. Her shoulders heaved with suppressed laughter.

"I am going to have a serious talk with Letha about spreading gossip," Mason said solemnly. "And for your information, and Aunt Pokey's and Letha's, we did not have a big fight. We had an um, discussion. But Celia is not gone."

"Are you still getting married?" Sophie asked, tilting her head to look at her father.

He looked out the window. "It's still under discussion," he said finally. "Anyway, that's nothing for you to worry about."

"Annajane could stay in my room with me. Right?"

"That's a very generous invitation, Sophie," Annajane said, giggling despite herself. "But if I do stay in Passcoe, which I'm not sure I will, I'll need to find a house of my own."

"Why?" Sophie looked puzzled. "Don't you like us?"

"I like you a lot," Annajane said. "But I've lived alone for a long time now. I'm used to my privacy, and doing things my own way. It would be best for everybody if we left it like that."

Sophie yawned widely and leaned her head back against Mason's chest.

"Time for you to go take a nap," he told her, gently sliding her down from his lap.

Sophie threw her arms around Annajane's neck. "Will you come over and watch *Milo and Otis* with me tonight?"

"Hmm," Annajane said. "I wish I could, Soph, but now I've got to go home and get my stuff all packed up to put in storage. But I promise, as soon as that's done, we'll have movie night again."

"Okay," Sophie said, trying to suppress another yawn.

Mason waited until Sophie had gone to find Letha before returning his attention to Annajane.

"Will you at least agree to come back to work at Quixie?" Mason asked. "I'm dead serious, Annajane. I told Davis I want you back on our team. You'd report directly to me. I know it'll be awkward, but that can't be helped. Will you do it?"

He gave her that slow, winning smile that had always worked on her in the past.

"I don't know," she said quietly. "I really don't want to get between you and your brother. Or Celia. I've complicated things enough already."

Tell her, damn it. You're only making things worse by talking her into staying.

"You're not what's between us," Mason said. "Davis and I have been having issues for a long time now. And Mama, she's got her own agenda. But I do want to talk to you about this new marketing scheme; I don't like it."

Annajane bit her lip, hesitant to trash Celia.

"You know," she said finally. "Yesterday, I was cleaning out my office and taking some old file boxes that had been in there for years and years out to the Dumpster. One of the boxes was so old it fell to pieces as I was unloading it. Inside it I found all the old magazine and newspaper mechanicals and tear sheets for Quixie ads from the '40s and '50s. They were so charming, so right, so *Quixie,* for want of a better phrase. For me, they just really captured the essence of what we're selling — fun, refreshment, and yeah, the idea of celebrating the moment. I honestly think that's what we've forgotten with all these slick, sophisticated campaigns we've bought into in the past few years."

Mason nodded thoughtfully. "I remember those old ads. There was one, from the sixties, probably, showing teenaged girls in a speedboat . . ."

"I saw that one," Annajane said. "It made me want to run out and get a permanent wave and a Jantzen bathing suit, maybe buy a

Chris-Craft outboard."

"Mama and my aunt Lu posed for that ad," Mason said. "They took the photo that the illustration was based on, out on the lake, back in the day. Dad had it framed and hanging in the basement playroom for years and years, when we were growing up."

"Those are the ads that *everybody* remembers," Annajane said. "Quixie is never going to be Coke. It's never going to be Pepsi. It shouldn't even try. The brand is iconic in its own way, and I think that's what the message needs to return to. Retro is in again, you know."

"My granddaddy always said he just wanted us to be the best independent regional soft drink company in the business," Mason said. "He never touched coffee, but he drank a bottle of Quixie from his own special Quixie icebox just about every morning of his life, as soon as his feet touched the bedroom floor. As far as he was concerned, our product was unique, and he really believed every bottle of Quixie that left the plant was the thing that would sell the next one."

He grinned. "That and ads with curvy girls in bathing suits."

Annajane stood up. "I better get going. I've still got to finish packing and, I suppose, start looking for a temporary place to live, at least until I figure out my next move."

"Think about what I said, will you?" Mason

said, touching her arm lightly. "I think you're on the right track with your ideas about returning to our original brand message. If I can just get Davis to listen, I think he'd realize it's brilliant."

"Maybe," Annajane said. "I will say that if he's dumped the ad agency, he's gonna have to come up with a new summer campaign in a big hurry."

"One more thing," she added, her hand on the back door. "I bumped into Celia as I was sifting through that file box I just mentioned. She urged me to throw all of it in the Dumpster, and not to bother you with any of that old crap, but I told her you might like it for the company archives. There are a bunch of the old original Quixie bottles, too, the ones with the ribbed glass . . ."

Mason looked horrified. "You didn't throw them out, I hope."

"Nope," Annajane said. "I put it all in a new box and stashed it in the trunk of my car, just in case."

"Great," he said. "I'd really like to see those ads, maybe use them to persuade Davis it's time to go retro. Hell, maybe we'll even resurrect Dixie the Pixie." He did a mock leer at Annajane's legs. "I'll bet you'd still fit in the suit. And the Fourth of July is just around the corner. Right?"

"No. Frickin'. Way," she said succinctly. "But maybe Celia would like to wear it."

28

Pokey picked up a plastic tub of winter clothing and balanced it on her hip. Annajane swiftly snatched it away from her.

"No lifting! Folding, packing yes, lifting no. How many times do I have to repeat myself?"

Pokey stuck out her tongue and took the tub back. "Don't you think that little chunk o' love Clayton weighs waaay more than these clothes? I tote him around all day long, just like I toted Petey when I was pregnant with Clayton. Relax, will you? I'm pregnant, not crippled."

Annajane looked around the loft at the barely controlled chaos. It was Wednesday morning. She was dressed in the only clothes she hadn't packed: a bleached-out Durham Bulls T-shirt and a pair of ratty cutoff jeans. Pokey wore an oversized blue and white oxford cloth dress shirt she'd borrowed from her husband and a pair of stretchy yoga pants. They'd been packing all night.

"I've got to be at the lawyer's office in three

hours," she reminded her friend. "And the movers I hired still aren't back from the storage place to pick up the second load yet. I honestly don't know if I'll be out of here by noon."

"You will," Pokey assured her. She held up her cell phone. "I just texted an SOS to Pete. He's sending over a truck and a couple of the guys from the furniture store to give us a hand. This is the last of your clothes to go into storage. So if you'll just get your rear in gear and pack up the clothes and toiletries you need for the next month or so, I think we've got it licked."

"You really think so?" Annajane pushed a strand of hair behind her ear. "I'm so overwhelmed I guess I can't see the forest for the trees."

They heard a horn honking out on the street, and Pokey ran to the plate-glass picture window and looked out. "See here? Pete's guys just pulled up, and your movers are right behind them. Why don't you grab some clothes and head over to our house? The boys won't be back from Pete's mom's house until two. You can get a shower and change into some halfway decent clothes and still have plenty of time to get to the closing. I'll stay here and supervise. You know how I love to boss around men with trucks."

"That would be great," Annajane said. "Are you sure Pete's okay with me staying with you guys for a couple of days? Just until I find a place of my own? I mean, I really could go to the Pinecone Motor Lodge . . ."

"Pete probably won't even notice you're there," Pokey said. "With everything going on at the new furniture store, he barely notices I'm there half the time. You, on the other hand, will probably get tired of the wild bunch way before we get tired of you. The boys are superexcited you're coming. Denning even offered to let you sleep in his tree fort, which is saying a lot. You know he's pretty antigirl these days."

"That's the second best offer of a crash pad I've had from a member of your family in the past couple days," Annajane said drily.

"Fascinating! Who made the first and best offer?" Pokey asked.

"Sophie did. I stopped by to check in on her after she got home from the hospital Monday. She heard me telling Mason my tale of woe about having to move out of the loft early, and she just piped up and invited me to sleep in her daddy's room."

"She didn't!"

"Oh yes, she did."

"Out of the mouths of babes," Pokey snickered.

They heard footsteps in the stairwell, so Pokey opened the door with a grand sweep, and the room began to fill with men and furniture dollies.

"Okay, then, I'm outta here," Annajane told Pokey. "Just as soon as I find the carton with all my clean underwear."

At eight that night, Annajane wearily dragged her suitcase onto the front porch of Pete and Pokey Riggs's cheerful pale blue Dutch colonial revival home. She opened the heavily carved mahogany front door with her hip and walked in unannounced, letting the door bang behind her.

The sound of a television echoed in the high-ceilinged hallway. She stepped out of her shoes and left them on the worn rug at the foot of the stairs.

"Is that you?" Pokey called from the direction of the back of the house. "If it is, come on back. We're in the den, and it's cocktail time."

Annajane made her way toward the den, stepping over a spilled box of Legos, a green rubber dinosaur, and an enormous cardboard box of Pampers. She found her best friend sprawled out on her back on an overstuffed bottle-green damask sofa, with her bare feet resting in her husband's lap.

Pete Riggs stood up and gestured toward a silver cocktail shaker resting on a tufted leather ottoman in front of the sofa. "Care for a martini?"

"I would kill for a martini," Annajane said gratefully. She slumped down into a wing

366

chair and looked around the room suspiciously. "It's awfully quiet around here. Where are the heathens?"

"It's grown-up time," Pete said, handing her a pint Mason jar. "Hang on a sec," he added, plunking an olive into her drink. "Now you're ready."

"The rule around here is, everybody under the age of eight has to be in bed by eight," Pokey said. She was noisily slurping on a large chocolate Blizzard. "It's the only way we keep our sanity."

Pete rejoined his wife on the sofa. "So — did your closing go all right? We were starting to get a little worried when we didn't hear from you earlier in the day, but Pokey didn't want to jinx things by calling you."

"We closed," Annajane said. "There was some minor panic when one of the loan documents still hadn't arrived at noon, but by the time we finished signing all the other paperwork, the courier had arrived with it. I'm no longer a homeowner."

"You'll find something else just as nice," Pokey said. "Here in Passcoe — right?"

Annajane sipped her martini appreciatively. "I guess. Susan Peters showed me three more listings this afternoon. That's where I've been all this time."

"And?" Pete asked. His red hair shone dully in the light from a pair of antique brass sconces on the wall behind the sofa, and, close up like this, Annajane noticed with a start that he was beginning to get just the slightest hint of silver around his temples and paunch around his midriff. He wore a pink button-down oxford cloth shirt, rumpled khaki slacks, and oxblood penny loafers with no socks.

She was struck by how much he'd changed since the first time Pokey brought him home to meet her family. Pete Riggs was a twenty-four-year-old stud, a rich, cocky kid from Charleston, who'd started on the varsity golf team all four years at Wake Forest, and he was enrolled in grad school when he'd met Pokey and gotten her pregnant right before the end of her senior year at Chapel Hill.

The Baylesses had been devastated, but Sallie had assured Pokey the family would take care of her and the baby, no matter what. Nobody could have predicted that Pete Riggs would do what he did — drop out of grad school, marry Pokey, and get a job working in his family's furniture business. And the biggest surprise, to everybody, including Pokey and Pete, was that the two of them would make a success of all of it — including marriage, parenthood, and, eventually, running and expanding Riggs Home Fashions.

"It's hopeless," Annajane said of her house hunt. "The cottage on Mimosa — the one she thought I'd be so crazy over? It's Old Lady Harrison's house. If I'd known that, I wouldn't have bothered to take a look."

"Eeewww," Pokey said, wrinkling her nose. "Mama used to make me sell her Girl Scout cookies every year when we were kids. She used to pay for the cookies with nickels and dimes that looked like they'd been scraped up out of a sewer or something. That house was nasty way back then, and she's been dead and gone at least ten years. I don't think anybody's lived in that house since she died."

"Correction," Annajane said. "There's a family of raccoons living there now. Or maybe squirrels. I didn't get past the living room, where they'd been nesting in an old sofa, so I couldn't say for sure."

"What else did you look at?" Pete asked, absentmindedly stroking Pokey's hair. "How about Clay Snider's house? I hear he and Whitney have split up."

"Yeah," Pokey said excitedly. "The Snider's house is fabulous. We went to a Christmas party there a couple years ago. You would love what they've done with the kitchen. They blew out the whole back of the house, and there's a patio and a pool house . . ."

"Susan sent me the link to their Web site. I'd love that house even without the patio and pool house. But alas, I do not have the eight hundred and fifty thousand dollars they're asking," Annajane said. She reached over to the tray on the ottoman and helped herself to a handful of roasted peanuts.

"I looked at a totally mediocre brick ranch over on Rosewood. It's a two-bedroom, two-bath, with a crazy floor plan. You actually have to walk through the master bedroom to get to the living room. But it was only eighty-nine thousand. And then I saw a butt-ugly contemporary house out past the country club. Gray cinder-block walls, smoked plate-glass windows — which were all across the whole front of the house. You'd feel like you were on display for anybody who drove past."

She sighed and took another sip of her martini, smacking her lips dramatically. "If Pete would promise to make me a martini like this every night, I might just threaten to move in here with you guys."

Pete raised his own Mason jar in a mock salute. "I live to serve."

"You know you can stay here as long as you like," Pokey said. "What have you decided about going back to work?"

"You're going back to work at Quixie?" Pete said.

"Maybe," Annajane allowed.

"You are," Pokey said. "You must. For my sake and the sake of my unborn child. Not to mention the rest of my whole nutty family."

"It's gonna depend on Davis," Annajane said. "If he won't listen to any of my ideas for a new marketing plan, it's a waste of my time to go back to work. And I really, really do not want to be around Celia. Especially now."

"Whooo," Pete chuckled. "I hear old Celia is pretty fired up about you, Annajane darlin'."

"What did you hear?" Pokey demanded, tugging at Pete's arm. "Tell!"

"Aw, no," Pete demurred. "I didn't really hear anything. Just a little trash talk in the men's grill at the club today."

"Peterson James Riggs, you better spit out what you heard at the club right this minute," Pokey exclaimed. "It's no fair teasin' us."

"Yeah, Pete," Annajane urged. "Tell. Come on, sticks and stones may break my bones and all that."

"You know I don't usually listen to that mess," Pete groused. "I was walking past Matt Kelsey at lunch, and I just heard him tell Ben Gardner that Celia was accusing you of being a home wrecker."

"You know Bonnie Kelsey is the one spreading that talk," Pokey said. "Her and Celia, that little bitch!" She pounded Pete's knees for emphasis. "Who does she think she is, coming into town and trying to take over Quixie and my brother?"

"Hey!" Pete protested. "Don't kill the messenger. I'm not agreein' with her. I'm just reporting. Anyway, who cares what those two girly men Matt Kelsey and Ben Gardner gossip about over lunch?"

371

Annajane plucked the olive from her half-empty drink and sucked on it. "It's a small town," she said finally. "And Mason is running the biggest business in it. People are always gonna talk about him, and the Baylesses. Face it. It comes with the territory."

"I might have to face it, but I don't have to like it," Pokey said. "Every place I go in town, somebody comes up and asks me if the boys are gonna sell Quixie. I'm getting really sick of telling people it's just a rumor."

"Jax Snax is no rumor, baby," Pete muttered. "They want Quixie, and they want it bad. The question is whether Mason or Davis is going to prevail. And how your mama's gonna vote."

"What about me?" Pokey demanded. "Don't you think Daddy left me any say in what happens to Quixie?"

"I sure hope he did," Pete said. "But let's face it, honey — you've not worked for the company since you were a teenager, and you never worked in management. Knowing your daddy like I do, I've got a feeling that when he divvied up the pie, he saved the biggest, juiciest pieces for your brothers. And your mama."

"I guess we'll find out who gets what next week," Pokey said. "But I called Davis today, and I told him flat out, if he lets Quixie close down, or move from Passcoe, I will never forgive him."

"What did he say to that?" Annajane asked.

"Oh, he just tried to bullshit me," Pokey replied. "Said nobody's discussin' closing it down or moving it. He says Jax Snax will only make the company better."

"And him richer," Pete quipped.

Pokey picked up the remote control from the tray on the ottoman. "All right y'all, enough talking about business. I am ready for some mindless television for an hour or so before I call it a night. Which is it — HGTV or Food TV?"

"You mean food porn or decorator porn?" Pete grabbed a pillow and wedged it under his wife's head. He stood up and dropped a kiss on Pokey's forehead. "I think I'll go watch baseball upstairs."

Annajane experienced a familiar pang of jealousy at Pete's tenderness toward Pokey. Her friend had so much — a home and a husband who adored her — and three rowdy but healthy children, with a fourth on the way. Did Pokey appreciate just how blessed she was? Or how hollow and envious Annajane sometimes felt in her company?

"Check on the boys, will you?" Pokey called absentmindedly while she flipped channels. "Make sure Denning isn't up there messin' with one of those doggone video games."

An hour later, after they'd both grown bored with *Real Housewives* and *Bridezilla* shows, Pokey handed off the remote to Annajane.

"It's all yours," she said, yawning.

"Nope," Annajane said. "I'm going to bed, too. I've got to save my energy for going back to Quixie in the morning."

"Good for you," Pokey said, nodding her approval. "And what about Mason? What's going to happen with you two?"

"Leave it be, Pokey," Annajane warned. "Everything is happening too fast. We're friends, okay? Can we just leave it at that for now?"

"Friends with benefits?" Pokey chirped. "Look, I just don't want you to let Celia Wakefield screw things up by guilt-tripping you," Pokey said. "You and Mason didn't do anything wrong. Not deliberately anyway. You acted honorably, so just hold your head high and ignore Celia."

"Celia, ugh," Annajane said. "I am not looking forward to running into her tomorrow."

"Oh my God," Pokey said suddenly. "I forgot. I finally did call Angela — my sorority sister, the one who's a buyer for Belk?"

"Does she know Celia?" Annajane asked.

"She'd heard of her, but she didn't really have any dirt on her. However, she did give me the name and phone number of a friend of hers who might know more about the details of Celia's clothing business," Pokey said. She reached in her pocket and handed over what looked like the page from a Bob the Builder coloring book that had been written on in red crayon.

"Her name is Katie Derscheid," Pokey said, yawning widely again. "I wasn't sure how to spell it. Just call her and mention Angela Hooker's name."

At some point in the evening, Annajane dimly recognized the sound of rain on the roof and the brush of tree limbs against the windowpanes. She opened one eye and saw a jagged flash of lightning streaking across the deep blue sky outside. She snuggled deeper into the down comforter and pulled a spare pillow over her head to drown out the noise, glad not to be out in the storm.

She drifted off to sleep again, but maybe an hour later was aware of a shaft of light streaming in through the doorway. She lifted her head off the pillow and spied a small, forlorn little body standing in the doorway.

It was Petey, clad in his cotton Thomas the Tank Engine pajamas, sucking his thumb and trailing a bedraggled but much-loved blue silk bordered blanket.

"Hey, buddy," she said groggily. "What's up?"

"I'm scared," he said, moving his thumb aside only long enough to speak.

"Want me to walk you back to your bed?"

He shook his head side to side, vigorously.

"Want to go sleep with your mommy and daddy?"

"The baby is with Mommy and Daddy."

She sighed and scooted over on the queen-sized bed. "Come on, then."

Petey favored her with a tremulous smile before crawling up into the bed beside her. Annajane rubbed his back the way she'd seen Pokey do so many times, and a few minutes later, she heard his breathing become soft and rhythmic. Smiling to herself, she turned on her side and fell back asleep herself, only dimly aware of the warm little body spooned up against her back.

Maybe an hour later, she heard the bedroom door creak open. Looking up, she saw Pokey silhouetted in the doorway.

"Hey," Pokey whispered. "Pete's in there snoring so loud I can't sleep. Okay if I bunk in with you?"

Annajane lifted the edge of the comforter to reveal the sleeping form of Petey.

Pokey laughed softly, and walked around to the other side of the bed, yawning widely as she shifted her young son into the middle of the bed. Moments later, mother and son were breathing in tandem.

Once again, Annajane managed to fall back asleep. The rain began to beat at the windows, heavier now, and the howl of the wind became ominous. She shifted in the bed and now felt a warm, damp spot where she'd been sleeping moments earlier. She sniffed the sheet, sniffed Petey.

"Crap," she muttered softly. Wrapping herself in the quilt from the foot of the bed, she tiptoed out of the room, headed for the sofa in the den. Tomorrow, she promised herself, she would either find a house to buy or check into a room at the Pinecone Motor Lodge.

29

Annajane felt small hands lightly patting her face. Opening one eye, she spied Petey, staring at her intently. *"Curious George,"* he said.

Sleep deprived, she turned over so that she was facing the back of the sofa. He shook her shoulder. *"Curious George,"* he repeated. She felt her head being struck with something, and reached back and caught his hand, which was holding the remote control.

"Petey! Leave Annajane alone."

Annajane rolled onto her back. Now Pokey stood over her, holding an outstretched mug of coffee.

The room was still in half darkness. "What time is it?" Annajane mumbled.

"A smidge after seven," Pokey said. She sat on the edge of the ottoman, and Annajane, with effort, managed to pull herself upright.

"Curious George," Petey said loudly. "I want *Curious George.*" He slung his damp, pee-scented blanket across her knees and climbed into her lap.

"Sorry," Pokey said, deftly scooping the child off Annajane and onto the ottoman. "Petey is our early bird. I've tried everything to get him to sleep late and let us alone in the morning, but it's no use. Little guys don't know numbers, and they have no concept of time. So now I've trained him to wait until the streetlights go off outside. Then and only then, he can come downstairs to the den and turn on PBS. He loves *Curious George* and *Dinosaur Train.*"

"Those are television shows?" Annajane took the mug and inhaled the hot coffee fumes.

"His favorites," Pokey said, clicking on the television. "How come you wound up sleeping down here?"

Annajane handed her the damp blanket. "Your son sprung a leak last night."

"Sorry about that," Pokey said with a laugh. "Welcome to my world."

"Yeah, about that," Annajane said. "It won't hurt your feelings if I find myself someplace else to stay?"

"Not in the least," Pokey said. "I'd stay someplace else if I were you. Hell, I'd stay someplace else if I were me, but I think my husband might object."

Annajane reached out and tousled Petey's strawberry-blond hair. "Don't kid yourself, sweetie. You've got the world on a string. A beautiful home, loving husband, great kids.

I'd trade places with you in a New York minute."

"I know you would," Pokey said softly. "But you'll have all that pretty soon, too, Annajane. I know you will, if you just hang in there and make up your mind that he's worth fighting for."

Later that morning, Annajane swung her car into the parking lot at the Quixie plant and groaned when she saw the familiar silver Saab parked in its customary slot.

You can do this, she told herself. *Celia is not the boogeyman. And you are not a quitter.*

Heads turned to stare at her as she walked through the reception area and into the back office. Obviously, everybody had heard the rumors about her and Mason.

She smiled and ignored the stares and whispers. She found Voncile at her desk, stationed right outside Mason's office. Voncile was on the phone, but when she looked up and saw Annajane, she waved her into Mason's office.

He'd just slammed down the phone and was staring intently at the computer monitor on his desktop, frowning, when she walked in.

"Hey," she said, feeling unaccountably shy. Hadn't she come just a flashlight beam away from hot messy car sex with this man just a few days ago?

"Morning," Mason said.

"Something wrong?"

Mason rubbed his chin and looked away. "Not good news. I've asked Davis to stop in for a chat, and I'll fill you in when he gets here."

He held up a can of Quixie. "Want one?"

She shuddered. "It's a little early for me to start on the red stuff. What gives?"

He took a long chug of the soda. "Just getting myself back to the brand, like we talked about yesterday. I hadn't realized how long it had been since I'd actually really stopped and tasted our product."

"Did you come to any conclusions?"

"As a matter of fact, I did," he said, leaning back in his chair. "For one thing, I think it's a pretty darned good waker-upper."

"Better than coffee?"

He shrugged. "I don't think we can claim that, based on the amount of caffeine in Quixie, but it's just as good as some of these high-priced energy drinks that are killing us at convenience stores."

"Hold that thought," Annajane said, grabbing a pen and a yellow legal pad from his desktop. "What else?"

"You were right about the taste of celebration. I'm thinking Quixie reminds people of good times, happy occasions, boat rides on the lake, summers at the beach, campouts under the stars. Fun, wholesome stuff. That's

381

what we started out selling, that's what we need to get back to."

"Riiiight," Annajane said. "We're on the same page so far."

They heard a tap on the door, and the sound of a throat clearing.

Davis leaned into the office, glancing from his brother to Annajane. "You wanted to see me?"

Mason stood up and walked around his desk, clasping his brother's hand. "Come on in."

"I'll talk to you later," Annajane said, making for the door.

"No, stay," Mason said. "But close the door behind you, please."

Davis, Annajane thought, was clearly uncomfortable being in a room with her. He tugged at the too-tight starched collar of his pale blue button-down shirt and made a point of taking a chair as far from hers as possible.

His face was jowly and sunburned, and his dark hair, already starting to recede, still bore damp comb marks. Unlike Mason, who usually wore khaki slacks and a Quixie logo shirt to work, Davis was, as always, impeccably turned out in an expensively tailored dark suit, a red silk tie with repp stripes, and black wingtip shoes polished to a low luster. A pair of flashy gold cuff links twinkled from the French cuffs of his shirt. He looked like a refugee from Madison Avenue.

When the three of them were seated, Mason solemnly handed cold cans of Quixie to his guests.

"Is this a stunt?" Davis asked, putting the can, untouched, on the edge of the desktop.

"Not at all," Mason said, edging the can back toward his brother. "Come on, Davis, at least take a sip. It won't kill you. You've been drinking it your whole life, for Chrissakes."

Davis rolled his eyes, sipped, and put the can back on the desk. "Happy now? Actually, I never liked the stuff. I'll take a Sprite or ginger ale any day."

Mason leaned back in his chair. "Well, that's one of the roots of our problem, right there."

"I resent that," Davis snapped.

"It's not meant as a personal criticism. I just don't see how you can sell what you don't like and don't believe in," Mason said, his voice mild.

"I believe in the company," Davis said. "I believe in profits. And I don't need a marketing lesson from you, thanks just the same."

Mason leaned across the desk, raising his hands, palm out, in a gesture of surrender. "Can we just have a friendly, nonconfrontational business discussion here?"

"You're the boss," Davis said. "What's on your mind?"

"Our marketing plan," Mason said. "Or the

lack of."

Davis's face reddened. "Look, if you want to second-guess me and rehire Farnham-Capheart, I guess you can do that, since you're the CEO. But I don't see the point in doing an end run . . ."

"I'm not second-guessing you," Mason said crisply. "And I have no intention of making an end run around you, which is why I asked you to meet with Annajane and me this morning. But I would like to point out that it would have been good if you, as a courtesy, had informed me that you intended to fire the ad agency we've been working with for more than thirty years."

"As vice president of marketing, that was entirely my decision to make," Davis said, glancing nervously over at Annajane. "If this Jax Snax deal happens, we'll be working with their agency, which happens to be the largest in the country, and anyway, Annajane, you said yourself you didn't like the tone of the new campaign . . ."

It was Annajane's turn to clear her throat. Her stomach roiled with nervousness, but something else was boiling up inside her. Anger.

"You deliberately sabotaged me," Annajane said quietly. "You and Celia suggested to Joe Farnham that he should hire me, because you were sure I would be 'uncomfortable' working with Celia after she and Mason got engaged. And then, as soon as I'd quit my job here, and days before I was to start there, you made sure I wouldn't have a job in Atlanta. That was petty, Davis. It was mean and it was low-down, and I really can't believe I've ever done anything to you to deserve that kind of treatment."

"Hey!" Davis said sharply. "This was nothing personal. It was business."

Mason looked stunned. "Is this true?" he asked Davis. "You angled Joe to give her a job — to get rid of her, because Celia didn't want her around?"

"I assumed you wouldn't want your ex-wife around," Davis said easily. "Because your fiancée sure as hell didn't. I just did what I thought you would have done — if you had any balls, which you apparently don't."

Mason's face darkened. "Annajane and I had managed to get along quite nicely for the past five years, without any help from you. She's been an important part of our team . . ."

"Oh please!" Davis broke in. "She came to work here because Dad thought she was a cute kid and she was married to you, and she stayed on after the divorce because you somehow felt guilty about the breakup. Well, that's on you, brother." He gave Annajane a pitying glance. "She hasn't had an original idea in years. Once Celia came on board, it was clear — to everybody but you — that we needed a new direction. I did what needed to be done. And I'd do it again."

Annajane felt her hands clench and un-clench with barely suppressed rage. Tears sprang to her eyes, and she blinked them back helplessly.

"That's enough," Mason roared. He pointed at his computer screen. "If you're such a marketing genius, explain to me why our sales have been sliding every quarter for the past two years. Also, explain why we're paying a six-figure promotional fee to a scum-bucket Nascar driver like Donnell Boggs, who not only hasn't placed in a race since we hired him, he's had two DUI arrests in the past six weeks." Mason flung a stack of auto-graphed glossy photos of Boggs, wearing a cap emblazoned with the Quixie logo, across the desk at his brother.

The photos fluttered to the floor. "That's the face you hired to be the face of Quixie?" Mason thundered. "Check the front page of today's *Charlotte Observer*. Or you can find the story online. It's on all the wire services. The Mecklenburg County Police arrested Boggs at a motel in Concord last night, where he'd checked in with a sixteen-year-old high school dropout, a quart of Tecate, and eleven hundred dollars' worth of Ecstasy."

Davis's ruddy face paled. "What? No. That's not possible. I talked to Donnell last night. He was heading to Spartanburg for the opening of a new Piggly Wiggly; then he was throwing out the first pitch at a minor league game in Greenville. It was Quixie night."

"He never made it to Spartanburg, or Greenville, thank God," Mason said. "He was too busy hooking up with a teenager he met online. I want him fired. Today."

"I can't fire him. He's got a contract," Davis said. "We've got all the summer promotional materials set. Cardboard cutouts of Donnell for all the displays, models of the number eight Quixie car. Supermarket openings, theme park promos. His picture is gonna be on the twelve-pack cartons. They go to the printers tomorrow. It's all set."

"Unset it," Mason said bluntly. "Do whatever it takes. Call our attorney and have him start the paperwork. I want that contract canceled based on the morals clause. I want the sponsorship deal ended, and I want our name painted over on his cars, even if you have to do it yourself. I don't want that degenerate turd's name mentioned in the same breath as Quixie."

"God," Davis said, burying his head in his hands. "We've spent thousands on this campaign. Hundreds of thousands. We'll have to do new ad buys, shoot new commercials . . . There's no time to create a new campaign from scratch."

"I can help with that," Annajane said.

Davis gave her a sour look.

"It's what Mason was just talking about. Returning to our roots. Retro. I've got all the old mechanicals and illustrations for the Quixie ads from the forties through the sixties," she said. "And I bet if I call Farnham-Capheart they've still got footage of the old commercials. We just clean up the graphics for the print ads, maybe reshoot some of the commercials, cut out the footage of Donnell and the Quixie car, maybe substitute with novelty bits from the old commercials. Make the new ones look like those old Dr Pepper ads everybody used to love. We can do Facebook pages, the works. If we get started right away, we should be able to pull it off."

"Fine," Davis said tersely. "You seem to have it all figured out. I'll leave it to you."

"Davis, enough!" Mason snapped. "Annajane didn't hire Donnell Boggs because she wanted to party with a bogus celebrity. You did. Now stop with the pissy attitude and let's get this fixed."

Davis stood abruptly and dumped his nearly full Quixie can into a metal trash can, where the sound of metal meeting metal made a hollow clang.

"You can't fire me," he told his brother. "And you can't stop the inevitable. You can slow it down, but only until next week, when old man Norris gets off his ass and tells us how the trust works. But we both know how it's gonna go down. Mama's tired of watch-

388

ing this company slide into the dumper. She'll vote to sell. And when that happens, you'll be out. I guarantee."

Mason watched his brother's exit with a pained expression on his face. He turned to Annajane. "Fun times, huh?"

She winced. "That was pretty brutal."

"At least we cleared the air," Mason said. "No more of this bullshit passive-aggressive radio silence. He knows how I feel, and I definitely know where he stands on things. Also, it's gonna be expensive, but at least we're shed of that slime-dog Donnell Boggs. I knew that guy was trouble the minute I laid eyes on him."

"I guess we're just lucky he got arrested before the new campaign rolled completely out," Annajane said.

"Luck had nothing to do with it," Mason said. "I've had a private investigator following him for weeks. As soon as he saw Boggs pull into the motel parking lot with that girl yesterday, he called me, and then he tipped the cops."

30

An unfamiliar woman's voice on the other end of the line asked, "Is this Annajane Hudgens?"

She glanced at the caller ID screen on her phone, but it said UNKNOWN.

"Yes," Annajane said cautiously. "Who's calling?"

"My name is Katie Derscheid. I'm a friend of a friend of your friend, Pokey Riggs. I understand you're interested in knowing something about Celia Wakefield and Gingerpeachy?"

Annajane's pulse quickened. She got up from her desk and closed and locked her office door. Just in case. She'd been working furiously all day, trying to rebuild and rebook the summer Quixie promotion, had even worked straight through lunch, so she'd fortunately managed to avoid Celia. But she wouldn't put it past Celia to be lurking somewhere nearby.

She sat back down at her desk and straightened her shoulders. "Hi Katie. I was actually going to call you today, until I got involved in putting out assorted forest fires around here." She lowered her voice til it was just above a whisper, and still deliberately avoided saying Celia's name out loud. Just in case. "So . . . you do know her?"

"Ohhhh yes," Katie Derscheid said. "She's, uh, not a friend of yours, is she?"

"No," Annajane said, a slight shiver going down her spine. "Definitely not."

"Oh goodie," Katie said. "Now we can really talk girl to girl."

Annajane laughed ruefully. "She's a bit of an enigma, isn't she?"

"She's a scorpion," Katie said. "Absolutely deadly. And not in a good way. She screwed my former company, Baby Brands, big-time."

"Interesting," Annajane said. "The company I work for, Quixie, hired, um, that person, as a consultant, based on her reputation as a sort of girl genius with branding and business development."

"Yeah, what's genius about Celia is her ability to totally bullshit her way through life," Katie said.

"Did she really sell her company for ten million? That's what we all heard. In fact, I think she kind of alluded to that herself."

"The purchase price was actually just under half that — five million," Katie said. "The deal was structured so that Celia would be paid in staggered amounts. She did take Baby Brands for more than a million in cash, but she'll never see another dime of their money — not if their lawyers have their say."

"Oh my," Annajane breathed. "So . . . what happened?"

"Smoke and mirrors," Katie said cryptically. "That was the essence of her company. When Baby Brands bought Gingerpeachy, they were told she had millions in orders from several chain retailers — Gymboree, Pottery Barn Kids, Macy's. We bought everything — the name, the outstanding orders, the inventory. And all of it was bogus. The order numbers were wildly inflated, and as for inventory — there was none. A couple bolts of fabric and a ton of factory seconds that were unsalable as far as we were concerned."

Annajane's eyes widened. "How did she manage to pull that off?"

Katie's laugh was the deep, throaty chortle of a woman who'd seen a lot. "Celia Wakefield has ESP — extrasensual perception. She meets a guy, and within a couple hours, he's begging her to 'beat me, hurt me, make me write bad checks.' "

"And that's what happened at your company?"

"She met the president of Baby Brands, Reeve Sonnenfeld, in the lobby bar at the Mansion at Turtle Creek, in Dallas, during the Winter Mart week. Celia was repping her own line in a little showroom at the time."

"I think I know where this is going," Annajane said. "She met my boss in the exact same way."

"Gotta love a gal who trolls hotel bars, right?" Katie said with a chuckle. "She's one step up from a whore, that Celia. Anyway, she strikes up a conversation with Reeve, tells him she's got this great line of dresses, reversible, all cotton — she even whips a sample dress out of her purse to show him. And then she acts all surprised when he tells her he IS Baby Brands. They have a couple more drinks; then Celia gives him her business card and takes off, leaving Reeve begging for another look, if you know what I mean. Of course, they meet later that night, after Reeve's wife Sandee has gone back to the suite."

"Right there in the same hotel with his wife?" Annajane asked.

"Oh, it was all business," Katie said. "At first. Reeve came back from Dallas raving about this brilliant young entrepreneur he was going to 'mentor.' It was revolting. I mean, she's two years younger than his daughter, for God's sake. Pretty soon, he's flying off to meet Celia in Atlanta and LA for Marts there, only those times, he made sure Sandee stayed home. Everybody in the company knew what was going on with those two.

Everybody but Sandee."

Annajane leaned back in her desk chair and looked out her office window. It was getting late in the day. The parking lot was emptying out. She got up and walked over to the window. If she stood at just the right angle, she could see Celia's parking space. It was empty. She exhaled noisily.

"Hey, are you still there?" Katie asked.

"I'm here," Annajane said. "What happened next?"

"The inevitable," Katie said. "Reeve got the brilliant idea to buy Gingerpeachy. As soon as the deal was inked, Celia and Reeve were history. And we were left holding a big bag of Gingerpeachy crap. It couldn't have happened at a worse time. You know what the economy's like."

"Is Baby Brands in trouble?" Annajane asked.

"They'll survive," Katie said drily. "Of course, it meant some belt tightening. Which meant I lost my job."

"Oh, wow, I'm sorry," Annajane said. "So, how does she get away with something like that? I mean, isn't what she did fraud or something?"

"Or something," Katie said. "It's all been kept pretty hush-hush. But yeah, I think Baby Brands has started legal action against Celia."

"You mentioned Celia met your vice president at a hotel bar," Katie said. "Are they

394

having a fling?"

"No. Davis was infatuated with her, but strictly on a professional basis, as far as I know," Annajane said. She was somehow reluctant to reveal to this stranger that Celia had targeted a much bigger fish at Quixie, in the form of Mason. "He brought her into the company as a consultant, based on what he thought was her marketing expertise and, of course, because of her track record starting and selling a successful retail business like Gingerpeachy."

Katie's laugh sounded sour. "Let me just fill you in on Celia Wakefield. First of all, is she still peddling that line of crap about how she designed the original PopTot dress?"

"Yeah," Annajane said. "I've seen the dresses. They really are adorable."

"They're very adorable," Katie said. "But there's some question of who actually came up with the idea for them."

"Really?"

"After Baby Brands bought out Gingerpeachy, *Parenting* magazine did a nice spread on the dresses," Katie said. "Not long afterwards, the reporter who did the piece called to let us know that *she'd* had a call from a woman claiming that Celia stole the idea from her."

"Why do I have a mental image of the theme music from *Jaws* in my head?" Annajane asked.

"A shark would be insulted to be compared to Celia," Katie said. "Celia happened to be working at a boutique and she got hold of one of this girl's sample dresses, which she was sewing at home with her mother. So Celia, sniffing an opportunity, drew up a business plan, hired a sewing room, and turned out a line of dresses exactly like the ones from the boutique. The next thing you know, she's the girl genius of retailing."

"Did you do anything to check out the other woman's claim?" Annajane asked.

"Nope," Katie said. "It's not like she trademarked the dresses. Anyway, there wasn't anything we could do about it. We listened to her story, but what could we do? We'd been victimized, too. By then, Celia was long gone."

"I know," Annajane said, putting down her pencil. "By then, she was here."

There was a knock at Annajane's office door. Her pulse quickened. "Katie, I have to go now. There's somebody at my door. Thanks so much for the information."

Mason stood in the hallway outside her office, his laptop case slung over his shoulder.

"Hey, you," he said, looking puzzled. "You're locking yourself in now?"

"Sorry," Annajane said. "I had so much going on; I just couldn't deal with distractions today."

"Wish I could lock myself in. Or other people out," Mason said. "Look, it's nearly six. Wanna go get some dinner?"

Annajane looked up and down the hallway. "I don't know," she murmured. "I've still got a ton of work to catch up on."

"Let it go until tomorrow," Mason said firmly.

"It's not just that," she said. "You know how people are. If they see us out together, it'll just fire up the rumor mill again."

"So?" He brushed his hand through his hair, impatient. "I've got news for you, Annajane. People in this town already think we're having some big flaming affair."

"I hate being the topic of gossip," Annajane said.

Mason rolled his eyes. "Me, too. Especially when I'm not even getting to do the things people suspect we're already doing." He caught her hand. "Come on. Please? We've wasted five years pretending we don't care about each other. I don't want to waste any more time. Do you?"

She felt so torn. She wanted to see him, be with him. Why was it so hard to say yes to making herself happy?

"Annajane?"

"All right," she said finally. "But I've got to finish up a couple things. I'll meet you. Where?"

"There's a new place, Blueplate, in

Creekdale. Where the old Emile's used to be? But it's silly to drive all the way over there in two separate cars. I'll go home, check on Sophie, shower and change, and meet you back here — in an hour?"

"It's a deal," Annajane said. On impulse, she leaned in and kissed him on the cheek.

He raised an eyebrow in surprise. "Now you're talking."

31

Blueplate was located in a small wood-shingled cottage set back from the road in Creekdale. Annajane had eaten there once when it had been Emile's, but hadn't cared for the ersatz French menu — or the haughty waiters.

Now, though, the place had been transformed. Rough whitewashed plaster walls replaced the overblown red damask wallpaper, and the furnishings were a friendly mélange of wooden tables and mismatched chairs. A small bar took up most of the entryway, and, beyond, they could hear the clatter of dishes and the hum of conversations in the dining room.

The hostess, a slender brunette with pale skin and tattoos wreathing both wrists, identified herself as Tabitha, the owner and wife of the chef, as she gathered up a menu and silverware for them.

"It's such an awesome night; I think we have a table out on the patio, if you want,"

Tabitha offered.

Annajane looked to Mason for approval. "That'd be great," he said. "We've both been cooped up in an office all day. It'll be nice to have some fresh air."

As they were led through the dining room, Annajane kept her face lowered and stayed a couple steps ahead of Mason. Realizing that she still felt awkward and self-conscious about being seen in public with him, she gave herself a mental scolding.

Stop hiding! You've done nothing wrong. Anyway, it's only dinner.

The patio was just as charming as the interior of the restaurant, with a rough-beamed peaked ceiling lined with twinkling white lights and a flagstone floor. Despite her earlier internal scolding, Annajane was grateful when the hostess seated them at a table shielded from the rest of the room by an enormous potted hydrangea whose platter-sized blue blossoms formed an effective screen.

They ordered drinks. Mason looked surprised at her order.

"Since when do you drink martinis?" he asked, sitting back in his chair and regarding her with interest. "You always used to like those girly drinks — what, cosmos?"

"Tastes change," she said lightly. "People change. But I know you still like bourbon."

"I've changed in other ways," Mason said.

400

"Older and wiser, I hope. More cynical, definitely."

A single candle in a low jar in the center of the table illuminated his face. She studied it now. His thick blond hair had a few streaks of gray, and crow's feet etched the corners of his eyes, which somehow seemed a deeper blue, not the clear blue she remembered from their youth. His jawline was still firm, and she realized, with surprise, that he seemed to have lost weight, his cheeks somewhat hollow, his worn blue blazer hanging awkwardly from his shoulders. And now that she thought about it, his khaki slacks bunched at the waist where his belt cinched them too tightly.

She wrinkled her forehead. "How much weight have you lost?"

He shrugged. "I don't keep track. Maybe twenty, twenty-five."

"You're not dieting, right? You never used to have a weight problem."

He shrugged. "Not dieting. Just kind of distracted with everything going on in my life."

Annajane laughed. "I wish I had that problem. I can't think of too many foods I don't like."

"Don't say that." His voice was sharp. "You're fine exactly the way you are."

The waiter brought their appetizer, a sizzling skillet full of sweet briny shrimp sautéed in garlic and olive oil, swimming alongside tiny Greek olives and feta cheese. A loaf of hot crusty bread accompanied the shrimp, and they busied themselves dividing up the shrimp, dipping the bread into the fragrant juices.

"Mmm," Annajane said appreciatively between bites. "Heaven. I like this place so much better than Emile's. I'll have to come back here."

"How was the rest of your day?" she asked, after the waiter removed the remains of the shrimp and brought their entrées.

Mason took a bite of his flounder, chewed, and considered. "Difficult. Davis is determined to battle me on every issue, large and small. Business decisions that should be routine, things like truck maintenance or contracts with vendors, all of a sudden, he's questioning, objecting to, second-guessing."

He shook his head. "It's like he feels like he has to stir every pot."

"Maybe he's trying to prove himself."

"To whom? He's family. It's not like I can fire him, as he so aptly pointed out today."

"I don't know," Annajane admitted. "Being an only child, your family dynamic is kind of hard for me to read. Maybe he feels he has to prove himself to himself. Or your mom." She took a sip of water and had another thought. "Or Celia."

"Celia," Mason put his fork down and frowned. "Much as it pains me, I think this is

402

a topic we can't keep avoiding."

"You don't have to talk about her," Anna-jane offered.

"Yeah. I do." He picked up his fork and took another bite of fish. And then another.

"It's like she casts this giant shadow over us. I can't get around it. Can't seem to get away from her."

Annajane giggled. "You make her sound like this huge presence, when in reality, she's this teeny-tiny little person."

He grimaced. "Her physical size is one of many deceptive aspects to Celia. I guess I found that out the hard way. It's like she . . . wills something, and it happens. She showed up at Quixie, and she was smart and hard-working . . ."

"And sexy," Annajane put in. "Glittery and fascinating and compelling."

"On the surface, maybe," Mason agreed. "But when you get her alone, one on one, after a while, you realize there's just nothing much there. She doesn't read, except busi-ness stories, doesn't watch movies or tele-vision, except CNBC. Really, the only thing I think she's passionate about is money. Mak-ing it, and spending it."

Annajane took a sip of the wine he'd ordered her, gathering courage. "You two did seem like an odd match to me."

"She was . . . different. I guess that's what fascinated me about her," Mason admitted.

"And okay, I was surprised she didn't go for Davis, the lady's man of the family. Maybe I was flattered that she was so openly pursuing me."

"Or your money," Annajane said, wondering if she should share what she'd just learned about Celia's business dealings with her ex-fiancé.

"Davis has as much money as I do," Mason pointed out.

"But maybe not as much power over the company. Anyway," she added, "I get what she saw in you — besides the financial aspect."

"And what would that be?"

She gave him a gentle smile. "Now you're just fishing for compliments."

"No. Seriously. Are you still attracted to me?"

Color crept into her cheeks and she looked away.

"Annajane?" His knee touched hers lightly under the table.

Another sip of wine. "I never stopped being attracted to you, but then you knew that. Even . . . when my world fell apart, it was so hard, being around you, seeing you, knowing what you were capable of."

He looked stricken. "How would I know what you were thinking back then? You deliberately cut yourself off from me. You wouldn't return my calls, or talk to me, or even listen to reason. And then Dad died . . ."

She sighed. "I was crushed. I couldn't stand to see you. It was so painful, knowing . . ."

"Annajane," his voice was even. He pushed his half-eaten dinner aside. "You've spent five years dodging me, hiding from me, even though all that time, I was right there. You told me earlier tonight that you've grown up. Matured. Are you finally ready to listen to me now?"

Her eyes met his. "Are you ready to tell me the truth?"

"I never lied to you about that night," he said, returning her gaze. "I was never unfaithful to you. Never even considered it. I loved you, and you were all I wanted."

She felt the old shame, the bitterness welling up in her throat. Unbidden, the memories of that night — the last night of their marriage — came flooding back.

"You never came home!" she said urgently. "You knew it was the company Christmas party, that I was counting on you. But you didn't even bother to call. I was humiliated. And then I really thought you'd been in an accident or something. You have no idea how terrified I was. But when you came home and acted as if I should have known it was 'just business' that you were out with that woman . . . Eva."

"Christ," he muttered. He leaned over and dabbed at her eyes with his dinner napkin.

405

"I'd completely blocked her name from my memory."

"I'll never forget her name," Annajane said, her voice wobbly. "Or her handwriting. On that CD I found in your car."

"Can I tell you something?" He took her chin and cupped it between his palms. "I couldn't tell you this that night. I wanted to, but I was so mad at you for thinking I'd cheated, my damned pride wouldn't let me."

"Tell me what?"

"You found that CD, but it wasn't mine. It was the company car, remember? I drove it to Atlanta and back, but it was the company car."

She stared. "Then, whose?"

"Dad's. God help me, it was Dad's."

She sat back, stunned. "Your father? He was the one having an affair with that Eva woman?"

Mason nodded sadly. "That's why we were so late getting back that night. We signed the papers for the Maxi-Mart deal, and we were all supposed to meet up afterwards at the Ritz-Carlton in Buckhead for dinner. Dad offered to drive Eva back to her hotel so she could change for dinner, and he made it clear to me that he didn't need me riding shotgun. So I stalled for a while, and finally caught a ride over to the Ritz with one of the Maxi-Mart guys. We had drinks in the bar, and waited . . . and waited. I kept excusing myself to go to the men's room, so I could call Dad's cell, but he wasn't answering. I didn't know what the hell to think."

"You had no idea he was seeing her?" Annajane asked.

"None," he said bitterly. "He knew I wouldn't put up with that crap. I caught him, once, years ago, with another woman. At the cottage at Wrightsville Beach. Pokey was with me. I confronted him; we had a huge blow-up. That's the summer I left town. I couldn't stand to look him in the face for nearly a year; I was so disgusted with him for cheating on Mom. On us."

"Pokey told me about that," Annajane admitted.

It was his turn to get taken by surprise. "She swore she'd never say a word. We both did."

"Relax," Annajane chided him. "She only told me the other night, at the hospital, while we were waiting for Sophie's surgery. She said that was how she knew you wouldn't have cheated on me. Because you didn't want to be like your dad."

Mason let out a long breath and sat back in his chair. "He was a hero to me in so many ways, you know? He was a great dad. As busy as he was with Quixie, he always had time to spend with us kids. And I know he loved my mother. You saw them together. He was devoted to her! So how could he? It made me sick to think about it."

"Your dad was a good man," Annajane said. "He did so much for this community, in Passcoe. He could have spent his time being just another rich prick, but he wasn't like that. He genuinely cared about people. And he did love your family. Especially Sallie. I guess maybe some men just compartmentalize things. They think sex and love are two different things, and it's okay to sleep around, as long as their wife doesn't find out and nobody gets hurt. I can't explain it, but I believe it's so."

"I'm not like that," Mason said evenly. "I'm not like him. Not that way."

"Tell me about that night," she urged. "I'm ready to listen now. I want to understand what happened."

He took a sip of wine and closed his eyes, remembering the evening. "It was getting late, so we finally ordered dinner," Mason said. "I was beginning to think I might have to cab back to the hotel and spend another night, because I had no idea where Dad and Eva were. Finally, at around ten o'clock, the two of them came strolling in, acting like nothing had happened. It was ten o'damned clock! We were the last party left in the dining room. The waiters were literally sweeping the floors and polishing the glasses in the bar."

"Did they have some kind of an explanation for where they'd been?"

"Dad had some lame-ass story about how they'd stopped for a drink on the way over and just lost track of time," Mason said, his lips curling in disgust. "It was a load of crap. He reeked of gin, and her hair looked like she'd just gotten out of bed. They were screwing their brains out in her hotel room. It didn't take an ace detective to figure it out. We ordered coffee, and finally, at eleven, I managed to drag him out of there. And then, on top of everything, it really did start snowing. The farther north of Atlanta we got, the icier the roads were."

"You should have called," Annajane said. "Just to let me know."

"I know I should have. Now," he said. "I was a selfish, self-centered idiot. I was so furious with Dad, I couldn't even speak. And he was half in the bag. He fell asleep as soon as he got in the passenger seat. I swear to God, more than once, as I was driving, I had the urge to reach over and throttle him. For what he'd put me through. And what he was doing to Mom. I didn't give a thought to you."

Annajane sighed. "Why didn't you just tell me that night — as soon as you got home?"

"I don't know," Mason admitted. "I remember how tired I was, and then you were so pissed at me; I just wasn't in the mood for a fight right then. I'd made up my mind, the next day, to have it out with Dad. I was seriously thinking, on that long drive home, maybe it was time to leave Quixie. Get out from under all the family drama, and see if I could make it on my own someplace else. I hated his guts that night."

"I wish I'd known," Annajane said.

"I shook him awake when we got to Cherry Hill that night," Mason said. "I didn't even cut the engine. I just said, 'We're home.' He got out of the car. He couldn't even look me in the eye. He could tell how angry I was. I think he said something like, 'Talk to you tomorrow,' and he staggered toward the front door. And I just drove off. Of course, the next time I saw him, he was barely alive. All I could think about was how I'd left it with him. 'We're home' — that's the last thing I ever said to my father."

"Oh, Mason," Annajane began.

Just then, Mason's cell phone began to ring. He looked annoyed but pulled it from his pocket and looked at the readout screen.

His expression softened as he saw who the caller was. "Hey, Soph," he said. "Everything okay?"

Mason listened for a moment, then laughed. "No, afraid not, punkin. Letha is the boss, and if the boss says you have to go to bed, then you'd better skedaddle. Okay? Hmm? Yeah, actually she's right here."

He handed the phone to Annajane. "Sophie would like a word with you."

"Hi, Sophie," she said.

"Annajane, Aunt Pokey says you spent the night at her house last night."

"That's right," she said cautiously.

"No fair!" the girl cried. "Petey and Denning and Clayton get all the fun. I want you to spend the night at my house."

"Not tonight," Annajane said. "Maybe the next time your daddy has to go out of town, I can come over and we'll have a spend-the-night party. Girls only! How would that be?"

"Come tonight," Sophie said.

"I can't tonight, sweetie," Annajane said. "It's a school night for you, and a work night for me."

"But Letha says I'm not going to school tomorrow, because I had an operation."

Annajane rolled her eyes at Sophie's logic. "I forgot about that. However, I still have to go to work. We'll have our slumber party. Soon. Okay?"

"Oh-kay," the child said reluctantly.

She handed the phone back to Mason, barely suppressing a yawn. "Speaking of skedaddling. Guess I better call it a night, too. I didn't get much sleep last night, and tomorrow, I think, is gonna be another killer day."

"We need to talk about something else," Mason said, keeping his voice low. "It's . . . about Celia."

Annajane put her wineglass down carefully.

"I'm listening."

"First, we need to talk about us," Mason said. "The other night, you told me — there was no us. There never could be. But then you broke your engagement to Shane. I'm kinda getting mixed signals here, Annajane."

She gave a wry smile. "I could say the same thing about you."

"Let me ask you something," Mason said, leaning forward so that his knees were touching hers under the table. "In a perfect world — where we hadn't split up, where there was no Shane and there was no Celia — do you think we'd still be together?"

"No," Annajane said.

His face fell.

"Not the answer you wanted, I know. But I just think our lives were veering so off track, we probably wouldn't have made it — even without the things that broke us up. Your family — mine — our jobs, our own selfishness, pride and insecurity, we had to work through all those things. I don't know about you, but I think I'm only just now really starting to figure out how to be a grown-up. So maybe now I'm almost ready to have a mature, committed relationship." She laughed. "Of course there's just one thing standing in the way of that."

"Celia."

Annajane shrugged.

"I can't," he started to speak, and then

reconsidered.

"No matter what else happens, I want you to know that I love you. I always have. That's never changed. Do you believe me?"

"I guess." Her pulse was racing. She glanced up at him, then looked away.

"No, that's not good enough," Mason said, taking her hand and looking directly into her eyes. "I need you to understand that there are things that are out of my control. Situations . . ."

She lifted her chin. "Why don't you just come right out and tell me what's going on?"

"She's pregnant," Mason said.

Annajane picked up her glass of wine and sipped slowly. She was aware of the hum of voices around them, the smell of a sizzling steak being carried to a table next to theirs, the easy jazz playing on the restaurant's sound system, the breeze rifling the fronds of the potted fern next to their table. A tiny piece of her brain noted these things and filed them away. *This is how it felt the night I learned I would never win the man I loved. I drank this wine and ate these foods, and I will never see or smell or taste these things again without thinking of that night.*

"What will you do now?" she asked, putting the wineglass down because her hand was starting to shake. She rested her left hand on top of her right, to keep it from trembling.

"I don't know yet," Mason said. "She just

413

told me a couple days ago."

Annajane bit her lip and looked away. "And she's sure?"

"So she claims," Mason said bitterly. "At first I couldn't believe it. I mean, we've been living apart for weeks now. She was obsessed with all this wedding stuff, and Sallie decided it didn't look right to Sophie for us to be living together, so Celia has pretty much been staying at Cherry Hill. Plus, I guess maybe I subconsciously knew I didn't want to go through with the wedding, because I just didn't have the desire . . ." His face colored briefly and he looked genuinely ill. "I couldn't even remember the last time . . ."

"I'll bet Celia could," Annajane said. She felt bile rising in her throat. Had Celia done this on purpose? Deliberately gotten pregnant just to make sure Mason would marry her?

"March," he said glumly. "She was on birth control, the patch. She claims it sometimes happens. But . . ."

Annajane was having a hard time catching her breath. It felt as though she'd been punched in the chest. She held up her hand, struggling to regain her composure. "I don't want to hear this, Mason. It's too personal."

"My God," he said, his voice breaking. "I never saw this coming."

Annajane sat back in her chair, easing her hand out from beneath his. She folded her hands in her lap, just for something to do.

"So now what?"

"Celia knows I'm in love with you. But she doesn't seem to care. She says she can't raise a child by herself. Not that I would let her. Celia's not really . . . maternal." He straightened his shoulders. "This is my responsibility. I'll just . . . have to figure out how to make it work."

Annajane could only nod. She felt her eyes filling with tears and was sure that everyone in the room was watching them. She fumbled with her napkin and tried to push her chair away from the table. But the chair caught on the edge of the tablecloth, and her glass of wine tipped over, sending a rivulet of sauvignon blanc flowing across the table and into his lap. "Damn. I'm sorry," she said, desperate for a way out. But her chair was stuck on the edge of a flagstone. "I need to leave. Right now. Please, Mason."

He caught the waiter's attention and asked for the check. In the car, he looked at her expectantly. "Where to? Pokey's?"

"No," Annajane said. "I don't think so. I'll just get a room at the Pinecone Motor Lodge."

He frowned. "A motel? Come on, that's crazy. I'll take you back to my place; you can have the guest room. It'll all be very circumspect. And if you're worrying about Celia, don't. She's been staying over at Cherry Hill."

"The Pinecone will be just fine for now,"

Annajane said. "It's under new management. It's clean and it's cheap, and that's really all I require for right now."

He gave it some thought. "That place is in the middle of nowhere. I don't like the idea of you driving out there at night like this. At least let me follow you there."

"Mason," she said calmly. "You forget I've been single for five years. I'm used to traveling alone, driving places by myself, checking into motels by myself. I appreciate your concern, but this really is no big deal."

"I don't like the idea of you staying in a motel. It's . . . seedy."

"This isn't really up to you," Annajane pointed out.

"I'm following you out there," he said, and the stubborn set of his jaw told her it was no use arguing.

The Pinecone Motor Lodge had been the only motel in Passcoe for as long as anybody could remember. Consisting of semicircle of a dozen small whitewashed frame cottages, it was set amid a thick grove of its namesake pine trees, and reached by a winding driveway leading off what had formerly been the main route into town.

Built in the postwar years as a tourist court, the Pinecone did a respectable business up until the 1980s, when the state built a bypass around it, traffic dwindled, and the Pinecone lost some of its luster. It changed hands a couple of times, then languished in foreclosure for two years, until a semiretired couple from Florida bought it to run as a hobby.

Mason had driven past the motel often in the past, duly noticing its slow deterioration. Now, though, he was relieved when his headlights revealed the changes brought about by two gay men and what must have cost several hundred thousand dollars.

The little cabins were gleaming white, with freshly painted dark green shutters with pine-tree-shaped cutouts. A neatly clipped boxwood hedge lined the front of each unit, and window boxes with perky red geraniums and trailing ivy flanked the doorways. Lanterns shone above every door, and on each miniature porch stood a pair of red-painted spring-back motel chairs.

She parked in front of a white bungalow with a small neon OFFICE sign. Mason pulled his car alongside hers. "Okay," Annajane said, when he rolled down his window. "See? It's perfectly respectable. You can go now."

"Nuh-uh," Mason said stubbornly. "Not til I see you safely inside."

The look she gave him was bleak and full of despair. "Just go," she said quietly. "Please?"

A small brass plaque on the office door requested that visitors RING BELL AFTER 10 PM. It was five past, so she hesitated, but then

417

pushed the doorbell. A moment later, a lean man with a deep mahogany tan and a shiny bald head opened the door.

"Come on in," he said, before she could ask about a room.

She found herself in a small entry hall. Her host, who was barefoot and dressed in a wildly flowered Hawaiian shirt and baggy white shorts, stepped behind a tall antique oak reception desk.

"I'd like a room, if you've got one," Annajane said.

"One? I've got eight or nine," he said. "You can have your pick."

"Oh," she said. "I'm sorry. Is business that slow?"

"Don't mind me," he said. "Thomas — that's my partner — he says I'm a chronic complainer. Actually, business is a little better than we'd expected. We've been full every weekend this spring, and word is starting to get around about our little restoration project and the new management."

"I've been hearing good things," Annajane said.

"Just a single tonight?" he asked, peering over her shoulder out the window, where Mason sat patiently in his car.

She blushed. "Yes. My, uh, friend just wants to make sure I get checked in all right."

"Ain't none of my business," he said airily. "We're strictly don't ask, don't tell around

418

here. Now. We're an entirely smoke-free facility, but from the looks of you, I'd say you're not a smoker anyway. Also, all the cottages have kitchenettes, with refrigerators and microwaves, a coffeepot, and toaster. But we also have a coffee hour here in the office-slash-reception area, from seven to nine every morning. We do fruit, and whatever kind of muffins Thomas feels like baking that day. And coffee and tea, of course."

"How nice," Annajane said.

He pushed the registration book toward her and turned to get a key. "Here you are," he said, pushing an old-fashioned brass skeleton key with a silken red tassel hanging from it across the desktop. "You'll be in unit six. It's my favorite — so quiet, and there's a pink rosebush just blooming its head off right outside your window. If you do decide to have company, there's a new pullout sofa and a spare set of sheets and pillows in the top of your closet."

"Fine," Annajane said absentmindedly as she tried to remember her car's license number. She handed him back the registration book, and he glanced down at it.

"Oh. You're from Passcoe?" He peered at the book through the wire-frame glasses perched at the end of a long, bony nose.

"Yes," she said. "I just sold my loft, downtown, and we had to close much quicker than I'd anticipated, so I'm sort of homeless for the moment."

He nodded. "I can offer you our weekly rate, if you like. It'll save you about twenty-five dollars a night."

"All right," she agreed. "I'm sort of in transition right now. I'm not really certain whether I'll even decide to stay in town, or for how long."

She opened her billfold, took out her credit card, and handed it to him.

"Annajane Hudgens," he said, reading the charge plate aloud. He stuck out his hand, and she shook it. "Welcome home, Annajane. I'm Harold, and I run the place. Have you always lived in Passcoe?"

"Just about," she said. "I'm a native."

"You're lucky to be from such a beautiful place. Thomas and I just love it here," he confided. "As far as we're concerned, you can have Miami."

Annajane put the credit card away. "You might change your mind come February, when it's fifteen degrees here, and in the eighties in Florida."

"Never," he declared. "Now, don't be a stranger. We'll expect to see you in the morning for coffee."

"Maybe," she said. "I leave for work pretty early."

"Where do you work?"

"Quixie. The soft drink company?"

"Quixie, we adore it! We've even been talking about buying cases of it, so we can put a bottle in every room. Guests love that kind of local stuff."

"Let me know if you want to pursue that," she said, ever the marketing professional. "I can get one of our sales reps to talk to you about adding the Pinecone to one of the regular routes."

"Perfect!"

She picked up her key. "Good night, Harold."

"Good night, Annajane."

32

Mason kept watch until he felt certain Anna-jane was safely inside her unit at the Pinecone Motor Lodge. Finally, when he saw lights blink on inside the cabin, he reluctantly drove home.

Letha had left the porch light burning for him. He didn't bother to drive around to the garage, instead parking by the front door and leaving his car there.

He went into the kitchen and saw that she'd left him a paper plate of food neatly covered with aluminum foil, which he dumped into the trash.

Stepping softly, he climbed the stairs to the second floor. He opened Sophie's bedroom door and peeked inside. A pink-shaded nightlight shone from an outlet beside her bed, and he could see her blond curls spilling out on her pillow. Mason sat lightly on the edge of the bed and looked down at her. Five years ago, he'd been terrified at the idea of raising a baby. She'd been so tiny, so sickly, so helpless.

He'd been lucky to find Letha, who was Voncile's sister-in-law and, like Voncile, a widow. She'd raised three of her own children and taken care of numerous grandchildren. She was as skinny as Voncile was stout, with improbably dyed frizzy red hair and pale blue eyes. Letha was calm and loving and untroubled by Sophie's bouts of colic and sleeplessness. But even with Letha hovering nearby, Sophie seemed to prefer Mason's presence to her nanny's. For the first six months after he'd brought her home, he'd fallen asleep in a chair beside her crib more nights than he could count, with the fretful infant hugged tightly to his chest.

Mason wondered what Sophie's reaction would be to having another baby supplant her in his affections. Sibling rivalry? And how would Celia treat Sophie after her own baby was born? She'd never really seemed the maternal type to him. He'd somehow managed to sublimate that during the short time they'd been dating. Celia was fun, she was lively, she was undeniably attractive, and undeniably attracted to him.

But there was an undercurrent there, a layer of dark and cold he could never pierce, and didn't actually care to try.

Sophie stirred and he laid a hand on her back. Her face relaxed, and he felt himself responding in kind. He wound one of the silky corkscrew curls around his finger. Finding out about Sophie's existence had been a shock, but now he couldn't imagine his life without her. He had to believe that he would come to feel this way about Celia's baby, too. Even if he knew he would never actually love her the way he'd always expected he would one day love the mother of his children. That love, Mason thought, belonged to another. To Annajane.

Sophie turned slightly, and the shift exposed her pocketbook, which she'd hidden beneath her bedsheet. It had been a birthday gift from Annajane last year and had quickly become his daughter's most treasured possession, which she rarely let out of her sight. Whenever anything small disappeared around the house, they all knew to check Sophie's pocketbook. She was especially fond of anything shiny. More than once he'd had to retrieve from the pink plastic purse a favorite silver Mont Blanc cartridge pen, various keys, and even a small antique sterling silver penknife that had been a high school graduation gift from his grandfather.

Soon now, he thought, they would have to discourage her unauthorized acquisitions. But for now, Sophie's hoarding of trinkets was harmless. He leaned down, planted a kiss on the top of her head, and stood up. He was suddenly exhausted.

Inside the master suite, he placed his watch,

wallet, and cell phone on the bathroom vanity. He brushed his teeth and stripped to his boxers, leaving his clothing in a heap on the floor, reverting to his messy bachelor habits.

Mason dropped onto his unmade bed and pulled the sheet up at the same time he glanced at the clock radio on the nightstand. It was just after 11:00 P.M. He bunched his pillow under his head. The pillowcase was warm! He turned on his side and a pair of sinuous bare arms wrapped around his own bare shoulders.

"Surprise!" Celia whispered.

"Jesus H.!" Mason exclaimed. He sat bolt upright in the bed and switched on the lamp. "What the hell are you doing here?"

Celia blinked rapidly. "For goodness sake," she said, laughing. "It's not like I broke in. I have a key, remember?"

She gave him a lazy smile and raised the hem of the sheet to show him that she was completely nude. "I didn't think you'd mind," she said, propping herself up on one elbow to give him an even better vantage point. She reached for his hand and placed it on her right breast.

He snatched it back.

"This isn't funny, Celia," he said.

Her eyes narrowed. "It's not supposed to be funny, darling," she said slowly. "It's supposed to be a turn-on. Do you have any idea how many men fantasize about coming home and finding a nude blonde in their beds?"

"I am not one of those guys," Mason said flatly.

She sat up in the bed, allowing the sheet to fall around her waist to give him a better understanding of the extent of her endowment. And she was admittedly gifted in that particular department. Celia's breasts would probably be considered one of the seven wonders of the modern world to any other man with a pulse. But right now they didn't do a thing for him. God help him. She parted her lips slightly and gave him a come-hither look that had once had an appalling effect on him. Now? Nada.

"Don't do this," he said.

"Do what?" She slid closer to him on the bed and casually rested her hand on his crotch. He jumped as though he'd been bitten by a rattlesnake.

He picked her hand up and dropped it onto the sheet. "That," he said, frowning. "I've had a hell of a long day, and I am really not in the mood for this kind of a stunt."

"It's not a stunt," she said, looking hurt. "I'm trying to remind you of why we got together in the first place. It's been so long. I love you and I've missed you. Is that a crime?"

He shook his head. "Does Sophie know you're here?"

"No," she said. "She and Letha were both

sound asleep when I let myself in an hour ago. Which reminds me. Where have you been all night? And don't tell me you were at the office, because I checked, and your car was gone." She leaned in closer and sniffed. "You've been drinking wine?"

"I was out," Mason said. "Having dinner with Annajane." Maybe, he thought, his mood black, if he infuriated her enough, Celia would leave.

"Oh Annajane," Celia said with a dismissive shrug. "Did you tell her about the baby? Or are we going to let Bonnie Kelsey break the news to her?"

"She knows," Mason said. He stood up, looked around, and saw where she'd neatly folded her clothes on the armchair at the foot of the bed. He snatched them up and threw them at her. "Come on, Celia. Get dressed. I don't want Sophie to wake up and find you here."

"Darling, please come back to bed and stop being such a prude," Celia said, patting the mattress. "We've made love lots of times right here in this bed with her in the next room, and it never bothered you before."

It actually *had* bothered him, he thought ruefully. But not enough to induce him to turn Celia out of his bed.

"I was a hypocrite," Mason said. "That stops now." He jerked his head in the direction of the door. "Please go."

"And what if I won't?" Celia said playfully. "Are you going to pick me up and bodily throw me out of the house? With Sophie and Letha sleeping right next door?" She gave a look of mock horror.

Mason's face hardened. He stomped into the bathroom and pulled on the clothes he'd just removed. He went back to the bedroom and sat on the armchair.

"Look," he said. "Don't make this any more difficult than it has to be. You and I are going to have to come to some kind of an arrangement."

"I can't wait to hear this," Celia said. "Do explain."

He hesitated. "I am willing to marry you, and be a father to our child. But that will be the extent of my obligation to you. I'm not in love with you, and I won't pretend to be."

She arched an eyebrow. "So . . . you're telling me you'll live with me, but you won't make love to me?"

He recoiled for a moment. "If that's how you choose to put it, yes."

Celia laughed. "That's so noble of you, Mason. So gentlemanly. And what if I tell you I don't want to marry you under those conditions? In fact, what would you say if I told you I might decide not to have the baby after all?"

He felt his heart contract. "You wouldn't do that," Mason said. "Because that baby is the only hold you have over me." He looked at her coolly. "I no longer kid myself that you're infatuated with me. I realize you only got involved with me because you had some notion of a payday."

"You have such a low opinion of yourself," Celia said. "It never occurred to you I fell in love with you?"

"It did," he admitted. "But then I realized what a fool I've been."

She leaned forward. "I really do love you, you know. I could make you happy, if you'd let me."

"Don't insult my intelligence," Mason said. "Just go, would you?"

Celia's eyes blazed. "If I leave here tonight, Mason, it will be for good. I mean that. You won't see me, or our child, again. Ever. You see, I'm an all-or-nothing kind of girl."

It was the one threat he feared, the thing that had gnawed at his gut since the moment she'd told him about the baby. He knew Celia would think nothing of depriving the baby of a father, if it meant getting vengeance against him. The idea of her raising his child, his own flesh and blood, gave him a sick, terrifying feeling. He would do anything in his power to keep that from happening. And she knew that, of course.

Celia knew she'd won. She leaned back against the headboard, allowing the sheet to slip downward again. "I'm tired," she said, raising her arms over her head for an exaggerated stretch. "It's much too late for a woman in my condition to be driving around at night. Anyway, we have a wedding to plan, don't we? How's Saturday for you?"

"I'll leave that up to you," Mason said. "But no church. No reception, none of that. Just you, me, and a justice of the peace."

"You really know how to romance a woman," Celia said bitterly.

"This isn't about romance. It's about duty. And decency," he added. "If you won't leave, I will. Just make sure you're gone before Sophie wakes up in the morning."

"Where do you think you're going?" Celia demanded.

"Anywhere but here," Mason said.

33

Annajane smelled baked goods as she opened the door into the Pinecone's office-slash-lounge. "Well, hello!" Harold was dressed in a different Hawaiian shirt and baggy blue jeans. He wore a faded baseball cap, and he was setting a tray with mugs and saucers on one of two bistro tables by the window. "I'm so glad you came in."

"Thomas?" he called out.

Another tall, skinny, bald man with a long nose came bustling out from what must have been the kitchen. He looked enough like Harold to be his twin brother, but he was wearing a white butcher's apron, and he held an enormous napkin-covered basket of muffins.

"You're just in time; these are still warm from the oven," the baker said, setting the basket down on the table with the mugs. "These are date-nut muffins. My grandmother's recipe."

"Thomas, this is Annajane, the young lady

I told you about earlier. She's going to stay with us for the week. And she works at Quixie. Isn't that fun?"

"Very fun," Thomas agreed. He held out his hand, which was dusted with flour; wiped it on his apron; and then extended it again. "So nice to meet you. I guess Harold told you we're complete Quixie fanatics. I'm serious. It's . . . so essentially southern tasting. Like grits or homemade peach ice cream. It tastes like Dixie, right?"

Annajane's eyes widened. "What did you just say?"

"What? The part about it being better than grits? Or the part about it tasting like Dixie?" Thomas asked.

"Ohmygod!" Annajane breathed. She reached for the pen on the reception desk and started scribbling. Then she turned around, waved the paper under Thomas's nose, and proceeded to kiss him on the mouth.

"What was that for?" he asked, clearly startled.

"I think you just came up with our new slogan," she told him. "Quixie — the Taste of Dixie!"

"I did that?" Thomas said, looking pleased.

She nodded enthusiastically.

"I did that!" Thomas told his partner.

Harold rolled his eyes. "There'll be no living with the man now. He's been tinkering with making Quixie muffins, you know. He's gone completely bonkers over the stuff."

"Totally kooky, right?" Thomas said. "So far, I can't get the consistency right, but I'm not giving up. I know there has to be a way to bake with that stuff."

Annajane sat down at the table, and Harold and Thomas joined her. Thomas poured her a mug of coffee, and she inhaled the fumes gratefully before taking a sip.

It was funny. Her life had come apart at the seams last night, and yet here she was, calmly having coffee and muffins with a pair of total strangers, still chatting about Quixie, selling the product for all she was worth.

Later on today, she would have to figure out how to start rebuilding a life for herself. But for right now, indulging in a decent cup of coffee and some hot sugary treats wasn't a bad beginning to a new day. Plus she had a new slogan. So maybe the day didn't totally suck. Yet.

"You know," she said, reaching for a muffin and peeling the paper liner off. "The company did a Quixie cookbook, way back in the '60s, I think. It has all kinds of crazy recipes in it — Quixie Jell-O salad, Quixie layer cakes, Quixie barbecue sauce. I'm sure there must be some kind of muffin recipe, too. I think there's still a box of them somewhere around the office. I'll bring you one if you like."

"I'd love that," Thomas said. "How long do you think you'll be staying with us, Miss Annajane?"

"Just long enough to figure out what comes next."

34

Annajane sat at her desk and forced herself to go through the motions of doing her job. It was the one thing she was good at. Doing her job. She dashed off a memo to Davis about her proposal for the new Quixie slogan and sent another to route sales, asking them to drop off six cases of soda at the Pinecone Motor Lodge.

Celia Wakefield had taken her man, but, so far, she hadn't succeeded in destroying that last piece of her life.

She had decided on the drive in to work that she would keep her promise to Mason. And she intended to go out with a flourish. The summer campaign, she'd decided, would break all sales records. And then she would hit the road. Annajane had no intentions of hanging around to watch Celia's belly grow and expand with Mason's child.

As luck would have it, she was just pulling into her slot in the parking lot when Mason drove up. There was no time to duck down in

435

the seat or pretend she hadn't seen him. She took a deep breath and got out of the car and locked it. She could maintain her dignity and act as though nothing had happened between them. Because essentially, nothing had. Or would.

"Good mor . . ." she started to say, but she thought better of it when she got a good look at him.

Mason's eyes were heavily shadowed, his hair uncombed. He obviously hadn't showered or shaved, and he was dressed in the same clothes he'd worn to dinner the night before.

"Are you all right?" she asked, picking a pine needle from the sleeve of his shirt.

"Fine," he said, hoisting the strap of his briefcase onto his shoulder.

"You look like hell," Annajane said. "Didn't you go home after you left me last night?"

"I did," Mason said, trying unsuccessfully to smooth his hair. "But Celia was there. In my bed," he added, with a scowl. "So I took an impromptu camping trip."

"Camping?" Annajane asked, bewildered.

"I slept at the lake house," Mason said, his tone sour. "Or tried to, anyway. Between the raccoons and the pigeons roosting in the rafters, I didn't get much rest."

He eyed her warily. "How about you? How was the Pinecone?"

"Delightful," she said. "I slept like a baby."

"Glad to hear somebody did," he muttered. They were standing at the employee entrance to the plant. He held the door open for her.

"Annajane," he started.

"Mason, I really need to get in and get started on my work," she told him. She squared her shoulders and headed down the hall. "We've gotta sell some cherry soda today."

Once at her desk, she spent half an hour scanning online job listings for marketing positions. She e-mailed her résumé to a couple of former colleagues from her Raleigh days and called Joe Capheart to let him know she'd used him as a reference.

Then she got back down to soft drink business. She went to the break room and begrudgingly fed four quarters into the vending machine for a can of Quixie, hoping for some kind of inspiration.

As always, the combination of carbonation and the sharp-sweet taste of cherries gave her a start. Quixie was something special, she reminded herself, something worth saving.

She got a begrudging "Good idea" e-mail back from Davis, approving the new "Taste of Dixie" slogan. Then she spent the morning on the phone, talking to bottle manufacturers about copying the Quixie glass bottle from the '50s. She'd located the old molds from the bottles in a dusty corner of the warehouse, and now her challenge was to find a company willing to copy the old molds and start producing new bottles immediately.

There was a soft tap on her office door. Before Annajane could call out, the door opened and Voncile stepped inside. "Annajane? Can I talk to you?"

"Sure," Annajane said, rolling her chair away from her desk. "What's up?"

Voncile closed the door and locked it, then sat nervously in a chair opposite the desk, pulling the skirt of her sensible brown cotton skirt even farther down over her knees.

She folded her hands in her lap and blinked rapidly, opening her mouth, then closing it again, before finally the words came out in a torrent, her voice shaking with fear and indignation.

"I have worked for this company since I was fifteen years old. I worked for Mr. Glenn, God rest, and then I was so happy to go to work for Mason. And when he brought Sophie home, I prayed about that, and I called up my sister-in-law, Letha, and told her he needed a good woman to take care of that precious baby. And I have been with this company for thirty-two years."

"I know that," Annajane said reassuringly, wondering what this was all about. "And I know Mason and the rest of the family appreciates you and Letha's dedication."

Voncile nodded. "Last year, Mason said he

438

was gonna have to quit naming me Employee of the Month because I'd already won it so many times it was making some people jealous. He said he was just going to go ahead and name me Employee of the Millennium and be done with it. But I never did get a certificate or anything."

"I think that was just Mason's idea of a joke, Voncile," Annajane said.

Voncile shrugged. "You know, Annajane, I've been praying for you and Mason to get back together. It was a sad day for all of us when you two split up. Miss Celia is nice, and she certainly seems to know a lot about business, but just between the two of us, I think you would make a better mama for Sophie. Not that it's any of my say-so."

"That's very sweet of you to say," Annajane said demurely. "And I appreciate your prayers. But I think it's best if Mason and I go our separate ways."

Voncile gave Annajane an appraising look. "You know I do not listen to gossip. The Bible says, 'A gossip betrays a confidence; so avoideth a man who talks too much.' That's Proverbs 20:19. You could look it up. But Troy Meeks is a good man, and he said the talk around town is that you and Mason have gotten back together again. Is that true?"

Annajane felt herself blush. "Well, uh, not really. I think maybe Troy misunderstood. Mason and I are just friends."

"But you didn't marry that boy down in Atlanta." She nodded pointedly at Annajane's left hand. "You're not wearing your engagement ring. And you didn't take that job down there," Voncile protested. "I thought that meant Mason was going to ask you to marry him."

"I'm afraid not," Annajane said, fervently wishing for an end to the conversation. "Was there something specific on your mind, Voncile?"

The older woman stared down at the floor. "One of the girls in accounting told me the company is in such bad shape, we might get sold off. She said she heard Davis is already talking to some company in New Jersey that wants to buy us."

Mason had sworn her to secrecy, but obviously news of the Jax Snax offer had begun to leak out. She didn't want to lie to Voncile, but she also didn't want to keep the rumor mill going.

"Yes," she said finally. "I do know that there is a company that's approached the family about selling Quixie. But as you may know, Glenn Bayless established an irrevocable trust shortly before he died that prohibited a sale for five years after his death."

"It was five years this past Christmas that Mr. Glenn passed away," Voncile pointed out.

"Right. And next week, I think, Thomas Norris, Glenn's attorney, is going to let the family know how Glenn wanted the company left to his heirs. Until the family finds that out, any talk of a sale is premature," Annajane said, trying to choose her words carefully.

"Mason wouldn't sell us out," Voncile said flatly. "He knew what this company meant to his daddy. And his granddaddy. He wouldn't let that happen. Right?"

Sometimes, Annajane thought, *doing the right thing means doing the wrong thing for the people you care most about.*

"Mason cares deeply about his responsibilities," Annajane said. "But I'm afraid it isn't just up to him. Davis and Pokey and Sallie will probably all have a say in what happens."

Voncile's breathing grew rapid, and two bright pink splotches appeared on her heavily powdered cheeks. "I was afraid of that. If outsiders buy Quixie, what will happen to all of us?" She nervously chewed her lower lip. "I need this job, Annajane. My Claude, rest his soul, didn't leave me hardly anything when he passed. If we get bought out, those New Jersey folks won't want a fifty-nine-year-old like me with bad knees and fallen arches, even with all my Employee of the Month certificates. And I'd lose my health care. Annajane, I have the sugar diabetes. And hypertension. I can't afford those pills without my health care plan."

Annajane nodded in sympathy. "Nothing's

been decided yet, Voncile, so please don't go getting yourself all upset. It's true that Davis is in favor of the sale. But Mason doesn't want to sell, and neither does Pokey."

"And what about their mama? Miss Sallie? She wouldn't let them sell Mr. Glenn's company, would she?"

"I'm not sure," Annajane admitted. "Really, nobody knows how this will all be settled until Mr. Thomas meets with the family next week to explain about Glenn's trust."

Voncile clucked under her breath. "Rest his soul. This company was Mr. Glenn's baby. I just pray he fixed it up good with the lawyers so things can stay the way he intended."

Annajane stood up and patted the older woman's shoulder. "I hope your prayers get heard, Voncile."

Voncile raised her eyes heavenward. "My faith is in the Lord," she said solemnly. "But sometimes, the lambs of the flock have to rise up and take care of themselves. Sometimes, it is up to the righteous to do the Lord's work here on earth for him."

"Okay, then," Annajane said, walking Voncile back out into the hallway. She wondered, for only a brief moment, what kind of measures the righteous would take to cast somebody like Celia out of Passcoe. And then she got back to work.

At midmorning, she ran to the ladies room down the hall, pushed open the heavy door, and ran smack into Celia herself, who was standing in front of the mirror, touching up her already-flawless makeup.

Annajane nearly did an about-face. But after drinking all that Quixie, she desperately needed to pee, and there was only one lady's room in the plant, and this small, two-stall bathroom was it.

She nodded curtly at Celia and went to open the door of the nearest stall. It didn't budge. She glanced downward and saw that it was occupied. As was the one next to it. There was nowhere to hide. Annajane crossed her arms over her chest and stood with her back to the paper towel dispenser, staring up at the ceiling as though it were the Sistine Chapel.

Celia was in no particular hurry. She took a large brush and dusted her face with tinted mineral powder. Rummaging in her cosmetic bag, she brought out an eyebrow pencil and applied short, feathery strokes to her pale brows.

A toilet flushed, and Patsy, one of the girls from accounting, emerged from the stall. She looked from Annajane to Celia and scurried out of the bathroom without even stopping to wash her hands.

Grateful for a reprieve, Annajane ducked into the stall. The toilet next to hers flushed, and she watched while a set of cheerful red ballet flats walked out of the stall. She heard water running, and then the sound of the bathroom door closing. She waited for another two minutes, just to make sure the coast was clear, before emerging.

Her heart sank when she saw Celia, standing at the mirror, fully made up, an odd, fixed smile on her face.

Annajane stood at the sink and washed and dried her hands. She stepped past Celia and reached for the door handle, but Celia neatly stepped sideways, effectively blocking her exit. "Excuse me," Annajane said.

"I'll only take a moment of your precious time," Celia said. "And then I'll let you get back to packing up your shit and getting the hell out of this company."

"This is not happening to me," Annajane muttered. She reached for the door again, but Celia slapped her hand away.

"Oh, honey, it *is* happening," Celia said. "So you better pay attention. Because I need to have a few words with you."

"Whatever," Annajane said. "What's on your mind, Celia?"

"*You* are on my mind," Celia said, poking her index finger into Annajane's clavicle. "Every time I turn around, Annajane Hudgens, there you are. At my wedding," she poked Annajane. "In the ambulance on the way to the hospital." Another poke. "At the freakin' hospital." Yet another poke. "Fucking my fiancé in a fucking cornfield. And, oh yes, at a restaurant, last night. Did you think I wouldn't find out about that?" She poked Annajane again. "Did you?"

Annajane caught Celia's hand roughly. "Do. Not. Touch. Me," she said. "Ever." She squeezed Celia's fingers together tightly and then released.

Celia laughed. "You have been messing with Mason's mind for months now. Making an exhibition of yourself. The whole town is laughing at you. Yeah. But that ends right now. I saw the two of you talking out in the parking lot this morning. Very touching. Heartbreaking, almost. Was he telling you good-bye? Did he mention that we've rescheduled the wedding for tomorrow?"

A wedding? Saturday? Annajane felt as though she'd been slapped across the face, but she would not give Celia the satisfaction of registering her shock.

"No," she said lightly. "He didn't get around to a wedding announcement. But he did tell me that last night he slept on the floor of the lake house, with the raccoons and the pigeon poop and the mildew and the roaches, rather than share a bed with you."

"Don't kid yourself that he's had a change of heart, Annajane dear. One little night apart won't hurt me. Because he'll be sharing my bed for years and years to come," Celia gloated. She stepped aside and held the bathroom door open with a flourish. "And

445

don't bother to wait on an invitation to the wedding. This time, it's strictly a private *family* affair."

35

"Voncile," Celia said, walking into Mason's outer office. Her voice dripped saccharine. "Don't you look nice today? I love that shade of chocolate on you. So flattering with your coloring."

Mason's assistant looked up at Celia. "Thank you," she said, preening just a little, patting her hair and straightening the collar of her blouse. "You look nice, too. But I'm afraid Mason asked me to tell people he can't be interrupted today. He's trying to catch up on work."

"Actually, I came in here to speak to you," Celia said. She perched on the edge of the chair opposite Voncile's. "I'm so excited," Celia confided. "We've rescheduled the wedding for tomorrow."

"Congratulations," Voncile said politely.

This traitorous Bible-thumping cow will be the first to go after we get back from the honeymoon, Celia told herself. *Mason needed a younger, smarter, more attractive woman for an administrative assistant. Although . . . not too much younger. And not much more attractive. At least he could find somebody with two years of college, for God's sake. Mason might put up a little resistance, but after he realized how much more time he would have for his personal life, once the office was running efficiently, he would be grateful for her input.*

"But I need your help," Celia said. "I have a million things to do to get ready by tomorrow and we don't want Mason to be bothered with the trivial details of a wedding, do we?"

"Well," Voncile said, reluctantly.

"Fine," Celia said. "I'll e-mail you the checklist. It's nothing really. We've already gotten the marriage license, of course. We're just going to have a very small, private ceremony, at Cherry Hill. Very cozy. So I'll need you to line us up a justice of the peace, and then you can call the florist and arrange for flowers. I've sent you a detailed memo about the flowers, so don't let them talk you into some tacky daisy and carnation horror. And talk to the caterer from the country club, see if they'll just do some nice appetizers and deliver them to the house. And wine, we'll need some champagne — I doubt if Sallie has anything decent at her house, so I need you to go to that nice wine shop over in Southern Pines. Get a couple bottles of Vueve Clicquot, and maybe a nice red. I'll research it and e-mail you what we need . . ."

Voncile had been dutifully scribbling notes, but now she put down her pen. "No ma'am," she said.

"Excuse me?" Celia said, staring.

"I am a godly woman. A deaconess. I've never set foot in a liquor store in my life," Voncile said. "And I'm not starting now."

"Oh, Voncile, of course you don't have to go into the store," Celia said sweetly. "I'll arrange to have them bring it out and put it in your car. All right? They can put it in your trunk so you don't even have to look at it."

"Well," Voncile said, not convinced. "What if somebody saw those men putting liquor in the trunk? I have people in Southern Pines. It wouldn't look right."

Celia narrowed her eyes. "Voncile, I really, really need you to do this. I'm sure Mason will be happy to give you a little time off so you can drive over there to pick it up for our wedding. And of course, we'll pay for your gas and mileage."

"All right," Voncile said reluctantly. She'd been outmanuevered and she knew it. "Since this is for your wedding, I will make an exception this one time."

"Fine!" Celia said brightly. "It will mean a lot to Mason to know you're doing this for our special day. And you'll let me know right away, won't you, as soon as you've lined up the justice of the peace?" She gave a self-satisfied little smile. "Since you work so

449

closely with Mason, I guess it won't hurt to let you in on a little secret. I'm expecting! And I want the ceremony done before I start to show."

Voncile's expression remained wooden. "Yes, ma'am."

Gone, Celia told herself, *as she hurried back to her office. That woman is so gone.*

She sat down behind her desk and went back to the list she'd been working on. Flowers. A bouquet for herself, something elegant but understated to go with the dress she'd actually intended to wear to the wedding reception before the church wedding was postponed. A boutonniere for Mason, and a corsage for Sallie, of course. Sophie? Definitely not. She wouldn't give the little brat a second chance at spoiling Celia's big moment.

Her cell phone rang, and she picked it up and answered without a second thought.

"Well hey, Lil' Sissy," a familiar voice said. "Long time, no talk to."

"Veronica? How the hell did you get this number?"

Her older sister laughed unpleasantly. "Our dear cousin Mallery gave it to me. Wasn't that thoughtful? She called me last week because Aunt Eleanor is in a bad way, and she just happened to mention that dear old Aunt Ellie had gone down to North Carolina to see you get married. Funny thing. I guess my invitation must have gotten lost in the mail."

Dammit. She should have known better than to have invited even one member of her wretched family to the wedding. But she'd thought it would look too odd not to have any family there, and Aunt Eleanor, her mother's aunt, was reasonably presentable. She should have left well enough alone.

"What do you want, Veronica? I'm at work, and I've got a million things going on today, so I'd appreciate it if you'd make it brief."

"Oh, Sissy," Veronica said mournfully. "You're about to hurt my feelings. I was just calling to catch up on old times. Hey, Mallery says you're quite the businesswoman. Had your own dress business, sold it for ten million dollars. Mama and Daddy and the girls and me, we hear you're rolling in the dough. Mallery says you even paid to fly Aunt Eleanor down for the wedding."

"Mallery doesn't know dick," Celia said. "I did sell my business, but there were . . . complications. The money's all tied up in stock options and stuff like that, so if you're calling to hit me up for a loan, you can forget it."

"A loan?" Veronica laughed. "No, see, I was calling you about the money you *owe* me. Remember? When you blew town, you stole my car? I'd say the car alone was worth six thousand. And in the glove box in that car was quite a bit of cash that belonged to Ed-

451

die? Like three thousand dollars?"

Celia clicked her fingertips impatiently on the desktop. "That piece of shit Cutlass had a hundred and sixty thousand miles and leaked oil like a sieve. It was worth maybe six hundred, tops. As for the cash in the glove box, it was only eighteen hundred. And since we both know the money was the proceeds from your ex-husband's sideline of selling oxycodone you stole from your nursing home patients, I figure he's probably not going to call the cops and report it missing. Six years later."

"Fine, you wanna quibble?" Veronica said. "We'll call it four thousand dollars even. And I won't even charge you interest, since you're family."

I have no family, Celia thought. *I am an only child and an orphan. And I intend to stay that way.*

"And what if I say I'm not giving you a dime?" Celia challenged.

"Well, then, I guess I'll just have to call up your ritzy-titzy *new* family, the Baylesses, and tell them all about your real family — the one you left back here in South Sioux City," Veronica said.

"Do that," Celia said, lowering her voice. "And I'll call the owners of that shithole nursing home you work at and suggest they check your personnel records at that hospital you got fired from in Lincoln. And then I'll call the sheriff in South Sioux City. Now, Veronica, I really do have to go. And I suggest you lose this phone number. Immediately."

She clicked End on her cell phone, tapped the Block Caller icon on her phone, and went back to work on her to-do list.

Celia looked down at her list and frowned. Mason had been adamant about no guests, but they had to have two witnesses. Davis? No. He and Mason had been at each other's throats all week long. And anyway, she thought, allowing herself a very small, very secret smile. She had another task for Davis. A very private task.

Matt Kelsey? She frowned. If she invited Matt, she'd have to include the insufferable Bonnie. You couldn't very well not invite the wife if you invited the husband, could you? She shrugged. After they were married she could tactfully unfriend the Kelseys. But for the immediate future, she needed them. In fact, she might as well put Bonnie's skills to work right now. She picked up her phone and tapped the icon for Bonnie's cell phone.

"Bonnie!" she cried. "Please tell me you and Matt don't have any plans for tomorrow afternoon."

"Well," Bonnie said. "Let me think. I've got a tennis lesson in the morning, and I don't know whether Matt's playing golf yet."

"I can tell you that Mason won't be playing

golf on Saturday," Celia said. "Because we've rescheduled the wedding."

"Oh, Celia!" Bonnie said. "I'm so happy for you. So . . . everything worked out with that unfortunate rumor about you-know-who?"

Celia held the phone away from her face and smirked. "Just ugly innuendo," she said. "I don't know how that kind of talk gets spread around town, do you?"

"I have no idea," Bonnie said. "But I bet I know who's behind a lot of the gossip."

"Who?" Celia asked, crossing her eyes. She knew damned good and well that the font of all gossip in Pasccoe was on the other end of the line.

"Don't be mad at me for saying this, but I think Pokey Riggs has been telling all kinds of stories on you, Celia."

"I wouldn't be surprised," Celia agreed. "She and you-know-who are thick as thieves. Anyway, I choose to rise above all of that petty stuff. And I know you do, too."

"Absolutely," Bonnie said. "Now tell me about the wedding."

"It'll be tomorrow afternoon at Cherry Hill," Celia said. "Very, very private and exclusive. In fact, we're not having any attendants at all. Just Mason and me, the justice of the peace, and Sallie. And our two very *dearest* friends. If you're not too busy."

"Really?" Bonnie squealed. "We would be

454

honored."

"Thank heavens," Celia said, rolling her eyes. "I was praying you didn't have any prior commitments."

"We'll clear our calendars," Bonnie said. "But why such a rush?"

Celia lowered her voice. "You'll keep this in strictest confidence, won't you, Bonnie?"

"You know me," Bonnie said. "Whatever you tell me, I'll take to my grave."

"I can hardly believe it," Celia said. "We really hadn't planned on starting a family this soon, but sometimes, you know, life intervenes . . ."

"Really? Celia, you aren't. I mean, are you? Pregnant?"

"I am," Celia said. "And Mason is over the moon. You won't tell a soul yet, right? We haven't even broken the news to Sophie."

"I won't breathe a word," Bonnie promised.

Celia hung up and laughed out loud.

"As if." The news would be all over town within a matter of minutes. Just a little additional insurance, in case Mason had any second thoughts about backing out on the upcoming nuptials.

36

Annajane sat at her desk and clenched and unclenched her fists. The encounter with Celia left her breathless with the kind of fury she'd never experienced before. She wanted to kick something, smash something, break something. Preferably something related to Celia. The bitch had actually ambushed her in the lady's room.

Poor Mason, Annajane thought. A life sentence with Cruella de Vil.

She busied herself with more work, more phone calls and e-mails, but couldn't manage to completely put aside the white-hot anger seething inside.

Pokey was already sitting at their usual table when Annajane arrived at Janette's Tea Room. She waved a carrot stick in Annajane's direction as a greeting.

"Sorry," she said, between chews. "I got here early, and I was starving, so I went ahead and ordered for us. You're having the chicken salad, yes?"

"Of course," Annajane said. There were no menus on their table, but after meeting her best friend at Janette's for lunch nearly every week of their adult life, they didn't need menus. Pokey always had the special salad with strawberries and pecans and chicken pot pie, while Annajane had the chicken salad plate. They always split a slice of chocolate silk pie.

Janette's dining room was a pink and green confection, a Lilly Pulitzer dress come to life, humming with feminine conversation conducted in sugary southern drawls. All the tables in the room were filled with women their age or their mothers', dressed in floral sundresses or summery pants outfits. Annajane recognized most of the women in the room and smiled and nodded at all of them.

Pokey sighed contentedly and patted her midsection when the waitress set their plates in front of them. "This baby has got to be a girl. I was hungry when I was pregnant with the boys, but this time around I am ravenous all the time!"

Annajane took a sip of her iced tea and laughed. "Well, I hope it is a girl, for your sake. When do you find out?"

"Next week," Pokey said. She ate a forkful of potpie and frowned. "Mama called right before I left to come over here. She told me about Celia's baby. I kinda threw up a little

457

in my mouth."

"Bad news travels fast," Annajane said, nibbling at a grape that was part of the fruit garnish. "Did Sallie also tell you about the wedding tomorrow?"

"No!" Pokey threw her fork against the side of her plate. "You really are doing your damnedest to ruin my appetite, aren't you?"

"At least you didn't have to hear about it the way I did," Annajane said. "I went to the lady's room at the plant and Celia was lying in wait for me. Just had to tell me the happy news to my face."

Pokey gaped. "She didn't."

"She certainly did," Annajane said. "She as much as told me to get my ass out of town before she kicked me out."

"Tell me you slapped the sass out of her," Pokey said.

"I should have, but I didn't," Annajane admitted. "I was too shocked to do anything more than stand there with my mouth hanging open. It was unnerving!"

Pokey took another bite of her lunch and chewed thoughtfully. "We're not gonna take this lying down, are we?"

"What can we do?" Annajane asked. "Celia's pregnant, and she just happened to have picked the one baby daddy on earth who actually feels obligated to do the right thing and marry her."

"I've been thinking about that ever since

mama shared the happy news," Pokey said. "Sallie is deliriously happy, by the way, at the thought of a Bayless grandbaby with a capital B."

"She already has four grandbabies, your three boys and Sophie," Annajane pointed out.

"Nuh-uh," Pokey said. "I'm just a girl. My babies are *Riggs* babies. So they don't really count as far as my mother is concerned. Even though Denning is named for Daddy. And then, of course, Sophie is what Sallie thinks of as a 'yard baby.' Although she would never dare come out and say so to Mason's face."

"A 'yard baby'?" Annajane looked puzzled.

"You know. Yard baby. Do you remember that housekeeper we had when I was little? Cora? I overheard her telling Sallie one day that she had six children at home, but two of them were actually her oldest daughter's 'yard babies.' Later on, I asked Mama about that and she told me a yard baby was a child born to a woman who wasn't married to the baby's father."

Pokey grinned suddenly. "Which prompted me to ask how a lady could *have* a baby if they weren't married. Let me tell you, Sallie Bayless was not prepared to have that conversation with an eight-year-old."

"I'll just bet," Annajane said, laughing.

"Back to Mason, though," Pokey said. "If he didn't feel obligated to marry Sophie's mama, why is he going ahead and marrying that bitch Celia? You know she deliberately got herself knocked up so she could trap Mason into marrying her."

"I don't know," Annajane said. "He never really talks much about Sophie's mother. All he told me was that they'd had a very brief fling, right after we were separated, and that the girl wasn't able to raise a child on her own. I think he's only agreed to marry Celia because he knows she'd totally be an unfit mother if he weren't around."

"We just can't let him marry her," Pokey repeated. "We have to do something."

Annajane poked at her chicken salad with her fork, separating out the bits of chicken and almonds and diced celery, but eating little.

"I think it's a lost cause, Pokey," she said sadly. "Unless we find out Celia is a convicted sex offender or bank robber or something by tomorrow, she's going to be your new sister-in-law."

"We can't give up now," Pokey said. "Did you find out anything else about her dress company?"

"I did talk to that woman, Katie Derscheid, who knows your friend Angela," Annajane said. "She confirmed our suspicions that Celia is a crook. After Baby Brands bought out Gingerpeachy, they discovered that she'd wildly inflated the value of the inventory and her orders. They're suing."

"Hmm," Pokey said. She finished off her potpie and pointed her fork at Annajane's plate. "Are you going to eat that chicken salad, or perform an autopsy on it?"

Annajane pushed it across the table toward her best friend.

"A lawsuit? That's pretty interesting. Wonder if we could get a copy of it?"

"I doubt if it would make much of a difference to Mason," Annajane said. "I'm pretty sure he has no more illusions about his bride to be."

"And this is the woman who's going to raise his child," Pokey said, making a gagging motion. "And Sophie. Perfect."

A pained expression crossed Annajane's face. "I can't bear thinking about that. You're just gonna have to shield Sophie from Celia, as much as you can."

"If she'll let me," Pokey said. "Remember, Celia hates me even worse than she hates you."

"You gotta give Celia credit for smarts," Annajane said. "Once she'd started up her own company, she immediately started looking for a way to trade up. She stalked the president of that other company, and then showed up in the hotel bar where he was staying during a trade show."

"Isn't that how she met Davis in the first place? In a lobby bar?"

461

"Sort of. According to Davis, Sallie actually tracked Celia down after buying a couple of dresses for Sophie. And then they just happened to be at the same conference in the same hotel at the same time." Annajane lifted a skeptical eyebrow.

"Yeah, I don't think there are a lot of coincidences where Celia is concerned," Pokey said.

The waitress came by and dropped off their chocolate silk pie, but Annajane shook her head when Pokey offered her a slice.

"Could you bring me a glass of Chablis instead?" Annajane asked the waitress.

"Hey, what goes?" Pokey asked. "You never drink on a workday."

"Extreme duress calls for extreme measures," Annajane said glumly. "Anyway, I doubt that anybody at Quixie is going to notice if I come back to work a little later than usual today."

A moment later the waitress was back with her wine. Pokey took the glass from her, waved the glass under her nose and sniffed appreciatively. "This is the thing I miss most when I'm pregnant. A nice little midday buzz. That, and seeing my own ankles."

"A midday buzz is just what the doctor ordered for me," Annajane declared, taking a sip of the wine. She looked over at her best friend. "As soon as I get the summer campaign lined up, probably next week, I'm gone."

Pokey started to protest, then changed her mind. "Where will you go?"

"Not sure yet," Annajane admitted. "I've got a little bit of a financial cushion, with the money from selling the loft. Maybe I'll travel for a while."

"You better come back here in time for my little girl to be born," Pokey threatened, blinking back tears. "Or I'll send the boys to live with you, wherever you are."

Annajane handed Pokey her napkin. "Don't be such a crybaby. Of course I'll come back."

37

Sallie Bayless beamed at her future daughter-in-law as Celia walked into the den on Friday night. They'd had an early dinner together at the country club, just a salad and some broiled flounder, although Celia had only picked at her food, pleading the case for morning sickness.

On their return to Cherry Hill, Celia had excused herself, saying that she needed to make a few quick phone calls. Now she had changed into form-fitting black slacks and a low-necked silver-gray halter top that showed off her tanned shoulders and slim, muscular arms.

"You look lovely, dear," Sallie said. "But won't you be chilly in that top?"

"Not at all," Celia said. "It's eighty degrees out."

"It's a shame Mason isn't here tonight to see you all dressed up. Have you talked to him this evening?" Sallie asked.

"Several times," Celia lied. The prick was

deliberately avoiding her, barricading himself in his office for the past few days, ignoring her e-mails, texts, and phone calls. He had Voncile aiding and abetting him in this subterfuge, and Celia was damned if she'd just break into her own fiancé's office. "He asked me to send his regrets. He's got so much going on at the office, he didn't think he'd get away for dinner tonight."

She'd tried once more to lure Mason into having sex, showing up at his house, their house, at dawn just that day, dressed only in a raincoat, a black garter belt, and her highest spike heels. It had been one of the more humiliating and ultimately futile encounters she'd ever had with a man. He'd laughed and slammed the door in her face.

Time was running out. She'd quit taking her birth control pills as soon as she'd hatched her plan and now felt sure she was about to ovulate. And if Mason wasn't going to cooperate, she was going to have to put plan B into action.

Celia picked up her car keys and slung her tote bag over her shoulder.

"Going out so late?" Sallie asked, with a slight frown.

Jesus, the old lady watched her every move. It was like she thought she was Celia's chaperone.

"Bonnie Kelsey and a couple of the girls from the tennis team are having a little get-together in my honor," Celia said. "Sort of a

465

bachelorette thing. But don't worry. I warned them, absolutely no male strippers!" Her giddy laugh echoed in the high-ceilinged room.

"I should hope not," Sallie said, looking horrified. She went back to reading her magazine. "If Mason calls, I'll tell him where he can find you."

Like that's going to happen, Celia thought. *But what if, by some chance, he did call his mother, and went looking for her? That could prove to be extremely embarrassing.*

"Now don't you go spoiling my fun by telling your son where he can find me tonight," Celia said gaily. She patted her tote bag. "This is strictly just us girls. Since it's probably going to be a late night, I'm planning to spend the night with Bonnie."

"Really?" Sallie shot her a disapproving look. "Aren't you a little old for that type of thing? I realize we're only having a small ceremony, but you do want to look your best on your wedding day, Celia. The photographer I hired is going to shoot a wedding portrait of you and Mason, and I know you don't want any dark circles or unfortunate puffy eyelids."

"The ceremony isn't until four o'clock," Celia said. "Don't worry, I swear, I'll get my full eight hours of sleep, and I'll be fresh as a daisy for the ceremony."

She kissed Sallie warmly on the cheek.

"Tomorrow's the day!"

She waited until she was almost to the gates of Cherry Hill before taking the phone out again.

"Heey," she said softly. "Are you busy tonight?"

"Not really. What did you have in mind?" he asked.

She was fairly sure he knew exactly what she had in mind, but if he wanted to play games, so could she.

"I was hoping we could get together to talk strategy. About the deal."

"Fine with me," he said. "Where and when?"

"Hmm," Celia said, playing along. "Someplace private?"

"I know just the place," he said.

38

Friday night. Annajane had listened to the tapes of the tinny recordings of the old Quixie radio ads a couple dozen times, trying for inspiration for a new jingle. Despite her gloomy mood, the vocals, done by what sounded like a group of midgets huffing helium, gave her an unstoppable case of the giggles.

Ask for Quixie in your glass
for a summer filled with sass!
It's the quicker fun-time drink
it's cool, it's cold, it's pi — iiinnk!

She glanced over at the tableau she'd set up on the desk opposite her bed at the Pinecone Motor Lodge.

She'd had one of the vintage magazine ads with the new "Taste of Dixie" sell-line on it blown up to poster size and dry mounted on a foam-core board with an easel backing. In front of the board she'd arranged smaller similarly mounted mock-ups of the summer fun ads from the '50s and '60s. And as a finishing touch, she'd filled one of the old green throwback Quixie bottles with a can of the cherry soda she'd picked up on the way out of the plant.

Shaded by the vivid vintage fringed barkcloth lampshade on the desktop, the green bottle gave off an eerie glow. The old jingles were funny and catchy, Annajane decided, but definitely stretched the truth. Quixie was not pink at all. It was definitely, decidedly red. Unless you added a scoop of vanilla ice cream, in which case it would lighten to an obliging pink.

She reached for the martini glass on her bedside table, took a long drink, and smacked her lips. She'd worked late, only stopping in the early evening to eat a bag of chips from the break room vending machine, and had been the last one to leave the plant at 9:00 P.M.

When she pulled into the parking lot at the motel, she'd been surprised to see that every slot in the parking lot was full, and most of the vehicles were vans or box trucks. Lights shone from all the units, and smoke curled from a barbecue grill that had been set up in the courtyard. Music drifted out from several of the units, and casually dressed men sat in front of several cottages, chatting and sipping from Styrofoam cups. The place was hopping. She followed the blacktop around to the back of the units and finally found an empty space behind the office.

Annajane was trudging back toward her own unit when the door of the office opened and Thomas, one of the owners, beckoned her inside.

"You're just in time for happy hour," Thomas informed her. He pointed to an overstuffed green chintz armchair. "Sit. I'll get you a drink. You can have anything you want as long as you want a martini."

"A martini would be fabulous," Annajane said. "But what's going on around here? Did you book a convention?"

"Kind of," Harold said with a grin. He was wearing a different Hawaiian shirt, and neatly starched beige linen pleated-front slacks. "There's a big florists' trade show that starts in Southern Pines tomorrow. One of Thomas's old boyfriends saw our Pinecone Motor Lodge ad in the North Carolina Pink Pages, and he sent out a few e-mails and voilà! We're nearly sold out with a full house of florists."

"He is not an old boyfriend!" Thomas protested with a blush. He handed Annajane an oversized glass and poured her drink from a bullet-shaped glass and chrome cocktail shaker. "He's just a kid. It was years ago. We had maybe one date before I realized he was too immature for me."

"Immature?" Harold said with a hoot. "They went out to dinner and Harold had to order him a Happy Meal."

"Would you stop?" Thomas said. "Annajane doesn't want to hear about my old flames." He went into the kitchen and came back with a dish of cheese straws.

"Yum," Annajane said gratefully. "I didn't have any dinner tonight."

"Were you at work all this time?" Harold asked. "We were beginning to wonder if you'd changed your mind about staying."

"I've got a big project I'm trying to wrap up," Annajane said quietly. "I've resigned effective next week."

"Oh, no," the men said in unison. "Does that mean you're leaving Passcoe, too?" Harold asked.

"For now," Annajane said. She stared into her cocktail glass. "I need a change of scenery."

Thomas exchanged a meaningful look with his partner. "Man troubles?"

She nodded. "You could say that."

Harold patted her on the shoulder. "Whoever he is, he's an idiot."

"Thanks," she said. She stood to leave and held out her half-empty glass. "He's getting married tomorrow. Would you mind pouring this into a go-cup for me? After the day I've had, I think I need a nightcap."

"Here," Thomas said, handing her the cocktail shaker. "Just take the whole thing with you."

The bad thing about staying in a genuine retro '50s motel room, Annajane decided, was that all that authenticity meant that she didn't have a television. She'd finally given up on her jingle project after an hour of staring at the old ads and listening to the old commercials.

Instead, she reached into the box of old Quixie recipe booklets she'd rescued from one of the boxes that had been headed for the Dumpster. She decided to look for anything approaching a muffin recipe that Thomas could use.

The booklets had apparently been produced in-house and given away at grocery store displays or as mail-in premiums. She was leafing through a booklet called "Quixie Entertaining Tips" when she came to a page featuring recipes for "Summer Quix-E-Que." Among the dishes was a Quixie-marinated barbecued chicken, the baked beans recipe Annajane had seen in an earlier advertisement, and a chocolate sheet cake recipe with "Choco-Quixie frosting."

On the page facing the recipes was a full-page black-and-white photo of teenagers enjoying a summer cookout. As she was marveling at the teenager's clean-cut outfits, she realized, with a start, that the perky brunette who was holding an upraised bottle of Quixie in her hand was none other than a teenaged Ruth Hudgens.

"Oh my gosh, Mama," she said softly. Her mother's dreamy-eyed smile was directed at a trim lad dressed in a madras short-sleeved shirt and sharply pressed khakis. He looked enough like Mason to take her breath away, but as she looked closer, she realized she was staring at a teenage Glenn Bayless, who had his arm around the very young, and very adorable, Ruth.

Annajane knew the photo had been staged, but as she studied the faces of the other teens, she realized that Sallie Bayless was not among the partygoers.

"Mama and Glenn?" she murmured. Had the two of them ever dated? Emboldened by the martinis she'd been sipping, she picked up the phone and called her mother.

"Hey, Mama," she said softly. After a few minutes of chatting about her job prospects and some sharp questions about why she didn't come to her senses and make up with Shane again, she finally managed to get to the point.

"Listen, Mama," she said, staring down at the recipe booklet spread out on her bed, "I was going through some old Quixie ads, and I found one with a photo of a barbecue layout that you were in. Do you remember that?"

"That old thing?" her mother chuckled.

"Good Lord, honey, I haven't thought of that in years."

"You were wearing a little cotton shift dress and had your hair in a flip; you looked so cute, a little bit like Jackie Kennedy back in the day," Annajane said.

"People did used to tell me that," Ruth admitted. "I bet I wasn't but eighteen when they took that picture. I made that dress myself. It was my favorite."

"It'd be right in style today," Annajane said. "Mama, in the picture, Glenn Bayless has his arm around you. And the two of you look pretty lovey-dovey."

"What?" Ruth sounded startled. "Annajane, the photographer posed all of us like that."

"You're looking at him like he hung the moon," Annajane said. "And he's looking at you the same way. Mama, did the two of you have a thing, back then?"

She heard Ruth sigh. "We went out a few times that summer, yes. I wouldn't call it a thing."

"Was this before or after Glenn started going with Sallie?"

"Now, why are you digging up all this ancient history? You are good and done with that family, I hope."

"Humor me, Mama, please?"

"I can't remember back that far," Ruth groused. "I think that was the summer after our senior year. Glenn and Sallie dated all through school, but then I seem to recall that they broke up right before the prom. And I ended up going with Glenn, and then we went out a few times that summer. But then your daddy came home from overseas, and I never gave Glenn another look. He and Sallie got back together right before he went off to college. And I ended up marrying your daddy. Now, can I please go on to bed?"

Annajane ran her finger over the old photograph. "Why didn't you ever tell me you'd gone out with Glenn?"

"It was years and years ago," Ruth said. "Way before you were born. What difference does it make?"

"I thought you hated all the Baylesses," Annajane said.

"I never said I hated them," Ruth corrected. "I just said I didn't care for the family. Especially the mother."

"All these years, I've wondered why Sallie didn't like me; this explains everything."

"Sallie Bayless didn't like you because she thought she was better than you and me and everybody else in this town," Ruth said.

"But she hated *you,* probably because she had some idea that you stole Glenn from her," Annajane said.

"Stole him! I did no such thing. Glenn was a nice enough boy, but even back then he had a wandering eye. I wasn't the only girl he was seeing that summer."

"But I bet he only went running back to Sallie after you threw him over for my daddy," Annajane guessed. "And to somebody like Sallie, that would be unforgivable. And unforgettable."

"That woman is bad news," Ruth said flatly. "How we were ever friends is beyond me."

"You were friends?"

"Best friends. In grade school," Ruth said. "Like you and Pokey always were. Although I will say that Pokey is nothing like her mother, thank the Lord."

"And then what happened to break up the friendship?" Annajane asked, fascinated.

"Boys!" Ruth said. "Sallie Woodrow was boy crazy. She didn't have any time for girlfriends once she discovered boys."

"Wow," Annajane said. "Just . . . wow."

"If that's all you wanted to know, I'll say good night," Ruth said. "It's too late for an old lady like me to be up this time of night. But honey?"

"Yes, Mama?"

"Send me a copy of that picture, would you?"

After talking to her mother, Annajane couldn't settle down. She'd tried reading, but couldn't concentrate. And her iPod was packed away in boxes with all the rest of her belongings. She could hear voices outside from the courtyard. People having a good time. It made her deepening depression even worse. Everybody in the world, it seemed, had a man. Except her.

The room did have an old hi-fi, though. Annajane lifted the console lid and picked up a half-dozen old record albums. Most of the artists were ones she recognized only because her step-father had inherited his father's old record collection. She wrinkled her nose in distaste at the selection: the Ray Conniff Singers, Perry Como, Brenda Lee. Pat Boone? Harold and Thomas were dears, but their musical taste definitely ran to mid-century cheese. She considered the last album in the stack, *Johnny's Greatest Hits,* by Johnny Mathis.

What the hell, she decided. She had to study the console switches and knobs for a few minutes to figure it out, but then she put the record onto the turntable, turned up the volume, and dropped the needle on the record.

Lush strings and background singers filled the room. Annajane stretched out on the bed, propped her head up on the pillows, and poured herself another martini.

"You ask how much I love you," Johnny crooned in his velvet voice, "Until the twelfth of never." She managed to make it through two more syrupy ballads, "Chances Are" and "Wonderful Wonderful," before she broke down in great, sorrowful sobs.

"That's it," Annajane cried, lunging for the

hi-fi's on-off dial. Much better. Thank God the proprietors of the Pinecone Motor Lodge's tastes didn't include vintage Journey, or she would have slit her own wrists with a dull nail file. She poured herself a little more martini and decided that was better yet.

The *Twelfth of Never,* she reflected, sipping her drink, could have been the theme song for her relationship with Mason, with never the operative phrase. They'd been so close this last time to finding their way back to each other. But close, her mother had always warned, only counted in horseshoes and hand grenades.

She found the old snapshot in her purse, where she'd stashed it while packing for her move, and studied it again, hoping to find a clue to that happy place they'd inhabited so long ago. Mason's eyes were shadowed by his sunglasses, but his lips curled in a carefree, unaffected grin that was nothing like the guarded, hesitant half-smile he'd affected these last few years.

And what about her own face? The Anna-jane of the photo gazed up at Mason in unabashed adoration that made her cringe today. Back then, she'd hidden nothing, held back nothing. Stupid, vulnerable girl. Couldn't know then what she wished she didn't know now. How she missed that girl.

Annajane heard a small ding come from the direction of her cell phone. It was a text.

From Mason.

I need 2 see U.

She glanced at the photograph again, looked at the happy face of that stupid, unguarded, vulnerable nineteen-year-old version of herself. One more time, she decided. One more chance. And the hell with the consequences.

Annajane grabbed her purse and her car keys. She opened the door. Mason stood on the threshold.

"I'm sorry," he said, but he never got to finish his sentence, because Annajane was kissing him.

"Don't say anything," she cautioned, when he managed to pull back from her. "Don't tell me you're sorry again."

"I won't," he promised, taking her face between his hands. "I tried to stay away tonight. But I couldn't. I had to see you."

"I know," Annajane said. "I've been sitting around here moping and crying all night long." She managed a laugh. "I was listening to an old Johnny Mathis album, for God's sake."

"I've been standing here for ten minutes, listening," Mason admitted. "Trying to get up the nerve to knock."

"I couldn't take any more," Annajane said.

"He was killin' me. My tear ducts are totally dry."

"I don't want you to cry," Mason said. He pointed toward the door. "Come on. Let's get out of here. I brought the fun car. For old time's sake. I'm selling it after tomorrow."

Annajane gasped. "You're gonna let her make you sell it? But you love that car."

"Not anymore," Mason said. "What's the point of keeping it? I think I'm done with fun."

"Sophie loves that car, too," Annajane pointed out. "And you promised to take her for a ride in it. All the way to the coast."

"She'll forget," Mason said with a shrug. "She's just a kid."

"Stop that!" Annajane said. "I can't stand being with you like this."

"I'm . . ." he started to say. And then he caught himself. "One more ride."

Annajane pulled away. "I don't think so," she said slowly.

His eyes widened. "Look, it's my last night. I've told her I love you. But after tomorrow, I can't come to you like this. I won't cheat. Not even with you."

"I know that," Annajane said. She turned her back to him and lifted her hair to expose the nape of her neck. "I think we should stay in tonight. Could you please help me with my zipper?"

He held her hair up with one hand and

kissed her neck. He inched the zipper down slowly, following its track with his lips.

Mason turned her around. He kissed her lightly at first, his lips brushing hers, almost a brotherly kiss, she thought, somehow dismayed at the casual nature of his embrace. But then he bent, and his lips strayed to her bare collarbone and the warm hollow of her neck. He pulled her closer, and Annajane's arms twined around his neck. Finally, his lips found their way back to hers. He kissed her slowly, gently, deeply, his tongue teasing as she opened her lips to him.

I remember this, Annajane thought, as she melted into Mason. She inhaled the scent of him, his soap, his aftershave. She was intoxicated with the scent of him, his nearness, dizzy with wanting him. With her fingertips, she traced the smooth skin of his jawline.

"I've missed you," Annajane started to say, but he kissed away whatever else she might have said. His hands cupped her butt, and then they finger-walked their way up her spine, and the shiver that worked its way up her body made him chuckle, as it always used to.

He eased his thumbs under the band of her bra, pushing her breasts upward, until they spilled out of the gaping neckline of her dress, and then he bent his head, raining feathery kisses at first, and then, nipping and kissing and caressing her exposed nipples, until her

481

knees buckled and her brain idly telegraphed, *I remember this. Oh. My . . .*

Somehow, her dress slipped to the floor. She pushed Mason's polo shirt up, and then over his head, and tossed it aside. A moment later, her lacy coral bra joined his shirt, and she pressed herself against him, wanting the sensastion of his nipples pressed against hers. She hooked her fingers briefly inside the waist of his jeans, and then ran them up his belly, laughing to herself as she felt his sharp inhale of arousal, and pleasing herself, running her fingers through his chest hair, over his now-taut nipples.

He buried his hands in her hair, kissing her so deeply, with such passion, he literally lifted her out of her heels. Then he set her gently back down, pressing her with his hips, until her back was to the cabin wall. Without her heels, she was four inches shorter than Mason. He braced one hand on the cabin wall, looking down at her with such ineffable tenderness it took her breath away. He bent, kissed her forehead, nuzzled her ear, traced the nape of her neck with his tongue, murmuring under his breath. "So sweet, so sweet . . ."

All the while, he worked his knee between hers, his hands roaming over her bare torso. He bunched the fabric of her lace panties with one hand, and then the other, effort-lessly sliding them from her hips. She gasped as he slid his fingers into her, and ripples of pleasure flooded her body. *I remember this. Oh. My. God. I want this.*

She slid her hand down his chest again, feeling the hard strain of him against the fabric of the worn jeans. She let her hand linger there for a moment, before unfastening the metal button. She inched the zipper down slowly with her thumb, letting the palm of her hand rest against the hardness for another long moment.

Mason's breath caught as she langorously unzipped his fly. She tugged at his waistband, and then, lifting one leg and wrapping it halfway around him, she pulled at the jeans until they puddled around his ankles, and he was forced to pull away, kick off his shoes and step out of the jeans.

She gave him a lazy appraisal. "Still a boxer man, I see."

"I'm the same as I always was," he said, taking her by the hand and leading her to the bed.

She pulled the covers down and slipped beneath them, and a minute later, he was beside her. He propped himself up on one elbow, and gazed at her so intently, she found herself blushing.

"What?" she said nervously.

He kissed her. "I've been waiting for this a long time. Five years. I tried to make myself forget you, but it didn't work. Nothing else worked. Nobody else was you."

Annajane kissed him back. She laid her cheek on his chest. "I know. Some nights, I'd leave work, and driving home, if I had the radio on, and a certain song came on, I'd completely lose it. I'd go to meetings at work so I could be near you, but then you seemed so cold and distant; I knew you hated me. It was all I could do to stay in the same room."

Mason ran his hands down the length of her body, and she shivered in delight, curling toward him as he stroked and caressed her, and she did the same, reacquainting herself with the contours of his body, the flat plane of his belly, his muscled thighs, even the smallpox vaccine on his upper left arm.

His voice was husky. "I never hated you. I couldn't. It was just . . . a defense mechanism, trying to keep you at a distance because I knew I'd blown my one chance with you. I never thought I'd get you back again."

"Tonight's the twelfth of never," she laughed, with a catch in her voice, as he rolled on top of her. And it was that easy, as they moved together, the dark, empty years receded, the cold place in her heart melted, and all was light and joy and pleasure, as their rhythms matched and their bodies coupled so easily, so naturally.

"Annajane," he said it over and over again, as though he'd just discovered the name of his long-lost love. "Annajane." His voice faltered, as they climaxed, in unison, waves of ecstasy washing over her as she arched her body to meet his. *I remember this. This is mine. For one last time.*

The soft buzz of Mason's snore awoke her. He was curled on his side, one hand cupped over her breast, the way he'd slept so many nights of their marriage. She smiled sleepily to herself and glanced at the clock radio on the nightstand. One o'clock.

"Mason!" His snores drowned out her whisper. She'd forgotten what a heavy sleeper he was. "Mason." She turned and shook his shoulder. "Mason, wake up."

"Why?" he said groggily, rolling over onto his other side, facing away from her.

"It's after one. You have to go home." She shook his shoulder again. "Come on. Get up, now."

"Sleepy. Stayin' here."

"No, you're not staying here." She hopped out of bed and rummaged in her suitcase for her robe. Knotting the belt around her waist, she gathered up the clothes he'd dropped on the floor earlier in the evening and took them around to the other side of the bed.

He was snoring again. "Mason!" Her voice took on a new urgency. "Look, you can't stay here. You need to go home."

"Celia's at Mama's house," Mason said.

"You need to go home to Sophie," Annajane insisted.

"Letha's there," he mumbled.

"I don't care. Sophie will wonder where you've been. I don't want her to think you're playing spend the night with me, when you're marrying Celia this afternoon. It's . . ." She searched for the right word. "Trashy."

He tugged at the shoulder of her robe. "Not trashy. It's romantic. Now come back to bed."

"Absolutely not," she said, yanking the covers off him. "You're going home." She shoved the bundle of clothes at him. "Here. Get dressed."

39

She followed him out of the cabin, missing him already, wanting him to stay, knowing she couldn't ask him to.

"Where's the Chevelle?" she asked, looking out at the quiet parking lot, half-empty now.

"I had to park clear out in back, right near your car," he said. "Just as well. Everybody in town knows the fun car by now."

"Are you worried about the gossip? About what Celia will think?" Annajane asked.

His jaw muscle twitched. "I don't give a damn what Celia thinks. But I'd rather not have another lecture from Sallie."

She nodded. "I'm not going to kiss you good-bye."

"Better not to," he agreed.

"I'm almost done with the promotion," Annajane said. "By midweek, I'll have it wrapped up. By the time you get back from your honeymoon, I'll be gone."

"Honeymoon?" He nearly spat the word. "I said I'd marry her, but there's just so far I'll go with this farce. I never said anything about a honeymoon. If she wants to take one, she's going solo."

There was so much she wanted to ask him, but the time had slipped away. They'd only had a few hours. She was glad they'd spent them loving each other. One last time.

"Have you told Soph you're leaving after all?" he asked, stuffing his hands in the pocket of his jeans to keep from touching her again.

"Not yet," Annajane said. "I'll figure something out. One good-bye at a time is all I can manage right now." She swallowed hard. Her tear ducts apparently hadn't dried up after all.

It was chilly out, and she was barefooted. She hugged herself and hopped up and down to keep warm. "Okay. I'm going in now."

"See ya," Mason said. Then he turned and walked right out of her life.

Sunshine flooded in through the slats of the wooden window blinds. She heard the slam of a car door and the murmur of voices from outside.

Annajane sat up in bed and peered groggily at the alarm clock. It was only seven o'clock. Her head throbbed dully, leading her to wish, too late, that she hadn't finished off the shaker of martinis after Mason's early-morning departure.

She showered and dressed in a pair of jeans and a pale blue Dandelion Wine T-shirt. Her mouth felt dry and cottony. Coffee, she thought, heading toward the motel's office, might be her only hope of salvation.

"Good morning," Thomas called, as she pushed into the little lounge area. He held up the coffee pot, and she nodded gratefully.

"You're an early bird this Saturday," Harold said, looking up from the computer screen behind the check-in desk.

"Too early," Annajane said, taking the mug of coffee Thomas offered. She looked out the window at the quiet courtyard and half-empty parking lot. "What happened to all your florists?"

"The Stallion Club happened," Harold said.

"It's an after-hours gay bar they discovered in Pinehurst," Thomas explained.

"They have gay bars in Pinehurst?"

"Bar. Singular," Thomas corrected. "Apparently it's quite the scene. A couple of the boys came knocking on our door at two, asking if we wanted to go along."

"Honey, we are too old for that kind of nonsense," Harold said.

"Now," Thomas added. He raised an eyebow. "But there was a time . . ."

"Annajane is a nice girl," Harold told his partner. "She doesn't want to hear about the scandalous behavior of our youth."

"You mean your youth," Thomas shot back. "I'm not the one who traveled with a Village People tribute band the summer I turned twenty-four."

"Were you the Indian chief or the construction worker?" Annajane asked.

"Both!" Harold said. He smoothed his hands over his nearly bald head. "But that was back in my drinking days. The strongest thing I drink now is your delicious Quixie."

"That reminds me," Thomas said. "We've got another guest staying here who works at Quixie."

"Really?" Annajane took another sip of her coffee. "I wonder who it is?"

Harold looked down at the old-fashioned ledger book on the reception desk. "Hmm." He laughed. "It says here his name is Harry Dix. And he paid cash for the room. Whoever he really is, he has a delightful sense of whimsy."

"Harry . . . oh, I get it," Annajane said, blushing slightly. "He used a pseudonym. But how do you know he works at Quixie?"

"He asked for the corporate rate," Thomas said. "Seemed like a nice guy. Dark hair, late thirties, getting a little bit of a paunch, drives a Porsche Boxster. There can't be that many of those around here."

"A dark-haired guy driving a Boxster?" Annajane said, her eyes widening.

"I'm surprised you didn't run into him

when you came over here this morning," Harold chimed in. "He's staying in unit twelve, on the end. It was the only room we had when he checked in last night."

Annajane felt the blood drain from her face. Davis Bayless drove the only Boxster in Passcoe that she knew of. And of course, according to Pokey, he'd been using the Pinecone Motor Lodge to shack up with his girlfriends for years. She'd totally forgotten he had a history with this place.

What if Davis had seen Mason's car here last night? Was he aware that Annajane was staying at his favorite motel?

Her head pounded. She took another gulp of coffee, and tried to reassure herself. Mason had parked on the other side of the complex, in the unlit back parking lot. And he'd left in the middle of the night. He'd been gone for hours now. Where was Davis's car?

She stood and gazed out the window, and, as she did, the door to unit 12 opened. Annajane's head was muddled, but her reflexes were fine. She hit the floor.

"Do I sense some drama?" Harold asked.

"Don't worry, hon, she's not even looking this way," Thomas said.

"She?" Annajane pulled up to her knees, crawled over to the window, and peeked out.

A petite woman in tight black slacks, a slightly askew silver halter top, and high-heeled silver mules peeked out the door of unit 12. She had short, white-blond hair and a large overnight bag slung over her shoulder.

Annajane gasped and ducked again.

"Oh my God," she whispered. "Is she looking this way?"

Harold walked over to the window and looked out. "Not really. She's talking on her cell phone. Do you know her?"

"Afraid so," Annajane said. "Her name's Celia. She's the one who's marrying my ex-husband today."

Now Thomas was standing at the window, too. "Hmm. She's certainly blessed. Do you think those are real?"

Harold went back to the reception desk and fetched his bird-watching binoculars. He studied the set in question. "Ooh, look, here comes Mr. Harry Dix."

Annajane's heart was pounding in her chest as she poked her head high enough to see out the window. Sure enough, a man had stepped onto the tiny porch of unit 12. His dark wavy hair looked damp. His white dress shirt was rumpled and untucked, and he carried his expensive pin-striped suit jacket over one arm. He glanced around furtively, ducked his head, and headed around to the back of the unit, in Celia's wake. A moment later, the black Boxster came roaring from the rear of the unit.

"Oh. My. God." Annajane breathed. "I should have known."

"So you do know him?" Harold asked. "What's his real name?"

"His name is Davis Bayless," Annajane said, standing slowly, hoping her head would stop pounding. "He's the groom's baby brother."

"Uh-oh," Thomas and Harold said in unison. They did a well-choreographed fist-bump. "Undercover lovers!"

40

Pokey was fifteen minutes late, which was actually early by her own standards. She slid onto the cracked orange vinyl dinette bench opposite Annajane and automatically reached for the oversized laminated menu.

"I already ordered your french toast and sausage," Annajane said.

The Country Cupboard was jammed as usual on a Saturday morning. There were other breakfast spots in Passcoe, but none as popular as the CC, as everybody in town called it. The long counter at the bar was filled with people tucking into their runny eggs, country ham, bacon, hash-browns, grits, and biscuits, and every table and booth in the restaurant on the town square was full.

"What's up?" Pokey asked.

Annajane took a sip of ice water and looked around nervously. She should have picked a quieter, more private place, she realized. The tables were set close together, and everybody in the CC knew everybody else.

"I have news," Annajane said, trying to keep her voice low.

Pokey eyed her best friend with unguarded curiosity.

"You look different this morning," she said. Annajane blushed.

"Wait a second. Oh, yeah. I remember that look. You've got afterglow!" Pokey exclaimed. "Or maybe it's beard burn. You did it, didn't you? Finally." She clapped her hands excitedly. "Yay! I'm so glad."

"Shh!" Annajane whispered. "Lower your voice! Everybody in here knows us, and they all think they know what we're talking about. So, can we *not* talk about what they think we are?"

Pokey leaned forward. "Okay, we won't discuss. Just nod your head, or tap your glass once for yes, two for no. Did you or did you not? Do it with you-know-who?"

"All right," Annajane groused. She tapped her glass once with the side of her spoon.

"Was it amazing?" Pokey demanded.

"Pokey! None of your business," Annajane said, and then, with a shrug, she tapped her glass once. "Now, can we change the subject? Because that is not what I need to talk to you about."

"Sure, after you tell me where the deed was done."

Annajane looked away. "Some things a lady doesn't discuss."

"I'm no lady," Pokey replied. "Despite Sallie's best efforts. Did you do it at his house? Or did you go back out to the farm?"

"No! God, no."

"Where? You might as well spit it out, because you know I'll get it out of you eventually."

Annajane did know. "All right. It was at the Pinecone."

"Oooh," Pokey said, rubbing her hands together gleefully. "Perfect. Your own little love nest."

Annajane glanced around the room and leaned her head toward Pokey's. "Not as perfect as you might think. Guess who else was checked in at the love nest?"

"The baby mama? For real?"

Annajane tapped her iced-tea glass once with her spoon.

"And she had company! When I saw him sneaking out of her unit this morning I almost wet myself."

"Who?"

"It was almost a family reunion," Annajane whispered.

"Davis?" Pokey's eyes widened.

Annajane tapped her spoon once against her glass. "And he'd signed the guest register with a pseudonym. Harry Dix!"

A plume of ice water erupted from Pokey's nose.

"Oh my God!" Pokey said, dabbing at her

496

face with a paper napkin. "You can't tell me that kind of stuff without a warning."

"I know," Annajane whispered.

"Day-yummm!" Pokey exclaimed. "Harry Dix! That must be his porn name."

Annajane snickered. "Wonder what Celia's is?"

"Lotta Lays?" Pokey offered. She reached for the basket of biscuits in the center of the table, selected one, and sliced and buttered it. She took a bite and chewed slowly.

Annajane sipped her coffee and waited.

"You have to tell Mason," Pokey said.

"No way," Annajane said.

"Somebody needs to. We can't let him marry that, that, woman. Not now."

"I can't be the person to tell him his brother betrayed him like that," Annajane said. "And neither can you. He and 'Harry' might not get along all the time, but it would destroy Mason to find out that 'Harry' slept with 'Lotta.' Anyway, we don't really know for sure what they were actually doing there."

"Oh, please. You saw good old Harry coming out of a room with you-know-who at the Pinecone Motor Lodge this morning. And we both know that's where Harry has always stashed his girlfriends over the years," Pokey said.

"Maybe he was just dropping off some papers to her," Annajane said. "Or they were plotting how to overthrow Mason at Quixie."

"And maybe I'll be the cover model for next year's *Sports Illustrated* swimsuit edition," Pokey said. "We always knew she was a skank. And now she's a double skank — sleeping with brothers. Eeeewww."

The waitress brought Pokey's french toast and set it down on the table. Pokey carefully drizzled maple syrup across her plate. "You're not eating?" she asked.

"Not hungry," Annajane said. "I'm just so . . . sad and mad. And maybe a teensy bit hungover. I wish I knew how to save Mason. I wish he wanted to save himself. But he's resigned to marrying her and making the rest of his life miserable."

"Don't forget he's ruining your life, too," Pokey added.

"I don't have to live with her," Annajane pointed out. She slumped against the back of the vinyl bench. "Are you going to the wedding?" she asked.

"I'm not invited," Pokey said. "Not that I'd go even if I were invited. I'm going to go pick up Sophie after I leave here and take her over to spend the night at my house."

"Sophie's not going to the wedding, either?" Annajane asked, raising an eyebrow.

"Nope. According to Mama, it'll just be her and the happy couple. Oh yes, and Bonnie and Matt Kelsey, who will be the witnesses."

"Interesting that old Harry Dix won't be

performing best man duties today," Annajane said.

Pokey gave a smirk. "My guess is, he's already performed for *Lotta*."

41

Mason sat behind the desk in his study, stone-faced, as his sister made one last attempt to change his mind.

"Don't do this, Mason," Pokey begged. "Please? You do not have to do this. You do not have to marry Celia."

"I appreciate your concern," he said quietly, "but I have to do what's best for the child."

"You don't even know that the child is yours," Pokey said bitterly.

"That's enough," Mason said, scowling. "You're talking about the woman I'm marrying. I know you've never liked Celia, but you won't make things any better for this family if you keep up this kind of talk."

"I don't care," Pokey said. "She's a liar and a phony, and I'll risk pissing you off if it means keeping you from marrying her."

"I have obligations," Mason pointed out. "And I won't run from them."

"Fine! Wait til the baby's born. Get some DNA testing. Pay Celia a shitload of child support and buy her a house. But don't, for God's sake, marry her. Look, you never married Sophie's mother, and nobody cared," Pokey said.

Mason clenched and unclenched his jaw. "That's different. For one thing, Sophie's mother didn't want to marry me. She barely knew me. I took Sophie because her mother wasn't equipped to raise her on her own. Maybe it was selfish of me, deciding to become a single father, I don't know. But I know now that Sophie needs a mother and a father. Two parents. And so will this baby."

"Jesus, Mason!" Pokey shouted. "Do you always have to be the big brother? Always have to look out for everybody else? Always have to know what's best? For me, Davis, Mama, the company? You're so worried about doing the right thing and keeping up appearances, have you even noticed what you're doing affects other people? And that maybe this one time you actually *don't* know what's best? What about Annajane? She loves you and you love her, and you're going to just throw that away? You're going to let her walk away — from you and her friends and her job?"

"Annajane understands," Mason said.

"Bullshit!" Pokey cried, her hands on her hips. "Bullshit. Bullshit. Bullshit."

"Aunt Pokey?" a small voice called from the hallway.

Sophie peeked around the doorway. Her

501

blond ringlets were a tangled mess, she had hot pink lipstick smeared around her mouth, and her sparkly pink glasses slid down her nose. "Are you and my daddy having a fight?" she asked timidly.

Pokey held out her arms to the little girl. "No, punkin," she said, looking shame-faced. "We weren't really fighting, we were just discussin'."

"And cussin'," Mason added. "But we're not really mad at each other. Right, Aunt Pokey?"

Sophie tiptoed into the room. She had obviously dressed herself in her second-best dress, a hand-smocked pink batiste dress she'd worn to her little cousin's christening, which she'd managed to put on backward, so that the tiny mother-of-pearl buttons fastened in the front. She wore a pair of unbuckled white sandals on her feet, and slung across her chest was her pink plastic purse.

"Don't you look nice," Mason said, looking down at her. "Are you all dressed up to go see your cousins?"

"I'm dressed up for the wedding," Sophie said. "But I can't wear my wedding dress, 'cuz Letha said she had to throw that nasty thing out after I got sick on it."

Her impression of her nanny was, as usual, uncanny, and both Mason and Pokey laughed.

Mason picked the little girl up and sat down

on the sofa with her on his lap. "I'm sorry, Soph, but you're not going to the wedding today. This is just for grown-ups. Me and Celia and your Nana. That's all."

Sophie's face crumpled. Her lower lip pooched out.

"I'm not even going to the wedding," Pokey said. "Who cares about a stinky old wedding, anyway? I bet they aren't even gonna have any cake."

"We're not," Mason assured her. "Not a lick of cake."

"But I wanna goooooo," Sophie wailed, huge crocodile tears running down her cheeks. "I wanna go with Daddy!"

Pokey plunked down on the sofa beside her brother. She patted Sophie's back. "Come on, punkin, don't cry. You and me are going to have a girl's night out. Do you know what that is?"

"Noooooo," Sophie sobbed. "I wanna go to the wedding. I don't wanna go girl's night out." She buried her face in Mason's starched white dress shirt. "I. Don't. Wannna. Idonwanna," came her muffled chant. "I donwanna. I donwanna!"

"Sure you do," Pokey said, attempting to shift Sophie onto her own lap. "It'll be lots of fun. We can bake some cupcakes. Pink ones. I bought pink sugar sprinkles just for us. And we can watch *The Little Mermaid*. And I'll make Uncle Pete sleep with the boys and it'll be just you and me in the big bed. I'll even make us pancakes for breakfast in the morning!"

But the little girl wrapped her arms tightly around Mason's neck and clung to him like a small, determined barnacle.

Mason looked stricken. "Help," he mouthed.

Pokey reached over and gently disentangled Sophie's arms, wrapping her in her own. "It's just for one night, Soph," she said. "And then tomorrow, Daddy will pick you up at my house and take you right back here to your own house and your own bed."

"Noooo," Sophie cried. "I donwanna."

Mason looked down at the hot pink smears on his shirt. "She's breaking my heart," he said. "What should we do?"

Pokey looked over Sophie's head at her brother. "Let's see if we can distract her," she whispered.

"Hey Soph," she said brightly. "Let me see that pretty dress of yours, will you?"

"No," the little girl said. But after a moment she slid out of Pokey's lap and did a slow twirl.

"It's bee-you-ti-full!" Pokey said encouragingly. Sophie did a faster spin, and the flap of her pocketbook opened, and a strand of silver chain slipped out and onto the carpet.

"You dropped your necklace," Mason said, picking it up to examine it. He frowned down at the chain. "Where did you get this, Soph?"

"It's my jewels," Sophie said, tucking the pocketbook protectively under her arm.

"Hmm," Pokey said, reaching out her hand to take the chain. "This is white gold, and that's a nice-sized sapphire stone. That's an expensive-looking jewel for a five-year-old."

"It's Celia's," Mason said. "I bought it for her at Christmas."

"Oh, Lawwwd," Pokey drawled. "If Celia finds out Sophie's been looting her stuff, you're gonna have hell to pay, brother."

"Christ," Mason muttered. "Like I don't have enough to deal with."

"Sophie," he said. "Have you been borrowing Celia's treasures? You know you're not supposed to get into her things."

"No," Sophie said petulantly.

"Sophie?" he said, a warning note in his voice. He held out his hand. "Can I see what's in your pocketbook?"

"It's my treasures," the little girl said, taking a step backward. "I found 'em."

"Okay," Mason said pleasantly. "But can I see what you've found? Please?"

Reluctantly, Sophie unwound the strap of the purse from her neck and handed it over to her father.

"Let's see," Mason said, reaching inside. He held up a silver-cased pink lipstick with a missing cap.

"Not mine," Pokey said. "I don't wear slutty

505

shades like that."

Mason shot her a warning look, but reached back inside the purse and brought out a handful of silvery objects, which he dumped on the sofa cushion. "Let's see what we've got here," he said, taking inventory.

"Couple sticks of chewing gum, some Quixie pop-tops, an earring . . ."

Pokey picked up the hand-tooled silver hoop earring. "I was wondering where that had gotten to."

Mason continued with the inventory. "Nail clipper, some kind of eye makeup thingy . . ." His voice trailed off and he held up a flat foil-wrapped package. "Pills!" He looked panicky. He grabbed his daughter's hand. "Sophie, you didn't swallow any of these pills, did you? Tell daddy the truth. Did you swallow any of these pills?"

Pokey reached over and took the packet, turning them over and reading the fine print of the label. A slow smile spread across her face.

"I didn't swallow any," Sophie said. "I only take pills Letha or Daddy gives me."

"Thank God," Mason said. "What are they, anyway? I wonder where Sophie got 'em?"

"They appear to be birth control pills," Pokey said, holding up the back of the packet so Mason could see. "And according to the prescription label, they belong to Celia Wakefield."

"What?" Mason said, taking the packet from his sister. "These must be an old prescription. Celia told me she was on the patch. That's how she got, er," he looked over at Sophie, who was listening attentively. "You know."

Pokey took the package back. "They're not that old," she told her brother. "According to the label, these were dispensed from the CVS Drugs out on the bypass, to Celia Wakefield, on April 1. That's two weeks ago. She picked them up a week before your wedding. And look," she said, pointing to the empty perforations in the foil. "There are ten pills gone. Seems to me Celia was on the pill, right up until three days ago."

She gave her brother a piercing look. "Isn't that when she told you she was pregnant?"

They heard the sound of the lock turning in the front door, and the sound of it opening and closing, and then the tap of high heels on the wooden floor.

Celia stood in the doorway of the den, with a plastic dry-cleaner's bag across her arm. "Mase? I picked up your suit from the cleaners. I knew you'd . . ." She saw Pokey sitting on the sofa beside Mason, and saw Sophie, seated on the floor, refilling her pocketbook with her treasures.

"What's going on?" she asked, sensing the hostility radiating from every pore of Pokey's body.

"Just a family conference," Pokey said.

"Giving it one last try, to convince your brother not to marry me, are we?" Celia asked, trying to sound lighthearted. "Mason's a better man than you give him credit for, Pokey."

Pokey held up the silver package of birth control pills. "And he's a smarter man than you give him credit for."

Celia snatched the pills from Pokey's fingertips. "Where did you get these?"

Pokey pointed to Sophie's pocketbook, which was once more slung across the child's chest. "Sophie has apparently been helping herself to some of your most secret treasures. We found these in her pocketbook, along with one of your lipsticks and some other things she picked up around the house."

"That's absurd," Celia said, but her laugh was hollow. She turned the package over. "I don't know where she found these, but I haven't been on the pill in months and months."

Mason stood up and took the package from Celia. "According to the label, you had this prescription filled two weeks ago." He pointed at the perforations from the missing pills. "What does this mean, Celia?"

Celia pulled herself up to her full five feet one inches of height. "It means I don't appreciate being interrogated like a common criminal." She shot Pokey a glance of unmitigated venom. "For your information, I *was* on the pill, months and months ago, but I switched to the patch right after Christmas. Anybody could have called the CVS and had this prescription refilled, and then planted it with Sophie to make me look bad. Darling, this is obviously some farce your sister has cooked up, to keep you from marrying me. But it won't work."

She turned on Pokey. "I just bet Annajane Hudgens is in on this nasty little plot of yours, isn't she? She'd do anything to try and get Mason back."

Mason glanced down at Sophie, who was watching the brewing storm with interest.

"Pokey," he said, keeping his voice pleasant. "Maybe you and Sophie should get started on that girl's night out."

"I don't wanna," Sophie protested, even while Pokey was taking her by the hand and attempting to lead her out of the room. "I wanna go to the wedding."

"Come on, Sophie," Pokey coaxed. "I don't think there's gonna be a wedding today."

"Over my dead body," Celia called.

Pokey turned and gave her a dazzling smile. "Oh, trust me, that can be arranged."

42

Celia stood by the fireplace, still clutching the plastic bag of dry-cleaning. But Mason had retreated to his desk. He had the package of birth control pills, and he kept turning it over and over. "Mason," she said, pleadingly. "You can't believe I would lie about the baby. Pokey did this. And Annajane. I swear, they refilled that prescription just to make me look bad, and then planted them with Sophie, so that you would find them. They'd do anything to keep us apart."

"Enough," Mason said. "You lied. Please don't make it worse by blaming my sister."

"You don't know them," Celia said, flinging the suit onto the back of a leather wing chair and marching over to the desk. "You think your baby sister is so perfect. And Annajane! You have no idea what that woman is capable of."

Mason kept staring down at the birth control pills.

"There never was any baby, was there?" he

asked, when he finally looked up at her.

"Of course there was!" Celia cried. "Would I make up something like that?"

The muscle in Mason's jaw twitched. "I think you did," he said, in disbelief. "I don't know why, but I do believe you cooked up a phony pregnancy because you knew that was the one way in the world I would go ahead with marrying you."

"No," Celia insisted. And then, her voice fainter. "No. This is Pokey and Annajane. They're out to get me. They refilled those pills . . ."

He sighed. "What would you say if I asked you to take a pregnancy test? Right now?"

"I'd say that proves you don't trust me," Celia said, her face growing pale. "That you'd take the word of your sister and ex-wife over mine."

"Unfortunately, I don't think I can trust you," Mason said. "I just can't understand why you would do something like this. You know I'm in love with another woman, but you'd go to this kind of lengths to trap me into a loveless marriage?"

"It wouldn't be loveless," Celia said. "Once we're married, and you see how good we are together, how happy I'll make you, you'll forget about Annajane. We'll sell Quixie, start a new business, have a family. I'm perfect for you. Everybody says so."

"No," Mason said. "Enough lies, Celia."

He picked up the telephone.

"Who are you calling?" Celia asked, her voice panicky.

"I'm calling Sallie," Mason said. "To tell her the wedding's off." He held up the receiver to her. "Unless you want to call her yourself?"

43

Mason Bayless was a man who lived up to his obligations. And the one he dreaded nearly as much as he'd dreaded going through with his wedding was telling his mother that he hadn't.

By four that afternoon, he'd arrived at Cherry Hill, removed the festive wreath of orange blossoms and hydrangeas from the front door, and poured his mother a stiff scotch and water and briefed her on the most salient details of the breakup.

"I don't understand," Sallie repeated, for the fifth or sixth time. "How could this happen? Are you sure this wasn't just some misunderstanding between the two of you?" She took a deep drag on her cigarette, tamped the ashes into the kitchen sink, then turned on the tap to wash them down the drain.

"No misunderstanding," Mason said drily. "There was never any pregnancy. Celia made it up, because she knew that was the only way I would marry her."

"That's just not like Celia," Sallie protested. "Such a lovely girl. With a wonderful head on her shoulders. I'm heartbroken. Really devastated." She studied her oldest son's lack of expression.

"Aren't you the least bit upset? About the baby, at least?"

"Relieved is the word I would use," Mason said. "Relieved and grateful."

Sallie sighed deeply. "And I was so looking forward to a Bayless grandchild."

"You have four grandchildren," Mason said sharply. "Remember?"

"Of course," she said quickly. "But Pokey's boys aren't Baylesses. They're Riggses. And Sophie, well, you know what I meant."

"No, Mother," Mason said, his voice icy. "What did you mean? That Sophie isn't a Bayless, because I never married her mother? Is that another reason you were so hot for me to marry Celia, so that you'd have a legitimate grandchild from me?"

"Stop it, Mason," Sallie demanded. "I won't have you speak to me like that. You know perfectly well that I've accepted Sophie as one of our own. I've always treated her exactly as I have Pokey's children. And I wanted you to marry Celia, and for her to have your children, because I believed she would make you happy and be an asset to this family. Is that so wrong for a mother to want?"

She took another drag on her cigarette and let the smoke curl from her nostrils, waving it away, as though she could wave away anything unpleasant or displeasing in her life.

"Whatever," Mason said. "It's done."

"But where will she go?" Sallie asked. "You'll let her stay on at the company, won't you? She has a consulting contract."

"Celia is gone," Mason said emphatically. "She's moving her things out of my house as we speak. As for Quixie, no, of course I'm not going to keep her on. We'll pay out what we owe her, but under the circumstances, it would be disruptive to business to allow her to stay on."

Sallie's eyes flared. "And yet you kept Annajane on. Even after the divorce."

"Yes, and thank God I did," Mason said. "No thanks to Davis. Or Celia."

Realizing that she was on shaky ground, Sallie quickly changed tack. She flicked a fingertip at the tray of plastic-wrapped crab bundles, the caviar-topped deviled eggs, and the bacon-wrapped chicken livers. "All this food," she said with a sigh. "For the second time in a week. And there are six bottles of champagne in the refrigerator and half a case of expensive-looking red wine in the dining room. And should I even mention the wedding cake? What on earth am I supposed to do with yet another wedding cake? I still have the top layer of the first one in the freezer down in the basement."

Mason shrugged. "I don't give a damn. I told Celia I didn't want any of it in the first place. Feed it to your bridge club. Throw it out. Or better yet, send it over to the nursing home, why don't you?"

Sallie winced. "I am not looking forward to explaining to the girls in bridge club about this latest debacle in your personal life. And as for sending caviar and chicken livers to a nursing home? Certainly not." She picked up the telephone on the kitchen counter. "We'll just have a particularly extravagant family dinner instead. Pokey and Pete and the children will come, of course, and I'll call Davis, too. You'll stay, of course."

"No thanks," Mason said. "There's somebody I have to see tonight. If she'll see me."

When she finally stopped laughing, Pokey hung up the phone.

"Was that Sallie you were talking to?" Pete Riggs asked, looking up from the DVD player he was trying to repair on the kitchen table.

"It was," Pokey said, still chuckling.

"What makes your mother such a laugh riot this afternoon?" Pete asked. He stabbed the Shuffle button, but the machine didn't move.

"Poor Mama," Pokey said, sitting down beside her husband. "I know I shouldn't have laughed right in her face like that, but she's really so clueless."

"What's she so clueless about this time?" Pete asked.

"Life. Family. All of it. She actually wanted me to call Mason and try to 'make him see the light' about his breakup with Celia."

"Like that was gonna happen," Pete said. He picked up a screwdriver and jabbed at the DVD player.

"And then when I told her I was thrilled that the bitch had been caught in her own web of deceit, she invited us all over to supper tonight — to eat the appetizers Celia ordered from the country club, for a wedding to which we were specifically uninvited."

Pete sniffed the DVD player and wrinkled his nose. "Does this thing smell funny to you? I think it smells like something crawled up here and died."

Pokey inhaled. "Eew. Rancid peanut butter. Probably Petey. I don't know what it is with that kid and peanut butter."

"So what did you tell her about dinner?" Pete asked.

"I said *hell* to the no," Pokey retorted. "Then she got her panties all in a wad because I told her I didn't think caviar and deviled eggs and chicken livers were ideal food for three little boys."

"But I love caviar and deviled eggs and chicken livers," Pete said plaintively.

"Pete! We are taking a stand here. We are not eating any food that has any connection to Celia Wakefield or her foiled attempt to drag my poor brother to the altar. Besides, we're having pizza tonight. And then Sophie and I are baking cupcakes. Pink ones."

"Okay, fine," Pete said. "I'm good with pizza. Also cupcakes, pink or otherwise. What does Sophie think about her father's canceled wedding?"

"Not fazed in the least." Pokey said. "She's really more upset about the fact that Mason made her give back that sapphire necklace of Celia's that she had in her pocketbook."

"Not to mention the birth control pills," said Pete, who'd already heard his wife's triumphant blow-by-blow account of the demise of Celia Wakefield. "Soph really saved the day, didn't she? If the kid hadn't found those pills and stashed them in her purse, and you guys hadn't found them when you did, poor old Mason would be celebrating his wedding night right now."

"Not a chance," Pokey said, jabbing at the back of the DVD player with a butter knife. "If Mason hadn't called off the wedding himself, I still had plan B."

"Do I want to know what that was?" Pete asked.

"Probably not," Pokey said. She got up, sat on her husband's lap, and patted his cheek. "Know this, Riggs. When it comes to messing with my family, Pokey don't play."

44

Celia Wakefield was an unholy mess. Her eyes were red and puffy from crying, and a nasty patch of acne had spontaneously erupted on her chin and was working its way north toward both her cheeks. She was hot and sweaty from lugging all the belongings she'd packed up from Mason Bayless's house and cramming them into the back of her Saab. She'd broken two nails and twisted her ankle.

And the very cherry on her parfait of personal misery was that she had gotten her period within the past hour. Two weeks early.

She'd been examining her options, and they didn't add up to much. If it weren't for the money she'd be losing out on, she'd have been positively giddy at the prospect of seeing Passcoe, North Carolina, in the rearview mirror. Where to next? Not Kansas. The lawyers from Baby Brands were making noises about a lawsuit, so she wouldn't be launching another children's clothing business anytime soon. Hmm. Texas? Or maybe

Florida? Lots of wealthy men with lots of lovely money. It was something to ponder. Now, she was already late for her meeting. Her cell phone rang and she snatched it up and answered without checking the caller ID, an impetuous decision she immediately regretted.

"Hey, honey," Cheryl's voice, coming live over the phone from South Sioux City, Nebraska, sounded like she'd been gargling with broken glass and battery acid. "Veronica tells me you're living in North Carolina now. I hear it's real nice down there."

"How did you get this number?" Celia demanded.

"Veronica give it to me," Cheryl said. "But that's not a very nice way to talk to your mama."

"Sorry, I'm having a really shitty day," Celia said. "What do you want?"

"Why do you assume I want something everytime I call you?" her mother asked.

"Because you always do. What is it this time? I hope it's not money, because I don't have any to spare. I just lost my job."

"Oh." Silence. "I wasn't calling to ask for nothing," Cheryl said, sounding hurt. "I just wanted your new address, so I could send your birthday present. Gene's got these real nice Louis Vuitton purses now, and I know you like that kind of stuff."

Her mother's boyfriend for the past ten

years was a grifter named Gene, who spent more time in lockup than he did in the house he shared with Cheryl.

"My birthday isn't until November," Celia said. "And how would Gene get his hands on Louis Vuitton handbags?"

"He's got his ways," Cheryl said airily. "Anyway, it's too bad about your job. I was thinking it might be nice to come visit you. I've never been to North Carolina."

"Why would you suddenly want to visit me now?" Celia asked. "Did Gene kick you out of the house?"

"Hell, no!" Cheryl said. "I just thought it would be nice to see you. It's been a real long time."

Not long enough, Celia thought. It had been six years and counting. She'd dropped in and out of college and was waitressing at a steakhouse when a good customer there offered her a job as a traveling sales rep for a company that sold a line of hospital linens. She'd "borrowed" her sister Veronica's car and headed out that night for St. Louis, with nothing more than the clothes on her back. The wad of cash she'd found in the glove box was a pleasant and unexpected bonus.

"Now is not a good time," Celia said flatly. *Never would be the perfect time to be reunited with her family.*

"Maybe you could come on back here,

while you're between jobs," Cheryl suggested. "There's plenty of room in the house. You hadn't even seen Jaymie's twins, and they're almost six. And Terri's boy Richie, he's a big old thing. Nearly twelve, I think. He's already started shaving, you believe that? And Jasmine, she's nine and just as tall as her mama."

"Are they all still living with Daddy in the double-wide?" Celia asked.

"I don't ask," Cheryl said. "Those girls don't care nothin' about their mama. I don't even get a card on Mother's Day. Doyle's the only family they care about."

Most likely, Celia thought, *what her two youngest sisters cared about was their father's latest disability check. Neither Jaymie nor Terri had bothered to graduate from high school, or to marry the various fathers of their children. Instead, they'd gotten an early and thorough education in the art of scamming from Doyle Wakefield.*

Celia peered through the Saab's windshield, at a booth near the window of the restaurant. "Look, Mama," she said. "I gotta go now. I'll give you a call with my new address when I get settled."

And when hell freezes over, she thought. *She really was going to have to get a new phone number now.*

"You do that, precious," Cheryl said. "And

you know, if you did happen to have a few extra bucks laying around, you could send 'em my way."

Davis Bayless sat across the table from Celia at the Waffle House on the bypass and wished he were somewhere else.

"You have to do something," she told him.

"What?" Davis said. "I can't hold a gun to his head, Celia. I can't make him marry you if he doesn't want to."

"He did want to," she insisted. "Right up until the minute that Annajane Hudgens crooked her little finger and decided she wanted him back."

Davis shrugged. "What can I say? My big brother is a big sap. Ole Annajane must know some tricks in the sack that we ain't heard of. Anyway, I'm the last person he's likely to listen to these days. My advice is, take what you can get and move on down the road. He offered to buy out your contract, right?"

"That's peanuts. If we'd gotten married, and the Jax deal had gone through, it would have been worth millions. To all of us. Now, I walk away with what? Maybe fifty thousand dollars? Screw that!"

Celia glared at Davis. "You have to make this right, Davis. I'm the one who brought Jerry Kelso and Jax to the table for this deal. Kelso had never heard of Quixie until I met him in that hotel bar in Atlantic City. I'm the one who made them understand what this brand is worth. Most importantly, I'm the one who sucked up to your mother, gained her trust, and then hammered it into her silly southern belle head just how much cash she will get out of this sale, and just how much she needs to get out of the godforsaken town of Passcoe, North Carolina."

"I know what all you did, and I appreciate it, Celia, I really do," Davis said soothingly. "And don't you worry. Once we get that deal with Jax inked, getting Celia Wakefield on board in an executive position, that's gonna be my number one priority. Jerry and I have already discussed it." He winked and then reached under the table and squeezed her thigh. "Davis is gonna take good care of you, baby."

She slapped his hand away. "I don't need taking care of that way. The only thing I want from you is an ironclad, signed agreement that I will be fairly compensated for my participation as a go-between in Jax's acquisition of Quixie."

"Sure thing," Davis said. "You have my word."

Celia's laugh had a nasty edge.

Like I would take the word of a man who'd fuck his brother's fiancée?

"I'd prefer to have it in writing," Celia said. "Just so there won't be any misunderstandings."

"Hey, now," Davis said, rearing back. "I'm on your side, remember? Didn't I help you out with that little problem you were having?"

"I don't know what you're talking about," she said.

Davis slid his hand over Celia's, trapping it on the tabletop. "Why, trying to get you knocked up, what else? Don't you think I figured out why you were in such a hurry to get in my pants Friday night? And me without a condom? I'll admit, my feelings were a little hurt when you first came to work at Quixie and immediately set your sights on Mason, instead of me, but I got over it eventually. Hell, I was even willing to take one for the team and let you pass off my baby as Mason's, if that's what it took to seal our little deal."

He glanced around the restaurant. It was only eight o'clock, past the dinner hour, too early for the night owls, and nobody he knew ever frequented the Waffle House, which was why he'd agreed to meet there.

"Hey, uh, you don't think Mason knows, do you? You know, about us? I mean, you didn't happen to mention that, right? Because that could make things kind of awkward. Him being my brother and all."

The seed of an idea took hold in Celia's imagination. *If you got right down to it, they were both from the same gene pool, so one*

Bayless was as good as the other, wasn't it? Davis wasn't the man Mason was. He never would be. But once the Jax deal was inked, he'd be just as rich.

"It's our little secret," she assured him.

She was about to pay for her coffee and leave when her cell phone rang. She grabbed for it, still not totally convinced Mason wouldn't have a change of heart. She saw the caller ID too late.

"Sissy! Is that really you?" Her baby sister Jaymie sounded drunk.

"Hey, Daddy! I got Sissy on the line," Jaymie called. "Hang on, hon, Daddy needs to talk to you real bad."

"Where did you get this number?" Celia said through clenched teeth.

"Veronica gave it to Terri and me," Jaymie said. "Listen, Sissy. Daddy's not doing too good. That last accident, he messed up his back. For reals. He's in a wheelchair . . ."

"I'm sorry, I'm afraid you have the wrong number again," Celia said pleasantly. She clicked the Disconnect button and dropped the phone into her purse. Davis was staring open-mouthed at her.

Celia took a deep breath. She really had to work on keeping her cool. "On top of everything else some lunatic keeps calling me over and over again. I'm going to have to get a new number."

"Yeah, tough luck," Davis said. He pushed

526

away the money Celia placed on the tabletop. "I'm glad we got together to talk tonight. Cleared the air. No hard feelings, right?"

She sighed and tried to look forlorn. It wasn't her strength. "Maybe it's for the best," she said, giving her imitation of wistfulness, standing to go, giving him the shot he was hoping for. She leaned over and gave him a lingering kiss, just to remind him of the good times.

"Good-bye, Davis. It's been fun."

"Well, hey," he said, confused. "It doesn't have to be good-bye, now, does it? I mean, I've got the evening free, and there's always the Pinecone Motor Lodge."

"That's so sweet," she said. "But I've had a really long day. I think I'll just drive over to Pinehurst and get myself a motel room and try to figure out my future."

"You do that," Davis said, beaming. "And give me a call when you get your new number."

"Don't worry," Celia promised. "You'll be hearing from me."

45

The florists were having themselves a high old time at the Pinecone Motor Lodge. A long banquet-sized table had been set up in the grassy courtyard and draped with a gauzy white cloth. A series of elaborate silver candelabras marched down the middle of the table, punctuated by raised epergnes of gorgeous centerpieces spilling lilies, hydrangeas, roses, tulips, and flowers whose names Annajane didn't know. The men, and a few women, were dressed in spring finery, milling about the tables, sampling from dozens of platters of appetizers and sipping wine from plastic champagne flutes.

She'd been holed up in her motel room most of the day, her phone turned off, all her focus turned toward the Quixie summer ad campaign, until, finally, Harold and Thomas had coaxed her out for a glass of wine shortly before dusk.

"I'm not really dressed for a cocktail party," she'd said, trying to beg off, but the men had insisted, so she'd changed out of her yoga pants and T-shirt into a somewhat respectable flowered, cotton ankle-length sundress and a pair of teal ballet flats. The dress dipped deeply in the front and criss-crossed with buttons at the shoulders. She pinned her hair up in a modified french twist and, in lieu of any real makeup, applied a quick bit of peach lip gloss.

"You look adorable," Thomas had assured her, handing her a glass of rosé and a stuffed mushroom cap. After polishing off the appetizer in two bites, she realized she hadn't eaten all day and gratefully accepted the plate full of food Harold fetched for her. "Much lovelier than that hussy who spent the night with your friend Harry Dix last night," Harold said. "You're like something out of *The Great Gatsby.*"

"Thank you," Annajane said, squeezing his arm affectionately. "Is flattery part of the package deal at the Pinecone Motor Lodge? If so, I might have to rethink my checkout date."

"We wish you would," Thomas said. "You're the first real friend we've made in Passcoe. People are curious about what we've done with the motel, but they seem a little standoffish. I mean, where's all that famous southern hospitality we've always heard about?"

"We've got to do a little marketing and networking for you," Annajane said. "Get you

529

out and about and meeting people in town. Seriously. If you haven't done it already, you should join the Chamber of Commerce. And either the Kiwanis or Rotary. And have you thought about hosting an open house here? People need to see what you've done with the Pinecone. Most of them probably still think it's this slightly sleazy no-tell motel it was for years and years."

"We *should* do that," Thomas said.

"This would be the perfect place to have out-of-town guests for weddings or the holidays," Annajane enthused. "It would be a great function space, too, especially if you built some kind of covered gazebo or pavilion. Passcoe doesn't really have that many places to hold gatherings, outside of the country club and the church social halls. You'd probably want to get a pouring license, too."

She gestured toward the elegant cocktail party spread out before them on the grassy courtyard. "You should take some photos tonight and put them up on your Web site and use them in all your marketing materials. The gorgeous flowers and food, and the light is so beautiful right now."

"Web site?" Harold said.

"Marketing materials?" Thomas said. "Annajane, we don't know anything about that kind of stuff. It's all we can do to keep this place up and running."

"If only we knew a good marketing person!"

Harold said, shooting a sideways glance at Annajane.

"Somebody with taste and talent and energy," Thomas said, looking squarely at Annajane. "You know anybody like that?"

"Sorry," she said. "I'd like nothing better than to work for you two. But I'm moving away after this week. Remember?"

"You said you were quitting your job," Harold said. "You'll need a new one, right? That doesn't mean you have to move away, does it?"

"I'm afraid so," Annajane said. "I've already given notice . . ."

"Ooh," Thomas said, interrupting. "Look at this cute car!" As he spoke, a flashy vintage red Chevelle convertible came cruising toward them. The top was down, and the driver's dark blond hair glinted in the late-day sun.

Harold turned toward Annajane, who had the oddest look on her face. "Somebody you know?" he asked.

"Used to know," she corrected him, watching as Mason parked the convertible in front of her unit. He spotted her in the courtyard, waved, and began to walk over.

"Excuse me, fellas," Annajane murmured.

Mason glanced around the courtyard at the men who were strolling the grounds, laughing and chatting and sipping wine. "What's all this?" he asked.

"It's a florists' convention of sorts," Anna-jane said. "Mason, what are you doing here? I thought we agreed not to see each other alone again."

"Don't you ever answer your phone?" he asked, sounding irritable. "I must have left you half a dozen messages this afternoon. And I'm pretty sure Pokey left a bunch. The wedding got called off."

She dimly heard her own breath catch. "Is that so?" She was trying for nonchalant, but her voice was shaky. She sucked at nonchalant.

Mason didn't look like much of a bride-groom. He wore a faded and rumpled pink oxford-cloth button-down shirt tucked into a pair of threadbare old jeans that rode down on his hips and sagged in the seat. His sock-less feet were jammed into a pair of beat-up Top-Siders that she was sure he'd owned since his high school days. He was paler than she could ever remember seeing him before. Celia seemed to have sucked all the life out of him.

He nodded. "We need to talk. Will you go for a ride with me?"

Annajane looked dubious.

"Not to the farm this time, I swear," Mason said. "Please?"

Her heart was thudding in her chest. She wanted to go, wanted to ride off into the sunset with him, but what happened after sunset? She'd been Mason's second choice, after Celia. What made this time any different?

He must have guessed what was on her mind.

Mason took her hand and swung her around to face him. His mouth softened, and his eyes took in the flowered dress that swirled around her ankles in the late-day breeze and the graceful arch of her bare neck and slim arms. Annajane wasn't model-thin. She had curves, real hips and thighs that he could see silhouetted through the thin cotton of her dress, and breasts that were round and promising. Her full lips were slightly parted, her large green eyes serious and sad. He'd hurt her badly, and had no right to ask for another chance. But how could he not?

He looked puzzled. "Have you always been this beautiful?"

Annajane cocked her head. "Mason? You've seen me five days a week every week for the past five years. I look like I've always looked. Except maybe a few pounds heavier and a few more wrinkles," she said ruefully.

"No," he insisted. "You're different. I can't describe it. Like a peach, perfectly ripe. Wait, that's no good. You were always pretty before. But now, it's like, you've grown into who you were supposed to be. Luscious. Yeah, that's it."

She blushed and looked away. "What am I supposed to say to that?"

"Say you'll come with me," he said. "One more time."

The sun was slipping toward the glowing green horizon as the convertible bumped slowly down the dirt road, washboarded by rains and tree roots. Overgrown branches slapped at the sides of the car and kudzu vines scratched Annajane's bare arm. She knew, of course, where they were headed as soon as they passed through the wrought-iron gates at Cherry Hill.

Annajane glanced at Mason's profile. He seemed more relaxed, steering with his left hand, his right arm slung casually over the seat back.

"I need to get out here with a sling-blade and cut back some of this stuff before it completely blocks off the road," he said. "I had to stop the car twice the other night to drag fallen trees out of the way. And, I swear, I think I saw a glimpse of a coyote."

She shivered and tucked her legs beneath her and turned toward him. "When was the last time you were out here before that?"

He looked chagrined. "Probably the day I moved the last of my stuff out. How about you?"

"The second anniversary of our breakup," she said. "I was in a particularly melancholy mood. Guess I just wanted to torture myself. I was shocked by how fast everything went to seed."

A moment or two went by, and then they turned a curve in the road and the stone cottage came into view. Annajane gasped.

Vines completely covered the stone façade, with the exception of the doorway, where Mason had obviously cut a path through the growth. Part of the chimney had tumbled down, and the camellia bushes had reached nearly roof height, completely obscuring the front windows.

"This is so sad," she said softly. "Much sadder than when I was here last."

He pulled to the side of the house, driving as far forward as he could, until the nose of the Chevelle protruded from a thicket of privet and they could see the glint of the lake in the fading daylight.

Mason got out of the car, went around to the trunk, brought out a long-handled pair of loppers, and proceeded to spend ten minutes shearing off enough of the privet until they had an unobstructed view of the water.

"It's a start," he said, wiping his hands on the seat of his jeans before climbing back into the driver's seat.

"Looks like you'd need a backhoe and probably a bulldozer, too, to get all the way to the edge," Annajane observed. She half-stood in the seat, trying to get a better look.

"It's getting so dark, I can't see the dock and the boathouse," she said. "Is it even still there?"

"It's there, but it's gotten so rickety it's not safe to walk out onto it," Mason said. "Guess I need to post warning signs. Now that the weather's warming up, I'd hate for somebody to come over here by boat and try to explore — and wind up getting killed when the dock collapses under them."

Annajane shivered involuntarily at the idea. Mason reached into the back seat of the car and handed her a blanket. "Here," he said, drawing it around her shoulders. "I'd forgotten how quickly it cools down out here after dark."

"What, no flask?" Annajane asked.

He reached under the seat and produced a leather-wrapped thermos. Uncapping it, he poured a drink into the cup-shaped top, and the sound of crushed ice chinked against the worn silver. "I wasn't sure you'd come tonight," he said. "But I thought if you did, considering what happened last time, maybe I should mix up a proper drink."

Annajane took a tentative sip and laughed. It was Quixie and bourbon. "Very nice. So. What did you want to discuss?"

"I have a proposal I'd like you to consider," Mason said, turning toward her. "And I know I have no right to ask. But I have to anyway. I came so close today to ruining my life, it scared me. Pokey was trying to talk me out of marrying Celia, and she said something that hit home. She said Celia would ruin my life if I went through with the wedding. But I knew, as soon as she said it, that I'd already damned near ruined it myself. Worrying about what other people think. About my mother, about people in town. I was so concerned with *my* image, *my* responsibilities. All I could think about was my big, selfless sacrifice. And how noble I was. Marrying a woman I'd come to detest, just because I thought she was having my child."

"Go on," Annajane said, taking another sip of bourbon and handing it over to him.

Mason took a long drink. He looked at Annajane. Her cheeks were pink, and her pinned-up hair had come undone. He reached out and touched a tendril of windblown hair. "You didn't listen to any of your voice-mail messages today?"

"No," she said. "I decided to just shut out the whole world, since the world seemed such an unfriendly place to be in. I was determined to get the Quixie promotion plans nailed down. I think I've got the radio and television ads figured out . . ."

Mason put his fingertips across her lips. "There isn't any baby," he said. "Celia faked the pregnancy."

Annajane's eyes widened. "How did you figure it out?"

He rolled his eyes. "When Pokey came over to pick up Sophie before the wedding today, we just happened to see a necklace that had slipped out of her pink purse."

Annajane nodded.

"You know how Sophie does. She's a little magpie, always picking up shiny stuff and hiding her treasures in that purse. Anyway, the necklace somehow fell out, just as they were about to leave, and it was an expensive thing I'd given Celia for Christmas last year. So we checked out the rest of the contents. Low and behold, we found a half-empty package of birth control pills, with a prescription label that said they were Celia's."

"I don't understand," Annajane said.

"I wouldn't have either," Mason said with a chuckle. "Celia told me she'd been on the patch — that's how she got pregnant, because she'd been taking antibiotics, and they'd counteracted the hormones in the patch. But as Pokey helpfully pointed out, the drugstore label said the prescription had been filled just two weeks ago, and it looked like Celia had been taking the pills — right up until the day she claimed she was pregnant."

"Ohhhhh," Annajane said.

"When Celia showed up at the house, I confronted her with the pills," Mason said. "She tried to lie her way out of it. It wasn't very pretty."

"What was her explanation?" Annajane asked.

He shrugged. "She tried to say it was an old prescription and that anybody could have had it refilled. She even suggested that you and Pokey had gotten the pills and planted them on Sophie."

"Me!" Annajane said indignantly.

"Doesn't matter," Mason said. "She's an expert liar, but this time, she really couldn't talk around the truth. And so . . . it looks like I'm not going to be a father again. Anytime soon." His lips twisted into a sardonic grin.

"Not a very convincing smile," Annajane observed.

He ran his fingers through his hair. "I never said I didn't want more children," Mason said. "I do want more. Sophie needs brothers and sisters. I'd almost convinced myself that everything would be okay with another child, as long as I was around to make up for Celia's shortcomings."

"But you changed your mind?"

"It's not enough to have a husband and wife living in the same house," Mason said. "If those people don't really love each other, it's not a family; it's a fraud, with or without a marriage license. And a child will eventually see through that. I don't want that for Sophie. Or any child."

"That's pretty deep stuff there, Mason," Annajane said.

"Jesus," he said. "I came so close to blowing it. You'll never know how close."

Annajane was almost tempted to tell him the full extent of Celia's deception. But she knew she wouldn't. It was a hurt he didn't need.

"What happens next? With Celia, I mean?"

He glanced at his watch. "She and her stuff should be gone by now. And her contract with Quixie has been terminated. I'll pay out the rest of the money she's due. And hopefully, that will be the end of it."

He took a long drink from the cup and passed it back to her.

She shook her head and handed it back. She needed to keep a clear head. "You said you had a proposal for me?"

Mason rolled to the right and reached into the pocket of his jeans. He turned toward Annajane, opened his fist and revealed a ring on the flattened palm of his hand. It was the engagement ring he'd given her their first time together. He waited for her reaction.

Nothing.

"I want," he swallowed hard. Mason didn't think of himself as a big talker. He wasn't really effusive. That was his brother's gift. He'd never had a problem talking to Annajane before. But tonight the words stubbornly resisted being formed into sentences. He'd been thinking about this moment off and on for five years, since the day she'd left. He'd

540

rehearsed the scene in his mind, trying to make it perfect.

She slapped at a bug on her neck and waited. He couldn't read what she was thinking. That had changed, too. Once, her face had been an open book, vulnerable, patient, expectant. Now, she was a mystery to him. Somehow it was frightening and sexy at the same time.

He took a deep breath. "I want to ask you for a do-over. I know I don't deserve it. And I have no right to ask for it. But I love you, Annajane. I can't lose you again. I just can't. And I know I'm doing this all wrong, blurting out stupid stuff, and it's crazy to think you'd take me back, after everything I put you through, but I can't help it. I'm going nuts here."

Annajane was still staring at him.

"Anything?" he asked.

"I'd like for you to kiss me," Annajane said quietly.

He carefully put the ring in the ashtray, then pitched the rest of the drink out the open window and tossed the cup into the backseat. Mason held her face between his hands. He rubbed his thumb across her lower lip, and then he lowered his face to hers.

Annajane's lips were warm and full and sweet, reminding him of ripened cherries. He teased his tongue into her, and laced his fingers in her long, thick hair. Her arms went around his neck, and he slid out from beneath the steering wheel, drawing her closer, letting his hand trail down the smooth skin of her bare arms. She smelled different than he remembered, not the girlish floral scent she'd worn during their marriage; this perfume was spicy, citrus, even exotic. He kissed her earlobes, and her throat, and the hollow of her neck, and his hands drifted downward; slipping one strap of her sundress from her shoulder, he nudged it the rest of his way with his chin, kissing her breast while she raked her fingers through his hair and down his back.

There were buttons on the straps of her dress, and he fumbled, trying to unbutton one, hoping she'd help him out, but instead, she sat back and assessed him with cool green eyes, before catching his hand in hers. She kissed him deeply, then drew back.

"What was the question again?" she whispered.

"I want you to marry me," Mason said urgently, his hands going to her other shoulder, tugging uselessly at the buttons. "But first, could we take this dress off?"

She kissed him, and nipped his lower lip with her teeth. "I'm afraid not. Not tonight anyway."

46

Mason wasn't used to being told no. He wasn't even used to maybe. He grinned that lazy grin of his, knowing full well the effect it had always had on her. "No, we can't take this dress off, or no, you won't marry me?"

She slapped at another mosquito that had landed on her arm and kissed him lightly. "Hmm. As much as I love this place, I really don't love getting eaten alive by mosquitoes. In case you haven't noticed, they are currently feasting on my flesh."

He looked stricken. "I'm sorry. I didn't stop to think. I mean, you always loved it out here at the lake. It was our special place. I just wanted to be out here with you, again, when I, you know . . ."

"Asked me to marry you?"

"You're really not going to make this easy on me, are you?"

"Not this time." She kissed him again, this time, slipping her tongue into his mouth, pressing herself against him, flattening her breasts against his chest.

He groaned and tried to pull her onto his lap, but she laughed again and moved away. She curled her arms around his neck. "I want you, Mason. I really do. I guess I never stopped wanting you, even after I should have known better."

"Annajane," he started, but this time she was the one doing the shushing.

"I'll give you a do-over. But this time, I need to feel wanted. I want to be courted and flirted with. I need to believe I'm the only woman in the world you want to be with."

He gripped her arm. "You are. You always were. I was just too stupid to realize it, and to realize that you needed to hear it from me. And you will. I swear, I will never take your love for granted again. I'll spend the rest of my life reminding you what you mean to me."

Annajane propped one elbow on the seat back and sighed contentedly. "God, I've missed you."

He took her left hand and tenderly kissed each finger, and then he slid the engagement band onto her ring finger. She cupped his chin in her hands and kissed him deeply, and then handed the ring back.

"I haven't finished," she said sweetly. "If I marry you . . ."

Mason frowned. "You mean, when. Right?"

"If," she said, lifting her chin. "I definitely

mean if. If I marry you, we can't go back to the way things were. I won't be the little woman back at the house waiting for your phone call that never comes."

"Annajane, I've changed," Mason said.

"Good, because I've changed, too," she said. "At least the divorce did that for me. I'm good at what I do, Mason. I mean, really good. If you'll let me, I think I can help save Quixie. This summer promotion, if we can get the production started on the ads and commercials and Facebook campaign right away, I think it might really work. And I don't care what Davis says; I know you're right about adding the new Quixie flavors. We've got to expand the brand, not retrench. But you're going to have to really trust in me and believe in my professional abilities. The way you trusted Celia."

He looked shame-faced. "You're right. I totally bought into her vision for the company. Until the shine began to wear off, and I saw what was beneath."

"It was a pretty beguiling package," Annajane said.

"All of it was sham," Mason said. "Me, the company, we were just a commodity to her, something she could pluck, polish, and then peddle."

"Was that pluck, or fuck?" Annajane asked, laughing at the shocked look on Mason's face. "See? I told you you've been underestimating me."

"Never again," he pulled her into his arms. "Are we done here?"

"Not quite," Annajane said, trying to sound stern, which was difficult while he was nuzzling her neck. "Do you get what all this means, Mason? I want us to be full partners. In everything. I won't be like your mama. I'm not interested in bridge or in running the altar guild. There's nothing wrong with those things, but they're not me."

He was kissing her again. "I am not marrying my mother. And you are not marrying a man like my father." He tipped her chin up. "I love you, and only you. I will never cheat on you, Annajane. You are the only partner I will ever want, or need."

She kissed him back. "I've been trying not to think about it, but what happens after next week? You'll find out how your father divided up the company. What if Davis gets his way? What if you have to sell the company after all?"

"Worrying about that now won't change whatever is in my dad's will," Mason said firmly. "And if we have to sell the company, at least I'll have a kick-ass partner to help me start a new one. Right?"

"Right," she said. She held out her hand and held her breath while he replaced the ring. She held it up to the moonlight to admire it. "I'd forgotten how much I loved this thing," she said.

"And me," he said helpfully, sliding her onto his lap.

"Yes," she said. "You, too." She pushed herself off his lap. "Now can we please go back to the Pinecone? You were going to court me, remember? If we're going to do it, let's do it right."

On the way back to the motel, she found the cassette tape she'd made and slid it into the player. When Steve Perry sang the opening lines of "Open Arms" she looked over and saw that Mason was singing right along with Journey at the top of his lungs. Shane had said Journey was cheesy. She didn't care. This was their song. They were getting a do-over. For once, their timing was flawless.

47

Annajane looked around the conference
room of the law offices of Thomas and Fleishman, attorneys at law, and saw that the lines
had already been drawn in what looked like a
troubling Bayless family feud. Sallie, dressed
in a chic black St. John Knits suit, black and
bone Ferragamo spectator pumps, and her
ever-present pearls, had seated herself at the
head of the sleek glass and chrome table.

Davis sat at her right hand, in his customary navy suit and striped rep tie. He'd scooted
his chair over until it was only inches from
his mother's, and their heads were bowed
together as they shared a whispered confidence.

By contrast, Mason had seated himself at
the far end of the table. He looked remark-
ably composed, Annajane thought. His pale
green dress shirt and khaki slacks were crisply
pressed and he wore a hunter green tie with
the red Quixie Pixie logo woven into it. Annajane smiled to herself when she saw that tie.

She'd custom-ordered the ties for all the Bayless men: Glenn, Mason, Davis, and even Pete, the first year of her marriage. Mason, who seldom wore a dress shirt, let alone a tie, swore he loved his Quixie tie. But she couldn't remember ever seeing him wear it again. The tie, she knew, was Mason's subtle way of letting his family know where he stood. With Quixie.

He glanced over at her, saw what she was looking at, and gave her a wink. Annajane looked away. How could he be so relaxed, knowing the company's fate — their fate — would be revealed in just a few moments?

She'd been a bundle of nerves all morning, trying on and discarding outfits until her room at the Pinecone was strewn with clothing, shoes, and jewelry. In the end, she'd decided on a slimly cut pale aqua sleeveless sheath with a matching jacket. She'd twisted her hair into a modified french knot and, on a whim, chose Grandma Bayless's diamond engagement ring as her only piece of jewelry — an unspoken declaration of her loyalty. To him. No matter what the day's outcome.

Annajane had nearly turned her car around when she arrived at Norris Thomas's law office above the Mid-State Bank. Why should she be here, she asked herself, for the tenth time that morning. This was Mason's battle, not hers. But when she saw Davis and Sallie drive up together in Davis's Porsche Boxster, she knew why she'd come. For him, yes, but mostly for herself.

Glenn Bayless considered her part of his family. He'd made that clear the day of her wedding to Mason, when he made a special trip to her house to tell her about his gift of stock in Quixie. No matter what Davis or Sallie thought, she too had a stake in Quixie's future.

She waited until Sallie and Davis went into the bank, gave them a five-minute head start, and then followed them in. Sallie's greeting to her when she entered the conference room was decidedly frosty.

Annajane was surprised to realize that for the first time she could remember, she wasn't fazed by Sallie's hostility toward her. "Hello, Sallie," she said sweetly.

The conference room door opened, and all eyes were riveted in that direction. Pokey rushed in, her face flushed, her hair mussed.

She wore a brightly flowered red, yellow, and purple linen maternity tunic; yellow slacks; and spangly purple thongs, and the oversized tote slung over her shoulder was actually a green and navy quilted diaper bag.

Sallie's eyes flickered briefly but meaningfully over her daughter's outfit. "There you are," Sallie drawled. "We were about to send out an all-points bulletin for you. You do know you're ten minutes late?"

"Sorry, Mama," Pokey said, sinking down

into the empty chair between Annajane's and Mason's. "The sitter was late, and then I couldn't find the car keys because Clayton had hidden them in the potty chair, and then I got stopped at the railroad crossing by a train that I swear was a mile long . . ."

"Never mind," Sallie said, waving away any other excuses. "Just so you're here. Did you tell the receptionist to let Norris know we're all present now?"

"She knows," Pokey said, reaching for the bottle of water sitting in front of her place at the table and taking a hefty swig. "She said to tell you he's on the phone."

"He needs to let one of his junior associates tend to the phones so he can tend to business," Davis snapped. He glanced down at his watch. "I'm about over all this waiting."

"Relax, Davis. We've been waiting five years," Pokey said. "Another five minutes won't kill us."

"Some of us give a shit," Davis shot back. "Some of us have a business to attend to."

"Davis!" Sallie said sharply, laying a warning hand on his sleeve. "That's enough."

But Pokey was undaunted. "It's not even ten thirty yet. No worries, Davis. You can sell off the company after lunch, and then you can hightail it to Figure Eight Island and still have plenty of time to spend your new fortune."

"Pauline," Sallie said sternly. "I want this unpleasantness stopped immediately."

"Whatever," Pokey said. "I guess we know whose side you're on, Mama."

"I'm not on anybody's side," Sallie said, struggling to retain her majestic bearing. She looked around at her three grown children. "We are all here for the same reason, and I'd appreciate it if you would all remember that. Your father would not have tolerated this petty bickering."

"Not so petty, Mama," Mason said. "Davis wants to sell to Jax Snax for thirty million. That's a lot of pepperoni popcorn."

Pokey giggled, but before Sallie could admonish her again, Norris Thomas walked into the room, a thick file folder clutched tightly under his left arm.

Annajane had met Thomas on several occasions and reflected now that he didn't seem to have aged in the past ten years, despite the fact that he must be in his late seventies. His build was storklike, with long legs and a slight paunch in the belly. His wiry white hair stood up in tufts above his high, patrician forehead, and the silver aviator-frame glasses he'd favored for the past thirty years had come and gone back into fashion again without his notice.

Davis and Mason got up and shook hands, and Sallie, still seated, coolly offered her own hand in greeting, deliberately making the elderly attorney a supplicant, rather than the trustee of a multimillion-dollar family fortune.

Pokey stood and gave the older man a hug. "Uncle Norris," she said. "How is Miss Faye?"

"She's good, spoiling the grandchildren rotten, and she sends her love," Thomas said. He turned and greeted Annajane warmly, before making his way to a chair in the middle of the table on the far side.

He cleared his throat twice, took a sip from the bottle of water at his place, and cleared his throat once more.

"All right, y'all," he started, flipping the file open on the table. "I do apologize for being tardy." He peered down his nose through the spectacles at the file, and then at the family members ranged around the table. "I'm happy to see that everybody is here today, and I trust that you all are enjoying good health?"

"We're fine, Norris," Davis said impatiently. "Busy, but fine."

Sallie shot him a look, but Davis shook it off. "The trust, Norris. We really need to know the details of the trust Dad set up for us."

Looking unperturbed, Norris began handing around five sheaves of stapled documents. "This is a copy for everybody concerned," he said. "The document you now have in your hands is the irrevocable trust drawn up by Robert Glenndenning Bayless. The trust provides for the division of stock in the legal entity called Carolina Carbonated Beverage Company, or Quixie."

As Glenn Bayless's widow and children bent their head over the document and began leafing furiously through the pages, Norris went on.

"As you all know, Glenn was proud of his family's ownership of Quixie, and of Quixie's contributions to this community. His greatest wish was that the company would always stay in Passcoe and that it would be run by his heirs. This was the reasoning behind the provision mandating that the company could not be sold for a period of five years following his death."

Norris was speaking, but Annajane was the only one listening. The others' eyes were glued to the thick document in their hands.

Norris took a deep breath. His gaze fell on Sallie's elegantly coiffed head, bowed over the trust agreement.

"Glenn wanted the division of the trust kept confidential for that same period of time," he said, "for reasons he did not divulge to me, but which I might guess at. It was always his intention to have the company run by his sons, Mason and Davis."

Davis nodded but didn't look up, still scanning the fine print.

"But," Norris went on, "Since you, Sallie, were provided for quite generously through Glenn's will, with ownership of real estate, stocks, cash, jewelry, and other real property, Glenn decided to divide ownership of Quixie amongst his children."

Sallie's head shot up, and her eyes widened. "What exactly does that mean?"

Norris coughed again. "Well, uh, the children inherit the company."

"Not me?" Her eyes narrowed. "Are you telling me I have no ownership in my family company? No vote in how it's run?"

"Glenn felt," Norris said, apologetically, "that since your commitment was to rearing your family and being active in the community, that you would not desire to be burdened at this stage in your life with ownership in the corporation."

"That's crazy!" Sallie cried. "Glenn depended on my advice. I was his partner, in everything!"

"Of course you were," Norris said soothingly. "Nobody questions that."

"Apparently he did!" Sallie cried, shoving the papers away from her. "My God! I can't believe this."

Davis reached over and rubbed his mother's arm lovingly. "It's all right, Mama. None of us will do anything about the company without your approval. You know that."

"Of course," Mason echoed, looking at

Pokey, who said nothing.

"Well," Norris said, "that, uh, leads us to the next matter. And I'm afraid this is going to be very awkward, but as trustee it's my duty to follow through with Glenn's wishes, to the letter."

"Awkward?" Pokey looked amused. "More awkward than telling Mama she's out of running the company?

"I'm afraid so," Norris said, two bright spots of red blossoming high on his cheekbones. "So let's just get to it. With the exception of the small, minority portion of stock Glenn left to you, Annajane, as his daughter-in-law, the rest of the stock is to be divided amongst the four living children of Robert Glendenning Bayless."

"Four?" Davis said. "What the hell?"

It was as though a live wire had been poked directly into the skull of everyone sitting around the conference room table. Everyone, that is, but Annajane and Norris Thomas.

"Four," Norris said firmly. "Mason Sheppard Bayless, Davis Woodrow Bayless, Pauline 'Pokey' Bayless Riggs, and, er, the minor child, Sophie Ann Bayless."

Dead silence.

Finally, Pokey spoke up. "Uncle Norris, I don't understand. You're saying Daddy left stock in the company to Sophie? We didn't even know Sophie existed until after Daddy died. And she's Mason's daughter. Daddy

556

didn't leave stock to any of the other grand-children, did he?"

Davis was leafing furiously through the trust documents. "What kind of crazy shit is this? You're saying Sophie, a five-year-old, for Christ's sake, has a share in Quixie equal to mine? That can't be."

Norris Thomas looked pleadingly at Mason, who had been strangely quiet. "Mason, you're going to have to help me out here."

"Yeah," Davis barked. "Help all of us out. Help us understand how you managed to have your illegitimate child inherit our mother's share of the company. I wanna hear this, *brother*."

Annajane felt something inside her stir. Mason was staring at his mother, and his eyes, riveted on hers, were filled with a sad-ness Annajane hadn't seen in him since that day in the emergency room, when he'd learned of his father's death. It was as though a fog had lifted, and she could suddenly see, with crystal logic, the meaning of everything that had happened over the past five years.

"Sophie's not my daughter," Mason said quietly. "Not biologically, anyway. She's Dad's." He looked at Davis, and then at Pokey. "She's our sister." He reached across the table and took Annajane's hand, squeez-ing it tightly. She squeezed it back and held on for dear life.

48

Every head in the room turned toward Sallie Bayless. "Mason, for God's sake!" she cried, her face drained of blood.

Davis jumped from his chair, fists clenched. "What the hell kind of slimy stunt are you trying to pull here? Ain't no way Sophie is Dad's. And I'll tell you what, we have all had it with your high-handed tactics. Blood or no, I am fixing to give you the ass kicking you have been begging for."

The room was dead quiet.

Mason looked directly at his brother. "Bring it," he said, unblinking.

Norris Thomas looked supremely uncomfortable. He coughed and cleared his throat and stared down at the stack of papers on the table.

Pokey was kneeling down beside her mother, ineffectively patting Sallie's shoulder. "Mama, did you know anything about this? About Sophie?"

"No," Sallie said, flinty-eyed. "And I refuse

to believe it. Mason, I cannot believe you would stoop so low. To accuse your father . . . it's . . ." She took a deep breath. "It's an unspeakable, unforgivable lie, and I want you to take it back. This instant."

"Um, Sallie, everybody?"

All heads swiveled toward Norris Thomas.

The elderly attorney tugged at the collar of his shirt. A fine film of perspiration beaded his forehead. "Mason is telling the truth. Sophie is the legal issue of Glenn Bayless. I understand that this is a shock to all of you, as it was a shock to me. Glenn was my oldest, most trusted friend, but I assure you, there is no doubt about the child's paternity."

"But, how?" Pokey asked, her voice catching.

Norris looked beseechingly in Mason's direction. Annajane squeezed his hand and gave him an encouraging nod.

"Mama, I'm sorry," he said, turning toward Sallie, his voice low. "I truly wish you wouldn't have had to find out this way."

"Mason didn't know what was in the trust agreement," Norris said. "I gave my word to Glenn that I would keep everything in confidence until the day I disclosed the details of the settlement."

"Mason?" Pokey asked.

"Dad . . . met this woman at a car rental place. At the Jacksonville airport. Her name was Kristy. They had an, um, relationship.

And she got pregnant. With Sophie."

"Glenn was made aware of the pregnancy shortly before his death," Norris volunteered. "We had already drawn up the trust mechanism some months earlier, after he'd experienced some cardiac issues."

"Wait," Pokey said. She glanced over at her mother. "Daddy had heart problems before?"

Sallie only shrugged, tight-lipped. "Of course not. Glenn was perfectly healthy, as far as I knew."

Norris Thomas did not contradict the widow, but it was obvious that he was working from his own set of facts.

"Glenn came to me, at that time, and he was, naturally, quite embarrassed about the, um, child. We drew up a confidential document that would provide financial support for the child's mother, and the child, of course. And at that time, Glenn determined that he wanted that unborn child to have an equal ownership share in the family company."

"Unbelievable!" Sallie cried. "He wanted some bastard to have what belonged to *my* children, his real family? And you went along with this lunacy, Norris?"

"Dad would never do anything like that," Davis said. "He would have never cheated on Mama. Never! This is the biggest cock-and-bull story I've ever heard." He looked to Pokey. "Are you gonna let Mason sit there and defame your father like this?"

"But Daddy did cheat on her," Pokey said sadly. "Mason and I caught him, years ago. And that's why I can believe he cheated on her again."

"What the *hell* are you talking about?" Davis said fiercely. "He would never. Goddamn it, Pokey! Are you in cahoots with Mason now, too?"

"It's true," Pokey said, watching her mother's drawn face. "It was years and years ago. Mason and I went down to the house at Wrightsville Beach on the spur of the moment. Daddy was there, with a woman. I was just a kid, but even I knew what they were up to."

"I don't believe it," Davis said. "You've got no proof."

"The Chevelle," Pokey said, blinking back tears. "Dad said he was giving it to Mason as a twenty-first-birthday gift. But it was a bribe. So he wouldn't say anything to Mama about that girl."

"Not that I would have," Mason said. "I hoped she'd never find out. About any of this."

"Mama?" Davis said.

"I will not have this," Sallie said, her voice strained. "I will *not* have you children dishonor your father's memory this way. Do you two hear me? Do you?" Again, she didn't raise her voice. She didn't have to.

Sallie fixed Norris Thomas with a withering stare. "How dare you? How dare you make these grotesque allegations about a man who is not here to defend himself? Norris, I would never have expected this of a man of your reputation."

"This bullshit trust won't fly," Davis added. "We'll hire our own lawyers and challenge it." He thrust out his chin aggressively in Mason's direction. "That bastard kid of yours won't get a nickel of Dad's money."

Thomas opened the folder in front of him and brought out a single sheet of paper. "Davis, I can't stop you from doing what you think is best. But you should know that your father was very specific about the trust agreement. I did try to convince him he might provide for his unborn child in other ways, but he was adamant that each of his children would have an equal share in Quixie. And I should also tell you that we've done DNA testing, and it absolutely proves that Glenn Bayless was Sophie's father."

He handed the paper across to Davis, who angrily batted it to the floor.

Thomas retrieved the paper without comment. He'd been a small-town estates and trusts lawyer for five decades. He'd witnessed more colorful dramas than this. He coughed, and his face colored slightly. "After Glenn's death, I contacted the child's mother, to let her know about the provisions of Glenn's will. Unfortunately, it was the first she knew that he'd passed away."

Pokey winced.

"The mother's pregnancy was normal and seemed to be going smoothly," Thomas went on, "but the baby was born somewhat prematurely."

"Sophie was in the neonatal intensive care unit at University Hospital in Jacksonville for six weeks," Mason said. "They really weren't sure she would make it and, even if she did, whether or not she would have lingering developmental problems." He reached across the table and took Annajane's hand again.

"Norris, uh, thought that somebody in the family should be aware that this baby, our half sister, was fighting for her life in the neonatal unit," Mason said. "It was a risk, but he confided in me. I went down to Jacksonville several times to check on her.

"She was so tiny," he marveled. "I'd never seen a baby that small. Theoretically, I could hold her in the palm of my hand. Except I couldn't, because they had her hooked up to all the tubes and monitors. They wouldn't let me hold her until shortly before they released her. But the first time I did, I knew she was ours."

He gave his weeping sister a pleading look. "She had Dad's blue eyes. My damned high forehead, and just the barest fuzz of blond curls. Just like Pokey's baby pictures."

"Stop it," Davis shouted, pounding the tabletop with his fist.

Sallie stood abruptly, pushing her chair back with such force that it went crashing to the floor. "I won't listen to another word of this," she said. She got to the door and looked over her shoulder at Davis.

"I'm leaving, too," he announced. The conference room door slammed behind them.

"Pokey?" Mason asked.

She shook her head and settled back in her chair, arms crossed over her chest. "I want to hear it. All of it."

Mason got up and walked around to the chair next to hers, the one Davis had just vacated.

"Kristy, that's Sophie's mom, isn't a bad person," he said. "She was only twenty-six when she got pregnant."

Pokey buried her head in her hands. "Oh God, Daddy," she moaned. "A twenty-six-year-old? How could you?"

"She looks a lot older," Mason said. "I thought she was about thirty-five when I met her. She's divorced, and she's smart, but she hasn't had an easy time of it. I think she really cared about Dad. He was good to her, you know?"

"Go on," Pokey said, sniffing. "How long do you think he was seeing her?"

"Kristy told me they'd been dating for about a year," Mason said. "He met her at the Hertz counter at the airport in Jacksonville, and he'd call her whenever he was in Florida on business, which was pretty often that last year he was alive, because we were chasing that Maxi-Mart deal. But I was totally in the dark about her. He knew I wouldn't put up with that crap."

Pokey wrinkled her forehead. "Wait — back up a minute. Uncle Norris, are you sure Dad told you he'd been diagnosed with heart problems?"

"Yes, Pokey," the lawyer said. "We had the same cardiologist. Blaine McNamara. Max Kaufman referred both of us to him. Glenn and I talked about it several times."

"But how could Mama not know Daddy was sick?" she asked, looking bewildered. "He wouldn't have kept that a secret from her, would he? I mean, was he on some medications?"

Norris Thomas looked distinctly uncomfortable. "We discussed the prescriptions he'd been given. He was, uh, worried about potential side effects."

"What kind of side effects?" Pokey asked. "Could that have been what killed him?"

Thomas tugged at his collar. "Well, um, I don't know that would be something he'd want me to discuss with his daughter, Pokey."

"He's been dead five years now, Uncle Norris," Pokey said flatly.

Mason chuckled. "I think Norris probably

doesn't want to tell you that Dad didn't like the fact that his heart meds affected his sexual performance," Mason said. "Does that about sum it up?"

"Well, uh, in a manner," Thomas said. His face was the shade of a glass of Quixie.

Pokey turned her attention to her older brother. "You two traveled a lot together. Did he talk to you about having a heart condition?"

"No," Mason said. "I know he had a bunch of pill bottles in his shaving kit, but we usually didn't share a hotel room." His face darkened. "His excuse was that he snored too much and didn't want to keep me awake. In hindsight, I suppose the real reason was that he had company in his room some of those nights. Like Kristy."

Pokey's eyes softened. "Tell me how you ended up with Sophie."

"The medical bills were pretty steep," Mason said. "But Dad had taken care of that. He'd put Kristy on the company payroll, so she'd have insurance coverage."

His sister rolled her eyes. "Oh God. If Davis found out about that he would blow a gasket."

"Yeah, especially if he heard her title. Taste Ambassador."

"Oh, no." Pokey giggled. "Taste Ambassador. That's just . . ." The giggle turned into a guffaw, and even the stern-faced Norris

Thomas managed a nervous chuckle, and then Annajane joined in, and soon the conference room echoed with the Bayless family's grief-tinged hilarity.

"Oh, God, Daddy," Pokey said, wiping her eyes with a tissue from the box in the center of the table. "Who knew you had such a delicious sense of irony?" She patted her brother's hand. "Thanks, I needed a little comic relief to cut all this drama. Finish telling me about Kristy. What's she like?"

"She's not a gold digger, or your typical home wrecker," Mason said. "I think she really thought she would be able to raise Sophie on her own. Her mom lived nearby and was going to help with the baby. But then her mom was diagnosed with breast cancer, and she was going through chemo, and Kristy was terrified and totally overwhelmed. That last time I was down in Jacksonville, I ran into her in the neonatal unit, and she just . . . came unhinged."

"The doctors had been trying to explain to her about the special care Sophie would need after she was discharged from the hospital and to warn her about the possible developmental issues," Mason said. "I walked into the nursery, where she'd been standing by the isolette, just looking down at the baby. Kristy was scared to touch her, to hold her, even though the nurses told her that's what Sophie needed most. 'You take her,' she said.

'I can't do this.' And she ran off."

"Not permanently ran off, right?" Pokey asked.

"No. She called me later that night and asked if we could meet. We did, and that's when she told me she couldn't take Sophie home. She was living with her mom in a tiny one-bedroom apartment, and it just wasn't going to get any better. Even with the money Dad left her, Kristy was not equipped to care for a baby on her own, especially a baby as sick as Sophie had been."

Mason shrugged. "What could I do? She had already started calling adoption agencies to try to get Sophie placed. I couldn't let strangers take her, Pokey. She was ours. And I couldn't tell Mama. She wouldn't have stood for me bringing home Dad's child by another woman. You saw her reaction today."

Pokey leaned over and hugged Mason. "You big dope. You know I would have taken her and raised her as my own. Everybody knows how badly I've wanted a little girl."

"No," Mason said. "Anybody who saw Sophie would know she was a Bayless. There would have been questions. And we'd be right back at square one. This was the only way. I adopted Sophie and Kristy gave up all rights to her. That's how she wanted it."

"You could have told me the truth," Pokey said. "I would have been shocked, yeah, but I could have handled it."

"I wanted to tell you," Mason said. "But if Mama ever found out you were in on it, she would have never forgiven you."

"Well, hey-yull," Pokey drawled. "It wouldn't be the first time I got cross-wise with Mama." She looked over at Annajane. "Did you know?"

"Not until Sunday night," Annajane said. "He told me right after he proposed."

"Lying to Annajane was the worst of it," Mason said. "Letting her think I went out and got some chick knocked up even before our divorce was final. And her having to put up with all the gossip and crap going around town, everybody assuming we split up because of Sophie."

"You did what was best for Sophie," Annajane said. "That's what matters."

"Man, oh, man," Pokey said. She gazed down at her belly, then pantomimed a telephone call. "You hear that, baby mine? We just found out your cousin is really your aunt. And that my niece is actually my sister. Or half sister. Crazy, huh?"

Norris Thomas looked pointedly at the clock on the conference room wall. "Well, I guess our family conference can probably be concluded, since half the family has decamped."

"Sorry about the histrionics," Mason said. "And I guess we can expect that the issue is not closed as far as my mother and brother are concerned. Should we be worried?"

Thomas was putting papers back in the file folder. "I don't think so. Glenn was very thorough with these kinds of things. He had me research the issues, and we reviewed every sentence of the trust agreement backwards and forwards."

"Davis won't care," Pokey predicted. "He just wants his money out of the company, and he'll do anything to get it. You watch, he probably left here and went right across the courthouse square to hire himself another lawyer." A new thought occurred to her. "Uncle Norris, could he get Dad's trust thingy overturned, on some kind of incompetency thing? It's ridiculous to even think about, but I wouldn't put it past Davis."

"Glenn Bayless, incompetent? Absurd," Thomas said. He stood up and touched Pokey's shoulder. "I'll tell you how incompetent he was. When we drew up the agreement, and the documents setting up the financial arrangements for Sophie's mother, he hired a videographer to record the meeting. At the time, I thought he was being overly cautious, but now, I suppose he was anticipating what your mother's reaction would be when she learned of the child's existence."

"Daddy might have had a wandering eye, but his mind never wandered," Pokey said. "Nobody was sharper. Lucky for Sophie. And us."

49

"I'm hungry," Pokey announced. "Let's get lunch."

"It's not even eleven o'clock," Mason protested.

"You can have coffee or something, but I am pregnant and starving, and I need to eat. Annajane?"

"Lunch sounds fine," Annajane said. "Where shall we go?"

Pokey looked around the courthouse square, past the gazebo and the confederate memorial statue. "The Country Cupboard," she decided.

They easily found a booth near the back of the room and placed their orders. After the waitress brought their drinks, Pokey put both elbows on the table and gazed across at her brother. "I've still got a lot of questions," she said.

Mason sipped his coffee. "I swear, I did not know anything about how the trust was set up. Norris never said a word to me, and I certainly had no clue Dad would leave Sophie part of the company."

She waved away his disclaimers. "I saw your face when Uncle Norris spilled the beans. You were as surprised as all of us."

"Not as surprised as your mother," Annajane said. "It's too bad it had to come out the way it did. She looked so hurt."

"Hurt?" Pokey said with a hoot. "Sallie wasn't hurt. She was red-hot furious. I haven't seen her that mad since the day I told her I was pregnant and dropping out of Carolina."

"She'll either get over it, or she won't," Mason said. "I can't be worrying about her hurt feelings. I've got a daughter to raise and a company to run." He nodded at Annajane. "And a wedding to plan."

"Yay!" Pokey said, clapping her hands. "When's it gonna be?"

"Soon." Mason said.

"After Memorial Day," Annajane said, at the same time.

They looked at each other and burst out laughing.

"I can tell y'all have spent a lot of time discussing this," Pokey said. "Do I get to be the maid of honor again?"

"Of course," Annajane said. "But I don't think we're gonna have anything elaborate. Just family."

"Half of our family isn't currently happy

with you two," Pokey pointed out. "So that ought to make for a real intimate affair." She looked at Annajane. "Have you told your mama?"

"Yes," Annajane said. "She told me I'm crazy as a bedbug. She's still furious that I broke it off with Shane. So I guess we can cross her off the guest list, too."

"More cake for me," Pokey said. "What did Sophie say?"

"Yippeee!" Mason said, in a girlish, high-pitched squeal. "She can't understand why Annajane won't move in right now. And I happen to agree with her."

"Nope," Annajane said, shaking her head obstinately. "You've got a whole lot of courting to do yet. Besides, I happen to love staying at the Pinecone Motor Lodge."

Pokey looked at Mason thoughtfully. "Will you tell Sophie about her real father?"

"Eventually," Mason said, reaching for Annajane's hand. "When she's old enough to process it. And hopefully before she hears it from somebody else. She does know that her biological mother lives down in Florida and that her mother couldn't take care of her and thus gave her to me. She has a picture of Kristy, but at this point she hasn't asked a lot of questions about her."

"Do you ever hear from Kristy?" Pokey asked.

"No," Mason said. "We kind of lost touch

after her mother died and Kristy moved. The last time I talked to her, about two years ago, she'd gotten remarried. Her new husband is actually her supervisor at the airport, and he knows about Sophie. So I think that's probably a good thing. She'll have some stability in her life."

"And she's never asked to see Sophie?" Pokey said, shaking her head. "I can't even imagine that."

"Me neither," Annajane agreed. "But then I haven't had the challenges she's had."

"Kristy knows how to reach me if she wants to," Mason said.

"Mason," Pokey said, toying with her straw, "Did you think Mama's reaction today was, well, odd?"

"She was furious that Dad didn't leave her any stake in the company. I think it's understandable that she'd be hurt," Mason said. "I guess we all assumed he'd leave her controlling interest. Instead, he completely cut her out. I was stunned. Weren't you?"

"I guess," Pokey said. "Although, when you stop to think about it, Mama was never all that interested in or involved in what went on down at the plant. And we all knew he wanted you and Davis to run the company. I guess I'm having a hard time wrapping my head around all of it."

"We all are," Annajane said. "Imagine finding out your husband had a child with another woman — who was being raised as your grandchild?" Annajane said. "That's a pretty big shocker."

The waitress brought their food, and Pokey sighed happily as she contemplated her club sandwich and french fries. She dipped a fry in the fluted paper cup of ketchup and nibbled. Annajane reached across the table and helped herself to a fry, too.

"I wonder," Pokey said, midbite, "if it really was a big shock to Mama that Daddy fooled around on her."

"You think she knew?" Annajane asked.

"They were married for forty-five years," Pokey reminded her. "Sallie was never naive. I can't decide if she just chose not to notice, or if she knew and chose to look the other way."

"Don't guess we'll ever know for sure," Mason said.

50

Annajane found Voncile in the break room, eating her lunch at a small table in the corner of the room: a tuna-fish sandwich on neatly sliced and trimmed white bread, a huge dill pickle in a plastic baggie, and a small container of baby carrots. Two route drivers sat at a table in the opposite corner of the room, arguing about the merits of Fords versus Chevys.

"Annajane!" Voncile motioned her over. The older woman's face was wreathed in smiles. Her hair had been freshly permed and colored, and she wore a muted navy print rayon dress.

"Mason tells me you have happy news," Voncile said, her voice low. "Praise the Lord!"

"Thank you, Voncile," Annajane said, twisting her engagement ring around to face her palm. "We're not really making a public announcement yet, but I know Mason couldn't wait to tell you himself."

"He was grinning ear to ear when he came

in on Monday morning," Voncile said. "I don't know when I've seen him that happy."

Annajane laughed. "I'm pretty happy myself, to tell you the truth."

Voncile sighed and shook her head. "That Celia sure had me fooled. I thought she was just about the nicest, sweetest girl Mason had ever dated — except for you, of course."

"She fooled a lot of people," Annajane commented.

"She took a nice check with her when she left, too," Voncile said indignantly. "Some people have no shame."

"Maybe so," Annajane said. She watched as the two route drivers gathered up their fast food bags and tossed them in the trash on the way out of the room.

"Say, Voncile," Annajane said, trying to sound casual. "Did you know anything about Glenn Bayless having heart problems before he had the heart attack that killed him?"

"Why do you ask?"

"Something came up today," Annajane said vaguely. "And it started me wondering. So, had he had symptoms in the past?"

"Oh, yes," Voncile said. "You know he had a spell here in the office, a few months before he passed. It about scared me half to death."

"Really?" Annajane said, leaning closer. "I didn't know that. When was this?"

She had to think. "I know it was summertime. One afternoon, he'd had a big steak lunch, probably at his Rotary meeting. He came back here, and his face was so pale; he looked awful. He swore he felt fine, but I knew he didn't. I got him a glass of water and some antacids, but it didn't seem to do much good. I'll tell you, Annajane, I fussed at him so much that day, he threatened to fire me. He finally did call his cardiologist, Dr. McNamara, over in Pinehurst, and of course when the doctor heard his symptoms, he wanted to call an ambulance for Mr. Glenn. Instead, I drove him over to Pinehurst myself."

"Was it a heart attack?" Annajane asked.

"I don't think so. But you know how Mr. Glenn was. He was that vain about his age. Never wanted to admit anything was wrong. I'll bet he never stayed home sick more than once or twice in all the years I worked for him."

"Mason is the same way," Annajane said. "Never gives in to a cold, flat denies the possibility he could ever get sick. So, Glenn had been seeing a cardiologist?"

"Sure," Voncile said. "You know, I made Mr. Glenn's appointments, business and personal. Even doctors, dentists, barbershop — everything. That way I kept everything on one calendar, so I could remind him. I made his appointments with Dr. Kaufman, and Dr. McNamara. And I got his prescriptions filled. I had to keep after him to take those pills every day."

"For his heart condition?" Annajane asked.

"And his high blood pressure," Voncile said. "We had the same prescription."

Voncile folded and unfolded a paper napkin. "Annajane, why are you asking me all these questions about Mr. Glenn?" she asked. "He's been gone all these years. Five years now. Are you going to tell me what happened at that meeting with the lawyers today? Mason looked kinda funny when you all got back from lunch."

"I'd prefer you to hear it from Mason," Annajane said.

Voncile's face fell.

"All right," Annajane said. "I know Mason had to get on a conference call after lunch. And I know he'd probably tell you this himself. So here it is. Glenn's trust left equal shares of the company to his children, but not to Sallie. His *four* children: Mason, Davis, Pokey, and Sophie."

Voncile raised an eyebrow. "You're saying Sophie is Mr. Glenn's child? Not Mason's? My goodness, that must have taken everybody by surprise. But how can a five-year-old own part of the company?"

Annajane sat back in the hard plastic chair and regarded Voncile. She had the best poker face she'd ever seen.

"As her legal guardian, Mason will control Sophie's share of the business until she comes of age when she's twenty-one," Annajane said.

Voncile processed that for a moment, then nodded her head slowly in understanding. "So, if Pokey and Mason, and Sophie, don't want to sell off the company, they outvote Davis, is that right?"

"Essentially," Annajane said.

"Praise the Lord!" Voncile said, raising her eyes heavenward. "My stomach has just been in knots all this week, thinking about what might happen to all of us if we got sold."

"Mine, too," Annajane admitted.

"And Sallie doesn't have a say in what happens to Quixie?"

"Nope," Annajane said. "According to Mr. Thomas, Glenn didn't think Sallie would want to be bothered with running the company at her age. And, after all, he'd already left her pretty well-fixed in his will."

"My, my," Voncile said. "I'll bet there were some fireworks when all of that came out. Especially the part about Sophie."

"You already knew about Sophie, didn't you?" Annajane asked.

The older woman allowed herself a small, private smile. "I guessed," Voncile admitted. "But I never said a word to anybody. And I never will. I'll take it to my grave."

"I know Mason will appreciate that. But how did you know?"

Voncile cut her sandwich half into quarters, and then eighths, but she didn't eat them.

"Mr. Glenn had me handle the paperwork to put that girl on the company payroll. We never had anybody working for us in Jacksoville, Florida, before. And then she'd call the office, sometimes, looking for him." She pursed her lips in disapproval. "Just how old a girl was she?"

"Young. Just twenty-six when she had the baby."

"Mercy." She shook her head. "Mr. Glenn knew I didn't approve of that kind of thing. He was a good man in so many ways, Annajane. He helped people in this town in more ways than you'll ever know. Paid doctor bills, got folks out of jail. Had to get a few folks put *in* jail, too. He bought people cars, gave them jobs."

Annajane smiled. "He gave me my first real job when I was fifteen, remember?"

"I sure do, honey. You were so serious and business-like. Such a good little worker. Mr. Glenn noticed that, too. You were always his favorite."

"And he was mine, too," Annajane said, feeling a little weepy. "Even before Mason and I got married, he always treated me like one of the family."

"Unlike some folks," Voncile commented. "Miss Sallie just never did take to you, did she?"

"Sallie . . . had an old, silly grudge against my mother," Annajane said. "And she always

581

thought Mason could have done better. Maybe she was right."

"Never," Voncile said. "I always thought you were Mason's one true love, even though I did get hoodwinked by that Celia. Mason is a good man, like his daddy. Did you know Mr. Glenn helped us buy our house? My husband, Claude, had been out of work, so the bank wouldn't give us a mortgage. Mr. Glenn held the paper on the house and let me pay off a little bit every week. Interest-free. He didn't go to church like Miss Sallie, but he was as fine a Christian man as I ever knew. Not perfect, though. He just had a weakness for the flesh is all. I used to pray about it all the time."

"Voncile," Annajane hesitated. "Well, maybe it's none of my business. Never mind."

"Go ahead and ask, honey. You're wanting to know if Sallie knew about the other women, aren't you?"

"Yes," Annajane said.

Voncile rewrapped the remnants of her sandwich into a neat wax-paper bundle while she thought about her answer.

"If she knew, she never let on to me," she said finally. "But she wouldn't have. She is a proud lady, and of course we didn't really have that kind of relationship. As far as Sallie was concerned, I was just somebody who worked for her husband at the plant."

"Did Sallie know about Glenn's heart condition?"

"I don't see how she couldn't have known," Voncile said. "With them living in the same house. I sure knew about my Claude's cancer. That man didn't have a hangnail or a hemorrhoid that I didn't have to take care of."

That made Annajane laugh. She remembered Voncile's husband. He was a skinny stick of a man, who always seemed to have an ailment of some kind. He'd taken early retirement from the plant in his late forties.

She decided to confide further in Mason's administrative assistant. "At the lawyer's office today, Sallie said she had no idea Glenn ever had any heart problems."

"That's not right. It can't be right," Voncile said. "Why, Annajane, that Saturday, the day he died, I talked to him on the phone that morning. With him not making it to the Christmas party the night before, I got a little worried that maybe he wasn't feeling too good. So I called to see if he was all right."

"What did he say?" Annajane asked, intrigued.

"He sounded funny; his voice was kind of weak," Voncile said. "He kept insisting he was fine, but he didn't sound fine. He sounded like he did the last time he was having chest pains. I told him he needed to call Dr. Mac or get over to the hospital."

"Did he agree to do that?" Annajane asked.

"He kind of laughed at me and said I was overreacting. He said Sallie was right there, and she'd take good care of him."

"What time was that?" Annajane asked.

"Hmmm." Voncile folded and refolded her paper lunch sack while she tried to remember. "It must have been around ten o'clock, because I needed to go out and do some last-minute Christmas shopping."

Annajane felt a chill go up her spine. "Did you check back later in the day to see how he was?"

"I tried," Voncile said. "I called his cell phone before noon, when I got back from the store, but my call went straight to voice mail, so I called the house. Sallie answered right away, and I asked her how Mr. Glenn was feeling. She told me he was fine, which kind of surprised me. He sure wasn't fine when I'd talked to him earlier."

"Did you tell her he'd been having chest pains earlier in the day?"

Voncile's face crinkled up in concentration. "It's hard to remember — it was so long ago. I think I asked to speak to him, but she said he was taking a nap or something."

"So you never did talk to Glenn again?"

"No," Voncile said, frowning. "I tried later in the day, around three, maybe, but all I got was a busy signal. I tried and tried, for half an hour or so, but then I kind of forgot about it because we were getting my granddaughter's angel costume ready for her Sunday School pageant. And then we drove over to Garner to spend the night with my daughter."

Now it was Annajane's turn to think back on that Saturday, with all its painful memories. She'd run into her mother-in-law at noon, at the country club, and Sallie had been oddly insistent that Annajane join her group for lunch.

She wondered whether Sallie was aware that her husband was having breathing problems and chest pains earlier in the day.

Voncile looked stricken. "Oh heavens. He must have had his heart attack right after I talked to him."

"I don't think so," Annajane said slowly. "Sallie said she found Glenn unconscious at around six that evening. That's when she called the ambulance. They worked on him at the hospital, but the doctors said it was too late."

"But that was hours and hours after I talked to him," Voncile said. "I thought . . . I mean, I always assumed he'd gone to the hospital earlier in the day, right after we talked. Are you sure that's right, Annajane?"

"Very sure," Annajane said soberly.

Voncile crumpled her paper bag into a tight ball. "I just don't understand. Why didn't Sallie call the doctor? Or take him to the hospital that morning?"

"That's what I'd like to know," Annajane told her.

51

Pokey Bayless Riggs stood on the doorstep of her brother's bachelor pad, a contemporary two-story wooden structure with soaring beams and weirdly jutting angles located on the grounds of the Cherry Hill estate, just out of Sallie's line of vision. She'd called in advance and left numerous voice-mail messages, but she had gotten no response. Now she was determined to have it out with him, face-to-face.

She'd been ringing the doorbell and pounding on the door with no luck. Finally, she took a step backward and, cupping her hands into a makeshift megaphone, began hollering, "Davis Bayless! I know you're in there, you weasel, so you might as well let me in.

"Davis! I'm not going away. I'll stand here all night if I have to."

Finally, she walked around to the back of the house, tried the kitchen door, and found it unlocked. She stepped inside and found Davis, seated at the smoked-glass kitchen table, eating a microwaved chicken potpie and washing it down with what looked like a very large tumbler of Dewar's.

His suit jacket hung from the back of his chair, and he'd loosened his tie and rolled up the sleeves of his dress shirt.

"Go away," he said sourly.

"Nope," she said, seating herself at the table, opposite him.

"I got nothin' to say to you," he said, fishing a large green garden pea out of the pot-pie and lining it up on the edge of the plate with a lot of other discarded green peas.

"Then don't talk," Pokey said. "Just sit there and listen."

"This is my damned house. I don't have to sit here and take any crap off of you," Davis said. "Why don't you go on home to your husband and kids?"

But Pokey had had a belly full of her brother. Now she had fire in her eyes and was ready for a showdown.

"Don't do this, Davis," she said, crossing her arms across her chest and regarding him with a mixture of regret and disgust.

"Do what?" he asked, innocence itself. "Eat a potpie for dinner? You should try one." He pushed his plate in her direction. "They're really good. Jax Snax just bought this company. Maydene's Home-Style Frozen Diner Dinners. Jerry sent me a big ole carton full of 'em. They got frozen pot roast, frozen chicken and dumplings, frozen mac n' cheese. I may never have to go out to dinner again."

"Stop trying to change the subject," Pokey ordered. "Everybody in town knows what you've been up to. You've hired a lawyer to contest Daddy's trust arrangement, and you're already starting to drag our family's name through the mud. And for what? More money?"

Davis placed his fork on the side of his plate with elaborate precision. He wiped his mouth with a paper napkin. "Look here, Pokey. I don't see why you're so hot and bothered about selling Quixie. I mean, let's face it. You ain't never really had to work a day in your life. Sure, you played at working for Daddy summers in college, and a little bit after you married Pete, but you're just a stay-at-home mama. And that's fine. You've got three swell little boys and another on the way. Pete makes a good living. Why do you wanna go messin' around with stuff that doesn't even really concern you?"

"Don't you dare patronize me, Davis Bayless," Pokey snapped. "I am not one of your stupid bimbos. I may not have worked in the day-to-day end of Quixie, but you better believe I know what goes on with our business, and I do care. I care deeply. Daddy knew that, even if you don't, which is why he left me an equal share of the business."

"Yeah, well, I wouldn't count on that trust

agreement standing, if I were you," Davis said lazily. "My lawyer says there's loopholes in that thing big enough to drive a Quixie truck through."

Pokey clenched and unclenched her fists and finally clasped them tightly together in an effort to keep herself from slapping the smile right off her big brother's jowls.

"Your lawyer is a jackleg Yankee just dying to take you for every dime you've got," Pokey said. "And in the meantime, you need to know that I will fight you every step of the way if I have to. Because I will be damned if I will allow you to sell off my heritage. And my sons'. I've taken a look at that Jax Snax offer, and it's a load of garbage. You know what happened to that family-owned pretzel business they bought? They shut it down. Yeah. Spun off the one product they really wanted, shifted production of it to one of their own plants, laid off two hundred and fifty workers, then sold the equipment for scrap metal. That town was already hurting, but losing the plant was like putting a stake through its heart. Half the houses in town are in foreclosure, and I read on the Internet that they've closed the town's only high school. They have to bus the kids forty-five minutes away to the next town over. I am not gonna sit still and let that happen here."

Davis shook his head. "You and Mason just don't get it. Frankly, Daddy didn't get it either. Even six, seven years ago, the hand-writing was on the wall. But he refused to believe it. Twenty years ago, there were nearly a dozen other family-owned soda companies operating in the Southeast. Now? You've got what? Three or four? If that many? You know why? Because it's a lost cause. Quixie is a dinosaur. We can't compete with the big boys. Not unless we become one of 'em."

"See!" Pokey said. "When you think like that, it's a self-fulfilling prophecy. We're still operating in the black, still have a good product, but I believe you actually *want* the company to fail. That's why you resist any kind of change in the product line or spending any money to update the plant or the distribution network. You're deliberately sabotaging Quixie."

"Me?" Davis laughed. "I don't have to do a goddamn thing to make that happen. All I have to do is sit back and let Mason keep on the way he's keeping on. Which I don't intend to do."

Pokey took a deep breath. "What's the matter with you, Davis?"

"Me? Nothin'. I am fine as frog hair."

"No, seriously," Pokey said. "You're my brother, and I love you, but I don't understand one thing about you. We were raised in the same house, by the same parents, but sometimes I wonder how you got to be the way you are. Don't you have an ounce of

591

loyalty towards our family?"

"I'm a businessman," Davis said, shrugging. "Family loyalty's got nothing to do with it. I love my big brother, but I have serious doubts about his abilities to run Quixie the way it needs to be run in this economy. I've tried to talk sense to him about that for the past five years, but to Mason I'll always be the dumb baby brother. The wannabe."

"You say you love your brother?" Pokey asked. "Is that why you slept with his fiancée?"

"I don't know what you're talking about," Davis said. He took a long drink of the scotch, and she noted that his hand shook. Just a little. "And this conversation is beginning to bore me, little sister. What say you get the hell out of my house?"

"I'll go when I've had my say," Pokey retorted. "And I believe you do know what I'm talking about. You and Celia have been in cahoots over this Jax Snax deal for a long time now. I just wonder how long you've been in bed together, literally."

"You're crazy," Davis said.

"Not as crazy as you," she said calmly. "Let's talk about Friday night, shall we? The night before Celia was supposed to marry Mason. Remember him? Your beloved big brother, the one you're so loyal to? How crazy could you be, Davis, taking Celia to the same motel you always take your sluts to? How stupid could you be, paying cash but making sure to ask about the Quixie employee discount? And what kind of lowlife, slimy horndog struts around calling himself Harry Dix?"

Davis looked away and closed his eyes slowly.

"You don't know anything," he said. "You're bluffing."

"Really?" She reached into her pocket and pulled out a photocopy of the registration book from the Pinecone and waved it under his nose. "That's my proof. Your handwriting, and the place where you wrote down the license number of the Boxster. Dumb shit. And you should know, Celia was seen coming out of that room with you the next morning by more than one person. You are so busted."

He opened his eyes. "Does Mason know?"

"No," Pokey said. She put the photocopy back in her pocket. "He already knows she's a lying, cheating piece of crap. I really don't have the heart to let him know his own brother is just as bad. Or worse."

"So, what? You're gonna blackmail me now?"

"No. I'm going to appeal to your long-dormant sense of decency. And your greed. Pete and I have had a long talk. We want you to sell us your share of Quixie."

"As if." Davis drained the scotch in his glass and poured himself another tumbler full. He took a long drink, smacked his lips, and drank again.

Pokey reached over and took the glass out of his hand. "Listen to me, Davis. We're serious. Jax was prepared to pay the family thirty million for Quixie. You own a quarter interest. Pete and I want to buy you out. We'll pay you seven and a half million cash. You take the money, go do whatever you want to do. Buy that house on Figure Eight Island, take a job with Jax Snax, or whatever. Or just sit back and count your money. But you walk away from the company. And you drop your challenge to Dad's trust agreement."

Davis got up and walked over to one of the gleaming ebonized kitchen cupboards. He got himself another tumbler, grabbed the Dewar's bottle, and poured himself another dose. He leaned up against the black granite countertop. "What if I don't take your offer? What if I decide to stay around and fight?"

"You'll lose," Pokey said, her chin jutting out. "And in the process, you will have antagonized everybody in this town. You will have trashed Daddy's good name, and you will have estranged yourself from your entire family. Including Mama."

"Mama . . ." he started to say.

"Mama is feeling hurt and betrayed right now, finding out about Sophie the way she did. Although I'm not really certain she didn't suspect all along that she wasn't

Mason's child. She'll get over it, eventually. And when she does, she will not want that piece of news broadcast all over some lawsuit and the Bayless family name dragged through the mud. And you had better believe she would never, ever, forgive you for the way you betrayed Mason by sleeping by Celia."

Davis jiggled the ice in his glass and smirked. "All of y'all are gonna have to get over this thing you have against Celia."

"And why is that?" Pokey asked.

He chewed on the ice for a moment before answering. "What would you say if I told you we're together now?"

"You and Celia? Is this a rhetorical question, or is this your ass-backward way of telling me the two of you are an item?"

He shrugged. "It was probably inevitable. We both tried to pretend we weren't attracted to each other, but hell, it is what it is."

Pokey shuddered. "What it is is grotesque, Davis. The two of you together? It's a bad reality show on a third-rate cable channel. But the sad thing is, the two of you deserve each other. I just hope Mason doesn't find out when the two of you hooked up."

"You just said you'd never tell Mason," Davis pointed out.

"I wouldn't. But if Mama were to find out . . ." Pokey shrugged. "You know what Passcoe's like. It's a small town."

"It's a shithole," Davis muttered into his

scotch. "A two-horse, two-traffic-light shit-hole."

"All the more reason you should take the money and run," Pokey suggested. "Delta's ready when you are."

"Maybe I will," Davis said. "Tell Pete to give me a call in the morning, if he's serious."

"No need to talk to Pete," Pokey said. "I handle all our family finances. I'll have our lawyer draw up an agreement, and I'll send it over to you in the morning."

52

The kitchen table was set with placemats and blue and white checked napkins and blue glass water goblets. A perky bouquet of daisies in a red bowl sat in the center of the table, and tall white taper candles burned from blue glass candleholders.

Mason stood at the stove, long-handled fork poised over a cast-iron skillet full of frying chicken, while Annajane sat at a high stool at the counter, preparing the salad.

Sophie came clomping into the kitchen and her eyes widened. She was wearing a pink ballet tutu over her purple pajamas and pink cowboy boots. "Are we having a party?" She climbed up on the stool beside Annajane's and plunked down a picture book, some paper, and a box of crayons.

"Yep," Mason said. "It's a Friday-night party. And you're invited."

"Who else?" Sophie asked, noticing that the table was set for three.

"Just us," Mason said. "It's a very exclusive

gathering. We used to have Friday-night parties a lot when I was your age, Soph. It was the only time my daddy ever cooked. And he only knew how to cook one thing, so we always had fried chicken."

"I don't like fried chicken," Sophie said, her eyes sparkling behind the thick glasses. "I love it!"

"Me, too," Annajane said. "How about we start the party with a cocktail?"

"For me?" Sophie looked puzzled.

"It's a kiddie cocktail," Annajane explained. She took a plastic highball tumbler from the cupboard. She poured in a couple inches of Quixie, added a splash of ginger ale, then topped it with a maraschino cherry before presenting it to the child. "Ta-da!"

"Mmm," Sophie took a delicate sip. "Am I allowed to have Quixie?"

"In very small amounts," Mason said. "For very special occasions. Like tonight."

Annajane reached over and picked up the well-loved picture book. By her own estimation she had read *The Runaway Bunny* to Sophie at least a couple hundred times. The edges of the board book were dog-eared, and the cover bore a couple of purple crayon doodles, but nothing had ever diminished Sophie's love for her favorite book.

Sophie picked up her crayons now and began to draw on the sheaf of printer paper she'd borrowed from Mason's office.

"Whatcha drawing?" Annajane asked, looking over.

"I'm ill-luss-stra-ting," Sophie said proudly, drawing out the word. "Miss Ramona lets us make new illustrations for books in school. This is my homework. I'm illustrating *The Runaway Bunny.*"

The child's pink glasses slipped down her nose as she bent over her picture, painstakingly drawing a very small bunny. She glanced over at Annajane. "In school, Miss Ramona reads the stories to us while we draw."

"Then allow me," Annajane said, putting her paring knife down, pushing away the salad bowl and the wooden cutting board, and picking up the book.

"Once there was a little bunny who wanted to run away," Annajane read. "So he said to his mother, 'I am running away.' "

Mason flipped the pieces of chicken over in the pan and covered it loosely with the lid. He stepped behind Annajane and, looking over her shoulder, read, " 'If you run away,' said his mother, 'I will run after you. For you are my little bunny.' "

Sophie poked out the tip of her tongue as she concentrated on drawing the rabbit's ears. "I would never run away from my mama, if I was the little bunny," she commented, filling in the middle of the rabbit's orange ears with a brown crayon.

"Even if it was just a game, like hide-and-seek, like we play sometimes?" Mason asked.

"No," Sophie said solemnly. "If I had a mama, I would never, ever run away."

Annajane glanced over at Mason, who looked stricken. "Sophie," he said gently. "Remember, you do actually have a mama. I told you that, remember?"

Sophie continued coloring, using a gray crayon to draw a lumpy version of the rabbit's body. "My real mama's name is Kristy. She lives in Florida now, and she loved me a lot, but she couldn't take care of me, so she asked my daddy to take care of me." Her voice was singsongy, but matter-of-fact.

"You're killin' me here," Mason muttered. "You know, Sophie, when you came here to live with me, I decided I would be your daddy *and* your mama for a while. Then I asked Letha if she would come and help take care of you while I'm working. And your aunt Pokey helped out, too, and also Annajane. So you're a lucky girl, because you have lots of people to love and help take care of you, instead of just one mama."

Sophie looked up at him thoughtfully. "The runaway bunny only needed one mama. The kids in school all have one mama. Except Lucy. She has two mamas. And Clayton and Denning and Petey all have one mama — Aunt Pokey. That's all I need, too."

Annajane and Mason exchanged worried looks, but Sophie, who knew the book by heart, was already onto her next illustration, drawing a fish, swimming in a stream. "Read some more, please," she told Annajane.

So Annajane read, " 'If you become a fish in a trout stream,' said his mother, 'I will become a fisherman and I will fish for you.' "

Sophie gave the fish a green body and a yellow tail and a red dorsal fin. She drew wavy blue lines to represent the blue trout stream, and beside the stream she drew a stick figure with long brown hair, wearing a dress and red high heels, holding a fishing pole.

"Who is that?" Mason asked, tapping the figure in the picture.

"That's the mama," Sophie said, rolling her eyes at her father's ignorance. "Duh."

"But she doesn't look like a bunny fisherman," Mason said.

"This mama is a real lady. Like Annajane," Sophie said. "See, she has brown hair like Annajane."

"And red shoes," Annajane added. "I have a pair of red shoes that look like that."

Mason wrapped his arms around Sophie. "We were thinking, Annajane and me, that when we get married, Annajane will be my wife. And she'll be your mama. Your only mama. What do you think of that idea, Soph?"

"We're not gonna marry Celia, right?" Sophie asked, adding a pink bow to her fisherwoman's hair.

"Nope. Celia and I decided that wouldn't be a good idea, because I love Annajane best," Mason said.

"Letha said Celia is gone for good this time," Sophie said.

"That's probably true," Mason conceded.

"We should marry Annajane," Sophie said, without hesitation.

Mason left one arm around Sophie, and put the other around Annajane's shoulder. "I think so, too. Definitely."

"See?" Sophie said, as if that settled it. She put the fish drawing aside and started on another one. "Keep reading, please."

Annajane read the next few pages, and Sophie's crayon flew over her paper. At one point, she looked up at Annajane. "What's a crocus? And why do they have a hidden garden?"

"I guess they have a hidden garden because the little bunny and the mother bunny are playing hide-and-go-seek," Annajane said, leafing ahead in the book. "And a crocus is a little flower that comes up from the ground in very early spring," Annajane said. "We can look online and find a picture of one, if you want."

"No, that's okay," Sophie said, reaching for another sheet of paper and drawing a daisy. "Keep going."

So Annajane read on, about the baby bunny morphing into a rock, then a bird, and a sailboat, and even a trapeze artist.

Mason hovered over his stove, adjusting the heat under the skillet and putting a pot of peeled potatoes on to boil. He poured a glass of wine for himself and one for Annajane, who nodded her thanks and kept reading aloud.

Near the end of the book, Sophie put her crayon down and sighed dramatically. "I hate this part," she announced.

"Why?" Annajane asked, almost afraid to hear the answer.

Did Sophie resent the fact that she didn't have a real mother like the bunny in the book? Or had she been dwelling on the fact that her own mother had, in a way, run away from her? Maybe they should think about having Sophie see a child psychologist. Especially since at some point, before Sophie got too much older, they would need to explain the complicated story behind her real father as well as her real mother.

"Yeah, Soph," Mason said, placing his hands protectively on the little girl's shoulders. "Do you hate this part of the story because you're sad about the runaway bunny and his mama?"

"No," Sophie said, frowning down at her picture. "I hate this part because I can't draw a tightrope walker, like the one in the book." She looked up at Mason. "You draw it."

"Hmm." Mason picked up a crayon and

sketched a brown rope, and then added an extremely detailed sketch of a little girl with eyeglasses and blond curls, wearing a pink tutu with a pink pocketbook slung over her arm and one dainty foot placed on the rope, the other poised above it. "How's that?"

"It's me!" Sophie breathed. "You drew me!"

"Not bad," Annajane said, regarding Mason with new respect. "I didn't know you could draw that well."

"I am a man of many talents," Mason said, bowing first to Sophie and then to Annnajane.

"Draw the next one," Sophie ordered. "The one with the bunny turning into a little boy and running inside the house."

Mason glanced over at the stove. "Can't," he said. "My dinner is just about ready. I've got to get my potatoes mashed. Are you two almost finished reading your book?"

"Almost," Sophie said, glancing over at the book. "Read the end, Annajane. That's my favorite part."

Annajane liked the ending, too. " 'If you become a little boy and run into a house . . . I will become a mother and catch you in my arms and hug you.' "

She stood and folded Sophie into her arms. Sophie wriggled contentedly and picked up her cue like a seasoned pro, reading in an uncannily baby-bunny-sounding voice.

" 'Shucks,' said the bunny. 'I might just as

well stay where I am and be your little bunny.' "

"Come on, you two," Mason called, dumping his mashed potatoes into a serving bowl. "My dinner is getting cold. Annajane, you need to finish making that salad."

"In a minute," Annajane said. She knew the last two lines of the book by heart. As did Sophie.

" 'And so he did,' " Sophie said.

Annajane reached into the salad bowl and snagged one of the vegetables she'd been cutting up.

" ' "Have a carrot," said the mother bunny.' "

Sophie took the proffered carrot and munched happily. "The end," she announced.

Annajane's cell phone rang just as she was wiping the skillet clean with a paper towel. Sophie had gone to bed, and they'd been discussing whether or not to watch a movie. She looked down at the caller ID. "It's your mother," she told Mason. "I didn't even know she knew I had a cell phone."

"This can't be good," he said. "Don't answer."

"I can't not answer when Sallie calls me," Annajane said. She punched the Connect button.

"Hi, Sallie," she said brightly. "This is a surprise."

"I'm sure it is," Sallie drawled. "Annajane dear, I was wondering if you could come over to Cherry Hill tomorrow morning for a little chat."

Annajane put her hand over the phone and lip-synched to Mason, "She wants to see me."

Mason shook his head vigorously. "Tell her no. Tell her hell no."

"Well, um, let me think what my morning is like," Annajane said, stalling for time, fishing for an excuse.

"I won't take up much of your time," Sallie said. "Just a quick little visit."

Put like that, she couldn't very well decline, Annajane thought.

"What time?" she asked.

"Ten would be perfect," Sallie said.

"Perfect," Annajane said gloomily.

53

They discussed the visit to Cherry Hill until midnight, right up until the moment Annajane reluctantly got in her car to drive "home" to the Pinecone Lodge.

"You do not have to go over there tomorrow," Mason said, his lips lingering at her collarbone. "She can't just call you up and issue a command performance."

"I'm going," Annajane murmured, her arms wrapped around his waist.

"She's still mightily pissed about me breaking up with Celia," Mason said. "Even after I told her about the fake pregnancy."

"And she's just as mightily pissed at me for marrying you years ago — and agreeing to marry you again," Annajane said.

"Which is why you should politely decline," Mason said.

"Nope," Annajane kissed him one last time. "I'm not running away from your mother anymore. I'm here to stay, and she can just like it or lump it."

In the bright light of Saturday morning, Annajane began to doubt the wisdom of a visit to the lioness in her own den. But it was too late to back out now. She played various scenarios over and over again in her head, planning a strong, assertive, take-no-crap offensive against Sallie Bayless.

She dressed carefully for the occasion, but not in the clothes she might formerly have worn for an audience with her mother-in-law. This time, she wore what she'd wear any other Saturday morning around town: a pair of red cotton capris, a red and white striped oxford-cloth shirt, an off-white cable-knit sweater, and a pair of navy-blue skimmers.

After she rang the doorbell at Cherry Hill, she repeated her mantra under her breath, as she'd done countless times on the drive over. "She is not the boss of me."

Annajane heard footsteps approaching from the other side of the heavy carved door. It swung open, and Sallie offered her a chilly smile. "Right on time. How nice."

Sallie was dressed in what passed for casual wear for her: black slacks, a peach silk blouse, and a black cashmere sweater that was looped across her shoulders. "It's such a beautiful morning; I thought we'd sit out in the sunroom."

Annajane followed her down the wide, marble-tiled central hall and out through a set of tall french doors onto the sunporch. She hadn't been out here since the divorce, but she doubted that anything had changed in five years. The room stretched the length of the back of the old house, with large, arched windows that gave a stunning view of the back garden and pool area. The floors were made of muted pink and gray brick pavers that had come out of the old smokehouse on the property, and the ceiling was high, with thick cypress beams. Fringy potted palms and ferns filled the corners of the room, which was furnished with comfortably battered white-painted wicker with flowered cushions. A ceiling fan whirred lazily overhead.

Sallie seated herself on a high-backed wicker armchair and gestured for Annajane to sit on a matching armchair opposite hers. A silver tray on the wicker coffee table held a pitcher of iced tea.

"Tea?" Sallie asked, pouring a glass. "Or I could open a bottle of Quixie. Glenn always thought it was so cute how much you enjoyed the stuff."

"Nothing for me, thanks," Annajane said. "I do still love the taste of Quixie, but I try to limit myself to one a day, and I had one for breakfast already."

"Oh," Sallie said, looking faintly nauseated

609

at the idea. "How sweet."

Annajane looked uneasily at her surroundings, wondering how long it would take for Sallie to get down to brass tacks.

"The garden looks beautiful," she said, looking out at the sweep of emerald lawn and the blooming flowerbeds. The turquoise of the swimming pool dazzled in the sunshine. It was a storybook setting, Annajane thought, as she had so many other times in the past.

Sallie waved away the compliment. "This is not our best spring. My tulips were anemic-looking, and, I swear, Nate's gotten so old and blind I believe he mistook most of my perennials for weeds and dug them up back in the fall. But that's not what I wanted to discuss with you today."

Annajane steeled herself. "What did you want to discuss?"

"Family," Sallie said, without hesitation. "I want to talk about my family. You know I love my children, unconditionally."

"Of course," Annajane murmured. Although she might have argued about the unconditional part. She'd seen how stingy Sallie could be with her affection if one of her children — especially Pokey — didn't measure up to her impossible standards.

"I never thought you were the right kind of girl for Mason," Sallie said flatly.

Wow, Annajane thought. *Way to get the niceties out of the way.*

"You've made that pretty clear over the years," Annajane said.

"Glenn felt differently about you," Sallie said. "He admired your 'spunk,' whatever that is."

"Glenn was lovely to me," Annajane said.

"And I . . . wasn't." Sallie reached under the cushion of her chair and brought out a pack of cigarettes and lit one. "Someday, if you ever have children of your own, Annajane, you'll understand what it's like, as a mother, to stand by and watch your child make a decision that you're positive they will regret. And maybe you'll understand why I treated you as I did."

Annajane felt her face go hot. "*When* I have children, and they grow up, I hope I'll trust their decision-making skills. Mason wasn't a child when we fell in love and got married, Sallie. He was an adult, and he was fully capable of deciding the qualities he wanted in a wife."

"Maybe," Sallie said, conceding nothing. She inhaled and then exhaled a long plume of smoke through her nostrils, waving ineffectively at it. She got up and opened the glass door that led to the patio and pool area. A cool wind swept the room, sending the pale green fern fronds swaying. "Better," she said to herself.

She gave Annajane an assessing look. "You know, you're much more attractive than your mother ever was. Your features are softer; you wear your hair in a much more flattering style; and of course Ruth, bless her heart, never did know how to dress."

For real? Annajane thought. *She expects me to sit here and listen to her insult my mother?*

"I disagree," Annajane said. "Mama was much prettier than me at her age. She had a way better figure, and if she didn't have the nicest clothes, well, that's because her parents never had a lot of money." She smiled. "It's funny you should mention my mother. Do you know, just this week I came across an old Quixie recipe booklet that had a photo of her at a cookout. In the photo, they had her posed with a bottle of Quixie, and Glenn was standing there, too, with his arm around her. They looked like a real couple. Funny, I'd never seen that photo before."

Sallie exhaled another stream of smoke, and her eyes narrowed. "Your mother never told you she dated Glenn?"

"No. She didn't even want to admit it when I called her that night to ask about it."

"I'm not surprised," Sallie said. "It's nothing to be proud of, stealing a friend's man."

That made Annajane laugh out loud. "Mama had a different perspective. She told me she went out with Glenn only a few times that summer, after he'd already broken up with you, but before my father got back from the army."

"That is *not* how it happened," Sallie said sharply. "Glenn and I were engaged to be engaged, and everybody knew it. But your mother had a huge crush on him. And why not? He was the best-looking boy in school, from the best family. He and I had some silly fight that spring, and I broke up with him. To get back at me, to make me jealous, he asked your mother to the prom. The biggest dance of the year, and I'd already bought my dress. Of course, Ruth knew all that, but she went with him anyway."

"And you never forgave her, or me, by extension," Annajane said. "She never forgave you, either, although she refuses to talk about her reasons."

"I wouldn't know either," Sallie said airily. "Ruth was always full of spite. Your mother is not a happy person, Annajane."

"Mama was in her early twenties when my father died. Driving a Quixie truck," Annajane said, her tone mild, pleasant even. "She was widowed with a young toddler. She had to go back to night school to get a nursing degree so she could support us, and she worked days to pay for the tuition. She hasn't exactly had an easy life."

"Oh, yes," Sallie said, rolling her eyes. "Here we go again, poor, poor Ruth Hudgens. The twice-widowed martyr with a chip on her shoulder the size of a two-by-four."

"Knock it off, Sallie," Annajane warned. "I'm used to your criticism, but I don't have to sit here and listen to you ridiculing my mother."

Sallie shrugged, unrepentant. "The point is, I knew what kind of girl your mother was, and I figured you'd be the same sort. I didn't want that for Mason. And besides, you two came from two very different worlds."

Annajane stood up. "Is there a point to all of this? Because if not, I can think of a more pleasant way to spend a Saturday morning."

"I'm almost finished," Sallie said. "Sit down, please."

Annajane glanced at her wristwatch. "Five minutes. That's how much more of my time you've got."

Mason was right again. She shouldn't have come. Despite all her best intentions, Sallie was getting to her yet again, needling, criticizing, and, yes, pushing her around. Annajane felt all the years of long-simmering resentment coming to a boil.

Sallie took a deep drag on her cigarette and flicked the ashes into the nearest potted palm. "All I wanted to do . . . all I wanted to say, is this: if you're going to become a part of this family . . . again, I want you to stop trying to tear us apart. That's it. In a nutshell."

"I'm tearing your family apart?"

"You think I don't know what you've been up to?" Sallie asked. "Pokey is furious with me over this mess with Celia, which she somehow thinks is my fault. Mason won't return my phone calls. He actually has Voncile running interference for him. And just last night, Davis came over here and announced that he was selling his share of the business to Pokey and possibly moving away." Sallie blinked rapidly, fighting back tears. Her voice cracked. "This is all your doing."

Annajane was speechless. For nearly a minute.

"You are unbelievable," she said, when she could finally gather her thoughts. "Me? Wreck your family? Let me clue you to the real world, Sallie, since you refuse to face it for yourself. Your daughter is furious with you because you let her know you don't consider her children to be 'real' Baylesses. Also, you treat her like shit, always criticizing her clothes, or her weight, or her housekeeping, always letting her know she isn't quite good enough."

"I never!" Sallie said. "Pokey knows I love her. And if I've given her constructive criticism, she knows it's because I want her to be the best she can be."

"I don't know what's going on with Davis," Annajane admitted. "It's news to me that Pokey and Pete are going to buy him out. But it's good news. He hasn't been happy at Quixie in years, and it's time for him to move on to something else if he doesn't believe in the company anymore. Besides, if he leaves Passcoe and quits trying to prove what a hot-shot he is, maybe he'll finally grow up and become half the decent, compassionate, loyal man his father was and his brother is."

"You have no right," Sallie said, stubbing out her cigarette in the palm. "I want you to leave this house right now."

"You asked me over here, and I listened to your bullshit, so now it's my turn," Annajane said. "Do you want to know why Mason won't return your calls? Why he avoids coming over here like the plague? It's because he's tired of having you tell him how to live his life. You helped destroy our marriage, years ago, and then you came damned close to pushing him into marrying a pathological liar. Earlier this week, you as much as accused him of lying when he finally told you the truth about Sophie. A truth you already knew."

"How dare you!" Sallie jumped up from her chair and stormed into the house. Annajane found her in the kitchen, unsteadily trying to open a bottle of wine.

"It's not even noon yet," Annajane observed, taking the corkscrew from her and applying it to the bottle herself. "But go ahead and have a snort. You're gonna need it by the time I've had my say." She took a goblet from the cupboard and poured the glass nearly to the brim.

Sallie gulped the wine, spilling some down the front of her blouse, a rare sight. "He had no right to tell those lies, to talk about his father that way," she said.

"He's telling the truth and you know it," Annajane said. "Mason loved his dad, more than you'll ever know. He loves you, too, which I don't think you fully appreciate. That's why he went down to Florida and brought Sophie back here after Glenn died. It's why he adopted her, rather than let her be raised by strangers, and why he let everybody believe he'd cheated on me. He did it out of respect for you and Glenn, because he couldn't stand the idea of a scandal. I don't think he had any idea he'd fall in love with Sophie as quickly or as deeply as he did."

Sallie took another gulp of wine. "This is unforgivable."

"You knew all about the cheating, didn't you?" Annajane asked. "You knew all about the other women, but it was convenient to look the other way, wasn't it, Sallie?"

"I didn't know anything," Sallie said, unconvincingly.

"But you guessed."

Sallie stared down into her wineglass. "The first time he cheated, I told myself it was just a slip. The children were so young; Pokey was still in diapers. He went to a ballgame in Chapel Hill for the weekend, and I stayed home with the children. When he came home, I just knew. The phone would ring at night, and if I picked up, she'd hang up."

She gave Annajane a tremulous smile and fingered the pearls around her neck. "He bought me these, afterwards. And the phone calls stopped, and I told myself all was well. Until the next time. It was years later. He'd gone up to Virginia to visit Mason, when he was in boarding school up there. I think he was actually sleeping with one of the teachers. That went on for three or four years."

"Why didn't you have it out with him?" Annajane asked. "Threaten to leave him if he didn't stop fooling around?"

"I didn't want to leave him," Sallie said. "I was in love with him. You knew Glenn. He was a good person. A wonderful father to our children. And so generous. He never denied me anything."

"Except your self-respect."

Sallie raised an eyebrow. "A highly overrated commodity, Annajane dear. We had a good marriage for a long time. It worked for us."

"Until things changed," Annajane said. "Like that last Christmas. The night of the company party."

"It was outrageous behavior!" she said, her nostrils flaring. "Even for him. I waited up all night, wondering whether he and Mason were even alive. He came stumbling into our

618

bedroom way after midnight, still drunk. And Glenn rarely got drunk. He stripped down to his underpants and fell into bed. I slept in the guest bedroom. In the morning, I found his clothes on the bathroom floor, where he'd left them. His clothes reeked of her perfume. That was a first. Before, he'd always been very careful to hide his . . . affairs. And then I went to unpack his overnight bag, to put the rest of his clothes in the laundry. I was emptying his pants pockets before I put them in the wash. He always left loose change and his pocketknife in his pockets, and I've ruined more than one load of laundry that way. But this time I found all that and a little bottle of blue pills I'd never seen before."

"His heart medication?" Annajane asked.

"Sildenafil citrate. Ever hear of it? I hadn't. I had to look it up on the Internet." Sallie put the glass carefully down on the counter, then picked up a sponge to wipe down any traces of the spilled wine. "He'd gotten himself a prescription of Viagra so he could perform like the young stud he thought he was. He didn't care if he couldn't get it up for his wife," she said bitterly. "But his girlfriends were a different story."

Sallie opened the cupboard under the sink and brought out a bottle of spray cleaner. She sprayed the already-immaculate formica countertop, then wiped it briskly, using nearly half a roll of paper towels, while Annajane stood, transfixed, waiting to hear the rest of the story.

"You think I'm a bitch," she told Annajane. "A mean, withered-up, spiteful old bitch."

Annajane shrugged. "Mean and spiteful, yes. But not so withered up."

That made Sallie laugh. "I spend a lot of money to look this good. I had a face-lift last year, did you know?"

"I wondered," Annajane admitted. "You had it done down in Florida?"

"Yes. There's a surgeon down there who does amazing work. I'm thinking of having a tummy tuck next. In fact, I've put in a contract on a little bungalow down in Palm Beach, and that's where I'll be wintering next year. I'm going to sell the Wrightsville Beach cottage. I never cared for it there anyway. It's much nicer in Highlands, and most of my friends have places there. A much more interesting social scene."

"Sounds like you won't be spending much time in Passcoe," Annajane said. "How long has this been in the works?"

"I've been thinking about it for a long time. And now, since I don't have any ties to Quixie, well, there's really no reason to stay around here. This house is beyond depressing. I'm only sixty-six, did you know that, Annajane? Glenn left me very well-fixed, so I intend to go out and live my life for myself now. Maybe even date. Who knows? I might even decide to remarry."

"Go for it," Annajane said. "But you were telling me about Glenn. About the day he died."

"I put the Viagra bottle on the bathroom counter, right beside his shaving kit, and then I waited for him to wake up and find it," Sallie said. "He came downstairs, still in his bathrobe. Glenn never left the bedroom unless he was fully dressed. It was a pet peeve of his."

"I remember, Pokey always had to get dressed before she came downstairs, even on Saturday mornings," Annajane said.

"I should have known he wasn't feeling well," Sallie said. "But I was so angry!"

"Did you confront him about the Viagra? About the woman he'd been with?"

"Eva. Her name was Eva," Sallie said. "He said it was just a . . . mild flirtation. We had a fight. I told him I wouldn't stand for being humiliated anymore. I asked him if he wanted a divorce, and he said no, of course not. He apologized, and I left shortly after that, to go to the country club for my bridge date. And when I got home," she said, biting her lip. "He was on the floor, unconscious." She opened a cookie jar on the counter and brought out yet another pack of cigarettes and a lighter. She lit a cigarette with trembling hands and blinked back tears.

"That's a nice story," Annajane said. "Too

621

bad it's not true."

"You're calling me a liar?" Sallie asked, her face deadpan.

"I guess I am," Annajane said.

54

Sallie flicked her cigarette into the sink, then turned on the tap to wash away the telltale ashes. She regarded Annajane as she might have regarded a cockroach who'd had the bad luck to wander into her immaculate kitchen.

"Why don't you tell me what you think happened?"

"I know for a fact that Glenn was having chest pains that morning," Annajane said. "Voncile called him on his cell phone, because she was concerned that he'd missed the company Christmas party."

"Did she now?" Sallie asked.

"Even she could tell, just from his voice on the phone, that he was having problems breathing. He admitted that he wasn't feeling well. Voncile begged him to call his cardiologist or to go to the emergency room, but he told her you were right there, taking good care of him."

"Cardiologist?" Sallie said. "I wasn't aware at the time that he had a cardiologist. Just one of the many secrets Glenn kept from me."

"You're a liar," Annajane said. "You knew he was on heart medication. Blood pressure meds, too. You had to know. If he was having . . . whatever, that he couldn't perform in bed . . ."

"Who said he was having problems in bed?" Sallie asked. "Didn't your mother ever tell you to have respect for your elders?" She tsk-tsked. "This is really not a topic for polite conversation, Annajane dear."

"I'm tired of polite conversation," Annajane said. "So let's get down to the nitty-gritty."

"Oh, please do," Sallie said.

"Voncile talked to Glenn at around ten o'clock that morning. He was having chest pains, which you had to have known. But you did nothing. I ran into you at the country club when you were arriving around noon. You knew he was probably having a heart attack. Did you hide his meds from him? Did you watch him gasping for breath, Sallie?"

"Absurd," Sallie said. "Glenn was fine when I left the house. He was watching the Carolina game and cussing a blue streak about the defense."

"The Carolina game? At noon? Really?" Annajane said mockingly. "That's interesting, because Mason was watching the game much later that afternoon. You know, it would be easy to look it up on the Internet, what time that game started. Are you sure that's right?"

"It was some football game," Sallie said. "I was so mad; I was distracted. But I do know that Glenn was fine when I left that house. He was alert and watching the game. And that's all that matters."

"Voncile told me she tried to call Glenn's cell again before noon," Annajane said. "But the call went right to voice mail. So she called the house and she talked to you. Don't you remember that, Sallie?"

"It was an awful day. My husband died that day, remember?"

"Voncile remembers it, because she was so worried about Glenn. You told her he was fine, but he was taking a nap."

"I just told her that to get her off the phone. He was watching the game!" Sallie repeated. "Glenn hated to be disturbed when he was watching football. The whole house could have burned down around him, and he wouldn't have noticed."

Annajane shook her head. "I don't think so. I think he was in full-blown cardiac distress. I think you knew it, and you were so pissed at him, you deliberately left him there to die."

She stood inches away from Sallie, whose back was to the sink. "Did he ask you to get his heart meds, Sallie?"

"No!"

"Did he ask you to call 911?"

"No!"

"Did you stand there and watch him dying?

625

Was he already unconscious when you left to go play bridge at the country club? Were you surprised to come home that afternoon and find him still alive? Is that why you called 911 when you did? Because you knew it was already too late?"

Sallie stubbed her cigarette out in the sink and turned on the tap and then the garbage disposal. The metallic rattling filled the room until she switched it off. She washed her hands, dried them, then carefully applied moisturizing cream to each of her elegantly manicured hands.

"I loved my husband," she said calmly. "I took care of him until the very end. And you can't prove otherwise."

"You're right. I can't prove a thing," Annajane said. "But I don't have to. Mason and Pokey are already asking themselves the same things I just asked you. They don't want to believe what you're capable of. But I know. And you know. And that's good enough for me."

Annajane left Sallie standing in the kitchen. She let herself out the front door and didn't look back. It was, she'd already decided, her last trip to Cherry Hill.

55

Mason pulled around to the front of the Pinecone Motor Lodge and parked in front of Annajane's unit. It was Friday night, the week before Memorial Day, and she was still putting the wedding off, still refusing to move out of the damned Pinecone Motor Lodge. It was a nice enough place, he guessed, but he was tired of playing this cat-and-mouse game. He honked the horn twice. Nothing. He was going to have to do this the hard way. Her way. He strolled up to the door and knocked.

"Who is it?" she called.

"It's the big bad wolf," Mason answered. "Open up, or I'll huff and I'll puff . . ."

The door swung open. Annajane was barefoot, dressed in a pair of white shorts and a beat-up Braves jersey. His lucky jersey. "And then what?" she asked carelessly.

He smiled and tugged her by the hand. "Come on," he said. "There's something I want you to see."

"Right now?" she protested. "Mason, I've

got stuff to do. I told you that earlier today. I'll come over in the morning, and we'll fix bacon and pancakes for Sophie, but right now . . ."

"Right now, you're coming with me," he said. "Please?"

"Just let me change," Annajane said. "I'm a mess. I was going to wash my hair."

"You're fine the way you are. In fact, perfect. Now let's go."

She finally managed to talk him into letting her put on a pair of sneakers and grab her phone, but five minutes later they were rolling through town in the Chevelle with the roof down, Journey blasting on the tape player.

"Are you going to tell me what the surprise is?" she asked.

"Wait and see," he said.

When they approached the gates to Cherry Hill, the sight of the discreet FOR SALE sign gave her pause. It had been six weeks since Sallie had announced she was putting the estate on the market and abruptly decamped for her new house in Highlands, North Carolina.

The rusted wrought-iron gates were open, and Mason easily swung the car down the driveway.

"Mason," Annajane said uneasily. "Look, I know it's your childhood home and all, but I really don't want to go up to the house

628

tonight."

"Relax," he said, pulling her across the bench seat toward him. "I have no interest in going there, either."

"Ever?"

His jaw muscle did that twitchy thing. "Mama offered to sell it to me. I told her no thanks. Pokey doesn't want it either."

"What about Davis?"

"Don't know," he said. "I haven't talked to him. But I doubt Sallie would sell it to him. They might be thick as thieves, but she has to know that if Davis did get the house, he'd tear it down in a minute, probably build mini-warehouses or something. Sallie's funny about the place. She doesn't want to live there anymore, but she doesn't want it torn down, either."

"I'm still shocked she put it on the market," Annajane said.

"Yeah, well, she knows nobody around here has got three point two million to buy Cherry Hill. Listing it, that's her way of thumbing her nose at everybody in Passcoe."

"Especially me," Annajane said.

He turned the car onto the dirt road leading to the lake house, but, to Annajane's surprise, the road wasn't dirt anymore. It had been paved so recently she could still smell asphalt and tar. The underbrush had been cleared, too; the huge old oaks picked clean of their coatings of kudzu; the shoulders stripped of the privet and weeds, with sod laid down; and ribbons of new shrubbery planted. She could see islands of azaleas and rhododendrons and camellias.

"Hey," Annajane said, craning her neck to see the new landscaping. "What's going on here?"

"The new owner made some improvements," Mason said.

"Sallie sold off the lake house?" Annajane didn't bother to hide the disappointment in her voice.

"She never came down here anyway," Mason said, a bitter edge to his voice. "It was too primitive for her taste."

"You were the only one in the family who ever really cared about the lake or the lake house," Annajane said. "I wish you'd told me before it closed. It would have been nice to come back and look around again, for old time's sake."

"That's what we're doing now," Mason said. "Once more, for old time's sake."

She caught a glimpse of something bright blue through the treetops as they got closer to the caretaker's cottage.

"What's happened here?" she asked, half-standing in her seat.

"You'll see," he said.

Without the tangle of fallen pine trees, kudzu, and privet, the old stone cottage stood proudly now on its point looking out over the lake, which could also be seen now. The blue she'd glimpsed earlier turned out to be a huge tarp that had been secured over the roof.

Annajane breathed a sigh of relief. "At least they didn't tear the house down," she said, turning to Mason. "If they're fixing the roof, maybe they're planning on trying to save the house?"

"Maybe," he said, bringing the fun car to a stop at a new graveled parking court that had been laid to one side of the cottage. "Whoever bought the place has obviously got more dollars than sense." He pointed past the house, and, even in the twilight, she could see the stacks of lumber and building materials and, beyond that, what looked like new pilings stretching out into the lake. "They've started rebuilding the dock. You believe that?"

"We used to talk about doing that," she said quietly. "Remember? We were going to build a two-story boathouse? With a fireplace and a deck on the top level?"

"And a screened-in sleeping porch," Mason added. He got out of the car and came around and opened her door. "Come on. Let's take a peek inside."

"No," she said. "I don't want to see. This was our special place, Mason. Even when it was rotting and falling down, I always thought, at the back of my mind, maybe someday we'd find our way back here. Knowing that can never happen now, even if it

631

wasn't ever really realistic, it's just so unbearably sad."

"Just one look," Mason cajoled. "Aren't you the least bit curious?"

"No," she said stubbornly. "Honestly, can we just go back to the Pinecone now? So I can wallow in self-pity for an hour or so?"

"Later," Mason said.

She reluctantly allowed herself to be escorted to the door, noticing, along the way, the new flowerbeds; the new walkway constructed of worn, antique bricks; and, finally, the cottage's front door, which had been newly sanded and painted a gleaming periwinkle blue.

"At least they kept my color for the door," Annajane said. She pointed at the worn brass hardware, which had been buffed up, not to a garish bright gold, but to the mellow color of good old brass. "And they saved the old hinges and even the old knocker."

Mason produced a key from his pocket and, noting her surprise, said only, "The new owner's a decent guy."

He let her walk in first. If the outside of the cottage was mostly unchanged, it was a different story inside. The tiny, cramped entry hall was gone. In fact, all the walls were gone.

She was standing in one large, airy room. It smelled of sawdust and cut pine, and what remained of the day's light poured in through a wall of new windows overlooking the lake.

The windows were open, and a slight breeze blew in off the lake. The water-stained plaster ceilings were gone, exposing age-darkened ceiling beams, and the old wooden floors were scarred and dusty, but intact.

"Oh my God," Annajane said, her voice echoing in the empty room. "They've gutted it!"

"Look at the views of the lake," he suggested. "Pretty cool, huh?"

"Unbelievable," she agreed. It was then she noticed a large old brass bed, situated in the right corner, near the fireplace, which looked like it had been recently reworked. The bed was dressed with white linens and an old quilt, which was neatly folded at the foot. A table had been fashioned from two-by-fours laid over a pair of sawhorses, and a couple of bright orange sheetrock buckets had been upended to use as chairs. There was a picnic basket on the table and a stub of a candle stuck into an empty wine bottle.

"Mason, look," she said, pointing at the bed and table. "The new owners must be staying here. Now I really do feel like a trespasser. We need to go, before they come back."

But he wasn't listening to her. He walked over to the table, picked up a box of matches, and lit the candle.

"What?" But she knew. Maybe she'd suspected as soon as she saw the bank of new windows.

"The new owners are right here," Mason said, giving her the brass skeleton key he'd used to open the front door. He took her by the hand and seated her on one of the buckets. He began extracting a number of foil-wrapped packets from the picnic basket, opening each one for her inspection. It wasn't the stuff of a romantic picnic. No imported cheeses or fresh fruit, pâté or crusty french bread. Instead, the meal he offered consisted of ham sandwiches on mushy white bread with bright yellow mustard and crunchy pickles, individual bags of potato chips, and store-bought chocolate chip cookies.

"You remembered," she marveled.

"Our first meal out here," he said. "You packed the food and I brought the beer. A very deliberate seduction on my part."

"Except the cookies I brought were oatmeal raisin. That was before I knew you were a raisin hater."

"A rookie mistake. Could have happened to anybody," he said graciously.

He sat on the bucket opposite hers and reached into the picnic basket one more time, bringing out two chilled bottles of Quixie. He unscrewed the caps and handed her one.

She took a drink. The essence of cherries lingered on her tongue and the bubbles tickled her nose. This taste thrilled her just as much as her first one had, nearly thirty years ago, at Pokey's birthday party. It still tasted new and full of promise. Mason was watching her. He held up his bottle, and they clinked them together.

Annajane got up and walked over to the windows. The sun was setting on the horizon, and the calm waters of the lake reflected the last amber glow of daylight. Mason stood by her side, and she nestled her head against his shoulder. They could hear the thrum of cicadas through the open windows and, from nearby, the soft hooting of an owl.

"You bought the cottage?" she asked. "And had all this work done?"

"Actually," he said. "Sallie gave it to us. As a wedding gift."

Startled, she turned to stare at him. "No way. She hates me. After the things I said the last time I went to Cherry Hill . . ."

"I was as shocked as you were when she sent the deed over," Mason said. "When I called to ask her about it, she just said she'd had a change of heart about us. And she said something about a down payment on self-respect, which I didn't get, but which she said you would."

Annajane shivered, and he put his arm around her, thinking she was cold. She'd actually been thinking about Sallie Bayless and her self-imposed exile from Passcoe. Was this, the gift of the lake house, Sallie's passive-aggressive way of admitting her guilt and asking forgiveness? Or was it the genuinely kind and thoughtful act of a loving mother?

"I didn't want to do too much to the place before I brought you out here," Mason was saying. "Mostly I've just been cutting back the jungle, planting some trees, and shoring things up. I knew you'd always wanted bigger windows looking out at the lake, so I went ahead and did that. And I had to evict the raccoons and have the fireplace relined and the masonry redone. All the rest, I thought we'd plan together."

She turned and kissed him. "You did all this for me? And kept it a secret?"

"For us," Mason corrected her. "But Sophie was in on it. She's already picked out the paint color for her bedroom. Princess pink."

"What would you think about adding a second story?" Annajane asked. "We'll need more bedrooms. And bathrooms. And a home office for both of us . . ."

They stood and looked out at the lake for a long time, eventually switching out the Quixie for a bottle of good red wine. As they watched the new moon come up over Hideaway Lake and marveled at the clarity of the stars in the night sky, they talked about their plans. For their new old house, for the company, for their all-new life together. When Annajane shivered again, this time from the chill seeping in off the lake, Mason went to the fireplace and lit the wood he'd already stacked there.

When he turned to remark on the lateness of the hour, he found that Annajane was already standing by the brass bed. She'd pulled back the covers, slipped off her shoes, and was pulling the lucky jersey over her head. He admired her smooth bare skin as the candlelight began to flicker out.

"Come to bed," she said.

And so he did.

EPILOGUE

The ruckus in the hospital room was close to
deafening. Pokey Bayless Riggs was making a
valiant but fruitless effort to look beatific
while surrounded by her brood. Three little
boys clambered onto the hospital bed, pushing and elbowing each other out of the way
in hopes of being the first to hold their new
sibling. "I wanna hold her." "No, me. I'm the
oldest," "You're too little." "Mama! Make
him stop!" while their father, who was trying
to capture the whole scene on video, called
out directions. "Look at the camera, Petey.
Clayton, take your finger out of your nose.
Denning, be careful, you're squishing your
mama."

"Peterson Riggs, don't you dare shoot a
second of film with me looking like this,"
Pokey cried above the din. She reached for
her lipstick and a hand mirror and gasped
when she saw her reflection. "I look like I've
been rode hard and put up wet."

"You look beautiful," her husband declared,

zeroing in on his wife's face. "Now hold her up a little higher, so I can get a shot of those big blue eyes and all that gorgeous red hair."

Pokey grinned and gently cradled the baby in the hollow of her shoulder. "Isn't she amazing?" she cooed, looking directly into the camera. "World, meet our daughter. Olivia Pauline Riggs."

Sophie stood close to her aunt's bedside, holding Annajane's hand tightly in her own. "My first girl cousin," Sophie said, not for the first time that day.

"That's right, Soph," Pokey said. "And you're going to have to help me figure out what to do with a little girl now. You can help me shop for dresses, and dolls, and all that girly-girl stuff for Livvy."

"I brought her a present," Sophie said, her eyes shining with pride. She reached into her pink pocketbook and brought out a lumpy package of pink tissue wrapped in what looked like a mile of cellophane tape. "I wrapped it myself."

"She wouldn't let me help at all," Annajane put in, squeezing Sophie's hand.

"I wanna open it," Petey clamored. "No, me," Denning hollered, shoving his younger brother completely off the bed, which set off a fresh set of howls from the injured party.

"That's it," Pete said, putting the camera down. "We're outta here." He leaned over and kissed Pokey and his brand-new daughter and extended a hand to the two boys remaining on the bed. "Come on, guys. Thanksgiving is only three days away. We've gotta get to the store and buy our turkey."

"And pies!" Denning said. "I want pecan. And pumpkin."

"And coconut custard," his father said, swinging Clayton onto his shoulders. "That's my favorite. Your mama makes me one special every year."

"But everybody's eating at our house this year," Annajane reminded him. "And I've already bought the turkey."

"Pete has to cook his own turkey, remember?" Pokey said. "He hordes his leftover turkey like it's a treasure from King Tut's tomb."

"My turkeys are a treasure," Pete proclaimed. "Wait til y'all taste what I'm doing this year. Deep-fried and injected with my supersecret sauce. Sweetest, juiciest thing you ever put in your mouth."

"Nuh-uh," Mason said. "Wait til you see what I've got up my sleeve. I bought a farm-raised free-range beauty from a farmer near Carthage. Then, I'm brining it for two days ahead of time. Kosher salt, cracked peppercorns, a bunch of other herbs Annajane's got out in the garden, and a whole liter of white wine. I got a bastin' sauce worked up with just the right essence of Quixie, too. You might as well leave that pitiful bird of yours at home, Riggs, because nobody's going to want it after they get a load of the bird from Maison de Mason."

"A brine?" Pete said derisively. "That's all you got?" He looked over at Pokey. "Honey, would you please tell this fool why my turkey rules?"

"Oh, good," Pokey said. "Dueling turkeys for Thanksgiving. This oughtta be interesting. Nothing like a good old-fashioned family food fight for the holidays."

"Speaking of family," Mason said, "What have you heard from the rest of our clan?"

"Sallie has been calling on the hour, demanding pictures and videos of Livvy," Pete said. "Says she's thrilled about us naming her Pauline after her mama."

"But not thrilled enough to leave Palm Beach to come see her new grandbaby," Pokey added, not bothering to hide her disappointment. "She wants us to come down for Christmas, even offered to buy us first-class plane tickets. As if! Like I'm going to load up all of us, plus a newborn, plus all the Santa Claus stuff, for a quick trip to Florida just to see her new house and meet her new boyfriend."

"She's got a boyfriend?" Mason asked, startled. "She's never said anything about that to me."

Pokey made a face. "Sallie doesn't come right out and call him that. His name is

Brewer, and she claims he's her investment guy. But every time I talk to her, it's 'Brewer took me to this fabulous new restaurant' or 'Brewer thinks I need a nicer car' or 'Brewer and I are taking a cruise in February.' From what she says, he's semiretired, and, I gather, just a teensy bit younger. Most importantly, to Sallie, anyway, he seems to have his own money."

"What about Davis?" Annajane asked, "Has he been by to see the baby yet?"

Pokey sighed and gestured toward a mammoth flower arrangement sitting atop a dresser near the window. It was a towering affair of pink lilies, orchids, tulips, and roses that was only dwarfed by the five-foot-tall stuffed bear sitting beside it.

"He sent those last night," she said. "With a very sweet card. Signed Davis and Celia." She wrinkled her nose. "Although I'm certain Celia has no idea her name was signed to that card."

Annajane shrugged off the mention of her former nemesis's name. Although Celia and Davis were living in a grandiose new subdivision on the outskirts of Passcoe, she rarely ran into either of them, and when she did, she managed to grit her teeth and smile graciously. "Do you think Davis will ever actually marry her?"

"Gawd, I hope not," Pokey exclaimed. "He'd never admit it to me, but I get the feeling there's trouble in la-la land. He stopped by the house last week, and I got the distinct impression he was running away from home because he'd had another big fight with you-know-who. After a couple drinks, he told me that lawsuit the Baby Brand people brought against her is starting to heat up. He was complaining about the huge legal fees, which, of course, she expects him to help pay. And, he mentioned, her daddy and her two trashy sisters showed up out of the blue two weeks ago for a 'visit,' and, so far, they don't show any signs of leaving. The poor sap. Her mother and her mother's boyfriend only just went back home to Nebraska. After showing up uninvited, eating them out of house and home for nearly a month, to top it all off, they backed into Davis's car on their way out of town and never offered to pay for the damage."

"Wait a minute," Annajane said. "Didn't Celia tell everybody she was an orphan? And an only child?"

"Wishful thinking, apparently," Mason said.

"Davis did call the house this morning while I was in the shower," Pete said. "He left a message on the answering machine with some lame excuse about why he wasn't going to be able to get over to the hospital to see you and the baby for the next few days. Something about his pool contractor and a gigantic screwup."

Mason scowled. "He's adding a pool now? Because a tennis court and a stable and a riding ring and a frickin' guesthouse aren't showy enough for two people?"

"He *had* to add a pool," Pokey said. "Because *we* had a pool growing up at Cherry Hill. And he *had* to build the biggest, gaudiest, most ostentatious house this county has ever seen, just to show everybody how rich and successful he is, since we bought out his share of Quixie. And to house all these freaky relatives of Celia's who keep showing up."

"And to demonstrate that he has the biggest pecker in Passcoe," Pete said.

"Way bigger than mine," Mason added, with a wink.

Annajane clamped her hands gently over Sophie's ears. "Little pitchers!" she reminded her husband and brother- and sister-in-law.

"Sorry," Mason said, glancing over at his nephews. "Sorry, guys."

But the boys and Sophie were busily helping themselves to the gift box of chocolates that had come with their Uncle Davis's flower arrangement and hadn't heard a word the grown-ups were saying.

"I better get these kids outta here before they start eating the flowers," Pete announced. "Sophie, would you like to come help us pick out the turkey that's gonna make your daddy's bird look like a Colonel Sanders reject?"

"Okay," the little girl said, polishing off a piece of candy. "But can we wait til Aunt Pokey opens my present?"

"Of course!" Pokey said, tearing at the multiple layers of tissue. A moment later, she held a small yellowed cardboard box in her hands. Lifting the top, she found a glittering object nestled on a bed of cotton.

She held it up for the others to see. It was a green rhinestone brooch in the shape of a pixie — a pixie holding an uptipped and intricately wrought ruby-red Quixie bottle.

"Sophie!" Pokey squealed. "Where on earth did you find this? I haven't seen one of these since my daddy gave me one when I was a little girl just your age. Of course, I lost it almost immediately. It's perfect. I love it."

Sophie beamed and wriggled with delight at her aunt's praise. "I have one, too," she said, reaching back into her pocketbook to produce an identical pin.

"Annajane found a box of them when we were going through stuff from the attic over at Cherry Hill," Mason said, his arm thrown across his wife's shoulders. "According to Sallie, Granddad had them made as Christmas gifts for the top distributors' wives back in the sixties."

"There are only a half-dozen left in the box," Annajane added, "but we found a jeweler in Asheville who's copying them for us. They'll be great little holiday giveaways for the women at the office."

"Along with cash bonuses, right?" Pete added. "After that kick-ass summer promotion upped sales forty percent, I think everybody in the company deserves something extra in their Christmas stocking this year."

Mason nodded in agreement. "Bonuses are definitely on the agenda for the next board meeting."

Pokey was busy pinning the brooch to her hospital gown. "Now that you mention it, I think I remember Grandmama Bayless wearing a pin just like this one at Christmas."

"Only hers was the real thing," Mason said. "Emerald and diamond chips and rubies. Sallie said she still has it but never wears it because she thinks it looks tacky."

Sophie looked up at Annajane with interest. "What's tacky?"

"Tacky is in the eye of the beholder," Annajane told her. "It's a word some people use for something they think is in poor taste."

"But this pin is not in poor taste at all. It's just beautiful," Pokey declared. She reached for her niece and gave her a hug. "And you're beautiful for thinking of me and giving it to me. And when Livvy gets as grown up as you, I'll let her borrow it for special occasions."

"Oh, we've got another one for Olivia back at the house," Mason said. "And we've got this, too, for a special toast."

He reached into a shopping bag he'd set on

the floor and brought out a bottle of champagne and a sleeve of plastic cups.

"Yippee!" Pokey said, grabbing the bottle and giving it an exaggerated smooch. "Hello, my old friend. Welcome back to my world."

Mason took the bottle and popped the cork, which brought a small "mew" from the startled Olivia, who looked around, took in the scene, and then promptly dropped back to sleep. He handed cups all around, and even poured a tiny bit for the children.

"To Pokey and Olivia," Pete said. "My two favorite girls in the whole wide world." He went through the motions of touching cups with the grown-ups and the children, and then settled on the bed next to his wife, dropping another kiss on the top of her head.

"Here, here," Mason said.

Pokey raised her own glass and took a huge gulp of champagne. "Come on, everybody," she urged. "Don't make me drink alone. I've been waiting nine months for a taste of something stronger than iced tea."

Denning, the oldest, took a wary sip. "Gross!" he said. "Quixie's lots better than this." He took his cup and dumped it into the sink, and Sophie and Petey loyally followed suit.

"Annajane?" Pokey said, pointing at her friend's empty glass.

"None for me, thanks," Annajane said, with a barely suppressed grin, looking over at her best friend and sister-in-law. "But if you had some skim milk — and some prenatal vitamins, I could go for that."

"What!" Pokey screeched. "Seriously? Does this mean what I think it means?"

"Yes," Annajane said, leaning her head on Mason's shoulder. "I'm pregnant. We just found out. Can you believe it?"

Pokey looked from her beaming brother to her teary-eyed best friend. "What I can't believe is that it took you this long."

Sophie giggled, and Pokey gave her a look of mock outrage. "You already knew, didn't you? And you kept it a secret from all of us?"

"Yup," Sophie said. She proudly removed her bulky quilted jacket to display the T-shirt she'd been hiding underneath. I'M THE BIG SISTER! was written on the white shirt in glittering silver letters.

Pete was pumping Mason's hand. "Congratulations. When's the big day?"

"Fourth of July," Mason said.

"Give or take a day or two either way," Annajane cautioned.

"It'll be the fourth, no matter what, as far as I'm concerned," Mason said. "The most important day of my life."

"Why's that?" Pete asked, looking from Annajane to Mason.

"Because that's the day Daddy saved Mama," Sophie volunteered. "It was a long time ago. She was dressed up like a pixie, that's an elf, kind of, for the Fourth of July parade, and some bad boys pushed her down, but then Daddy rode up in the fun car and saved her."

"And she saved me right back," Mason said, wrapping his arms around Annajane's waist.

"And they lived happily ever after," Sophie declared. But Annajane snaked an arm around Sophie's waist and drew her into an embrace that had finally, finally come full circle. "*We* all lived happily ever after," she said, gently correcting her daughter.

The cottage had been abandoned for years. As children, she and Pokey had appropriated it for a playhouse, furnishing it with cast-off furniture from the big house, a wobbly kitchen table, a pair of rickety wooden chairs, and an army cot for campouts. They played at cooking with a battered saucepan, once nearly burning the place down after attempting to heat up a can of SpaghettiOs on Davis's Boy Scout camp stove.

And yes, she and Mason had snuck away to the caretaker's house for stolen hours in the first few months after they'd started dating.

At first, Annajane had been enchanted with the quaint honeymoon cottage, with its deeply pitched slate roof, leaded-glass windows looking out onto the lake, and stacked stone fireplace.

But living there was a different matter. The kitchen's warped wooden cabinets didn't close, the refrigerator barely cooled, and that adorable roof had a spot that leaked — directly over their bed. It was drafty in the winter and hot in the summertime, and damp and mildew from the lake seemed to creep in year-round. Also, there were mice. There was no washer or dryer, which meant they had to either troop into town to the coin Laundromat or drag their basket of dirty clothes up to the big house, like a couple of college students.

All that Annajane might have cheerfully accepted. She hadn't grown up in a mansion, as Mason had. Her family's two-bedroom brick ranch had one window air-conditioning unit — in Ruth and Leonard's bedroom — and just one bathroom. The real problem with the cottage was its location — directly in the looming shadow of Sallie Bayless, a constant presence in their lives, who was prone to dropping over uninvited to offer Annajane unsolicited advice on everything from housekeeping: "Annajane dear, you really must use lemon oil every week on Mason's grandmother's walnut dresser, to keep the wood from drying out"; to cooking, "Annajane dear, we never, ever use dark meat in chicken salad"; to marriage itself, "Annajane dear, no man wants to see his wife in the morning before she's fixed her hair and her makeup — and his breakfast."

Her mother-in-law never came right out and criticized the new bride in front of Mason. That wasn't Sallie's style, but the slow drip-drip-drip of her constant nitpicking had the effect of sand in Annajane's newlywed sheets.

Annajane knew it was no good trying to extricate their life from Mason's family, or his family's business. They were too tightly woven together now.

And it was all Pokey's fault.

She'd shown up, unannounced, at Annajane's studio apartment in Raleigh, on a

96

freezing weeknight in February.

"Guess what?" she'd demanded, as soon as she'd stepped into the room. "I'm pregnant!" And next came, "You're gonna be my maid of honor. And I won't take no for an answer."

Pokey had been in no hurry to finish college. She'd declared herself on the six-year plan, until she met Pete Riggs at a fraternity party in Chapel Hill. He was from a wealthy Charleston family who owned a chain of fine furniture stores. He was tall and redheaded and had earned a full four-year golf scholarship to Wake Forest. Fun-loving Pokey called Annajane that night, dead serious, to announce that she'd met her future husband. And as always, what Pokey wanted, Pokey got.

Before Annajane knew it, she was being dragged to bridal boutiques for fittings and, yes, back to Passcoe, for a seemingly endless round of brunches, teas, dinners, and showers.

Mason was a no-show for all of the prenuptial hoopla. He was working as a regional manager for Dr Pepper, in Memphis, with his father's blessing, to gain experience outside his own family's business. He was, Pokey confided, being a major pill about the whole thing. "Mason doesn't approve of Pete, and he doesn't approve of me getting married and dropping out just a semester short of graduation, and he most definitely doesn't approve of me having a baby. He threatened to put a beat-down on Pete for knocking me up, until I admitted I actually got myself knocked up on purpose. But if you ever tell that to Sallie, I'll never speak to you again," Pokey said.

"Too bad," Annajane had murmured, trying to sound unconcerned about Mason's opinions. She was desperate to see him again, and desperate to pretend he'd never entered her life. It wasn't until she had to walk up the aisle on his arm, the day of Pokey's wedding, that Annajane allowed herself to remember how she felt when Mason Bayless touched her. It wasn't Mason, she told herself, it was just spring fever.

Still, she tried to avoid him at the reception, dancing with every man in the room who was under the age of seventy and hiding out on the veranda of the country club, behind a huge potted palm, between dances.

That's where he found her, leaning against the veranda railing, sipping a glass of lukewarm champagne toward the end of the evening.

"Shoes hurt that bad?" he'd asked, gesturing toward the high-heeled silver slingback sandals she'd slipped out of.

"They're killing me," Annajane said, taking a large sip of champagne, hoping he wouldn't notice her suddenly flushed face in the darkness.

ABOUT THE AUTHOR

Mary Kay Andrews is the *New York Times* bestselling author of *Summer Rental, The Fixer Upper, Deep Dish, Blue Christmas, Savannah Breeze, Hissy Fit, Little Bitty Lies,* and *Savannah Blues.* A former journalist for *The Atlanta Journal Constitution,* she lives in Atlanta, Georgia.

The employees of Thorndike Press hope you have enjoyed this Large Print book. All our Thorndike, Wheeler, and Kennebec Large Print titles are designed for easy reading, and all our books are made to last. Other Thorndike Press Large Print books are available at your library, through selected bookstores, or directly from us.

For information about titles, please call:

(800) 223-1244

or visit our Web site at:

http://gale.cengage.com/thorndike

To share your comments, please write:

Publisher
Thorndike Press
10 Water St., Suite 310
Waterville, ME 04901